THE HUN

"Hiya, Doc," Spider-Man said, perched on the jib of a nearby tower crane. "Where you off to?"

It was then that Strange noticed the rips in Spidey's costume, and the fresh, oozing wounds beneath.

"Not to steal Deadpool's shtick, but you look like a salsa-smothered burrito in that cloak," Peter continued, his voice slurred. "And I'm hungry, Doc. So hungry."

Strange didn't need to hear more.

Spider-Man and the others had definitely been injured, but Strange had no idea what had infected them. He thrust his hand out toward Peter, and a miniature black hole appeared behind the webslinger.

Behind where he *had* been.

And then the Sorcerer Supreme found his arms pinned to his sides and his mouth clogged with sticky webbing as Spider-Man drew near, like his namesake arachnid bearing down on its doomed prey.

"You can't possibly imagine how hungry, Doc. But you'll know soon…"

More Super Hero Action

Marvel Crisis Protocol
Target: Kree by Stuart Moore
Shadow Avengers by Carrie Harris
Into the Dark Dimension by Stuart Moore

Marvel Heroines
Elsa Bloodstone: Bequest by Cath Lauria
Black Cat: Discord by Cath Lauria
Silver Sable: Payback by Cath Lauria
Mockingbird: Strike Out by Maria Lewis
Rogue: Untouched by Alisa Kwitney
Domino: Strays by Tristan Palmgren
Outlaw: Relentless by Tristan Palmgren
Squirrel Girl: Universe by Tristan Palmgren

Marvel Legends of Asgard
THE CHRONICLES OF HEIMDALL
The Head of Mimir by Richard Lee Byers
The Rebels of Vanaheim by Richard Lee Byers
The Prisoner of Tartarus by Richard Lee Byers

The Serpent and the Dead by Anna Stephens
Queen of Deception by Anna Stephens

The Sword of Surtur by C L Werner
Three Swords by C L Werner

Marvel Multiverse Missions
You Are (Not) Deadpool by Tim Dedopulos
She-Hulk Goes to Murderworld by Tim Dedopulos
Moon Knight: Age of Anubis by Jonathan Green

Marvel School of X
Sound of Light by Amanda Bridgeman
The Phoenix Chase by Neil Kleid
The Siege of X-41 by Tristan Palmgren

Marvel Untold
The Harrowing of Doom by David Annandale
Reign of the Devourer by David Annandale
The Tyrant Skies by David Annandale

Dark Avengers: The Patriot List by David Guymer
Witches Unleashed by Carrie Harris
Sisters of Sorcery by Marsheila Rockwell

Marvel Wastelanders
Wastelanders: Star-Lord by Sarah Cawkwell

Marvel Xavier's Institute
Liberty & Justice for All by Carrie Harris
First Team by Robbie MacNiven
Triptych by Jaleigh Johnson
School of X edited by Gwendolyn Nix

MARVEL ZOMBIES

THE HUNGER

MARSHEILA ROCKWELL

ACONYTE

FOR MARVEL PUBLISHING

VP Production & Special Projects: Jeff Youngquist
Editor, Special Projects: Sarah Singer
Manager, Licensed Publishing: Jeremy West
VP, Licensed Publishing: Sven Larsen
SVP Print, Sales & Marketing: David Gabriel
Editor in Chief: C B Cebulski

First published by Aconyte Books in 2023

ISBN 978 1 83908 245 0

Ebook ISBN 978 1 83908 246 7

Cover art by Blake M Kandzer

Distributed in North America by Simon & Schuster Inc, New York, USA
Printed in the United States of America
9 8 7 6 5 4 3 2 1

ACONYTE BOOKS

An imprint of Asmodee Entertainment Ltd

Mercury House, Shipstones Business Centre

North Gate, Nottingham NG7 7FN, UK

aconytebooks.com // twitter.com/aconytebooks

Librarians like Zelma Stanton are super heroes in their own right, even when not apprenticed to a Sorcerer Supreme. This book is dedicated to librarians everywhere, but especially to my elementary school librarian, Mrs Kimpton, who recognized a hungry reader and let me borrow whatever books I wanted, allowing me to discover such varied literary luminaries as Edith Hamilton and Judy Blume. Being able to escape into books undoubtedly saved my life, and is the main reason I wanted to become a writer – to create those escape hatches for others who might need them, if only for a few hours or a few hundred pages.

(This is why we don't ban books, BTW. Stories can save lives. Suppressing them can only ever do the opposite.)

CHAPTER ONE

On the snowy, windswept plains of Canada, Elizabeth Twoyoungmen, better known as the super hero Talisman, looked up from the drum circle, frowning. A discordant note had sounded, but it hadn't emanated from the throats of any of the singers here, or from their instruments. She closed her eyes and checked the magical wards around the Tsuut'ina Nation. They held. A threat loomed, but it had not reached them. Yet.

In the steaming jungles of Haiti, Jericho Drumm's eyes snapped open, his meditative trance shattered by an ominous sense of impending doom. But the man known as Brother Voodoo was alone in the quiet clearing. Still, he frowned. He knew that this fragile tranquility could not last. It would be broken, and soon, by whatever dread thing had sent its foul tendrils questing along the edges of his concentration.

In upstate New York, the witch Agatha Harkness stepped out onto the porch of her imposing manor, Whisper Hall, drawn by an impulse she could not name. Thirteen crows had gathered in the nearby cemetery, each perched on a different headstone. They stared at her in utter silence, their black eyes unblinking. Agatha frowned and couldn't stop a shiver from skittering up her spine at the ill omen. Something was coming.

Something bad.

In Manhattan, Doctor Stephen Strange jolted awake in his Sanctum Sanctorum, heart pounding from a nightmare he couldn't remember. He had fallen asleep in the high-backed library chair he often used as a haven for his physical body while he traveled the astral plane. But this morning he had not been gallivanting about in spirit form. He had instead been pondering the deep unease rippling through the magical community of late when the last several sleepless nights of unrelated research finally caught up with him. He might be the Sorcerer Supreme, but he was still mortal, still formed of flesh and blood and bone, and still subject to their many limitations.

He was in the middle of a jaw-cracking yawn when a sudden echoing boom sounded like a death knell from somewhere outside his Bleecker Street brownstone.

Strange was airborne in moments, his Cloak of Levitation speeding him across the bustling city to Midtown, where black smoke rose to mingle with purple, lightning-laced clouds. Below him, he could see many of his fellow Avengers already gathered around the impact crater. The white star on Captain America's blue suit shone like a beacon of hope in the gloom of skyscraper shadows.

Though Strange couldn't make out details as he hovered, he saw Cap confidently waving his teammates away before descending into the smoking crater of what the sorcerer assumed was a meteorite impact. And then Cap came lurching back out again, hand clutched to a bloody wound on his neck, shredded flesh trailing out from beneath it like bizarre streamers at a tacky Halloween party.

Strange had originally believed Manhattan to be the unfortunate victim of an undiscriminating space rock. But space rocks tended not to tear chunks out of people's throats.

After that, it was like watching a horror movie on fast-forward. Cap stumbled into the group of assembled Avengers, which had grown considerably as news of the impact spread. Cap yanked the closest hero – Hank Pym – toward him, tore a mouthful of flesh from the scientist's left bicep and gulped it down, then moved on to his next victim, shoving Pym into a nearby cluster of their fellow Avengers. Several went down, then Hank rose up and started ripping *their* flesh off and gobbling it down, even as blood still spurted from his own wound. And then it was like super hero dominos – whatever had infected Cap radiated out in a wave, first to the super powered, and then to the humans. For the most part, the heroes were only infected.

The humans, however, were slaughtered. And then eaten.

Aghast, Strange knew in moments that no spell he could throw at this threat would end it – too many of the most powerful Avengers had already succumbed, and he was not remotely prepared. He would need the magical tomes and artifacts back in his Sanctum Sanctorum if he had any hope of stopping this contagion before it overran the world. And judging from what he had just witnessed, he didn't have much time.

He turned, his cloak already responding to his thoughts and moving him back toward Bleecker Street. But he found his tactical retreat obstructed by a friendly neighborhood interruption he did not need right now.

"Hiya, Doc," Spider-Man said, perched on the jib of a nearby tower crane. "Where you off to?"

It was then that Strange noticed the rips in Spidey's costume, and the fresh, oozing wounds beneath.

"Now, Peter," Strange began, his left hand forming the Tarjani Mudra, his intent to cast a Conjurer's Cone spell and send Peter safely elsewhere to be dealt with later.

"Not to steal Deadpool's shtick, but you look like a salsa-smothered burrito in that cloak," Peter continued as if he hadn't heard, his voice oddly slurred. "And I'm *hungry*, Doc. So hungry."

Strange didn't need to hear more. He thrust his hand out toward Peter, and a miniature black hole done in shades of sparkling gold instead of ebony appeared behind the webslinger.

Behind where he *had* been.

Strange whipped around, the cloak moving him quicker than thought, but Peter was even faster. The Sorcerer Supreme had only one chance.

Spider-Man and the others had definitely been injured, but Strange had no idea what had infected them. It could be a parasite, a spaceborne virus, even a form of supernatural possession.

He only had a quick spell for one of those, so he put his money on blue.

"*Corelli Distinctov Smiteth!*"

Strange focused the exorcism spell through the Eye of Agamotto, using the technique of the Warriors of the Free Spheres and imagining the removal of an unwanted pest. In this case, a spider.

A pulse of blue energy erupted from Strange's amulet, rocking the sorcerer backward, much like the kick of a powerful firearm. The cerulean wave washed over Peter with no apparent effect.

And then the Sorcerer Supreme found his arms pinned to his sides and his mouth clogged with sticky webbing as Spider-Man drew near, like his namesake arachnid bearing down on its doomed prey.

"You can't possibly imagine how hungry, Doc. But you'll know soon…"

CHAPTER TWO

Zelma Stanton lounged on her bed in her room adjacent to the Bleecker Street library, pillows stacked behind her back, legs up and crossed to form a human easel for her laptop, earbuds running up from it to hide beneath the edges of her ever-present beanie. She was rewatching the series arc where her favorite television witch became hooked on magic, slipping down a long, plot-greased slope that began with having some harmless fun at the local club and ended with her becoming the season's Big Bad. Zelma had always found the metaphor a bit heavy-handed. In the real world, being overly dependent on magic cost you lives, not friendships. It was laughable seeing the show treat the use of magic for personal gain as a moral failing. But Zelma supposed the puritanical view of magic, even for a character whose whole reason for existence on the show had become the wielding of it, wasn't all that surprising. Things hadn't changed much since Salem – those without magical power still feared those who had it. They'd just found newer and more subtle means of persecuting its users.

Still, decent witch-rep was hard to find in the mainstream media, and this show scored points in that regard more often than it fumbled. Zelma also liked its emphasis on friendship, so she was willing to give its moralistic leanings a pass. Besides, you could only watch so many twitching noses and talking cats before you started seriously considering throwing your laptop across the room.

The episode was just about to reach one such laptop-chucking moment when the annoying buzz of the Emergency Alert System sounded in Zelma's ears, startling her into a sitting position.

"This is not a test…"

Zelma looked reflexively out the window, but all she saw were storm clouds, which weren't unusual for New York City at this time of year. She didn't remember hearing anything about any hurricanes making their way up the coast, or any cold fronts making their way down from Canada, but she clicked over to a local news station, just in case.

There was a shaky helicopter-cam view of Midtown Manhattan that zoomed in suddenly on a smoking crater.

"…Jim Hansen is live at the scene, where a meteorite seems to have struck Midtown Manhattan. Jim, we're not getting many reports from on the ground, but from what we *are* hearing, it looks like some Avengers who responded to the initial impact may have been injured. Can you confirm–"

But Zelma never heard what the anchor wanted Jim to confirm, or what Hansen's response might have been, because the screen went black, then snowy, and then showed nothing but a color test pattern. It was the same on every other local station she could find, and a quick glance at social media showed nothing but cell phone and drone footage of widespread panic as rumors of Avenger and civilian casualties mounted.

Zelma had seen and heard enough. Heart pounding, she slid off her bed, shoving her laptop aside and yanking out her earbuds. Then she ran to the library where she knew she'd find Doctor Strange. She had left him there earlier, safely nodding off over a scroll describing druidic portents; enough to lull anyone into a coma of boredom, super hero or not.

He would know what was happening, and what to do. If there was really something out there killing Avengers, he might be the only one who did.

There was a small, selfish part of Zelma that was secretly glad her mentor wasn't among the Avengers who'd first responded to… whatever this was. That he wasn't among even the rumored casualties. Not just because he was her friend. As much of a friend as it was possible for a man who purposely held himself aloof from those under his protection to be, anyway. That was the largest, truest portion of her relief, of course.

But it was also true that while she might be just a magician's librarian and apprentice right now, someday she wanted to be the magician herself. Maybe not a Sorceress Supreme – she wasn't sure she wanted that kind of responsibility, or even had the aptitude or courage for such a calling. But a master of the mystic arts? Definitely. Maybe even with capital letters. And for that, she was going to need more than she could glean from the books in Doctor Strange's library, no matter how many of them she memorized. For that, she needed a teacher.

She needed him.

Then she opened the library door, and all thoughts of friendship and ambition were driven from her mind. For a split second, Zelma thought there was something wrong with her eyes, or with her glasses, because what she saw in the room that had heretofore been her trusty peaceful refuge was incomprehensible.

But the problem wasn't with her eyes. The problem was with what they were seeing – Doctor Strange, face and clothes already thick with coagulating blood, taking another bite out of Wong's stomach. Or what was left of Wong.

"Doc…?" Zelma ventured hesitantly, having halted on the library threshold, unable to process the horror unfolding before her.

Then she saw a flash of green behind Strange. Rintrah's minotaur-like corpse lay crumpled on the floor, the R'Vaalian's abdomen ripped open, his shredded entrails scattered about like trick-or-treater candy wrappers on Halloween.

She had once told Doctor Strange that the state of his library before she took over its curation was the most horrifying thing she had ever seen.

She had been so very, very wrong.

Zelma was pretty sure she screamed at that point, and tried to run, but Doctor Strange had looked up from his feasting, his eyes suddenly clear, and Zelma felt herself pulled all the way inside the library, the door slamming shut behind her.

"You have to help me, Zelma," Strange said, his voice somehow not monstrous coming from that gore-coated mouth. "While I still have my wits about me. Before the hunger grows unbearable again."

His intense blue gaze pierced Zelma's heart like a stake.

"You have to kill me."

Frank astonishment warred with her fear and revulsion.

"I have to *what* now?"

As before with her sight, Zelma now wondered if there was something wrong with her hearing. Surely he hadn't just had the gall to ask for her aid, while bits of her friends' flesh still freckled his blue coat?

Surely he hadn't just asked her to do what gods and demons and magic-wielders far more accomplished than her had been trying and failing to do for decades?

Maybe she was dreaming. She'd fallen asleep while watching her witch show, maybe during some excursion into a vampire den, and her subconscious had substituted the faces of her friends for those of the actors, like a bad *Wizard of Oz* remake.

Or the weirdness of seeing the world through a magical lens had finally become too much, she had snapped, and this was all a psychosis-induced hallucination.

Deep down, Zelma didn't really believe that, but she knew Wong had always worried that the price of her association with Doctor Strange would be her sanity. Wong, who was – who'd *been* – a stalwart friend as well as a fellow disciple of Doctor Strange. And also an amazing cook, a kickass martial arts instructor, a mystical guardian in his own right, and a self-described insatiable adventurer.

There'd been some friction when Zelma first became Strange's apprentice, but it'd had nothing to do with her, and everything to do with how she'd acquired the power to take that position.

Or rather, how it had been thrust upon her.

When she'd done the transference spell in WeirdWorld to take Doc's illness upon herself, she had fully expected to die. It had seemed like a ridiculously simple bargain. Her boring, inconsequential life for the life of the Sorcerer Supreme, Earth's mystical protector? Done.

But it hadn't been that easy. Nothing with Doc ever was.

Once they'd made it back to Earth and the Sanctum Sanctorum, Strange had chosen to infect her with magical antibodies rather than let her die. He had no idea how those antibodies would affect her, only that they would *change* her, open her up to the world of magic in a way few mortals ever experienced. She would see the world as he did – through three eyes instead of two – whether she wanted to or not.

And he hadn't known if that change would be reversible.

Wong had objected.

"'Exposure to magical energy changes a mortal body,' Stephen," he'd said, apparently quoting the good doctor back to himself. "You know that. No one should be forced into the dangers of your world without consent; if they want to enter it of their own free will, that's one thing. Making that choice *for* them is another thing entirely."

Unsurprisingly, Doc hadn't listened to Wong's counsel, though he had once told Zelma that Wong was the only man alive he trusted completely. Doctor Strange had deemed Zelma's life worth the cost, even though he wouldn't be the one paying it. That unilateral decision had been a bridge too far for Wong; once he knew she'd survived the introduction of the antibodies into her system, he had taken his leave of the Bleecker Street brownstone, and the subject had remained a sore spot between him and Doc for a long time.

Not long enough, apparently. If they hadn't reconciled recently, he wouldn't have been here to serve as an entrée to Rintrah's appetizer. Somehow, Zelma didn't think Wong would have any problem with her agreeing to Doc's deadly request.

But she wasn't Wong, and even if she wanted to comply, it was impossible. Kill Doctor Strange? She didn't have that kind of magical ability. She wasn't sure anybody did.

And it might be a trick, a way to lure her closer so she could become the dessert course. Though he'd pulled her into the library, he'd released his hold immediately after the doors closed behind her. She supposed if he'd wanted to eat her, he could have just pulled her all the way in, straight to the supper table. She readied a seraphic shield all the same, knowing full well the Sorcerer Supreme could cut through it like a New York City winter through one of the Big Apple's innumerable homeless camps.

"Zelma," Strange said, finally realizing his mouth was a bloody mess and trying to wipe at it ineffectually with his equally bloody sleeve. "We don't have much time. This… infection… is spreading among the super hero population at an unimaginably fast rate. Most of the Avengers are already either truly dead or like me–"

"Zombified?" Zelma interrupted helpfully.

That brought Strange up short.

"Well, no," he replied, his voice taking on its familiar lecturing tone as he mansplained to her what a walking corpse was. "Not in the traditional voodoo sense. Not even by the classic horror movie standard. But for practical purposes, they – we – have become the ravenous reanimated, and we hunger for flesh. Other supers taste best, but we'll gladly settle for human.

"The Sanctum Sanctorum's existing defenses will keep the others from finding you here, but it won't keep me from hurting you once this period of lucidity fades.

"You have to make sure I *can't* hurt you before that happens." He avoided looking at the body in front of him. "That I can't hurt anyone else, ever again."

"And just how exactly do you suggest I do that?" Zelma asked, unable to keep the frustration from creeping into her voice, or the tinge of sarcasm, even in a situation as horrific and dire as this one. Maybe precisely because it *was* so grim. Anger was her only defense against paralyzing fear and the grief that underlay it. "Kill you? Aren't you kind of already dead? And even supposing re-killing you is possible, we still wind up back at that pesky 'how' part. Do you have some secret weakness not even Mordo or Dormammu could find?"

"Don't be ridiculous," Strange snapped, zombification having done nothing to improve his patience or his temper. "There are any number of spells that could do it, as long as I don't try to counter them."

Doc's Cloak of Levitation twitched at that. A defenseless Doctor Strange? Not on its watch.

"We don't have time for this," Doc repeated, his exasperation aimed at the cloak this time. "Cloak. Go to Zelma."

The crimson cape shuddered around Strange's shoulders, but otherwise did not move.

"*Now.*"

Zelma wasn't sure if a compelling spell underlay the word, or if the brusque intonation alone was enough to overcome the cloak's reluctance, but the mantle undid itself and floated from Doctor Strange's shoulders to settle, uncomfortably, on hers.

As if the cloak were somehow imparting wisdom as well as its ability to fly, the gravity of Doc's words finally sank in.

Most of the Avengers had been infected with a seemingly unquenchable lust for human flesh.

They were in some serious trouble.

Although "they" assumed there were even any humans alive besides her. That was starting to sound like a stretch.

Still, if there *was* anyone left to rescue, it was her job to help them. With limited power came little ability to change things, but huge quantities of guilt.

"OK," Zelma said, determinedly pushing the horror of the situation aside, squaring her shoulders beneath the heavy cloak, and taking a deep, steadying breath. "What next?"

"Like I said. You kill me. Depending on your level of satisfaction with your tutelage thus far, I suppose you could do it slowly, via poisoning with the Vipers of Valtorr, or dissolve me with the Ribbons of Nihility. Or do it faster, with Sarnios's Sword of Storms. Or even use Bolts of Bedevilment to incinerate me." He paused for the briefest moment. "On second thought, use that one. I'm not convinced merely cutting me into pieces would do the trick. Best to make sure there's no body – or body parts – left for the infection to reanimate. And faster would be better."

When he looked at Zelma again, there was an odd gleam in his eyes.

"I'm starting to get a bit peckish."

"OK, OK," Zelma said, holding up a quick hand. "I get it. Speed is of the essence. But... why do I have to- to *kill* you?" Even after all this talk, even with her friends' dead bodies lying on the floor in plain sight, the coppery smell of their blood hanging heavy in the air, it was still hard for her to say the word, to wrap her head around the concept. "Why can't we just lock you up somewhere safe where you can't hurt anyone until we can find a cure? There's got to be one, right?" When he didn't immediately respond, she repeated herself, "Right, Doc?"

"Hmm… what?" he replied, a faraway look on his face. Then his expression cleared. "Sorry, Zelma. I was thinking of one of the last dinners I had with Clea… steak tartare at Vauclause on Park Avenue… it was sublime…"

"Great story," Zelma interjected, trying to get him off the subject of food before he started wondering how Stanton served rare tasted. "But we were talking about keeping you confined somewhere while we look for a cure. No one else has to die. Or, die again." She still wasn't quite sure of the mechanics of this thing, and since there was no detectable rot or odor other than the smell of blood, it was hard to think of Doctor Strange as one of the restless undead.

As if her words had reminded him of his own misdeeds, Doctor Strange finally looked down at Wong's half-eaten body in front of him. He stared at it for long minutes before raising his gaze to meet hers again. Zelma didn't like what she saw there.

"You're going to need to look away, Zelma," Strange said, his voice taking on a rough edge. "You're not going to like what I have to do next, but it's the only way to keep you safe."

"You- You're going to… eat… more of him, aren't you?" Zelma asked, her voice gone faint and wobbly. Probably because she was pretty sure she was about to vomit.

"Better him than you," Strange replied bluntly.

Unable to argue, Zelma looked away. When the chewing and slurping noises started, she put her fingers in her ears. It helped block out the sound. Most of it.

Not enough to keep her from losing her noodle lunch all over the library floor, though. The same lunch Wong had cheerfully prepared for her earlier that day. When she had teased him about it being some ancient family recipe, he'd replied that it was ancient leftover takeout, and they'd both laughed.

Zelma choked back a sob and got a throat full of bile for her trouble.

After what seemed like an eternity, Strange spoke.

"You can unplug your ears now, Zelma. I'm done, and sane again. It should last a while longer, this time."

She turned to see Doctor Strange standing, his face clean now, the bodies of Wong and Rintrah nowhere to be seen.

"But I can't yet gauge for how long, so we need to get moving. We have a lot to accomplish." Strange paused meaningfully. "And I've just run out of carcasses."

CHAPTER THREE

"First things first," Strange said as he led her to the Chamber of Shadows, which was really just a glorified library alcove. There, he strode over to the three-legged glass Cask of Concealment that housed the Orb of Agamotto. "I've got to contact Clea."

Zelma frowned.

"Look, Doc. I know it's the end of the world and all, but is this really the time to be phoning up your on-again off-again?"

Strange quirked an annoyed eyebrow at her.

"It's time for Earth's Sorcerer Supreme to warn the Sorcerers Supreme of other dimensions about this threat, yes. It's bad enough the infection is spreading here. I imagine it will get off-planet soon enough. I'd prefer to keep it contained to one universe, if possible."

He didn't wait for a response as he began concentrating on the orb. The glass covering rose of its own accord and set itself on a nearby table. Freed, the orb floated in the air, cloudy and humming with arcane energy. Shadows flitted within the heart of the globe, only sharpening into focus once Strange murmured his ex-wife's name.

Instantly, an image of Clea appeared, her silver hair obscuring her face as she concentrated, head bent, on the map table before her. She looked up, sensing Strange's gaze.

"Stephen? What's wrong?" Her eyes narrowed. "What's wrong with *you*?"

"No time," Strange replied curtly. "There's an unstoppable plague spreading here. I've been infected, and given this thing's apparent rate of transmission and the abilities of those I've already seen succumb, most of the other Avengers and super-powered community will also have been infected by now – those that aren't dead. They're turning into flesh-eating monsters and decimating the human population on Earth. It won't be long before one of them gets the bright idea to hop dimensions. You can't let that happen. This must end here."

"But, Stephen," Clea began, a horrified look on her face. "What about you? Surely there's some kind of treatment…?"

"That's what I said!" Zelma exclaimed, earning her inscrutable looks from both Sorcerer and Sorceress Supreme.

"If there is, no one has found it yet, and with the rate at which this thing spreads, no one ever will. All our best minds have already fallen to it: Richards, Stark, Banner, Pym, McCoy. All dead, or worse.

"No, Clea. That's not an option. This dimension is as good as lost. The rest of you must close off access to your domains and save yourselves. I need you to tell them. Save your people. As I could not." That last part was just a murmur; Zelma heard it, but she doubted Clea had. Which was probably for the best. If Clea thought Doctor Strange had fallen into the clutches of self-pity, his ex-wife was just as likely to bring an army of her mother's Mindless Ones to rescue him as she was to close the door to the Dark Dimension and throw away the key.

"But what about the summoning spell?" Clea ventured, obviously still grasping for a way to save the man many said she still loved.

"It hasn't been cast in thousands of years. I'm not even sure I could do it in this state," Strange replied, gesturing to a grisly bite wound on his shoulder Zelma somehow hadn't noticed before. "And I can only maintain rationality for so long. It would be like summoning the holiday ham to the serving platter."

The silver-haired sorceress nodded, her expression both grave and grief-stricken.

"I understand, Stephen. I'll do as you ask and alert the others. But I hope to the Vishanti that you are mistaken."

"As do I, my dear. As do I."

Strange dismissed Clea's image after that, cutting off whatever final reply or endearment she might have made. He turned to Zelma.

"That will stop anyone but another Sorcerer Supreme from escaping this dimension."

He was still sporting the Eye of Agamotto, despite his recent atrocities, and Zelma got his meaning immediately.

"I can't kill you, Doc. I just *can't*. Not when I was already willing to give up my own life for yours once before. How does that even make sense?"

"You're right, Zelma. It was selfish of me to ask you," Strange replied. He immediately followed that "who are you and what have you done with the real Doc" statement with another. "You don't have to kill me. I'll do it myself."

As if to suit word to deed, Strange began to move his hands in the patterns Zelma knew would invoke Bolts of Bedevilment.

"Stop!" she yelled. When Strange paid her no heed, she turned to her only ally. "Cloak! Stop him!"

The cloak needed no further urging. It flew across the room, crossing the distance between apprentice and sorcerer in the space between Zelma's racing heartbeats. It wrapped itself tightly around its erstwhile master, effectively cocooning Strange from nose to knees. His arms were trapped against his sides and his mouth was covered.

But he could still send his thoughts.

Zelma. Stop this nonsense. Let me do what must be done.

"You don't know that it must be done! You don't know for sure there's no cure, or that we can't find it! You're just… giving up!" She spat the last two words out like they were acid, but she wasn't sure which of them they burned more, her or Strange.

Bowing to the inevitable is not the same as succumbing to despair, Zelma.

Zelma squinched her nose so hard her glasses bounced. Even his thoughts could sound patronizing.

I heard that.

"Then hear this – I'm not going to let you kill yourself," she said stubbornly. "At least not until we've exhausted all other options. I'm not going to let you eat me or anyone else, either. So that only leaves one option. Locking you up."

And what cage do you suppose would hold a Sorcerer Supreme bent on freedom? What shackles could withstand the magic at his command?

He had a good point. As long as Strange had access to magic, there really was no way of stopping him from doing whatever he wanted. Which right now was to rid the world of the danger he presented to it, but in a few minutes could be chomping on her brains. It wasn't like that cloak was going to keep him mummified forever.

As if to demonstrate the truth of that thought, a shudder went through Strange and the red shroud slipped off him like satin pajamas on silk sheets, pooling at his feet. Zelma tried to ignore how much the quiescent cloak looked like a puddle of fresh blood.

Well, OK then. Obviously, they had to get rid of Strange's ability to access and use magic. But how?

"Destroy the parts of my brain where memories are stored."

"What? No! Then even if we did find a way to cure you, you'd… never be *you* again," Zelma protested, appalled at the mere suggestion. But would it really be worse than killing him?

She thought about what it would be like not to be able to remember any of the books she'd ever read, to maybe lose the ability to read altogether. To be unable to remember the moments in her life that mattered most to her. To forget what few friends she had as if she'd never had any at all. Then she imagined multiplying that bereft feeling by a gazillion to give her some idea of what it would feel like for Doc to lose his memory of all those things and decided that, for him – and probably for her, too – that loss *would* be worse than death. Infinitely more so.

"No!" she repeated, pushing up her glasses and fixing him with her best librarian's glare. "We're not doing that."

She thought for a moment.

"What about a spell of forgetfulness? Thinker's Folly?"

She'd seen that last one in a book she'd filed recently. It wasn't frequently used, since it required a willing subject, but in this case, they had one.

Strange shook his head.

"No. I might not be able to remember the spells to leave this dimension, but they would still be there, in my head, and another skilled magician could find them, pluck them out, and use them to infect Agamotto knows how many other worlds. I won't risk that."

Zelma chewed on the inside of her cheek as she thought. She was no neurosurgeon like Doctor Strange had been before becoming the Master of the Mystic Arts, but she was well and widely read, and she knew a decent amount about brain structure, psychology having been a subject of particular interest to her before her life became all magic, all the time. She recalled that short-term memories were stored in the hippocampus and longer-term memories were stored in the prefrontal cortex, while the emotions associated with those memories were stored in the amygdala.

"Could we just… take out those parts? Store them somewhere safe, then put them back in once there's a cure?"

"You want to take out my entire prefrontal cortex?" Strange asked, looking at her like she was a few fries short of a kids' meal. Or like he was wondering if she'd taste good with ketchup.

"…Maybe …?" she replied uncertainly. It was probably a stupid idea. He was the master, after all. She was just the animated mouse who wanted to try on his hat.

Strange frowned, his eyes taking on a faraway look. Zelma readied her undoubtedly useless seraphic shield.

"I can't do that," he finally said. Zelma deflated with disappointment. She'd been scraping the brain barrel with this one – if it wouldn't work, she was out of ideas, and she might as well start basting herself now. Then Strange added, "But you can."

"What?" Zelma asked, startled out of despairingly concocting recipes for roasted apprentice. "Me? How?"

"The M'Casta Spell of Item Transference." Then he cocked his head to the side, brow creasing as he weighed the innumerable heavy thoughts of a Sorcerer Supreme. Or maybe what side dish to have with her corpse. "Well, the M'Casta-Strange Spell of Transference. I've made some… alterations. Most people would consider them improvements." Which made Zelma wonder about the ones who wouldn't think his changes were an improvement, and why. But she was sure Doc would never tell her, even if she did someday manage to bring him back to himself.

"Doesn't that just teleport something out of someone else's hand and into yours? How does that help?" Zelma asked. "Besides, if you already had your brain in your hand, there'd be no need to even cast the spell."

"You'd be mostly right if we were talking about M'Casta's spell," Strange agreed. "But this is the M'Casta-Strange spell. It doesn't have those limitations."

"Explain, please," Zelma said, knowing she'd just invited a lecture that they did not have time for. Not when she had no idea how much of Doc's "while longer" they'd already used up.

"M'Casta's spell is widely thought to be a simple item teleportation spell, but it's not. At its heart, it's a spell about maintaining balance. Yes, it takes something from one person and gives it to another. What most people don't realize is that it also takes something of the caster's and gives that to the spell's target – and the caster doesn't get to choose what that 'something' is. Because balance must be maintained.

"The M'Casta-Strange spell, on the other hand," he continued, chuckling slightly at his own pun, "allows the caster to choose what they give up, and it doesn't require that the item be something the spell's target is holding. Just that it be something on their person. Or, in this case, *in* their person."

Zelma grokked his meaning immediately.

"OK, but what do I put it in to keep it… fresh, or whatever… until we need it again? And what do we do with you in the meantime?"

"My prefrontal cortex can go in one of Golden Claw's terra cotta warriors I got from Jimmy Woo. I've rigged it up as a sort of magical Canopic jar. What's in the jar now won't be any worse for wear sitting in my skull for the time being.

"And as for me?" Strange's sudden smile was tight and mirthless. "You're taking me to the basement."

Zelma gasped. Of all the horrors the day had held thus far, this one might be the most terrifying. In all her time here, she'd never been allowed through that door, down those stairs. All she knew was that something waited at the bottom, and that to face it was to choose doom.

"You can't mean…?"

He nodded gravely.

"Yes, Zelma. To the Thing in the Cellar."

CHAPTER FOUR

Collecting the preemie-sized terra cotta figurine and getting from the Chamber of Shadows to the cellar was no simple task. They had to navigate through Escherian staircases winding in impossible directions and leading to floors that shouldn't exist, past doorways that opened onto other dimensions – which Doc summarily destroyed – and down hallways lined with portraits sporting real eyeballs that tracked your every step. At Doc's suggestion, Zelma had grabbed a drab green military-style backpack that contained pitons, a hammer, and a coil of seemingly endless nylon rope that had been stashed in a cabinet beside an ivory idol with the same disturbingly blank face carved into it over and over – she'd guessed it might be related to Ikkon, but decided against asking about it.

Zelma drove the first piton into the floor outside the library, tying one end of the rope securely to it. She was initially reluctant to pound the metal stakes into the brownstone's floors until Doctor Strange impatiently snatched one from her hand, hammered it in, and yanked it back out again. The wooden slats healed over like something alive. She decided not to ask about that, either.

She placed pitons with rope strung through them at various junctures along their route; at the tops and bottoms of the mind-bending staircases – because they might not be oriented in quite the same direction the next time she saw them – and at dozens of hallway intersections, all indistinguishable from one another, to mark which way to turn. At some point along this fantastical journey, the Cloak of Levitation, having recovered from whatever spell Strange had cast upon it, floated blithely through the air to settle once more upon Zelma's shoulders. The cloak had no features to define a face, so was incapable of facial expressions. Still, Zelma had the distinct impression it was snubbing its former wearer.

The path to the basement led through the living room, which was a vast jungle expanse split in twain by a river that sprang from one wall and disappeared into the far one, miles away. In addition to the white rush of rapids, Zelma could hear bird calls, monkey screeches, the distant roars of great cats, and possibly the sound of an elephant trumpeting. The room was humid and she soon found the long-sleeved shirt she wore beneath her thick white sweater sticking to her like a troll on social media.

Feuding tribes lived on either side of the river, but seldom approached its banks. Doctor Strange had declared the flowing water their shared boundary, promising dire misfortune to any who dared cross it, or him.

The living room was also home to two talking snakes, Aleister and Anton. Zelma had only ever been in the room once, on her first visit to the brownstone, and Doc had warned her then never to speak to the serpents, though she still didn't know what their story was.

One of the snakes – she couldn't tell them apart – hissed at them from a slithering knot atop the coffee table.

"Sssay, Ssselma," it said, "What'sss that awful sssmell? Trying out a new perfume? It does not sssuit you. I'd keep sssearching."

A second scaled, triangular head popped up out of the serpentine tangle.

"I don't think it'sss her," it said, flicking its tongue out. "I think it'sss–"

"Zelma!" Strange interrupted, his voice urgent.

"I know, I know," she groused. "Don't talk to the snakes."

"No," Strange replied. "*Duck.*"

Months of obeying the Sorcerer Supreme without question served Zelma well. Her knees bent of their own volition, bringing her eyes even with Aleister and Anton's heads.

Which turned out to be a mistake as, to her horror, Doctor Strange magically leap-frogged over both her and the table, then whirled, grabbing the two snakes just below their heads. He then bit those heads off, swallowing them whole before gobbling down their bodies like spaghetti, their blood providing the sauce.

Zelma turned her head and puked onto the moss-covered wood of the living room floor. Her heaving brought up only rank, sour bile after the last bout of vomiting induced by Zombie Doc's gluttony. Seriously, hadn't his great-grandmother Eunice ever taught him to chew with his mouth closed?

When the slurping noises stopped, she dared to look up to find Strange wiping his mouth with his sleeve. He shrugged when he met her gaze.

"I never liked them, anyway. They talked too much."

She'd had limited experience with the serpent duo, but if Doc thought they were too chatty, Zelma wondered how in the world she'd kept from getting evicted from the brownstone ages ago. Given current circumstances, she was almost sorry she hadn't been.

There was still time for that, of course. They'd reached the basement door.

Zelma placed the last piton and tied off the nylon rope, which was magically the exact length she needed it to be. Then she set the backpack on the floor, removed the terra cotta figurine, and straightened, feeling very much like Theseus about to enter the minotaur's labyrinth. But that thought made her think of Rintrah, whose R'Vaalian race bore such a close resemblance to the creatures from Greek myth. And the last time she had seen her friend, he had been sprawled out, gutted and lifeless, behind Doctor Strange, who himself had been in the process of snacking on Wong.

With her gorge threatening to rise again, Zelma turned her mind forcefully back to the task at hand. She'd never been this close to the cellar before, and despite all the dire warnings and fearful whispers about what it held back, she had still somehow expected to see just a normal door. Not one with a huge iron bar and the words THE CELLAR – NEVER ENTER carved clumsily into its oaken surface, along with a crude rendition of a skull.

Strange turned to her, fishing something out from an inner pocket. This close to him, she could finally smell the fetid odor the snakes had detected. It was probably her fear-primed imagination, but the bite wound on his neck seemed to be growing, and necrotizing as it did so, as if he'd been infected by Zombie Ebola on steroids.

Maybe he had been. Zelma had no way of knowing if what had felled him and all the others had been some spaceborne super-flesh-eating bacteria, or something more mystical in nature. Or maybe something entirely new, like nothing anyone had ever seen before. She didn't think Strange knew, either.

She supposed it didn't matter. Remedies for mundane ills might be easier to come by, but ultimately all cures were the same. You gathered particular components and synthesized them in specific ways, applied them, and hoped they worked. Collection of mystical ingredients and the mixing thereof were more difficult, but the overall process was still the same. Even for a malady never before encountered, the general principle should still apply.

There was *always* a cure to be found, given the right resources and enough time; Zelma firmly believed that. But resources and time were often in short supply, and even when they weren't, sometimes the price was just too high, or the cures wound up being worse than the disease.

"Here," Strange said, shoving a glittering key on a simple leather thong at her. As the key spun and bounced with the movement, its coloration seemed to change, cycling through every hue of the rainbow and beyond, to colors Zelma didn't even have the words to describe, let alone name. "Take this. Keep it safe. If by some miracle you do wind up finding a way to make things right, and you still want to save me – if there's still something left to save – you'll need it."

"What's it unlock?"

"The Thing in the Cellar."

Zelma had had enough of coyness. She'd seen the bodies of her friends used as memory supplements and just watched her zombified mentor pull an Ozzy Osbourne in the living room jungle. She thought she deserved some answers, plainly spoken.

"What *is* the Thing in the Cellar? What is so terrible down there that, of all the horrors that might lie behind any given doorway in this house – including the fridge door, I might add – this is the only one off-limits? Just what exactly are you keeping in the basement, Doc?"

She could only describe the expression that came over his face as sorrow, but of course that couldn't be right. She was pretty sure sadness wasn't in Doctor Strange's emotional repertoire. He couldn't afford for it to be. He was Earth's Sorcerer Supreme. Or at least he had been; to her surprise, he no longer wore the Eye of Agamotto. Zelma wondered when it had disappeared and whose neck it now adorned. She wasn't really sure what the rules of succession were regarding reanimation.

"The cost of magic, Zelma. The price we all pay, sooner or later. Even you." His intense gaze seemed to bore into the uncomfortable, shadowed places in her soul. "Pain. Suffering. Loss."

She didn't understand. Wasn't sure she wanted to, now. But she'd left the option for ignorance in the rearview the day she accepted her position as Doctor Strange's librarian.

The day she'd decided she wanted in on this magical life, whatever the price might be. Back then, she'd thought it would just mean giving up her banal existence as a single librarian living alone in New York City.

Back then, she had been very naive.

"Every spell a magician casts has a consequence beyond the results of the spell itself," Strange continued. "Most spells are small, infrequently used, so the magician might not notice a new bruise here or there, or might not connect his or her use of magic to the short bout of depression that follows. But the more magic you use, the bigger those bruises become and the longer that depression lasts. And when you are Sorcerer Supreme, you do nothing *but* use magic."

"So you're a walking bruise taking a pharmacy's worth of antidepressants?" Zelma quipped, but there was no real spirit to her sarcasm. She thought she knew where he was going with this, and it was nowhere she wanted to be.

"No one person can sustain that much pain and heartache without dying or falling into madness, not even a Sorcerer Supreme. But that's the job description, so you find a way to deal with it, or you fail, and the mantle passes on.

"I don't like to fail."

He paused, waiting for the inevitable question.

She had to ask it.

"So, what way did you find to deal with it?"

The look of sorrow, if that's what it had been, was replaced with a tight, hard smile.

"The Thing in the Cellar. The living embodiment of all the pain and suffering I could not endure and still do my job. My bar tab come to life. While I'm the one it has the score with, in the end, I'm not sure it really cares who pays up."

"And we're walking right into its lair because…?" Zelma waved an inarticulate hand in the air; words could not encompass how foolish this endeavor sounded. And she was a librarian. She was pretty good with words.

"Because it's made of my pain, my debt. The shackles I built to hold *it* are the only things on Earth I know for sure will hold *me*."

Well, when he put it that way...

"I still don't understand. The key unlocks the shackles that hold the Thing. But we need them to hold you. So... we're letting it out?"

"Not exactly," Strange replied. "The shackles themselves are empty."

Now she was *really* confused. And even more convinced this was an epically bad idea.

"But... if the shackles are empty, where is the Dweller in the Cellar?" she asked.

"Oh, it's there, lurking. The shackles bind it to the cellar, not to any particular cell. They'll be a bit more restrictive for me."

He slid the iron bar aside and opened the door. Zelma half-expected the Pain Monster to jump out at them like some B-movie boogeyman, but the only thing that assaulted them was dust and a few cobwebs.

"Normally I'd say, 'ladies first', but you'll have to excuse my lack of manners," Strange said as he moved past her to go down the stairs. Zelma shrank away from him; who knew if his infection could be spread by simple touch, and the biting part was just for fun? She didn't want to find out.

She followed him down the wooden staircase into a normal-looking basement. Normal, that is, except for the multiple ritual circles inscribed on the floor, the tunnels branching out in every direction, the various medieval implements of torture scattered about the room, and a set of shackles already holding a skeleton that had been picked clean of flesh long ago.

"Doc...?" she began, but he waved away her concerned tone.

"Halloween prop. Wong thought it was funny."

Zelma wasn't sure she believed that, but Wong wasn't exactly here to prove the lie, so she didn't press the issue.

There was another set of stairs that led even deeper under the brownstone, but Strange avoided those and led her through a tunnel already lit with torches spitting oily smoke.

It only took a moment to find their destination. It was the first opening on the left; a cell, complete with rotting straw on the floor and shackles on the wall that glimmered like the key now tucked safely down Zelma's shirt. There were other openings further down. Zelma wondered how many of them were cells. How many of them were occupied.

Strange stepped into the shackles, then nodded to her. Zelma carefully placed the terra cotta figure on a mound of straw that looked marginally less mildewed than those around it, then stepped forward herself, withdrawing the key Doc had given her. She quickly locked the cuffs on his ankles and wrists, wondering if he might, zombie-like, not just chew off those appendages and crawl along the basement floor without them, leaving a slimy trail behind as he looked for food. Zelma shuddered at the image.

"We should hurry," Strange said. "There's no telling when our friend will realize he's not alone down here and decide to come investigate. The aura of the shackles should keep him from entering the cell, but it's a long way from here back to the basement door."

Not a comforting thought.

"Now the spell," Strange continued. "Open the top of the

figurine, make sure your feet are touching stone and firmly planted, and then repeat these words after me."

"Wait!" Zelma said, hastily replacing the key and retrieving the rust-colored warrior, then unscrewing its head. "What's in here that we're swapping for your brain?"

"Nothing its owner ever missed," Strange replied with a dismissive shrug. Looking down, Zelma saw a shriveled, blackened heart, still beating. She wrinkled her nose and looked away. She kicked aside some straw, clearing the flagstone beneath her, then nodded her readiness to Doc, who began the spell.

"By the wisdom of Oshtur,
And magic, her son's domain,
Exchange these items now,
The balance to maintain."

Zelma wasn't sure what she'd expected – some sort of otherworldly nimbus stretching from the figurine to Strange, where she could watch the black heart and Doc's gray matter pass each other by as they were magically swapped.

Instead, Strange cried out, his face contorted in an agony she wasn't sure his zombification allowed him to truly feel. She watched his hands reaching for his head, only to be stopped short by his chains and clench in impotent rage. She saw the light of intelligence fade from his eyes.

And heard the last word he might ever say as it did so.

"Run!"

CHAPTER FIVE

She ran.

As Zelma dashed down the short tunnel and across the ritual chamber, she felt more than heard something moving behind her. There was no sound of pursuit, no echoing footfalls or telltale flap of wings, no scrape of slithering scales or sucking ooze of some gelatinous mass, just a feeling of creeping dread that got closer with every step she took. As if someone were stalking her as she walked home alone through Central Park, and she'd left her pepper spray in her other jeans.

Zelma redoubled her pace and raced up the staircase, knowing all the while that with her perpetually clumsy feet moving so fast, tripping was inevitable. It was just a question of where it happened on the stairs and how quickly she could recover.

If she could recover. The Dweller in the Cellar – whatever it actually was – was right on her heels. She could almost feel the heat of its breath on her neck, almost smell its putrid stench.

Or maybe that was just the rank odor of her fear-sweat.

She had almost made it to the top, could see the thin

rectangle that promised safety, when her self-fulfilling prophecy of clumsiness came to be, and she stumbled over an untied shoelace. Lurching forward, she bruised both knees and skinned one palm and the other elbow on the rough edge of a step as she clutched the terra cotta warrior close. She tried to use the momentum of her fall to lunge for the door, her nails scrabbling for the wood of the frame.

Just short.

Zelma could almost feel claws sinking into the fleshy part of her calves as she lay there, sprawled across the stairs, could envision fanged, slavering jaws clamping around her ankles…

And then the cloak was lifting her up and propelling her through the doorway, where she landed stomach-first on the wooden floor with a painful thud, barely tossing the terra cotta figurine aside before it was crushed beneath her.

Quickly regaining her bearings, Zelma flopped over onto her back and kicked the door behind her closed just as an amorphous tar-black mass appeared at the top step, the white blur of a theater mask serving as some sort of face. Two hands reached out to stop the door from shutting, one with far too many fingers, all ending in snapping mouths, and the other covered in eyeballs like pus-filled boils. But the heavy oaken slab slammed closed before they could escape and Zelma scrambled to her feet and heaved the iron bar home with resounding finality.

Then she fell against the wall beside the barred door, panting, heart still hammering in her throat. Only after catching her breath did she remember the figurine, which had rolled across the hallway until it bumped up against the opposite wall.

Zelma hurried over and picked it up, hoping Doc had reinforced the clay figure magically at some point. She was relieved to see that the top was still securely in place, though upon careful examination, she noticed a hairline fracture that started at the bottom of its left foot and went up the back of the figure's leg to mid-thigh. She didn't know if she'd damaged the rust-colored vessel when she threw it or if it had already been cracked, but either way there wasn't much she could do about it. She figured as long as there was no gray matter dripping out, it was probably fine.

Probably.

She placed the figurine in the backpack she'd left by the door, then shouldered it and made her way back through the living room, following her Ariadne-inspired rope trail. She pulled up the pitons as she went; if the Cellar Dweller did somehow manage to get out of the basement, she didn't want to lead it straight back to her.

The animal noises seemed louder now, almost frantic, as though the creatures somehow sensed that the master of their domain was no longer in charge. Zelma wondered how long it would be before the tribes dared to cross the river and reignite their war, or before the jungle animals decided they were tired of being cooped up in the brownstone's living room, vast as it was, and started making their way out into the rest of the house, or the city proper.

She didn't really think that would happen; Doc's wards should hold without his being cognizant enough to maintain them, and they could stop things from leaving the Sanctum Sanctorum just as effectively as they kept them from entering. Especially things that didn't know how to bypass the barrier spells, like she did. So elephants rampaging down Bleecker Street was unlikely to be one of her problems. Which was unfortunate; *that*, she knew how to deal with. Finding a cure for the zombie apocalypse to save her mentor – and anyone else who could still be rescued – was another thing entirely.

But even if Doctor Strange's warding gave way, the brownstone's protections were unlikely to do the same. The building had been constructed on hallowed ground atop a cluster of ley lines. It had variously been a potter's field, the site of a house of torment, and then of a church. Then a satanic supper club, a well-known hedonistic speakeasy, and a flophouse. Later still, it had been the home of the Strange Memorial Metaphysical Institute, and the headquarters for two separate teams of super heroes. Even without Doctor Strange around, 177A Bleecker Street was perfectly capable of safeguarding itself.

The same could not necessarily be said of Zelma. As she made her way through the living room, a boa constrictor fell out of the branches of the tree nearest her, startling Zelma out of thoughts that had been sneaking perilously close to self-pity territory. She was almost grateful, until another heavy serpentine body plopped onto the grass, and then another, and another. Soon it was raining snakes, which didn't even deserve a song title, let alone a "Hallelujah!" and Zelma had to run and dodge them like taxis on a New York City street. The big difference being that if a taxi hit you, it would probably just keep going; none of the constrictors moved after hitting her, or the ground.

Zelma didn't have to be a herpetologist to know the animals were dead, and she could guess the reason, though she prayed to the Vishanti and any other higher powers who might be listening that she was wrong.

Doctor Strange's enchantments *were* weakening, after all. The creatures he'd played zookeeper to were freaking out and/or dying. That could just be because Doc was essentially braindead at this point.

Or it could be because he was *dead* dead.

Doc had said the magic of the shackles' aura *should* keep the Thing in the Cellar away from his cell – a word with a disturbing amount of wiggle room. Maybe he was right and the living bar tab would stay away from him because it feared the shackles that bound him, which it must know could also bind it. But how long would it take for the creature to overcome that fear, if it did exist, once it realized Strange was in no condition to defend himself?

Zelma supposed she could look inside the terra cotta warrior – if the part of Strange's brain therein was dull and lifeless, then no doubt he was, too. But she had no idea what opening the figurine might do to his prefrontal cortex if it was still active.

Great. Doc had created Schrödinger's Brain. She hadn't seen that one coming.

Once outside the confines of the living room, Zelma closed and bolted the large double doors that led to the jungle expanse. They wouldn't hold forever, but she wanted to be long gone before they failed.

She followed her nylon lifeline up one of the two curving staircases that connected the brownstone's foyer to what was usually its second floor, then navigated a confusing trail of twists and turns before coming to a piton driven into the top of another set of stairs. This stairway, however, felt no need to make even a polite nod to the laws of gravity, spiraling up into the air and arching over a vast, bottomless stairwell. The other piton was driven into the impossible staircase's bottom step, on the other side of the Stygian abyss, Zelma's lifeline drawn taut like a tightrope between the two looped metal stakes.

Well, now what?

Walk the tightrope? Checking the "Big Nope" box on that one.

Pull herself across, hand over hand, trusting her life to questionable upper body strength while she dangled precariously over the void? Check the "Not Happening" box.

Then what? She could probably manage a flying spell, but it would be much easier if she were in Doc's library with access to his vast collection of spellbooks. In her frazzled state, she wasn't sure she could pull one off from memory alone. Sure, she might get over the chasm. Or the spell might give out halfway across. Or turn her into something with handy wings but without the correct vocal equipment to reverse the enchantment once she'd landed on the other side.

Something tickled her neck. She brushed at it in annoyance as she tried to come up with a solution. Bugs had never been a problem in the brownstone while Doc was around. Not mundane ones, anyway.

She knew there was more than one way to get back to the library. She could strike out along a different, unmarked route, and hope for the best. Of course, she could end up wandering the maze of magicked corridors for the rest of her life if she tried that – which would be brief if that route didn't pass the kitchen. Even if it did, she'd have to contend with the newly escaped contents of the fridge, so she probably wasn't long for this world if she struck out on her own, regardless.

Her neck itched again, and this time she slapped at the spot, hoping to crush whatever creepy-crawly had the unmitigated nerve to be biting her right now. Her hand touched soft fabric and her sudden laughter was two parts relief and one part self-deprecation.

Of course. The cloak.

She replaced the hammer in her backpack alongside the extracted pitons and the clay figure, then closed it and made sure she was holding on to it very securely.

"Cloak," she ordered. "Once around the block, please!"

When the cloak didn't immediately respond, she laughed again.

"By which I mean, 'Take me across this big scary abyss leading to the pit of who knows what hell, please,'" she said, and this time the cloak answered, lifting her gently into the air and carrying her across the chasm, then setting her down softly on the other side, not so much as a piece of her already ruined coif out of place. Still, she didn't open her eyes until she was sure both of her feet were firmly planted on a horizontal surface.

"Thanks, Cloak!" she exclaimed, reaching up to pat the garment where it lay across her shoulder, which instantly seemed awkward and which she vowed not to do again. She settled for a compliment. "You know, they say dogs are man's best friend, and diamonds are a girl's best friend, but I'm pretty sure a cloak that's smarter than you is a magician's best friend."

The cloak was already red, but she liked to think that if it had been a paler hue, it might have blushed at the praise.

Then she bent down and started to pull the rope through the piton on this side of the chasm. The far end fell into the darkness as she wound the nylon into a coil, surprised to find that it felt heavier than usual. She soon discovered why when she pulled the last part up out of the stairwell only to find two chittering monkeys attached to it.

Her first inclination was to shoo them away, but then they lunged at her, and she saw their mouths were bloody. She didn't know if the infection that had felled Doc also affected animals, but she couldn't risk it. With a squeal of mixed anger and disgust, Zelma booted the nearest monkey off the landing and back out into the abyss, a screeching sacrifice to the void.

The other monkey's fury intensified as its fellow's howls faded away, and she ordered the cloak to wrap it up before dumping it, too, into the darkness.

"Won't ever look at Curious George quite the same after that," she muttered before remembering that talking to yourself was often a sign that you were starting to lose it. Though "starting to" just at this moment might be overly generous.

Once she removed the piton on this side of the gorge, she turned to see where the yellow nylon road would lead them next, and was delighted to see it disappear down a familiar hallway and end tied to a piton in front of a most welcome door.

The library. At last.

"Well, Cloak," she said as she started toward the door. "Now the hard part starts."

CHAPTER SIX

Zelma replaced the faded green pack in its cabinet once she was safely back inside the alcove currently doubling as the Chamber of Shadows (formerly located down the hall from the library, but rendered unusable a few months ago in an explosion). She didn't bother to take the brain-housing terra cotta warrior out of the backpack, figuring there was a fair chance she might need to bug out at some point, and it would be better to keep the clay figure with her than leave it somewhere it could fall into the wrong hands. Meaning necrotized ones.

Once Doc's brain was securely tucked away, Zelma spoke the spell he had helped her devise to summon the books she wanted without her having to spend hours traipsing through the shelves to gather them. It wasn't that she didn't know where they were – she had organized and indexed every book Doctor Strange owned, even the non-magical ones – it was just that there were so many of them, so spread out through a library that kept expanding to match the size of its collection, that one person trying to assemble a handful of tomes would take days. And she needed way more than a handful and probably didn't have all that many days to spare.

As she sat down on the carpeted floor, books began floating into the alcove chamber and arranging themselves in neat stacks around her, some opening themselves to certain pages as if awaiting her approval. There were spells for healing skin diseases and broken bones, others that could restore blood lost from mortal wounds and even restart a death-stilled heart. Zelma pored through them all, rejecting one after another. This wasn't a curse – if it had been, Doc would presumably have lifted it himself – so spells to cancel hexes were useless. She found an incantation that would spark a plague, but it required the blood of a newborn baby, so reverse engineering it wasn't really an option.

More books floated in to take the places of the ones she discarded, and Zelma had no idea how many she'd gone through when she felt a tap on her shoulder. She twisted, half-rising to one knee, heart banging out a staccato beat of sheer terror against her ribs. Had Zombie Doc escaped? Or the Thing in the Cellar?

But there was no one there.

Zelma scanned the room, eyes narrowing. She peered hard at the bookshelves; their long shadows could hide any number of unpleasant things. Including decomposing ones that might want to eat her.

She saw nothing out of place, except the books that continued to make their way from the farthest reaches of the library, drifting along on a magical current, pulled inexorably toward her by a force stronger than magnetism.

It was probably just her overactive imagination, she decided. There *were* ghosts in the Bleecker Street brownstone, but they'd been banned from the library when one of them had decided to pop out of a book as Doc opened it, causing him to spill his tea. Still, with him currently unable to enforce said ban, who knew what the haunts might decide to get up to? "Terrorize the librarian" seemed to be a perennial favorite with most library ghosts.

She realized with a start that it was getting dark out, and she wondered just how long she'd had her nose buried in the yellowing pages of Doc's ancient tomes. A sudden rumbling in her stomach reminded her that she hadn't eaten since lunch, and that didn't really count, since she'd thrown that up afterwards.

But the food was downstairs, in the pantry. And the pantry was in the kitchen. And if the living room's denizens had already been breaking out of their heretofore insulated environment, she could only imagine what the fridge's occupants were doing. By now they'd likely overrun the entire kitchen, maybe the whole first floor. She doubted anywhere in the Sanctum Sanctorum other than the library and the Sanctum Machina were truly safe at this point, because Doc had layered several more sets of wards over them in addition to the ones that kept unwanted visitors out of the building proper.

Well, it wouldn't be the first time she'd pulled an all-nighter sans food. Sans caffeine was another thing, but nothing ventured, nothing gained. Or something trite like that.

She'd just sat down and gone back to flipping through another volume of spells, this one focused on death gods and necromancy, when she felt another tap at her shoulder.

This time, though, she caught a glimpse of the tapper and immediately felt like an idiot.

It was the cloak, of course. She should have realized it sooner; it was the same tactic the crimson raiment had used to get her attention when it had helped her over the staircase abyss.

The cloak unclasped itself and tried to float so that it was in front of her, but she was sitting on a good third of its lower length. It tugged ungently, struggling to extricate itself.

"Oh, sorry!" Zelma exclaimed and scrambled to her feet, freeing the cloak to assert its fabric autonomy. Once it was floating in the air before her, it shook itself, perhaps to remove the wrinkles that had formed while Zelma sat on it. Then one end of the cloak's high, stand-up collar pointed toward her stomach, which growled as if it had just been given stage directions.

"I'm a little hungry." She shrugged. "Not much we can do about it."

Luckily, there was no chance of her dying of thirst. Wong had insisted on installing water dispensers throughout the library years ago, as Doc had a bad habit of getting so lost in his research that he forgot to eat or drink. He would often become dehydrated, so the dispensers were now stationed at intervals throughout the library such that it was impossible to be out of sight of one. Doc still became dehydrated, even so, but now it was only once every few weeks instead of every few days.

Well, it had been.

The cloak's collar pointed at her and made a back-and-forth motion, like a teacher wagging a finger, correcting her for being naughty. Then the cloak pointed to itself and made an up-and-down motion. It took Zelma a moment to catch on.

"I can't do anything about it, but you can?"

The up-and-down motion repeated.

Zelma thought about it. She supposed the cloak could get to the kitchen with little trouble; it had been living – if that was the right word to use – in the brownstone for far longer than she had and knew the building's ins and outs far better than she did. And whatever lived in the fridge or had escaped from the living room or any other place where Doc's wards might be failing would probably have little interest in eating what was essentially a flying blanket hoodie with some fancy embroidery on the edges. Assuming they could catch the cloak in the first place; Zelma had seen it in action when Doc had worn it, and it could move surprisingly fast when the need arose.

But the cloak could still be damaged, and Doc had entrusted it to her. She didn't like the idea of knowingly sending it into harm's way. Though she supposed that was what Doctor Strange did every time he donned it, seemingly without qualm. She doubted Strange anthropomorphized the garment the way she was doing; to him, it was just another tool, like the Orb of Agamotto, or its title-bestowing Eye, and its job was to protect him, not the other way around. He'd undoubtedly meant for it to do the same for Zelma. She supposed she shouldn't look a gift cloak in the seam.

"OK, but stick to the shadows and be careful. And don't bring anything back here except food!"

She started to walk over to open the library door for the cloak, but it flew past her in a flutter of scarlet, turning the handle with its prehensile collar and disappearing into the hallway, the door closing automatically in its wake. Like the wards on the Sanctum Sanctorum itself, the library's magical shielding was keyed to the residents of the brownstone; they could pass, as could anyone they willingly brought with them, provided those guests had no ill intentions.

Satisfied that the Cloak of Levitation could handle itself, Zelma sat back down and returned to her books, poring over volume after volume to find some way to reverse not just Doctor Strange's zombification, but that of everyone else who had been infected. But no spell she found could do everything she needed it to, and thus far, no combination of them could, either.

She wasn't sure how long she'd been engrossed in her reading when she felt a sudden tap on her shoulder. Even though she had been expecting it, she jumped and let out a small scream.

The cloak had returned with a box of cheese crackers, an unopened box of livestock feed masquerading as cereal, some peanut butter and half a loaf of bread, and a cannister of slimy prunes that was half full and had expired three years ago.

"Thanks, Cloak," Zelma said as it dumped its loot on the floor in front of her, surveying it with a critical eye. Then she sighed. "We are most definitely going to die here."

CHAPTER SEVEN

Zelma and Cloak – she'd come to think of the magical mantle as a sentient being in its own right – kept up this routine for several days. Zelma read through books until the words blurred on the page, gobbled down the ever-dwindling supply of pantry spoils when she remembered to eat, paced around the library arguing with herself, and sometimes even slept. Cloak foraged less and less successfully for food and acted as Zelma's blanket whenever she fell over from sheer exhaustion.

Doctor Strange hadn't bothered to cover the Orb of Agamotto after finishing his conversation with Clea – to be fair, it wasn't as if they'd had boatloads of time. Zelma looked into it periodically, trying to gauge how the world outside the Sanctum Sanctorum was faring.

That answer was "not well".

Early on, she'd wondered if she might be able to reach out to other people through it, as Doc had done. Preferably uninfected magic-using people who could help her figure out how to save Doc, because she couldn't imagine how she was going manage it on her own. But she'd take whoever she could get at this point.

As if responding to those thoughts, the roiling clouds within the sphere had begun to coalesce. She hadn't been thinking of anyone in particular, but Doc had been with the Avengers when he got bit, so they had been on her mind, and the Orb had shown her scenes of various heroes across the world. Zelma had watched, horrified, as they fell to either infection or their fellows, again and again, the same drama repeating no matter where the orb cast its gaze.

In the skies above New York, the orb had shown her Falcon, his only visible injury a missing ear, catching Archangel in the air and tearing off his wings, muttering about Happy Hour menus as the mutant screamed in agony.

The next day, or the one after that – Zelma had already lost count – the orb had broadcast a gruesome scene beneath the surface of the Atlantic Ocean. A zombified Namor had been attacking Namorita, ripping off her foot-wings like an unwanted garnish before beginning to consume her from the ankles up, constantly glancing over his rotted shoulder as he hurried to devour his cousin before the group of insatiable aquatic zombies a scant nautical mile behind him arrived demanding their share.

Now she looked into the orb, and the sphere of horrors focused in on an island off the coast of Scotland, where Gambit was flinging his magically charged playing cards at an incapacitated Rogue, or what was left of her – her head, torso with the right arm intact, left leg ending at the knee. Zelma wouldn't have recognized the heroine at all if not for the telltale skunk streak running through the other woman's brown hair. It wasn't until Rogue stopped dragging herself along the ground and Gambit hurried over and began feasting on her remains that Zelma realized he was the infected one, and not his wife, Anna Marie.

As she shivered with revulsion, she recalled that Rogue had once led the Avengers Unity Division, which might be why the orb thought her worth including in its Avengers-themed murder montages. But if it was only showing her Avengers, and had now gone this many degrees away from Kevin Bacon, did that mean that Avengers-adjacent heroes were all that were left alive?

As if confirming that despairing thought, the orb switched back to America, homing in on a group of teens in what was likely Los Angeles, given the palm tree-lined streets and the ocean in the background. A glimpse of the iconic Hollywood sign confirmed it. Zelma racked her brain trying to think of what Avengers-adjacent heroes might be in the City of Angels; she could only see their backs, and they were moving fast. Pursuing, or being pursued, Zelma couldn't immediately determine.

Then the orb zoomed in a little closer, and Zelma could see that one wore a sort of short red cape around his shoulders and carried a staff from which he projected energy bolts. Another wore a questionable purple ensemble and was releasing explosive arrows from a bow.

Wiccan and Kate Bishop, aka Hawkeye? That would make this group the Young Avengers, although they were on the opposite coast from their usual stomping grounds. But Zelma had always been more interested in magic than in super powers or mutant abilities, and she didn't really keep up with who was with what group or where they were headquartered. She recognized Wiccan because of his considerable arcane ability and his relationship to the Scarlet Witch and her mythical chaos magic. Doc had still been skeptical of the true source of Wanda's reality-altering abilities prior to his zombification; he obviously had no thoughts on that matter now. Or on any other.

The orb moved in like a cameraman, coming up just behind the heads of the two heroes in the lead, Wiccan – aka Billy Kaplan – and Teddy Altman, the shapeshifter commonly known as Hulkling, due to both his extraordinary strength and his preference for transforming himself into a teenaged version of the Hulk.

Scratch that; these two were heroes no more. The view from the orb showed the back of Billy's head, the wound on his neck now clearly visible beneath his short hair. Zelma hadn't noticed it at first because the blood blended into the crimson of his cape. And Teddy didn't even *have* a whole head. Part of it had been caved in by what Zelma could only assume had been a massive haymaker. He had to have sustained at least some brain damage from that, but it wasn't slowing him down. Zelma took note. Pop culture rules pretty much agreed that shooting, stabbing, or otherwise causing a brain injury that would be fatal to a living person would put a zombie down for good. So either pop culture was wrong (gasp!), or Hulkling hadn't been wounded in just the right spot. Given that prevailing wisdom also said that the lumbering dead only hungered for human brains, and Doc had eaten a lot more than that, human and not so much, she was going to err on the side of caution and just assume everything she'd ever seen, read, or heard about zombies that didn't specifically come from a practitioner of Vodou was flat-out bull.

More worrying was the fact that the zombified Young Avengers seemed to be chasing another group of teenagers. Zelma recognized the pastel lightshow emanating from one girl's hair and the donut-capped staff another wielded. These were the Runaways – or what remained of them.

Zelma was first stunned and then elated to see that they weren't zombies.

Yet.

Karolina Dean, who was part alien of some sort, was floating in the air, surrounded by a cotton candy-colored nimbus that made her look like an angel from a child's picture book. The solar beams she sent out to blast craters in Teddy's head and chest, however, were anything but innocent. The bolts threw him back into the rest of the team behind him, knocking them over like bowling pins. Wiccan was the only one left standing.

He howled and pointed his staff at Karolina.

"You'll pay for that!" he shouted, then began to cast a spell. His powers, like Doc's, were seemingly unaffected by his apparent demise. "*Quenchherlight. Quenchherlight. Quenchher–*"

He didn't get to finish. The other girl Zelma recognized, Nico Minoru, had leveled her own staff at the young warlock. Zelma was surprised to see that the hand Nico clutched the staff in was made of a silvery metal, but then the other witch spoke a single word that chased all thoughts of bionic arms from Zelma's mind.

"Cease."

Whether Nico had meant for him to stop breathing or simply stop speaking, what she *got* was Billy ceasing to… exist. The other magic-user abruptly burst like an overlarge bubble, spraying everything and everyone around him with a fine scarlet mist. His staff fell to the ground with a clatter and lay there, useless.

"You've gotta be faster than that, Billy," Nico said grimly, shaking blood droplets out of her night-black hair. "Don't use three words when one will do."

"You want fast?" asked a voice from out of the air beside her. "I'll give you fast."

The air distorted, and suddenly Tommy Shepherd appeared beside her out of a blur of motion too swift to be seen. His iconic green leotard with its white racing stripe had been clawed nearly off his torso, making Zelma wonder which zombified hero had gotten to him. Wolverine? Or perhaps it had been the Runaways' pet dinosaur, Old Lace? Neither it nor its bonded human, Gertrude Yorkes, were anywhere to be seen. Whoever or whatever had managed to carve the speedster up had been infected, because the edges of the parallel wounds were rotted away. Or maybe he'd been zombified before he ever got attacked. No way of knowing.

Tommy – Billy's brother – was true to his word. He lunged toward Nico, his hair a smear of white as he went for her neck. The Runaway couldn't hope to cast a spell in time to save herself.

But Zelma could.

"By Munnopor's Mist,
Here, now, I insist!"

Doc would have had her scrubbing the floors for a week if he'd heard it, but the impromptu teleportation spell worked. Nico disappeared from Los Angeles just as Speed's teeth were about to clamp down on her jugular. She reappeared in the Bleecker Street library, still in the process of bringing up her metal arm to protect her throat while jerking futilely away from the coming attack. Unable to check her movement, Nico fell backward into a stack of books, scattering them and sending herself sprawling.

She quickly regained her bearings and wasted no time asking questions. Nico clocked the floating orb as she scrambled to her feet, rushing over to it just in time to witness Karolina's rainbow light being extinguished as the hungry Young Avengers who remained descended upon her.

Nico turned on the apprentice with an anguished cry.

"Why didn't you save her, too?"

Straight and to the point. No time squandered on unimportant things like gratitude.

Still, her tone wasn't accusing. Nico Minoru was a witch; more, she was a witch whose powers required never repeating the same spell twice. Zelma imagined she'd had her fair share of backfires and failures.

"I'm sorry," Zelma replied contritely, the quick shift from elation to sorrow almost giving her whiplash. "The only spell I know that can do that is the Teleportation Spell of the Vishanti, and that requires complete calm and inner peace. Those are in short supply right now."

"Then why didn't you save her instead of me?"

"I–" Zelma began, then stopped. There was no answer to that question that would assuage the pain she saw in Nico's eyes. Especially since it had never even occurred to Zelma to save the alien Runaway. She'd seen a fellow witch in jeopardy and instinctively – maybe selfishly – acted to save one of her own. One whose magic might be able to help her save Doc. "I'm sorry."

Nico squeezed her eyes shut, her lips compressing into a thin white line. She bowed her head so that her bobbed black hair obscured her features. Zelma suspected it was because she didn't want the librarian to see her grief. Maybe because then she'd have to acknowledge it herself.

The two witches stood that way for several minutes, Nico's breath hitched and her shoulders trembling, Zelma looking on helplessly, not knowing what, if anything, she should do.

At last, Nico raised her head again, swiping her right hand – the non-metal one – across her eyes and glowering at Zelma, as if daring the librarian to speak. When Zelma stayed silent, Nico's expression relaxed somewhat and she looked around the room, finally seeming to take stock of the alcove and the library beyond and noting the cloak Zelma wore.

"Doctor Strange?"

Zelma shook her head.

"He's been... neutralized... for the time being. Until I can find a way to fix this."

Nico barked out a short, bitter laugh at that.

"Look around you," she said, using her silver arm to gesture at the orb, which continued to show heroes dying and turning. "There's no fixing this. There's only doing the one thing Karolina and the others couldn't manage."

"What's that?" Zelma asked curiously.

"Try not to die."

CHAPTER EIGHT

Nico Minoru knew where she was – you couldn't use magic in this corner of the universe and not know of the Earth's Sorcerer Supreme and his Sanctum Sanctorum. She even knew who the anxious, bespectacled young woman drowning in an overlarge sweater was – by name, at least, and reputation. Doctor Strange's librarian-slash-apprentice, Zelma Stanton. The woman who had saved her.

Her, and not Karolina. But Nico was not going to think about that. Because she knew if she did, the fragile composure she was barely maintaining – all that was keeping her from collapsing into a sobbing heap, paralyzed by loss – would crumble to nothing. And considering that self-control was pretty much the only thing Nico had left at this point, she really kind of wanted to hang on to it.

Nico took in a deep, steadying breath and exhaled it slowly, trying to focus and take stock of the situation.

OK. It looked like it was just her and Glasses Girl. Great. If they were all the good doctor and the rest of the world had to count on, they were all doomed.

They needed help.

Nico nodded to the floating crystal sphere currently streaming Romero's greatest hits.

"Can you control that thing? Make it show you what you want to see?"

Zelma blinked at her, owlish.

"More or less."

"Good. Then tell it to find someone who might actually be able to do something to end this horror show we've found ourselves in. I don't know about you, but this is *not* how I want to make my movie debut."

"OK," Zelma replied slowly, blinking again. "Who did you have in mind?"

"The Scarlet Witch," Nico answered without hesitation. Though she had just offed the witch's reincarnated son; Wanda wasn't likely to be particularly happy about that, even if it had been justifiable self-defense. "On second thought–"

But it was too late. Zelma had already turned her attention to the orb, a look of concentration furrowing her brow beneath her black beanie.

Suddenly, the image in the orb went snowy, like an old-fashioned television that had lost its antenna in a windstorm. Then it resolved again, inside a ballroom of what might have been the Avengers Mansion, not that anyone would recognize it now. All the windows had been boarded over and the room's only light came from scattered candelabras.

Even if it was the home of the world's mightiest heroes, the dance unfolding on the polished hardwood was anything but noble. The floor was covered in bodies, most of them seemingly human. Nico couldn't be certain, but she thought they were still alive; she could see involuntary twitches of movement here and there, the kind you made when you were trying not to be noticed.

But even if some of them were still alive, that didn't mean they were safe. Far from it.

The synthezoid Vision, apparently the shepherd of this mostly unconscious flock, was carrying the body of one of his sacrificial lambs over to a pile of cushions and pillows no doubt scavenged from parlors and bedrooms throughout the grand abode.

What lay atop that pile was beyond horrific.

The Scarlet Witch, now just a head perched on a bloody silver platter, salivated as her android lover brought her his version of a box of chocolates, ripping off limbs and feeding them to her bit by bit, like the choicest of truffles. The crude beginnings of a headless metal skeleton lay on a lab table in the background, and Nico wondered if Vision was fashioning Wanda a new body for her head, rebuilding her in his own image.

"Eww," she said, unable to keep the disgust out of her voice or off her face. "That's just gross."

"How is she even eating that?" Zelma asked, nose squinched and mouth puckered. "She doesn't have a stomach!"

Nico shrugged.

"Looks like it doesn't matter," she replied flatly, schooling her face back to impassivity, or something like it. Somebody needed to keep a cool head here. And if playing Ice Queen helped Nico keep her thoughts off Karolina and the others, that was just gravy. Or maybe some other metaphor that didn't involve food, considering. "She's still hungry, and Vision seems more than happy to feed her."

"I thought they were divorced, though?" Zelma half-asked, though it seemed to Nico more like she was questioning her own card catalogue of memories than asking for the Runaway's input. Which was fine by Nico; she didn't make a habit of keeping up with the love lives of the Avengers. She was usually too busy running – sometimes *from* them. She didn't care who they were hooking up with, just which one had her and her team in their sights.

Not that she had a team anymore.

"Doesn't he have a robot family somewhere," Zelma continued, oblivious to Nico's dark musings, "with a robot dog and whatever the robot equivalent of a white picket fence is?"

Nico shrugged again.

"Just because you break up with someone, that doesn't necessarily mean you stop loving them." Nico couldn't help but think of Alex Wilder, her fellow Runaway whom she'd had feelings for long before they and the others had ever learned that their parents were super villains and part of the Pride, a human-sacrificing, Gibborim-worshipping cult. Long before they'd crossed that cult and been forced to run. That Alex had ultimately wound up betraying her and the rest of the Runaways to their parents had broken Nico's heart, and he'd died because of it.

But that hadn't stopped Nico from caring about him. She'd even tried to resurrect him using Marie Laveau's Black Mirror, but the less said about that disaster, the better.

And Karolina, whose heart Nico supposed she herself had broken by rejecting advances she hadn't been ready for at the time, and then rebounding into a relationship with Victor Mancha, who in turn betrayed Nico by falling in love with someone else.

Some stars, once crossed, could never be uncrossed. Whether you wanted them to be or not.

Zelma was nodding.

"I suppose that's true. I mean, look at Doc and Clea. They're technically divorced, but she was the first one he thought to contact when he'd fed enough to temporarily regain his sanity. Who knows, maybe if they hadn't both been sorcerers of the supreme ilk–"

"Wait. What?" Nico interrupted. Had Zelma just so casually said what Nico thought she had? "Back up. Strange went to the Dark Dimension? After he'd been infected? It's already spread that far?" She suddenly felt like an Ice Queen in truth, with liquid nitrogen flowing through her veins, freezing her from the inside out. Like someone had not just stepped on her grave, but decided to set up camp there.

"No, of course not," Zelma replied, looking affronted, though Nico didn't much care about offending the librarian's delicate sensibilities. Not if Strange had already doomed not only this world, but potentially all of them. "He used the orb to warn her to close off her dimension, and to spread the word for all the other Sorcerer Supremes to do the same. He was trying to *keep* it from spreading."

Well, that was a relief. But that wasn't the only thing Zelma had said that had caught Nico up short.

"And you said he… *regained* his sanity? After he'd eaten enough to… what? Satisfy a hunger so intense it has lovers devouring each other? What on Earth did he eat that managed to do that?" Then she realized that was the wrong question. "*Who* did he eat?"

Zelma's eyes glistened for a moment, then she blinked quickly several times and her gaze hardened.

"Don't ask questions you don't want to know the answers to."

It was then that Nico realized she hadn't seen Strange's manservant, Wong, whom she'd expected to find hovering about like some father-figure-slash-butler to a bratty billionaire who was in severe need of trauma therapy.

Zelma was probably right. Whoever had been the catalyst for Doctor Strange's brief return to sanity, there was nothing Nico could do for them now. She couldn't dwell on the people she hadn't been able to save. That way lay madness.

Nico turned her attention back to the orb.

"Okay, Maximoff isn't an option. Maybe… Agatha Harkness?"

Agatha was an old witch, rumored to have watched Atlantis fall and to have escaped the burnings in Salem. She'd been both Franklin Reed's nanny and the Scarlet Witch's teacher – before Wanda had killed her during a nervous breakdown with world-changing consequences. But death hadn't kept Harkness in its clutches for long. No one knew how powerful she really was, and no one was willing to cross her and find out.

Zelma nodded and concentrated on the orb again. This time, the sphere went snowy, and stayed that way.

"Maybe she's dead? Again?" the librarian ventured after a moment, a bead of sweat forming at her hairline.

Nico frowned at that. She had no idea how the orb worked – it clearly wasn't your average crystal ball – but typically if you scryed for someone who had passed, you could at least locate their spirit. You wouldn't just come up blank.

Unless they had completely ceased to exist in any form, anywhere.

Or they were shielded. Nico fervently hoped it was the latter.

"Maybe she's hiding somewhere magic can't find her. That's what I'd be doing." She glanced about the library alcove, wondering what sort of defenses the Master of the Mystical Arts had in place. Then she looked at Zelma, her eyes narrowing. "That's what I *am* doing. Right?"

Zelma gave an apologetic half-shrug.

"As far as I know. The Sanctum's wards are holding. Doc's wards are... mostly holding. But I don't know how long that will last if we don't find a way to cure him, and soon."

Nico snorted at that. She doubted there was a cure – if there was, surely some smarty-pants Avenger scientist or Wakandan princess would have figured it out by now. Even if it had only been, what... less than a week? How was that even possible?

"Well, that's encouraging," she replied, not bothering to hide her sarcasm. It was beginning to look more and more like she'd gone from the frying pan into the crockpot. Either way, her goose was getting cooked – fast or slow was the only real question now.

"Maybe Doctor Voodoo?" Zelma ventured.

Nico snorted again.

"I'd take Doctor Doom at this point." Actually, Doom wouldn't be a bad choice. He wasn't exactly the hero type, but he knew his way around a spellbook.

"I'll try both," Zelma said, grimacing. Nico wondered if the librarian had been trying for a plucky smile. If so, she'd failed spectacularly.

The orb remained snowy.

"Magik. Enchantress. Daimon Hellstrom."

Nothing.

"Morgan Le Fay."

Finally, movement. The orb cleared briefly to show the image of a shadowed iron cauldron, but there was no clue as to its location or contents.

"Great. She left her 'out of office' cauldron on," Zelma muttered. She kept trying, her voice gaining octaves of distress with each subsequent failure. "Margali Szardos. Elizabeth Twoyoungmen."

The orb snowed back over.

"Maybe you broke it," Nico offered after a few moments, smiling brightly at the annoyed look Zelma flashed her. Once she had the librarian's attention, though, she stopped smiling, her face settling into more serious, familiar lines. "Look, this isn't working. If there are any unzombified magic-users of any skill left, they're smart enough to have either skipped dimensions before the shutdown or gone into hiding. We're not going to find help that way."

"We still have access to Doc's entire library," Zelma replied, gesturing to the stacks of books surrounding her like a wall of eager puppies starved for attention. "I've catalogued and indexed every one of these. There's got to be something in one of them that can help."

"Even if there is, how long will it take to find that one spell in a collection this vast? How long have you already spent looking?" Nico asked. There had to be tens of thousands of books in Strange's library, and those were just the ones she could see from the alcove. And having access to a spellbook wasn't the same as being able to use it. She said as much to Zelma.

"Well, what do you suggest, then?" the librarian asked, irritation edging her words. Nico imagined she was getting on the other woman's nerves, but Zelma would just have to deal with it. The zombie apocalypse wasn't going anywhere, and it was equally unlikely that Nico's often untimely candor would choose a crisis like this to take a vacation.

"We've clearly got a monster plague on our hands," Nico replied. "So we'd be best served by finding a monster hunter. Luckily, I happen to know one. *And* where we can find her."

"Her?" Zelma asked, frowning. "Her, who?"

Nico smiled again, this time with just a hint of smugness. Well, maybe more than a hint.

"Elsa Bloodstone."

CHAPTER NINE

"Bloodstone? As in Ulysses Bloodstone's daughter?" Zelma asked, seeming to perk up at the thought of recruiting a renowned monster slayer. "Great! Tell me where she is, I'll have the orb find her, and then we can teleport her here."

Nico shook her head.

"It won't be that simple," she replied. As if anything ever was. "The Bloodstones have been hunting monsters for centuries. You don't live that long in that business without learning how to cover your tracks – conventionally *and* magically. Your little crystal ball won't show us squat."

"It's not a–" Zelma began indignantly, but Nico cut her off.

"Doesn't matter. It won't work–"

"Elsa Bloodstone!" Zelma said defiantly to the orb. As Nico had expected, it continued to show its blizzard of nothingness. She didn't bother with an "I told you so". Instead, she continued speaking as though she'd never been interrupted.

"If we want Elsa's help – and trust me, we do – then we're going to have to go to her."

Zelma paled and gulped awkwardly, as if she was trying to swallow something that didn't want to stay down.

"You mean… leave the Sanctum Sanctorum?"

You'd think Nico had suggested eating babies or banning pumpkin spice or something equally indecent, not just abandoning the protection of what was likely one of the safest places left on Earth.

"When it comes to magical protections, I think Bloodstone Manor can hold its own," she replied, though that was just an assumption on her part. A reasonable one, to be sure, but still an assumption, seeing as she'd never been there.

"So we're going to England? I thought I read about a Bloodstone Lodge there? Though Ulysses Bloodstone had bases all over the world, of course."

"Boston," Nico corrected quickly, hoping Zelma wouldn't notice the look of surprise that must have flashed across her face at Zelma's mention of the British-based manor. She'd forgotten there was another manor in England. Nico had met Elsa's younger brother Cullen several years before she'd met Elsa – if you could call trying to kill each other as part of a sociopath's deranged gladiatorial games "meeting" someone. She knew that Cullen had gone to boarding school in England, though most people wouldn't consider Braddock Academy anything quite so mundane, but she hadn't quite remembered him having a home there. A forgivable lapse, given the whole murdering each other part of the "her meeting Cullen Bloodstone" equation. Still, it made perfect sense, since that was where Elsa had largely been raised, and why her vocabulary consisted almost entirely of proper-sounding expletives like "bollocks" and "sod off".

"Not sure that's any better," the librarian remarked, "considering the east coast was Ground Zero for this thing."

"Flights are cheaper?" Nico offered, earning her the side-eye from Zelma. Then the Runaway grew serious. "We can teleport to the manor grounds; those shouldn't be warded. The house is also a museum of sorts, so it might have simple protections to keep out thieves; nothing we can't handle. The real test will be the basement."

Zelma made a face.

"The basement. Why did it have to be the basement?"

"Just lucky, I guess," Nico replied sardonically. She wasn't too thrilled about knocking on Elsa Bloodstone's cellar door, either; she'd seen Elsa in action, and the monster hunter fought dirty. Any boobytraps she'd laid for would-be intruders were likely to cause a great deal of pain before they killed you.

Zelma was silent for long moments as she considered Nico's idea. Finally, she sighed.

"OK," she said reluctantly. "For the record, I think this plan sucks like a black hole, but I don't have any better ones. Just let me grab my backpack and some supplies before we go."

"Whatever," Nico said with a shrug. She thought the plan sucked, too, but she wasn't about to admit that to the librarian. If it was up to Zelma, they'd spend weeks scouring through ancient tomes trying to find a way to reverse whatever had happened, and even if they somehow succeeded, by the time they did, there wouldn't be anybody left to save *but* Doctor Strange. As much as she knew the bespectacled apprentice wouldn't want to hear it, there were some things magic just couldn't fix. At least not alone. It wasn't an idea Nico found all that comforting herself.

Her natural inclination was to run. That's what you did when the world went crazy. But she'd learned that there were only two directions you could run in – away from trouble, or toward it. Running away meant turning your back on something that probably wanted you dead, thereby increasing the likelihood of said deadness occurring. Running toward trouble meant you could see what was coming, and maybe even take steps to avoid it. You might still wind up dead, but at least you'd go down swinging.

And after watching Karolina being swarmed by the Young Avengers, and even some of the Runaways, Nico wanted to do some swinging. She wanted to hit something and keep hitting it until the pain of watching her Majesdanian friend's light be so brutally extinguished didn't stab grief and regret into her heart with every breath.

Until the horror of watching the super-strong little sister of their team, Molly Hayes, getting her heart vibrated out of her chest by Tommy Shepherd stopped playing out on the insides of Nico's eyelids every time she dared close them. Until the sight of Molly, her chest now a gaping, flesh-fringed hole, getting up, chasing down Gert and wrenching her teammate's head from her body didn't make Nico want to start screaming and never stop.

Nico was not a "glass half-full" kind of person; she tended to think that if the glass *were* half-full, whatever it was full *of* would probably kill her. Most likely in a slow, painful, and gruesome fashion. So unlike Zelma, she imagined the chances of them finding any kind of cure for this super-powered zombie apocalypse probably lived somewhere in the Negative Zone. If they could find it and turn some people back to normal, great. But at this point, all she really wanted was some payback.

And nobody did payback quite like Elsa Bloodstone.

She'd met Elsa by chance, when they'd both sought respite at the remote hot springs outside Ouray, Colorado, and instead stepped into a Kafka story. Nico had been running from Captain Marvel and Queen Medusa of the Inhumans, who were the de facto leaders of A-Force while Jennifer Walters – aka the She-Hulk – had been left comatose after a battle with Thanos. The two heroines had sought to arrest Nico for a potential future crime foreseen by the Predictor, Ulysses Cain. Cain had had a vision of Nico murdering an innocent named Alice, and apparently that was all it took to destroy the fragile bonds of loyalty left among A-Force's members in the wake of Jen's forced departure.

So Nico had done what she did best and booked it. She had safehouses all over the country, for when things went sideways – and they always went sideways eventually, even when working with supposed allies. She'd chosen this one for her escape because of the nearby hot springs. After fighting against the sorceress Countess, then having her friends turn on her, she'd needed to destress a little.

Unfortunately, the universe had other plans.

She'd opened the door of the rundown safehouse – more of a safeshack, really – and stumbled into a swarm of human-sized flying insects, nearly getting mowed down by one piloted by a foul-mouthed redhead.

Enter Elsa Bloodstone.

The bug people had been changed by their queen, who was hiding in an abandoned mine in the mountains overlooking the town. A queen who had once been a young human girl... named Alice.

Nico and Elsa had bonded over the fact that they both

had artificial limbs. Nico had gotten her silvery witch-arm when possessed fellow Runaway Chase Stein ripped off her flesh-and-bone one during the same "games" where she had met Elsa's brother. Elsa's original hand had been torn off by her father, and now she directed the power of her bloodstone through what she called her "fancy bloodstone hand". The two had jokingly decided to form a club – the "Badass Chicks Who Lost Appendages Thanks to Jerks," or the BCWLATJ. They'd agreed that Misty Knight should be an honorary member, though the name might need a little work.

And then they had kicked bug abdomen, and Nico had sort of killed Alice at the girl-slash-bug-queen's request, but then Alice transformed into something new and removed herself as a threat, and all the bugs metamorphosized back into people with very sore abdomens, and so maybe Nico hadn't really done anything wrong, after all. Not that it mattered. She still felt guilty.

And that had been the last time Nico had seen the gun-toting monster-killer with the mouth of a dozen sailors. They'd parted at the hot springs, a scantily clad Elsa bathing in the water's balmy embrace and inviting Nico to join her. Nico had declined; she'd needed to get back to check on Jen's condition. It hadn't occurred to her until much later to wonder why that brief exchange still burned so brightly in her memory.

Had Karolina known something Nico didn't? Was Nico giving out some sort of signal? She *did* think Karolina was beautiful and *had* been sorely tempted to join Elsa in the hot springs, but that didn't necessarily mean she was attracted to them. Did it?

She gave Zelma a measuring glance as the black-haired

librarian returned to the alcove, a bulge beneath Doctor Strange's Cloak of Levitation making it look like she'd come to audition for the part of Quasimodo. Nico hoped the other woman didn't have any ideas about the Runaway wanting to play the role of La Esmeralda. Even if she was interested in girls – and the jury was still out on that subject – she didn't think Zelma would be her type. The librarian reminded Nico too much of herself, or at least of how she'd been before the Runaways found themselves on the mean streets of Los Angeles. Whether you had access to magic or powers or not, that sort of thing changed you. Usually not in good ways.

"OK," Zelma announced, tossing the cloak back to reveal a drab olive-colored backpack that gave off a slight aura of magic; Nico assumed it had been spelled to either hold more or weigh less than it normally should. Clever.

As Zelma's cloak settled, tiny shards of what Nico thought might be glass cascaded in a sparkling rain from the librarian's beanie. She considered asking what had happened, then thought better of it. She probably didn't want to know.

"I picked up some things from the Mystic Forge," Zelma continued, "and gathered up the last of the pantry offerings. Peanut butter and admittedly stale gluten-free pretzels. Doc wasn't – *isn't* – one for snacking."

If that was the extent of the food selection, Nico didn't blame him.

"Mystic Forge?"

"Doc's Sanctum Machina. It's where he plays mad magical scientist. It's got a Faltine Furnace and a Wall of Infinite Elements. He makes weapons there, mostly. It's pretty cool." Zelma paused for a moment, her enthusiasm quickly replaced by sorrow. "He'd never have let me in there if he were of sound mind and body."

"So what did you grab?" Nico asked, her curiosity more than piqued. If the world weren't burning down around her, she'd pay real cash money to explore Doctor Strange's laboratory. She supposed world-saving had to come first, though. Being a hero sucked sometimes.

"The Amulet of Agamotto, for one," Zelma replied, pulling said amulet out from under her shirt collar, along with a glittering key on a cord, which she quickly stuffed back under her sweater. The amulet was a golden square with a blue eye in the center that could have been carved sapphire or an actual functioning eyeball; Nico was pretty sure it winked at her. "It sees things we can't – physical, magical, even psychic. Might be useful if we're going to be skulking around in the dark. Though I brought a flashlight, too. A little operational redundancy never hurts."

True, but there had to have been something better than a magical nightlight to borrow from Doctor Strange's mystical armory.

"So you got yourself a fashion accessory. Great. Did you get anything actually useful?"

Zelma glared at her.

"It's all 'useful', or it wouldn't be in the Forge in the first place," she replied, a frown furrowing the patch of forehead not completely covered by hair and beanie. "I got a dagger, some scrolls, a few crystals–"

Nico groaned.

"You're not one of *those* witches, are you? We can't raise our consciousness or balance our chakras out of one of Elsa's boobytraps."

The librarian sniffed haughtily.

"Please. These aren't chunks of quartz from your local new age shop. These are relics, and in the right hands, they're deadly."

Zelma didn't specify if her hands were the right ones, and Nico decided it might be better not to ask.

"Fine," she said. "Fortunately, I don't need to be calm to teleport people. So, if you're ready...?"

Zelma gave the alcove one last longing look, then turned her gaze back to Nico and nodded.

Nico planted the end of the Staff of One into the carpeted alcove floor.

"Manor."

A bolt of lavender electricity snaked out from the circle atop the staff to create a bright blue-white hole in the floor a few feet in front of Nico. She gestured to it with her free hand.

"Ladies first."

Zelma side-eyed her dubiously, a look Nico imagined would become quite familiar the longer they remained in each other's company, but the librarian stepped into the glowing blue portal without hesitation and disappeared.

Nico followed. She felt a rush of icy wind around her as the world turned the color of a sunlit glacier, and then she was standing on a well-manicured lawn next to a sign that read "Bloodstone Curios" in a pretentious, flowing script. Zelma was standing a short distance away, surveying the area. She looked at Nico as the blue portal closed beneath the Runaway's feet.

"So... which way to the manor?"

Nico looked around. The grassy expanse they stood on was interrupted only by the sign and a paved driveway that cleaved a neat rectangle through the perimeter hedge. All she could see was green, as if she'd transported them to Boston's downtown St Paddy's Day festivities instead of to the manor grounds located several miles outside that city's limits. Though manor-*less* grounds might be a more accurate description.

Nico frowned. Had Elsa cast some sort of invisibility spell to protect her home and base of monster-hunting operations? That would make sense; if she were hunting zombies, she wouldn't want them following her back to her lair.

Zelma seemed to have the same thought, for she reached up to touch the amulet she wore, murmuring words Nico couldn't hear.

"It's not cloaked, to magical or mundane sight," Zelma announced after scanning the area. "It simply isn't here." Then she cocked her head to the side, as if trying to hear the amulet better.

"What's it saying?" Nico demanded, worried about being out in the open. They didn't know how the zombies tracked their prey, but she knew several of the super-powered Avengers and villains used scent, and the two women hadn't thought to disguise theirs before coming here.

"There is something… a pile of blackened timbers?" Zelma squinted through her lenses, and Nico turned to see what the librarian was looking at.

Nico swore. She hadn't noticed the rubble before because she'd been looking higher, searching for an intact, multi-story building. But there it was, a darkness in the center of all the green, a burnt-out husk, victim to some fire that couldn't be quenched, its flames hungrily consuming everything in their path, leaving little more than the building's foundation.

Bloodstone Manor was gone, and with it, their only way to find Elsa.

Nico swallowed down the sludgy lump of despair-flavored failure that threatened to choke her.

Now what?

CHAPTER TEN

Nico wasn't as good at hiding her emotions as she thought she was. Zelma could tell the other woman was distressed by this wrinkle in a plan that, in fairness, had needed a few more cycles in the dryer. She didn't understand why, though.

Yes, the manor here in Boston had burned down, but that didn't mean Elsa had been in it at the time. Even if she had, if she hadn't made it out alive, the monster hunter would have shown up in some form when they searched for her with the orb. She'd obviously fled somewhere else with magical protections before the fire got to her, and the logical choice would be the London manor, since it was probably spelled even more heavily than this one had been. But maybe Nico knew something about the various Bloodstone homesteads that Zelma didn't.

"She's not dead, if that's what you're worried about," Zelma said, reaching out to place an awkward hand on Nico's shoulder. She meant the gesture to be comforting, but it was stiff and robotic, and Nico pulled away from her touch.

"I know that!" Nico snapped, her dark eyes narrowing. The

expression she wore, along with the ragged purple and black dress and striped tights, could have made her look like every little kid's idea of the iconic scary Halloween witch. But with her studded leather bracelets, black hiking boots, and shaggy bob, she was more likely to pass for your average angry teenager going through a goth phase.

Except goth girls couldn't usually kill you with a word. Though they could make you wish they had.

"Then what are you so upset about?" Zelma asked. "Let's just go to London, to the other manor, or whatever."

"I- I just… I don't know," Nico finally spluttered, her cheeks flushing a dark pink that stood out prominently against her hair and dress. "It's just… this wasn't how this was supposed to go."

Then Zelma understood. Nico wasn't flummoxed by the manor's destruction or even what it might mean for her friend, Elsa. Zelma was sure their inability to locate the monster hunter must weigh on the Runaway's mind, but it wasn't the heaviest burden Nico carried. That one was self-imposed.

Nico was upset because she had been wrong.

Zelma had seen this happen with Doc. When you were responsible for the lives of other people, when they looked to you to protect them and your decisions were a matter of life and death for them, you couldn't afford to make mistakes. So even though this minor misstep was easily corrected, to Nico, it still counted as a failure. And failure was not to be tolerated.

"Get over yourself," Zelma said impatiently, words she'd wanted to say to Doc a hundred times but had never had the temerity to voice. "Everybody makes mistakes; it's not the end of the world. Arguably, failure is the only way anyone ever learns anything. How can you course-correct if you never even know you're off course?"

"*Arguably*," Nico spat back at her, "somebody somewhere made a mistake, and it *is* the end of the world."

"Well, then, see? Nothing for you to worry about. The worst has already happened."

Nico opened her mouth as if to argue the point – or possibly to do something nasty and irrevocable with the Staff of One – but then she clamped her lips shut again and just glared.

Zelma was about to open her own mouth to tell the other witch to get on with it when the amulet began to vibrate. The Amulet of Agamotto, a second cousin three times removed from Doctor Strange's Eye of Agamotto, did not share the bulk of that artifact's powers. But a blue ray of light suddenly shot out of the amulet's eye. It ended at the still-smoldering ruins of Bloodstone Manor.

"Didn't you say that thing could see things we can't?" Nico asked, her ire fading as they were faced with this new puzzle.

"Yes. It can penetrate illusions and detect magical emissions. It's kind of like a carbon monoxide monitor and a drug-sniffing dog all rolled up in one – except it detects magic, not deadly gases and illegal substances." Truthfully, Zelma wasn't sure how it worked. Since Doc hadn't meant for her to have it yet, he'd never briefed her on its exact capabilities. But she'd read about it in several of the library's books on Agamotto and the creation of magic, so if she was off target, it wasn't by much.

"So it's detecting… what?" Nico asked, her brow creasing in thought. "The residual energy of whatever magic was used to torch the manor? What's left of whatever magical boobytraps Elsa had set up there? Or of the curios she had in the museum?"

"Only one way to find out," Zelma replied.

"Then what are we waiting for?"

Zelma nodded and began walking toward the blackened shell of Bloodstone Manor, Nico following. Zelma only had sneakers on, not hiking boots like Nico, so she had to select her footing with more care, both because of the debris and the heat still radiating from it. As she did, she noticed something peculiar.

She stopped and gestured widely at the charred timbers and bits of broken glass and twisted metal at their feet. Wind whispered across the ruins, clearing away the hovering ash and perhaps sharing the very secrets they sought, but in no tongue known to man- or mage-kind.

"Why aren't there any bodies?"

"What?" Nico asked. "What are you talking about?" She was looking at Zelma as if the librarian had lost her mind. But that didn't bother Zelma; she was used to it. If you worked with Doctor Strange for more than five minutes, you were going to get looks like that. It came with the magical territory.

"There aren't any bodies. No burglars." Zelma paused dramatically. "No zombies."

"So… what? Less cleanup for the local biohazard team?" Nico asked sarcastically. "Assuming the biohazard team hasn't already been turned into biohazards themselves, which I'm not putting any money on."

"*So*, whatever defenses were triggered here, they weren't activated by an intruder. And it wasn't some spell cast from afar; there's residual magic here, but not enough to account for that kind of attack."

Nico's dark eyebrows came together in a frown. She scanned

the ruins with a critical eye, perhaps confirming with her own magical senses what Zelma had already determined with the help of the amulet.

"You're saying this fire was set intentionally."

It wasn't a question.

"Yes."

Nico now sported a unibrow and a dubious glower.

"Presumably by Elsa."

"Presumably," Zelma agreed.

"But, why? The manor was probably just as well-spelled as your space-time-defying brownstone on Bleecker Street."

"Maybe," Zelma conceded, "but maybe she wanted a kind of protection wards couldn't afford."

Nico heaved out an exaggerated sigh.

"Well, you've obviously cracked the case, Velma. Quit showboating and pull off the villain's mask already so we can all have our obligatory dog snacks and go to commercial."

Zelma's smile was both amused and satisfied.

"Who's going to come looking for you if they think you're already dead?"

CHAPTER ELEVEN

Zelma's gaudy bauble of an amulet led them toward the center of the manor's still-warm corpse. Judging from the heat coming off the scorched foundation, it hadn't been dead all that long. Although Nico imagined that a building's carcass probably retained heat far longer than a human's would.

As she followed the librarian through the ruins of Elsa's home, Nico wondered what the manor had looked like before it had burned down. She'd seen a picture of it once, briefly, on social media, but only recalled it having several stories, all of them old and creepy. The image had only caught her attention because of the sign. Seeing the Bloodstone name had reminded her of Elsa and the hot springs, but that had been shortly after Karolina had kissed her and Nico had been dealing with a lot of complicated emotions at the time. So she'd shoved the ones the picture stirred up into a box in her mind marked "Later", then stuck it on the mental conveyor belt that shunted everything uncomfortable off into the dark corners of her consciousness until she was ready to deal with them. Which was usually never.

"This is it," Zelma announced, dragging Nico's attention back to the here and now. The librarian gestured to a mound of blackened timbers in front of them. "This is where the magical traces are coming from." The amulet's blue ray abruptly disappeared, punctuating her statement.

"You think it's the entrance to the basement?" Nico asked. "And the amulet's picking up on wards or boobytraps or something?"

"Maybe? It picks up on things we can't see, so that would make sense. Or maybe—" Zelma stopped abruptly mid-sentence and looked at Nico, eyes widening. "Elsa's bloodgem is magical, right?"

Nico nodded, confused by the change of subject. She was beginning to think Zelma might have ADHD, the way the other woman flitted from one topic to another without warning. But then, Nico secretly thought all magic-users were neurodivergent in some way or another; it took an atypical mind to believe in magic in the first place, let alone manipulate it to any degree.

"You think that's what the amulet is sensing?" she asked. "Elsa's hand?" Which would most logically be attached to Elsa, though there was no guarantee of that. Or that, if it were attached, Elsa herself was still alive to wield it.

"Let's get some of this junk out of the way and find out." Zelma pointed at the jumble of logs that had no doubt once ribbed a high, vaulted ceiling. "Cloak!"

The scarlet cape obediently unclasped itself and rose from her shoulders, floating over to the pile of rubble and wrapping itself around the topmost crossbeam. It easily lifted the heavy timbers, moving them away from the heap, and soon a round patch had been cleared, revealing smooth, uncharred flagstone beneath.

Zelma stepped over a broken bookcase and entered the circle as the cloak returned to her shoulders unbidden. Nico followed, broken bits of glass, crystal, and plastic crunching loudly under her boots. The sound seemed to echo eerily in the quiet of the manor's grave, but she was sure that was just the product of an overactive imagination primed by watching too many horror movies as a kid. On the big screen, silence was suspect, a precursor to a monster jumping out from the shadows. In real life, Nico had found that silence often signaled less obvious but more sinister dangers, like complicity and submission. She'd take the jumpscares any day.

Her companion was bent over, peering at the stone floor as she walked slowly back and forth across it. Her sweater was white and not orange, but otherwise she looked very much like her cartoon counterpart. Nico was tempted to summon a magnifying glass for her.

"What are you looking for?" she finally asked as Zelma made her third seemingly fruitless pass across the cleared space. "A secret door? Why not ask your necklace to light it up for you?"

Zelma looked up at her, blinking.

"It only shows what we *can't* see, remember?" she replied. "Ergo, the source of the magic it's detecting is somewhere below this portion of floor, but the mechanism to *reach* that source should be visible to the naked eye."

"Maybe your eyes are wearing too much," Nico joked, but then wondered if Zelma's glasses really were interfering with her ability to find the entrance to the basement. Regardless, another set of eyes, spectacled or not, never hurt. "Let me try."

Zelma straightened and gestured toward the ground with an unnecessarily gallant flourish.

"Be my guest."

Nico wasn't so churlish as to go back over the ground Zelma had already covered; she trusted that the librarian's magic and mind were both competent enough to have found anything there was to find, and she wasn't going to second guess the other woman on that point without a good reason. She knew what that felt like, especially as the de facto leader of the Runaways – it was easy to question decisions when you weren't the one making them.

So, where Zelma had focused on the center of the cleared area, Nico began to walk along its perimeter. She wasn't sure what she was looking for, or if there was even anything there to find. Maybe Elsa used magical floor polish and that's what Zelma's discount store Eye of Agamotto had detected.

Well, not Elsa. Elsa Bloodstone had much more important things to do than clean floors. She was a "monster hunter extraordinaire" and monsters that needed hunting were never in short supply. But someone had to take care of the day-to-day chores at the manor. Nico wondered what had happened to that person.

Nico's circuit took her back to where the two women had first entered the circle, by the toppled bookshelf, which still miraculously had a few somewhat intact volumes on its last remaining shelf. The only title she could make out was *Anatomy of the Monstrous*, which seemed apropos given its owner's occupation. The letters shone gold against a red leather binding, and Nico realized suddenly that only this tome, out of all those that had survived, seemed unharmed. There was no scorching on its spine, though the books on either side, one on demonology and one whose subject had been forever obscured by the fire, were both charred, their covers gone and their outermost pages flaking off, ashes of lost knowledge being carried away on the gentle breeze.

"Hey, Velma," Nico called softly, still leery of making too much noise. "I think I found a clue."

"Zelma," the other woman corrected as she started over to where Nico stood, but her voice was more amused than chiding. Once she was at Nico's side, she immediately saw what the Runaway had seen.

"That's some tough binding," she commented.

"Either that," Nico agreed, "or..."

She leaned down to pull the book off the remnants of the shelf. It didn't budge.

"Curious," Zelma remarked.

Nico didn't bother replying. She pushed away the carcasses of the books on either side, ignoring the twinge of guilt as large chunks of both volumes disintegrated into so much word dust.

Anatomy of the Monstrous stood unsupported, its cover as unblemished as the day it was first printed. Or, more likely, inscribed. Most of these sorts of books existed long before Gutenberg.

"And curiouser," Zelma said.

This time when Nico grabbed the book, she tried tilting it backward, like she'd seen done in so many movies with hidden rooms and staircases behind bookshelves. Nothing doing.

"See if you can open it," Zelma suggested, but Nico was already in the process of doing just that. And there, beneath the cover, was an unassuming white button.

"Ha!" Nico crowed. "Natural twenty on 'detect secret door!'" And then she pushed the button.

There was no sound, but suddenly a portion of the cleared floor slid away to reveal a curved stone staircase leading down into darkness.

Zelma murmured something inaudible and a wide-angle beam with a more diffuse light sprang from her amulet.

"Ladies first," she said, smiling and once more gesturing Nico forward with a flourish.

"I think the rule is 'Flashlights first'," Nico replied.

Zelma considered that for a moment before nodding. As she turned to lead the way toward the yawning opening, though, Nico was pretty sure she heard the librarian mutter something that sounded an awful lot like, "Scaredy cat".

CHAPTER TWELVE

The stone staircase spiraled as they descended, so they could never see more than a few feet in front of or behind them. Though they couldn't hear it, Zelma knew the secret door had closed above them when the glow from the amulet seemed to brighten, the only source of light once daylight was blocked out.

Zelma had a seraphic shield spell at the ready. Nico had gone on and on about Elsa's boobytraps; every step they took that didn't trigger one made the librarian increasingly anxious.

Finally, though, they reached the bottom of the stairs, after going down what seemed like several stories. Here, the floor opened up into some sort of warehouse. Rows of closely spaced metal shelves were lined up like silent soldiers, stacked to the low, pipe-lined ceiling with file boxes, trunks, barnacle-encrusted chests, books and scrolls, rolled up rugs, lamps and vases of various shapes and sizes, and more, each lit up for a moment and then returned to shadows as Zelma panned the amulet's wide ray across the cavernous room. If she didn't already know it had been gathering dust in the bottom of Doctor Strange's wardrobe for decades, Zelma would not have been surprised to find the Ark of the Covenant sitting on one of Elsa's shelves; it would be right at home.

Then there was a click and a buzzing noise and Zelma jumped back, heart pounding as she waited for the trap she'd been expecting all along to fling something deadly in their direction.

"Now who's the scaredy cat? I've heard of people being afraid of the dark, but being afraid of the light is new," Nico said mockingly from behind her as arrays of fluorescent lights flickered on overhead. "Well, for the good guys, anyway."

Zelma scowled over her shoulder at the other witch, adrenaline coursing through her system. She wasn't wrong to be on her guard, and she knew it. She certainly didn't need Nico teasing her about it.

Wrangling her attention back to the warehouse, Zelma had to admit she was impressed with Elsa's inventory. Larger even than Doctor Strange's collection – at least the parts of it Zelma had access to – it stretched from the staircase into darkness on all sides. But she supposed that made sense. Elsa was a monster hunter, her quarry ranging from infestations of giant psychic bugs to millennia-old vampires. Doc, on the other hand, had concerned himself with rarer, more existential threats, like rising old gods and inter-dimensional conquerors. Zelma wondered where on that spectrum zombie apocalypses fell.

As they continued through this magician's version of a candy-slash-toy megastore, Zelma started to think less about boobytraps and more about what some of these items were intended for, where they had come from, and if Elsa would mind terribly if she took a few of them back to Doc's for safekeeping. Or just plain keeping.

"Some of this stuff should probably be at the Sanctum Sanctorum," she whispered reverently, not quite daring to touch any of said stuff. She doubted the things in Elsa's basement had gotten there because they were pretty, innocent trinkets. Chances were that if an item had wound up here, it had belonged to someone or something nasty, and was likely to be as dangerous as it was shiny. There was a reason these things were gathering dust dozens of feet below ground and hadn't been in the museum when it went up in flames.

"We are supposed to be looking for Elsa, not planning on how to 'borrow' things from her collection," Nico said sharply.

Zelma kept her enthusiasm to herself after that, her head swiveling back and forth between the shelves on either side of them as they walked down the seemingly never-ending row. The librarian was in the middle of mentally cataloguing the assorted magical mirrors they'd just passed and thinking about where she might put them in the brownstone when Nico's voice startled her out of her artifact-induced reverie.

"I think we've finally reached the end of the rainbow," the Runaway announced, gesturing with her head.

Zelma looked, and the other witch was right; they seemed to have found the underground warehouse's far side. At first, it was just a dark smear, but as they neared, it quickly resolved into a stone wall, much like those in Doc's basement.

And, like those in the Bleecker Street basement, this wall seemed to double as part of either a prison or a torture museum, with various sets of shackles imbedded into the stone and a handful of iron maidens, racks, and stocks, all interspersed with freestanding cages.

But unlike the Bleecker Street basement, not all these cages were empty.

A figure clothed entirely in red and black spandex sat cross-legged on the floor inside one of the cages to their left, head bowed and thumbs twiddling. Zelma thought she could hear soft singing, but she couldn't make out the words. Next to the cage, within easy reach of the prisoner, was a metal tray on which sat a utility belt, a set of sheathed katanas, and a bandolier. Also a surgeon's scalpel, some bloody bandages, and on the floor nearby, a bucket of ruddy water.

The red-visaged head lifted and Zelma saw two large black patches covering the figure's eyes, almost like butterfly wings. At the same time, she heard Nico gasp.

"Is that… *Deadpool*?"

Zelma realized that it was. His suit did not look torn or bloody – admittedly hard to tell given the costume's color scheme – and there were no visible signs of injury, bite, scratch, or otherwise. But he was covered head to toe in spandex, and who knew what might be lurking where they *couldn't* see?

"D'you think he got zombified?" Nico asked. "And Elsa captured him?"

"Captured him but didn't kill him?" Zelma countered. "Why would she do that?"

"Maybe she couldn't? Doesn't he regenerate, or something? Like Wolverine? Maybe he can't be killed?"

Zelma supposed that was possible. But why leave his weapons where he could grab them anytime he wanted to? For that matter, why wasn't he in chains inside the cage? Something didn't add up here.

"Maybe," she replied, frowning, "but why this?" Deadpool stood as she gestured vaguely toward the cage. "Surely if you had to permanently imprison a zombie you couldn't kill, you'd find something less… Houdini-able… than this glorified kennel?"

"Hey," Deadpool protested in a hurt voice, his hands around the bars of his cage. His mask fit like a second skin, so every expression was evident, including his current pout. "I'm *right here*, you know. I can hear you." Then he perked up. "Say, neither of you ladies would happen to have a chimichanga hidden somewhere on your person? Maybe in your camel hump?" He pointed at Zelma's backpack.

Zelma and Nico just stared at him.

"Yeah, I didn't think so," Deadpool answered himself, sighing resignedly.

Nico turned to her.

"Do zombies eat fried food?" she asked in a whisper.

"I can still hear you," Deadpool said, but the two women ignored him.

"They seem to prefer it fresh," Zelma replied, remembering Doc eating Wong. And then immediately trying to forget it again.

But she realized that she could still detect that same underlying odor of rot here, like she could when she'd gotten too close to Doc. She hadn't recognized it immediately because she'd been inundated with the scents of dust and time and secrets since the moment they'd entered Elsa's underground storage room, and the smell of decay didn't stand out much against that olfactory onslaught.

"Maybe he's... *not* a zombie?" Nico ventured hesitantly.

"Still right here."

"Maybe not," Zelma replied, "but somebody here is. I can smell them."

Nico inhaled deeply and then her lips puckered and her eyelids fluttered like she was trying to keep from gagging. Or like someone had just given her a swirlie in a compost pile.

"Ugh, that is *rank*!"

The distinctive sound of a round being racked into its chamber echoed off the stone walls, and the two witches whirled to find themselves staring down the twin barrels of a shotgun.

"Oi, now, that's just rude," Elsa Bloodstone said, perfect teeth gleaming at them through a smiling cheek that had partially rotted away.

CHAPTER THIRTEEN

"Gun ja–" Nico began, but Zelma threw her arm out, clamping her hand across the other woman's mouth before she could complete her spell with the Staff of One.

"Don't!" she said urgently, and probably unnecessarily, since she had effectively muzzled the Runaway. But the librarian didn't want to stand that way indefinitely. Especially if she was wrong about her hunch.

The wound on Elsa's cheek was clearly visible, but Zelma saw no other injuries, despite the monster hunter's bare midriff. Elsa also sported a long trench coat the color of sun-bleached asphalt, and that could cover a multitude of sins. Including those committed against fashion, though Zelma was nobody's go-to girl on that front.

Regardless, Elsa's blue eyes were as clear as Doc's had been during his temporary bout of sanity. She might have been zombified, but she seemed to be fighting off the ravenous hunger that came with it. At least for now.

But then why did she have Deadpool in a cage?

The notoriously mouthy merc chose that moment to interject.

"I told her that natural deodorant stuff wasn't working, but she's all like, 'Monsters can smell chemicals,'" he said, his voice raising several octaves as he imitated Elsa. "I'm pretty sure they can smell decomp, too. And which one are they more likely to avoid, I ask you?"

On second thought, maybe the question should really be why the monster hunter had only caged and not gagged him.

Elsa lifted her shotgun to sight over Zelma and Nico's heads.

"I told you – I have no qualms about shooting you," she said to Deadpool. "You'll just regenerate, anyway; I'd get a few moments of blessed quiet without even having to endure a mildly tweaked conscience for it."

"You wound me," the mercenary said, actually sounding hurt.

"I will," Elsa promised, moving her finger off the guard and onto the trigger.

By this time, Nico had pried Zelma's hand off her mouth.

"OK, time out! Why does everyone else seem to know what's happening here but me?" Nico demanded, her patience obviously eroding rapidly.

"What makes you think *I* know what's happening?" Deadpool responded, continuing to sound aggrieved.

"Shut it!" Elsa snapped, lowering the shotgun to aim at the women once more. As she did, Zelma realized that she and Nico were standing close enough together that Elsa could probably take them both out with one shot. But before she could rectify that troubling situation, the monster hunter spoke again. "Actually, I'd like to know what's going on here, too. Why are you here, Nico and… friend… and why shouldn't I put you both out of my misery right now? Talk fast."

"Oo-ooh," Deadpool sing-songed. "Someone's getting han-gry."

Through some inhuman force of will that Zelma was sure had nothing to do with being a zombie, Elsa ignored him.

"We came here to get your help," Nico replied icily. "As you've obviously discovered for yourself, we have a bit of a monster problem. We thought the 'monster hunter extraordinaire' would be just the one to solve it. We never dreamed she'd turn out to be one of the monsters herself."

Zelma still had a seraphic shield ready, but now she wondered who needed it more – them, or Elsa. The frost that limned Nico's words was the kind only generated by deep anger or deeper hurt, and Nico didn't strike the librarian as the type to sit quietly with her feelings, especially when they involved being disappointed by someone she'd considered a friend. If the Runaway was smarting, she probably wouldn't be satisfied doing it alone.

"Monster is as monster does," Elsa replied with a shrug. "Seeing as I've been spending my time rescuing humans instead of having them with tea and crumpets, I'd say that puts me pretty squarely in the 'not-monster' category. Can't say the same for you."

Zelma frowned at that, disconcerted.

"What do you mean?"

Elsa eyed her, finally seeming to register the Cloak of Levitation.

"Doctor Strange?" she asked.

"Indisposed," Zelma replied, biting the syllables off.

Elsa nodded, unfazed.

"Lot of that going around," she said. She appeared distracted, and Zelma wondered if her rationality was beginning to wear off.

"You didn't answer my question," Zelma pressed. "Why can't you say the same for us?"

"How'd you get in here?" Elsa countered. "If you'd managed to teleport through my wards, you'd be much... bloodier."

"We found your secret bookcase door," Nico replied. Zelma noticed that the other witch had moved a few inches away from her, perhaps having also come to the realization that if she didn't put some distance between them, Elsa could kill them both without even needing to reload.

Or the zombified monster hunter would decide to eat them. There wasn't much room to maneuver here between the ends of the tightly packed aisles and the assorted torture devices and cages. If Elsa's current bout of sanity passed, fighting her was going to be tricky.

"Ah," Elsa said. "And I don't suppose you thought to... I don't know... *cover your tracks* when you came through it?"

Nico and Zelma exchanged an uneasy glance. Zelma realized the sickly-sweet smell of rot seemed to be getting stronger.

"No-o-o-o," Nico answered slowly. "Why?"

Elsa spun to her left, firing off two shots in quick succession.

"Try asking them," she said as she did, pulling out a pistol from behind her back and firing that, too.

Zelma and Nico whirled in the same direction, Zelma instinctively casting the Shield of the Seraphim she'd had readied all this time.

Which was the only thing that saved them from the mass of zombies now rushing at them from the warehouse aisles.

CHAPTER FOURTEEN

Nico could barely process what she was seeing. Back when this had all started, she and the other Runaways had just gotten word of the meteorite strike and subsequent super hero casualties when they'd happened upon the Young Avengers. Nico knew Billy from past encounters and had been relieved to see him and his brother. They were the Scarlet Witch's reincarnated kids; they'd have spoken to their mother. They'd know what was going on and what to do.

But then, horrifically, Tommy had killed Molly, pulled out her heart, and started eating it. And the other Young Avengers had piled on, trying to tear little Molly's corpse apart, arguing over who should get which parts. But they had forgotten about the girl's superhuman strength, which hadn't diminished just because she had technically died. Molly had thrown them all off, climbed to her feet, and set her eyes on Gert, drool trickling from the corner of her undead mouth.

Nico and the other Runaways, realizing there was something seriously wrong with the other teens, did what they were best at – they ran. Ran, and hid.

But they couldn't shake the Junior Super Squad, and a running, pitched battle had ensued, one that lasted days and took them across the entire landscape of Los Angeles, from the sewers to the smoldering heights of skyscrapers. Glimpses of rotted, tattered flesh on their pursuers made it clear to Nico that her team had somehow become extras in a horror movie, and its title ended in "of the Dead".

But even that nightmare had not prepared her for this fresh hell. There were so many of them, pouring into the area where the cages were, clogging the aisles, even toppling some of the heavily laden metal shelves.

"Aim for their heads! For their brains!" Elsa yelled. "Something above the neck keeps them going, and we need to keep them 'not going.'"

"Heard!" Zelma yelled, like she was on some sort of baking competition show and one of the hosts had just given a time call. But then she curled back some of the fingers of her right hand, flung it out in the air, and began to chant.

"*Bolts of Bedevilment turn and consume*
The brains of my foes inside this room!"

Instantly, white bolts leapt from her hand, bursting through the yellowish bubble of her shield and slamming into the heads of the nearest zombies. The air was suddenly filled with the sound of popping and the stench of burning, like someone had left a bag of popcorn in the microwave too long, only this burnt odor was that of cooking flesh, not of overdone corn kernels and charred paper. Zombified heroes collapsed before they could reach the three women, creating a temporary wall around them.

"I can't get them all!" Zelma exclaimed through gritted teeth.

Bedeviling rays leapt from her hand, but more slowly now, the popping sound becoming less frequent. "They just keep coming!"

Meanwhile, zombies had surrounded Deadpool's cage. He stood in the center, out of reach of their many outstretched arms, slicing off any appendages that came too near with the katanas he had retrieved. He spun and pirouetted like a music box ballerina and Nico was pretty sure he was singing, but she couldn't tell for sure over the sounds of gunfire, spell detonations, and general zombie bedlam.

A zombie that hadn't been popcorned by Zelma's spell came at her, wielding two swords, much like Deadpool. Nico wondered if it might possibly be the assassin Elektra, but the scraps of red costume on the tattered body could have belonged to any number of supers.

Nico blocked one of the blades with her witch hand, twisting to avoid the other, which just skimmed her right bicep, drawing a scarlet line across her black sleeve. But letting her blood was the original way Nico had accessed the Staff of One's power, and it would only make her spells stronger.

She slammed the butt of the metal rod against the floor and cried out "Crumble!"

Instantly, the maybe-Elektra zombie now swinging both swords at her dissipated into a pile of gray dust, metal blades clattering to the stone floor atop it, scattering it in every direction.

But there were more waiting to take that one's place, and Nico suddenly realized why.

The door.

Elsa had asked if they'd covered their tracks, and Nico finally understood the question. The fire and debris had been meant to make the zombies think there was no food for them here, so they would turn their attention elsewhere. But when she and Zelma had uncovered the door, even though it had closed behind them, they had basically left a "Free Food" sign pointing down to Elsa's warehouse of wonder. And these guys were hungry. Always so hungry.

Well, the door at least was a mistake she could correct. She brought the staff down again.

"Throw away the key!"

She couldn't see or hear it, but Nico knew that the secret bookcase door was now closed, locked, and covered, and no one would look twice at the pile of rubble on top of it again. Unfortunately, no one inside was going to be able to use it again, either – it was permanently locked. Which could be a problem if there wasn't another exit out of Elsa's basement, but only if there was anyone left alive to worry about it.

A blast of titian eldritch energy lanced over her left shoulder to take out the heads of three zombies in a row. Elsa had either run out of bullets or decided they were less effective than magic and was using her bloodstone hand now. Nico thought she recognized the second super in the downed trio, or at least the "X" on the hero's belt. But with no head now and a body quickly buried under the onrush of more zombies, it was hard to say for sure.

What she *could* say for sure was that, even if she'd stopped the influx of ravening zombies, there were still far more than she was comfortable with streaming into the now-crowded dungeon area of the underground warehouse. They climbed blindly over their fallen comrades, like Black Friday shoppers intent on snatching the last sale-priced gaming console before anyone else could.

Beside her, Zelma was chanting again.

"Vapors of Valtorr, stream forth and corrode
Let my foes fall before me and their progress be slowed
Winds of Watoomb, fill the air around me
And around all my allies; keep it Vapor-free!"

A thick chartreuse mist rose around Nico and Zelma, around Elsa, and around Deadpool in his cage. At the same time, a slight breeze sprang up, swirling around the allies, ruffling the women's hair. Within moments, Nico could see only a few inches in any direction. Zelma was a dark green shadow; Elsa and Deadpool just voices on the wind.

Then the screaming started as the mist began to scour the flesh from the zombies it enveloped. The wails Nico heard were not of pain – she wasn't sure the zombified supers could even feel anything besides hunger pangs. No, the zombies were howling in frustration and rage because they were being denied their repast. Even as the corrosive mist ate away at what was left of their flesh, finally reaching the brains that animated them, all the zombies could think of was assuaging their terrible appetites.

After some interminable time, the last of the groaning and snarling faded away and the vapors, no longer having any of Zelma's foes to consume, melted away into nothingness. All that remained of the zombies were their bones, shining an almost unearthly white beneath the fluorescent lights. Nico let out the breath she hadn't realized she'd been holding.

"That was fun," Deadpool said. "Can we do it again?"

CHAPTER FIFTEEN

"Well, that's left a bloody mess. Which one of you spell-slingers is going to clean up my floors now, hmm?" Elsa asked. The zombie woman had her shotgun leveled at them again, though Zelma didn't think she'd actually had a chance to reload it.

"Not it!" Deadpool exclaimed, quickly touching a finger to his nose. To Zelma's knowledge, his magical ability equaled his social awareness – he seemed to have little to none of either. She ignored him for now.

"Maybe you want to tell us why we shouldn't just sling one of those spells at you?" she countered, knowing it was a dangerous ploy. But Zelma had felt the pulse of energy when Nico sealed the staircase doorway with her staff, and she knew they were safe for the time being. So now that the other zombies were taken care of, they had to figure out what was going on with *this* one. Even if she did have a nasty looking gun trained on them and a scowl on what was left of her face.

Which made Zelma angry. Elsa might have saved Zelma and Nico from becoming zombie food at the outset, but the two witches had held their own in that fight, and kept more than a few of the undead gluttons off the monster hunter's back. And now she was pointing a gun at them again? Zelma wasn't having it.

"Same reason I shouldn't pull this trigger, I'd wager," Elsa replied. "We both want to kill zombies. Though I'm usually a bit tidier about it."

"But you *are* a zombie," Nico snapped. She seemed pretty mad about the whole thing herself, but Zelma thought the Runaway's anger stemmed from a different place. The staff-wielding witch seemed to take Elsa's infection as a personal affront, though Zelma didn't understand why. If heroes like Doctor Strange and the Scarlet Witch could succumb, anyone could, even a kickass warrior like Elsa.

"A zombie who keeps the hunger at bay while she hunts other zombies and ferries humans to safety when she can? Yes, guilty," Elsa replied saucily. "Quite."

"I've only seen one way of keeping the hunger at bay for long enough to do anything other than plan your next meal," Zelma said, pushing away the images of Wong and Rintrah's gutted corpses that her words instantly evoked.

Elsa cocked her head to the side in feigned curiosity, the movement causing her high, red ponytail to fall over her shoulder and the side of her face, masking the hole in her cheek. She almost looked normal.

"Do tell."

"*Eating* humans. Not saving them." Well, and mutants, too, Zelma supposed. And aliens. And who knew what else for sure, really? But definitely humans.

"So *how* are you doing it?" Nico chimed in. "If you really do belong in the 'not a monster' category, as you claim?"

Elsa didn't even bother to answer, just jabbed her chin in Deadpool's general direction with an annoyed grunt.

"Under ordinary conditions, locking Deadpool up might get you hero status, sure," Nico said, earning a "Hey!" from the mercenary as she continued, "but right now things are anything but ordinary, and we're going to need a better answer."

But Zelma thought she understood. There had been a scalpel on the tray next to Deadpool's cage, and now that he was standing, she could see that his spandex-like suit was in fact damaged. Not torn, but cut precisely, creating a small flap over his left butt cheek, like he was a prospector in a union suit. But she doubted either the bum flap or the bucket that had been overturned and kicked who knew where were for bodily functions.

"You're feeding off him, aren't you?" she guessed. "In some way that doesn't infect him?"

"Ding! Ding! Ding!" Deadpool crowed delightedly, while Elsa eyed her with renewed interest.

"Your caliber of mates has improved since the last time we saw each other, Minoru," she said approvingly. "And, yes, Ms...?"

"Stanton. Zelma," Zelma supplied helpfully.

"Zelma. You'll be Doctor Strange's proxy for this adventure, I'm assuming?" Zelma didn't know quite how to answer that, so she just nodded. "Yes, I'm 'feeding off' him, as you so succinctly put it. A bit off the old glutes every so often keeps me in fighting shape, and since the wound heals over lickety-split, he's better than one of those multivitamins for the fifty-plus crowd."

Deadpool scoffed.

"Yeah, because I actually *work*."

"For some definitions of that word, I suppose," Elsa retorted. She'd lowered her gun, though, which Zelma found to be more calming to her nervous system than even the vaporization of the attacking zombies had been. She'd known Elsa for less than an hour and already knew she didn't want to be on the monster hunter's bad side. Ever.

"Wait, but…" Nico began, brow furrowing as she looked back and forth between Elsa and Deadpool. Her gaze finally settled on Deadpool. "You're *OK* with this arrangement?"

"For some definitions of that word, I suppose," he parroted back to her, making a face at Elsa.

"Wade…" Elsa said warningly, and the mercenary raised his arms in mock surrender. Zelma hadn't noticed when he'd put his belt and bandolier back on and sheathed his katanas, but his hands were empty now.

"Fine, fine. No, I'm not OK with being stuck in this cage, but I *am* OK with Elsa leaving my handsome mug intact on top of these broad, muscular shoulders. Gotta keep the looks up, you know? Hot mercs make more money."

"Waaade…"

The barrels of Elsa's gun started to rise again.

"OK, OK! Sheesh, don't shoot me! I'm just the incredibly good-looking messenger."

Nico glanced over at Zelma, frowning.

"Do you have any idea what he's babbling about?"

Zelma just shrugged and shook her head. The odds were decent that he'd get around to telling them before Elsa's trigger finger got itchy. Decent, but not good.

"Now why don't you tell these lovely ladies why you're in

a cage, hmmm?" Elsa prodded. "And be quick about it, won't you? I've worked up a bit of an appetite."

Zelma wondered if there would ever come a time when that once-innocuous phrase would cease to give her chills.

"OkaysoElsasavedmeandthenIwashelpingher," Deadpool said in a rush, then took a huge breath and barreled on, "butthenI–"

"Right, that's it. I'm shooting you," Elsa declared impatiently, raising her shotgun to shoulder level and taking aim to do just that.

"Don't waste the ammo," Nico said, holding up a hand to forestall Elsa as Deadpool fell to his knees with his hands clasped penitentially in front of his face. "Allow me." She brought the Staff of One up in front of her.

Zelma was surprised at this sudden shift in the other witch's attitude, but she suspected it was a ruse of some kind. If Elsa hadn't already killed the mouthy mercenary, she was unlikely to do so now. After all, he was – according to the monster hunter – the only thing that was keeping her sane.

But Nico had no such misgivings, and she'd already shown herself to be impatient and quick to anger, at least in Deadpool's presence. He'd be less likely to know if she was bluffing, and less likely to call that bluff, even if he suspected she was.

Come to think of it, Zelma wasn't entirely sure herself.

Nico had opened her mouth and begun to say something – what, they'd never know – when Deadpool finally caved.

"OK! OK! No need to poof me!" Deadpool crossed his arms in front of his chest sullenly and huffed. "I kept getting in the way, all right? I was too flashy, talked too much, made too much noise when I offed a couple of zombie Avengers, then almost led the rest of their group straight back here and got both us *and* the humans we were trying to save eaten. And then... well, I might have done it a couple of other times. So she locked me up, for everyone's good. Is that what you wanted to hear me say, Elsa? Are you happy now?"

Elsa smiled and lowered her gun.

"Quite."

CHAPTER SIXTEEN

Nico and Zelma worked on cleaning up the zombie remains while Elsa found and righted the silver tray table. She located the scalpel, bandages, and now-empty bucket and headed over to a spot on the back wall that Nico had not noticed contained a large utility sink. It might have been white plastic once, or even stainless steel, but now it was just black, no doubt covered in decades worth of monster blood, and probably some of Elsa's, too.

Nico frowned, pondering as she watched the monster hunter move to the sink, refill the bucket and begin washing out the bandages. She had liked Elsa when they met. A lot. And Elsa had seemed to like her, a rare connection for both of them.

Maybe, after watching Karolina die, Nico's motivations for suggesting they find the extraordinary redhead weren't entirely pure. Maybe some part of her, here at the end of the world, had wanted to track down Elsa because Nico had already lost the only other people she had ever felt that kind of connection with. Maybe she just didn't want to die without knowing there was at least one person left in the world who cared about what happened to her.

But now the monster hunter had gone and gotten herself infected and Nico didn't know who she was angrier at – Elsa, for spoiling the Runaway's little fantasy, or herself, for having harbored it in the first place.

It hardly mattered now.

She watched, still inwardly fuming, while Elsa brought the bucket and damp bandages over to Deadpool's cage. The monster hunter produced a key from somewhere inside her long coat and touched it to one of the metal bars. A section of that cage wall faded away, as if it had been an illusion, and Elsa entered the small space with Deadpool.

The mercenary was still armed. If he wanted to, he could try to escape. Elsa had left her shotgun back at the sink. She still had her bloodgem, of course, and probably her pistol and a dozen other weapons hidden inside that coat of hers, but the odds were somewhat more even now.

Deadpool's hands didn't so much as twitch toward his weapons. Instead, he turned, bent over and lowered the flap on his red suit to give Elsa access to what Nico supposed was probably the only part of him that had any fat. Nico watched in mixed horror and fascination as Elsa pulled the scalpel she'd cleaned back at the sink from within what Nico was becoming increasingly convinced was really a coat-shaped Bag of Holding, then used her bloodgem to cauterize it. Then Elsa leaned forward, presumably to shave a bit off the mercenary's behind, though it was by no means in need of any sculpting. Nico couldn't see her making the cut, and Deadpool made no sound, so she only knew the deed was done when they both straightened and stepped away from each other, almost sheepishly, like lovers caught in a compromising position.

"You know," Deadpool remarked, "normally that'd cost you dinner and a movie."

"Dinner part's taken care of," Elsa replied as she turned back to the two witches-slash-scullery maids with a smirk, her mouth stained bright red. "Good luck finding a cinema still up and running, though."

"Not really your shade, Elsa," Nico commented, unsure if she were sniping or just trying to lighten the mood. That was the problem with sarcasm – the word's etymological root meant to rend flesh, but it was a blade that cut both ways, and even a skilled wielder could find herself nursing a nasty cut after its use.

Elsa grinned wickedly, then deliberately licked her lips.

"Better, darling?" she asked mockingly. Nico knew enough about British slang and Elsa to know the word wasn't an endearment.

"Quite," Nico replied, mimicking Elsa's earlier smug response to Deadpool. Then she grew serious again. "Look, we came here because we needed your unique expertise in monster-slaying. I will grudgingly admit that having been infected does not seem to have altered your capabilities in that regard. But can you even help us? You said you've been saving humans from becoming Hamburger Helpless meals. How, exactly? And is it something we can replicate on a wider scale?"

"'Wider scale?'" Elsa repeated.

"You are regaining your sanity after you've eaten enough,"

Nico clarified. She didn't specify enough of *what*. She didn't have to. "That happened with Doctor Strange, too. You can't be the only ones. If we found a way to duplicate the arrangement you have with Deadpool here, could we… bring them back?"

Elsa shook her head.

"Wondered that myself, but after some observation, seems like the ability to regain use of your faculties for more than a hot minute isn't universal. From what I've seen, only the chaps who use magic – or sort of have it embedded in them, like me – can do it. And it usually gets them killed."

Zelma frowned at that.

"What do you mean?"

"Bit of a shock, don't you think, being a good guy, then waking up to realize you've eaten the folks you're meant to have been protecting?" Elsa replied with tight grimace. "Probably knock you off your game for a minute or two. Which is all it takes to get dead for keeps."

Nico hadn't really pinned any hopes on some sort of *Soylent Green*-inspired end to the apocalypse, but she felt a surge of disappointment all the same. She spoke quickly to cover it, and to fill the uncomfortable silence that had followed Elsa's words.

"OK, so then, how are you rescuing humans?" she asked. "Maybe that's something we can up-size."

"D'you want fries with that?" Deadpool quipped.

"Chips," Elsa corrected automatically before answering Nico. "I go out into the city, get a bead on some bad guys who're tracking humans – it's usually quicker than trying to find them myself, since I don't have the benefit of super senses, abilities which being technically dead does not seem to have dulled in any of these pillocks, more's the pity. Then I try to get the humans out from under their noses, and when I can't, I kill them before they can ring the dinner bell and invite any more suits to the party. Not much to it, really." She shrugged.

Not much to it, except Elsa wasn't talking about killing your garden-variety vampires and werewolves here. She was talking about mutants and magic-users and other hero-types who were generally the butt-kickers, not the kick*ees.*

"Probably killed a few dozen by now," Elsa added.

"Hey, I killed some, too!" Deadpool interjected.

"And you don't think they might have figured out there was a zombie hunter operating in the area when both their buddies and their prey started disappearing?" Nico asked, her frustration mounting.

"Don't get your knickers in a twist, darling. Of course they know they're being hunted and stolen from; they're zombies, not imbeciles." Nico wasn't sure, but she thought she saw Elsa's gaze flick toward Deadpool. "Knowing I exist and being able to find me are two vastly different things, though, aren't they?"

"Just like Big Foot," Deadpool stage-whispered to Zelma, who looked at him with undisguised concern.

"Which, I might add, is part of the reason I was so miffed when you left footprints leading straight to my front door," Elsa continued pointedly.

"When you say, 'get the humans out', where exactly do you take them?" Zelma interrupted, her worried gaze shifting to Nico. "Has a sanctuary been set up? Some sort of safe zone?"

Elsa snorted.

"Pish! Wouldn't that be the bee's knees?" She tossed her head, which had the unfortunate effect of baring her rotted cheek again. "I'm not running a bloody Underground Railroad here."

"Well, then, what *are* you doing?" Nico demanded, nearing the end of her patience, her fingers tightening reflexively around the Staff of One. Maybe Zelma was right to be concerned about her.

"There's a warren of tunnels down here; not even I know where they all lead."

"So you're not going to tell us," Zelma interpreted.

"Bright as a button, that one," Elsa said to Nico in an aside before addressing Zelma directly. "No. I'm not going to tell you. For your safety as much as for theirs."

Deadpool opened his mouth, but Elsa's murderous glare shut it before anything came out.

"And before you ask, he doesn't know, either. Though he might try to convince you otherwise."

Oh, that was clever. Now, even if the talkative merc *did* reveal something, she and Zelma wouldn't know whether to believe it or not.

"But we found you here," Zelma pointed out. "And it wasn't even all that hard, given the right tools." She gestured to the amulet she wore.

Elsa nodded.

"True enough. Sadly, this place has likely outlived its usefulness. Too bad, really. The boobytraps are all preset, and the cages come in handy. Not to mention all of this…" She trailed off as she waved an arm toward the aisles upon aisles of artifacts that had been collected over the decades, many priceless and some probably even rarer. "Though I won't miss doing inventory."

"Bring some of it," Zelma suggested.

Elsa frowned at her.

"Bring it where?"

"Back to the Sanctum Sanctorum. You can continue your zombie-hunting exploits from there; it's a much safer base of operations."

"What's the catch?" Elsa asked, eyes narrowing suspiciously.

"The catch is you won't be freelancing anymore," Zelma replied, suddenly looking less like a mousy librarian and more like a worthy successor to Doctor Strange as she stood taller, chin raised. "You'll be working with us. And not just to slap band-aids on a gunshot wound. To dig out the slug, sew up the patient, and nurse her back to health."

"'Her', being…?" Elsa asked curiously.

The question caught Zelma off-guard.

"What?" she asked, flustered. "Oh. I don't know, Mother Earth? Whatever. It doesn't matter; it was just a metaphor. That's not the point."

"I mean, I was wondering, too," Deadpool said to no one in particular.

"Seen and not heard," Nico whispered, tapping the butt of her staff against her hiking boot. She didn't think either Elsa or Zelma noticed, but a muffled and quickly silenced protest assured her that her spell to keep Deadpool muzzled while the grownups talked had worked.

That probably wasn't fair. She knew he had done some good things, and was a hero in his own way. And he had, by Elsa's own admission, been helping her with her hunt-and-rescue operations. Well, until he hadn't been.

But Nico's patience had run thin enough it could dilute paint. Silencing him temporarily with a short-lived spell was better than any of the multitude of ways she could have chosen to do it permanently.

"The point is," Zelma continued, seemingly oblivious to both Nico's actions and her internal rationalizations, "that we need to do something that will end this nightmare for good for everybody, not just kick it down the road for the select few you – or we – manage to save."

"And you've found a way to do that, have you?" Elsa asked skeptically.

"No," Zelma replied without hesitation. "Not yet. But having a monster hunter extraordinaire on our team increases our odds of success considerably once we *do* find it."

Elsa thought about it for a moment.

"Well, the safety of this place has already been compromised. So I suppose we haven't a great deal of choice, have we?" It was a rhetorical question, and no one bothered to answer. Elsa heaved an exaggerated sigh. "Then, in the immortal words of every doomed enterprise ever, 'What could possibly go wrong?'" She looked over at Deadpool. "You good with that, mate?"

Nico let her spell drop so he could answer.

"The four of us, roomies? Like much younger and better-looking *Golden Girls*?" he asked, clapping his hands together in delight. "Are you *kidding* me? Where do I sign? But I get to be Dorothy! Bea Arthur is the absolute GOAT. Kinda like me." He grinned through his mask and gave Elsa two big thumbs up. Which was a good thing, since nobody seemed to follow his reference otherwise.

One thing Nico did understand, though, was the look he gave her behind the monster-hunter's back. It was pure venom.

CHAPTER SEVENTEEN

A simple "Return from manor" from Nico and her staff, along with the appropriate passwords from Zelma, and the four were back in the Sanctum Sanctorum. The library wards did not seem to be at all sure about Elsa, however, and held her in suspended animation until Zelma sternly repeated the phrases that unlocked both the brownstone's shielding and that of the bibliotheca itself, with hands on hips. Then the wards dropped Elsa unceremoniously on the floor.

"Bollocks!" the British-reared monster hunter swore as she stood up, rubbing her backside.

"I thought you couldn't feel pain?" Deadpool asked curiously. The wards, Zelma noted with interest, had had no problem with him. She wondered if they needed to be recalibrated.

"Only to my pride," Elsa replied.

"An' your pride's located in your arse, is it?" Deadpool asked, mimicking Elsa's accent. The impression wasn't half bad.

"Why shouldn't it be?" Elsa countered. "It's every bit as fine as yours."

Deadpool didn't seem to have an argument for that, Nico

was nodding in agreement, and Zelma didn't know how either of them could tell when the body part in question was covered up by Elsa's coat anyway, so that ended that.

"If we could maybe focus for a moment, please?" Zelma asked, trying to keep her voice soothing and her tone mild. Part of being a librarian was learning how to hush people who either didn't know how to or just didn't want to be quiet on their own. Usually, it was just school kids and college students who were easily settled, but every so often you'd get a belligerent panhandler or entitled housewife with no volume control, seemingly hellbent on creating chaos in Zelma's curated calm. Those, she ousted, often with prejudice.

But not only was she uncertain that she *could* oust any of these library patrons, she needed them to help her help Doc. That required a more diplomatic hand. Unfortunately, since she'd started working for Doctor Strange, Zelma's ability to play diplomat had not only gotten rusty, it had completely succumbed to the harsh elements of necessity and desperation and crumbled away into unsalvageable dust.

Diplomacy – at least as practiced by Doctor Strange – was often just a pretty name for manipulation, and that was something Zelma had neither the skill nor the taste for. On the other hand, she wasn't at all sure that appealing to their common sense would work, either. Common sense dictated that one should run away from danger, not toward it, but heroes in suits and capes and long trench coats like these three usually did the exact opposite. Meanwhile, the ones who *did* follow the dictates of common sense and get civilians away from danger remained largely unsung, even though their actions were just as important. Sometimes more so.

To Zelma's surprise, the others stopped their bantering and looked at her. She was caught momentarily off-guard, and unsure of what to say. But then her gaze moved past the others, to the spot where she'd discovered Wong and Rintrah dead, and Doc feasting on their corpses. The carpet there bore no stain, but the shape of it was burned into her brain, and she would always see it, every time she so much as glanced in that direction.

She wished there were some way she could *unsee* it.

More than that, she wished that she could un*do* it. Make it so none of this had ever happened. Then there wouldn't be anything to fix. The world would go back to being as unbearably beautiful and wonderfully awful as it always had been.

But they'd only brought one lamp from the warehouse, and the genie inside it didn't grant wishes, just carried Elsa to locations where her skills might be needed, homing in on conflict. The only other things they had rescued, much to Zelma's disappointment, were two coolers full of microwavable tamales and umpteen boxes of ammunition for Elsa's guns, which now numbered a half dozen, though Zelma had no idea where the woman was putting them all. Elsa had lamented more than once being unable to get into her subterranean weapons range, located somewhere *above* the warehouse, where the bulk of her custom firearms was kept. But the biometric locks failed to recognize her in her infected form, the place had anti-magic shielding to prevent teleportation and other similar means of entry, and none of the more mundane failsafes she had in place seemed to be available.

Deadpool *had* made a crack about someone named Adam who would have been able to get into the room if he were still around, but Elsa's face had gone purple – an impressive feat for a zombie – and she had punched him in the gut so hard he'd puked. Surprisingly, Deadpool hadn't hit her back, and no one mentioned the name again, so Zelma had no idea who the mysterious Adam was, but it seemed safe to assume he was probably dead.

By now, everything else in that delightful magician's megastore had been reduced to smoking slag by the pre-placed magic-enhanced explosives Elsa had set to go off right after they left, ensuring that none of the artifacts would fall into zombie hands and that the warrens beneath the basement would be sealed off from discovery forever.

Zelma opened her mouth to speak, then closed it again abruptly.

Make it so none of this ever happened. Then there wouldn't be anything to fix.

"Focus?" Deadpool repeated into the unexpected silence. "You first. Sheesh."

His reply snapped Zelma's attention back to the here and now, where it took her a moment to realize he was talking about *her* focus. Or, more precisely, her lack thereof.

"Listen," she said. "I know we've been talking about fighting and trying to find a way to cure or reverse this infection, and that's what we're all here for."

"Not me," Deadpool interrupted. "I'm just here for the microwave. Elsa shot ours when I microwaved tea in it. You do have a microwave here, right?"

"Don't make me put you on mute again," Nico warned, earning her a quirked brow from Elsa. Zelma had been aware of the Staff of One's use prior to their teleportation to Bleecker Street, but she had assumed Nico was laying the groundwork for that spell, not casting a completely different – and mostly self-serving – one. Also perhaps a trifle too temporary, given the distinct absence of continued Deadpool muteness.

"I bet I can slice you in two before you can get the first word out of your mouth," Deadpool replied, and for the first time, there was no trace of amusement or feigned innocence in his voice. Suddenly, moving in a blur of black and red too fast for Zelma to track, he was standing behind Nico, a naked blade held across her throat. "See?"

"The Staff likes blood," Nico answered, sounding unperturbed as she started to lean into the naked steel, though Zelma saw something primal flare in the Runaway's eyes, quickly tamped down before it could catch fire.

"That's enough!" Zelma yelled, having lost patience with all of them. Rear ends and microwaves and power plays were not why she'd brought any of them here, and apparently someone needed to remind them of that fact. That the someone had to be her only annoyed Zelma more. She might be ready to take on the mantle of Queen of the Library Stacks and all she surveyed from atop them when necessary, but she didn't actually like being in charge of things that weren't books. Books didn't second guess you or talk back. Usually.

They also didn't tend to die if you made the wrong choice. If you messed them up beyond repair, you could usually find another copy. That wasn't quite so easy with people.

Once again, the others quieted and looked at her, and Zelma was dismayed to realize that was exactly what they expected her to do – take charge and lead them. The thought would have paralyzed her with anxiety under normal circumstances.

But not now. Now, she had their fleeting attention. That

might not be the case in another five minutes, or even another thirty seconds. She had to take advantage of it.

Zelma took a deep, steadying breath. Cloak snuggled tight against her shoulders, as if encouraging her.

But before she could say anything, there was a thud against one of the library windows. They all looked up, startled, to see a stunned pigeon flying away in a flurry of feathers, leaving a greasy outline behind on the glass.

That was not a good sign.

While the wards wouldn't view pigeons as a threat, the fact that they were letting the winged rats through at all when they had never done so before was concerning. And not just because Zelma hated pigeons.

It meant the Sanctum's outer wards were beginning to fail now, not just Doc's inner ones that had once kept monkeys and fridge-dwellers in their proper places.

They needed to hurry. They couldn't risk the Sanctum falling into the hands of zombies, especially not the library. The zombies wouldn't need to pry secrets from Doc's brain if they could just look everything up themselves.

"We came here to fix this," she began again, her voice taking on a renewed urgency. "And I'm convinced we could do that, given enough time and resources. But we're running out of time; the Sanctum's wards are obviously weakening. Even if we did find a way to cure this plague, as fast as this thing spreads, who would be left to save? Super heroes who annihilated the very people they swore to protect? How long before they succumbed to grief and guilt over what they'd done to survive and ended things themselves? And then what good would we have done, really?"

"Saved the rest of the universe, even if Earth's a wash?" Nico supplied.

"Maybe one of the ones who didn't 'end things' could find a way to fix things," Elsa suggested. "Like your mentor, the Sorcerer Supreme."

"Earth doesn't have a Sorcerer Supreme right now," Zelma said flatly. "At least not one who isn't hiding in the shadows like a craven instead of doing his or her duty."

She had managed to avoid thinking about it up to this point, but Doc had said contacting Clea and getting her to spread the word about the infection had been his last act as Earth's Sorcerer Supreme, and he had been right, or close enough that it wasn't worth quibbling over. He'd still been wearing the Eye of Agamotto when he spoke to Clea. He hadn't been wearing it when they'd reached the basement door. Zelma had no idea at what point in between those two moments the Eye had left him to find a successor; all she knew was that successor had not come to Earth's aid in any appreciable way since gaining his or her title. And that was all she needed to know. Whoever wore the Eye now didn't deserve it.

All the more reason to get it back to its rightful wearer.

"We came here to fix this," Zelma repeated. "To figure out how to end this scourge, to save the Earth *and* the rest of the universe. To save humanity. And all the mutants and magic-users and unclassifiables who make up our super population."

"So just… everyone and everything, then?" Deadpool clarified sardonically, his trademark tone having returned intact, apparently no worse for the wear after its temporary banishment. He had sheathed his blade but was still standing behind and to one side of Nico.

"Exactly," Zelma replied with a smile, nodding. She was quickly warming to the idea blossoming to fullness in her mind. She thought it could work.

Mostly because it had to.

Elsa let out a snort, then grabbed a chair from its place at a nearby book-covered study table, spun it around backwards, then sat heavily, straddling it.

"That all, then?" she scoffed. "Zelma, darling, no offense, but I'm beginning to think you're a sandwich short of a picnic."

"I'm not... whatever disparaging thing that means," Zelma insisted. "I've just realized we've been thinking about this all wrong."

"Fixing it is wrong?" Nico asked, her lips twisting in that special way she had of expressing complete skepticism without ever actually coming right out and saying she didn't believe a word exiting your mouth. From her face, it was clear she'd sided with the others when it came to sandwiches and picnics.

"No reason to fix what isn't broken," Zelma countered. She could see she'd totally lost them all now. Nico was no doubt moments away from conjuring a straitjacket.

"It's... *not*... broken?" Deadpool ventured into the uncomfortable silence that followed her statement. She could have hugged him for teeing up her conclusion so perfectly. She might even let him use the microwave, assuming it could be retrieved from the kitchen.

"Oh, no. Unlike our microwave, it's totally broken," Zelma said, much to the confoundment of the others. Except Deadpool, who'd heard the word "microwave" and clapped his gloved hands in quiet glee. "*Now*. But it wasn't always."

"What bloody good does *that* do us?" Elsa demanded. She

looked like she was thinking about reaching for one of her guns. Zelma was glad the monster hunter had left her shotgun on the floor where she'd landed after being teleported. "Not sure you're aware, but we're sort of *in* the 'now.'"

"Obviously. But who says we have to *stay* here?"

CHAPTER EIGHTEEN

"Well, she's right crackers," Elsa said, throwing her hands up in mock despair. "Anyone else got a plan?"

"No," Nico replied. She leaned forward on her staff and stared hard at Zelma. Was the apprentice suggesting what Nico thought she was suggesting? "Let's hear her out. It's the end of the world. Nothing's off the table."

"Nothing?" Deadpool asked, his eyes widening with melodramatic and completely bogus surprise as he stared at her meaningfully. Nico rolled her own eyes but didn't respond. Instead, she motioned for Zelma to continue.

"OK," Zelma said, her eyes brightening behind her glasses as she spoke. "We all agree that the current timeline sucks and we'd rather be in a different one, given our druthers." Deadpool raised his hand to ask a question, but Nico and Elsa both glared at him until he meekly lowered it again. "But we're in what is arguably the most well-stocked arcane library in the world. There are dozens of time travel spells in here, ripe for the casting. Why not go back to before this ever happened? Warn the Avengers and whoever else so they're prepared to negate the threat before it develops? Have a cure on hand or, better yet, destroy whatever struck Manhattan before it enters our atmosphere?"

"And if they can't?" Elsa asked. "Time-hopping's all fun and games until you actually end up making things worse."

"How could it be worse?" Zelma replied, looking askance at the monster hunter.

"Are you serious?" Elsa responded, her expression a study in incredulity, its overall effect somewhat marred by the necrotized hole in her cheek. She raised her bloodhand and began ticking off fingers.

"One: Time's running out and they haven't found a cure or a way to prevent the impact. Maybe they don't even know how the strike happens, since there were no reports of anything remotely close to hitting the Earth beforehand this time around. But they try to save humanity anyway, because they're heroes, dammit, and that's what they do.

"They gather the humans together and ferret them away in various overcrowded and completely mislabeled 'safe havens', where they just become buffets for the infected when things eventually play out exactly the same way as they did in this timeline.

"Two: Same scenario, but Strange isn't able to warn his sorcerous counterparts to close off their dimensions, so this plague not only overruns our planet, it overruns *all* the planets, *all* the dimensions, *all* the universes. That'd be worse.

"Three–"

"OK," Zelma interrupted her, making a face. "There are obviously some kinks that will need to be worked out, but–"

"*Kinks*?" Elsa looked over at Nico in frank amazement,

her eyebrows climbing up to hide beneath her red bangs. "Does that word have some other meaning on this side of the pond besides the two I'm aware of? Like when you Yanks call something a 'sandwich', but instead of being a nice bit of cucumber or egg and cress on little triangles of bread like at a proper tea, it's some monstrosity with half a deli's worth of food on a twelve-inch bap? Except in reverse, so the word means something very small here, but to the rest of the civilized world, it is in fact something quite large and rather more alarming?"

"No, not really," Nico replied, compressing her lips into a thin line to keep from smirking. Not only did she not want either of the other women to think she was laughing at them, she also didn't want to give Deadpool a reason to chime in with his definition of "kink". She doubted it would be helpful, and while it might be enlightening, it was knowledge she would rather do without. "She's calling it a molehill and you're convinced it's a mountain. Personally, I'd be inclined to agree with you, but we're talking about magic here. That tends to knock relativity all out of whack."

"Thanks for that," Zelma said to Nico, giving her a grateful look. "I think." She turned back to Elsa. "Listen, we're just brainstorming here–"

"Ix-nay on the ains-bray," Deadpool stage-whispered. "It's offensive to zombies." He indicated the monster hunter by flicking his eyes meaningfully in her direction several times, as if anyone was unclear who he might be talking about.

"Oh, do shut up, Wade," the zombie hunter said, frowning in annoyance. She waved her bloodhand at Zelma in a "move it along" motion. "Fine. It's just a preliminary idea. A bad one, but let's leave that aside for now. Pretend I'm chuffed. All ears and whatnot."

"OK," Zelma said. "To recap – this timeline sucks. We have the means, so why not change it? We can go back to before the plague-laden meteorite or whatever it was ever hit, to either stop it or give enough advance notice that a way can be found to neutralize or contain its contagion. Which, as Elsa so colorfully noted, has some issues. But that's not the only way we can change things. We can go back and–"

"Wait," Nico interrupted, a sudden thought occurring to her. All eyes turned in her direction, Zelma's annoyed, Elsa's curious, and Deadpool's gleeful.

"What now?" Zelma snapped, her patience tank now the one running on empty.

Nico didn't care. The librarian had the right idea, but she was looking at it all backwards. Nico flipped the puzzle pieces around in her mind, and she could suddenly see how they might all fit together and make Zelma's plan truly workable.

"Why do we keep talking about *us* being the ones to go back in time?" she asked, not quite able to mask her sudden enthusiasm. "Why not send *them*?"

CHAPTER NINETEEN

"Lovely. Everyone's crackers." Elsa shook her head in disgust. "I should have stayed back in Boston where I only had the gobby one to worry about."

"Speak English," Zelma grumbled.

"Ha! That's bloody rich," Elsa replied with a short laugh and a raised brow. "To quote our ever-annoying companion here, 'You first.'"

Perhaps because Elsa had chosen to invoke Deadpool, Zelma chose to respond to her in the same way she usually responded to the mercenary – by ignoring the other woman. Instead, she looked at Nico.

"What do you mean, send *them* back in time? What good would that do, except maybe end the world before we were even born?"

"That *would* solve our problems," Deadpool said. For once, Nico couldn't argue with him. But that was definitely a "nuke it from orbit" type of solution, and not what she'd had in mind.

Not that Nico really knew exactly what she'd had in mind when she blurted out her idea. She only had the first glimmerings of a plan, not the full-blown blueprint. She just knew that there was no way to guarantee that having their little team take a trip back in time would produce the results they wanted. She'd traveled back in time with the Runaways once before. It hadn't seemed like a good idea then, and it didn't seem like a good one now. It was impossible not to change *something* when you went back – there was always that butterfly you didn't realize you'd crushed, and sometimes the alterations were so subtle it might take lifetimes to fully comprehend their impact.

No, them taking that trip had way too many potential fatal flaws. So that meant the other party had to go.

But Zelma was right. If they just sent the zombies back in time – even assuming they could somehow round them all up and get them to go through whatever portal the four of them managed to open – they would only end up destroying mankind that much sooner. Even sending them to the pre-primordial beginnings might not be enough, since there was no way of knowing how long the zombies could go without food, or what would happen if the hunger that gnawed at them ceaselessly wasn't sated. Assuming they didn't just go mad and destroy themselves, maybe they'd just sit around kumbaya-ing and waiting for life to develop. Maybe they'd shepherd evolution until they'd created mindless herd humans, a potentially endless food source.

Nico didn't really see that happening. So far, only a few zombies seemed able to control their appetites long enough to function at anything resembling their former levels. The vast majority were like kids at Halloween, stuffing themselves with candy before they even made it home, gorging on sweets until they were sick, and then eating more, either just because they could, or because they couldn't stop. Regardless, she didn't really think any zombies would be waiting around long enough for their multi-celled forebears to come crawling out of the sea.

But there was no way to be sure. These weren't regular horror movie zombies, after all. They were zombified Avengers, and all bets regarding what they could and couldn't do, given millennia in which to do it, were off.

So just sending them back wouldn't work, either, unless there was some way to make it so they didn't stop in any one place long enough to do any lasting harm. Like putting them on some sort of temporal hamster wheel that they couldn't get off, no matter how fast they ran.

Something like…

"A time loop?" Zelma said suddenly, as if reading her mind.

Nico blinked in surprise, then nodded.

"That would work, don't you think? We could tap into the timestream and create an infinite loop, open a portal to it, gather all the zombies together, and… get them to go in it. Somehow."

Elsa stood up, swinging her leg over the chair seat like she was dismounting a horse. Nico saw that the monster hunter's stance was loose and ready; she was expecting a fight. Or was about to start one.

"Listen to yourselves. You sound like the Queen of Hearts with her list of impossible things." She raised her bloodhand and began ticking things off on her fingers again. "Tap into the timestream. Create a time loop. Open a portal to that loop. Gather all the zombies together in one place." She paused on her ring finger, her bloodgem flashing with orange-red fire in the low sunlight streaming in through the library windows. "Oh, and, by the by, if we're doing that, why are we even bothering with time travel and not just wiping them all off the face of the planet in one fell swoop?" Then she raised her pinky. "And then, once gathered, we somehow get the entire group of zombies we have for some unknown reason chosen not to destroy to trot on into the loop. Perhaps by asking nicely? Or with a written invitation?"

Elsa shook her head, disgusted. Her red hair bounced about her face, some strands getting caught in the hole in her cheek. She didn't seem to notice; she was too exasperated.

"This is not a plan. This is madness. And I won't be part of it. Deadpool and I will be getting off the bonkers train now, thank you very much. Just show us to the door."

Nico's heart plummeted to somewhere near the tops of her hiking boots at the monster hunter's words. Not because Elsa thought their idea was lunacy – it definitely was. Which didn't mean it wouldn't work. But that wasn't the cause of the empty feeling in Nico's chest or the sudden constriction of her breath, and she knew it.

She desperately didn't want Elsa to leave the Sanctum.

Nico knew it was ridiculous. She wasn't even sure *why* it was so important to her that Elsa stay. It wasn't as if they were BFFs, though Nico thought maybe they could be.

She was attracted to Elsa; Nico could admit that to herself now. And Elsa's being a zombie had done little to lessen her appeal – she was still the same smart, sassy, competent woman Nico had first felt drawn to, just on a strict new diet that the witch preferred not to think about too closely.

But she didn't think that was it. It wasn't as if that attraction was ever likely to go anywhere, and deep down she knew it. And it wasn't even because they had a connection that, given time, could make them ride or dies.

Nico hadn't known Zelma or Deadpool pre-apocalypse, so they would only ever be associated in her mind with the fear and horror and creeping hopelessness of this moment, even if they did somehow manage to change the timeline. But Nico had met Elsa *before*.

Before she'd seen Karolina and the rest of her team torn to pieces by ravenous heroes who had once been allies. Before Zelma had pulled her into Doctor Strange's library and her quest to save him, and what was left of humanity.

Before the world had ended. Back when it was normal, As normal as it ever got for people like her, anyway.

Elsa was her last tenuous link to that world. The one where things made sense. The one where, even if she was still running for her life half the time, she wasn't always running scared, or alone.

Nico realized that was why she'd been so disproportionately angry to discover that Elsa had been zombified. But other than the hole in her cheek and a new paleo diet, it hadn't changed the monster hunter in any appreciable way. She was still Elsa.

And if Elsa left, she took Nico's hope of returning to that world with her.

It didn't make sense, Nico knew, but that didn't matter. It just *was*.

Nico couldn't let the monster hunter leave. She had to find some way to convince Elsa to stay, to go along with their time loop plan.

She just had to. Otherwise, the despair she'd been barely

holding back would swell up like a tidal wave and engulf her, and she would drown.

To her utter astonishment, it was Deadpool who provided her lifeline.

"Actually, Ellie, I think I'll be staying."

The three women looked at him in astonishment.

"What?" he asked defensively. "Like you said, let's take them out all at once – time loop, nuke, who cares? It has to be better than slicing me up every day just to get rid of a few zombies at a time. Though I secretly think you just use it as an excuse to grab my butt." He shrugged. "Anyway, it's crazy, but it's my kind of crazy. I'm in."

Then he gestured toward Zelma.

"Besides, you heard her. These guys have a working microwave."

CHAPTER TWENTY

Elsa, evidently seeing that she was outnumbered, gave up.

"Righto, then," she said with a sigh. "If that's how you all want to go out, I guess there's no point in chinwagging about it. Not the hill I would have chosen to die on, but then that boat's already sailed for me."

Zelma was surprised at the monster hunter's easy acquiescence, but she supposed Elsa had no choice but to stay if that was what Deadpool wanted to do. At least if she wanted to remain a monster hunter, and not become the monster hunted.

Which made Zelma wonder – how had Elsa gotten infected in the first place? Or, more to the point, how had she regained her sanity and realized the implications of doing so? That she could continue to be herself – or a reasonable facsimile thereof – as long as she had an available, replenishable, willing food source? And how had she gotten Deadpool to agree to be that source?

Knowing the answers to those questions could be important. They could give Zelma some insight on how to lure the other zombies to the time loop once it was open. So Zelma did the one thing she was better at than organizing and reading books.

Asking questions.

"How did that boat sail, again? I don't recall you saying."

"That's because I didn't, it not being relevant," the redheaded zombie replied, her frown causing small fissures to form in the skin around the hole in her cheek.

"Oh, but it is," Zelma insisted. "Extremely so. Because we know next to nothing about this… virus, or whatever it is. We know slightly more about the zombies it creates, largely due to information you gave us. You have insight into how the infection spreads and how to keep the hunger it causes at bay. If you can shed some light on the zombies' behavior and how they operate, then we can use that to flesh out our plan." She regretted the word "flesh" as soon as it left her mouth, but luckily Deadpool did not take the opportunity to chide her for using it as some imagined anti-undead slur. Still, it was hard to think of the zombies as anything other than mindless mouths that would do anything to fill themselves.

Which was why Zelma didn't understand Elsa's reluctance. It wasn't as if the monster hunter had asked to be chomped on. The librarian said as much.

To her surprise, Deadpool waved a flat hand in front of his throat, a "cut" motion Zelma believed was meant to get her to stop talking, though it was impossible to tell with that one. He might have just passed gas.

And, anyway, it was too late. Whatever line in the sand Zelma had unknowingly scuffed her shoes through had already been obliterated. There was no taking it back, as evinced by the hard, cold look Elsa leveled her way.

"Didn't I, though?" the monster hunter retorted, retaking her still-reversed seat. She placed her elbow on the top of the chair back, then leaned forward and put her chin on her fist. Her thumb tapped out an indecipherable pattern against the skin of her good cheek. "Any hunter who lets herself gets turned into prey *is* asking for it. In my book, anyway."

"Guessing it's not a bestseller," Deadpool quipped. Oddly, Zelma thought she detected a note of something else under the sarcasm. It couldn't possibly be… compassion?

But then Zelma realized what was going on. As far as Elsa was concerned, her getting zombified was a first-class failure. A disgrace of the highest order, a permanent stain on the Bloodstone name. It didn't matter *how* it had happened – the fact that it had was a black mark on the monster hunter's record that could never be erased, no matter how many of her fellow zombies she killed after the fact.

Which Zelma the apprentice totally understood. She'd screwed up royally so many times under Doc's tutelage that she was continually surprised he kept her on as a student. She was pretty sure he still hadn't forgiven her for turning him into a slug; maybe that memory would stay gone once he got his brain back and in working order. One could only hope.

But Zelma didn't believe failing was a sin. It was the only way you really learned anything – trial and error… and error, and error, and eventually, success. It was a feature of human existence, not a bug.

Unless you let it stop you. And that was what Elsa was doing now. Letting her perceived failure hold her back from doing what needed to be done.

Zelma wanted to tell her the same thing she'd told Nico

when the other witch had thought she'd missed the chance to find Elsa – to get over herself. But, arguably, that wasn't possible in Elsa's case.

She was a zombie, one of the "ravenous reanimated", to use the term Doc had so colorfully coined. There was no "getting over" that. At least not until they found a cure, or a way to reverse the infection's effects, which would amount to much the same thing. But until then, Elsa was pretty much… what would the Brit say? Buggered?

Zelma didn't think that was the only source of Elsa's reluctance to describe her experience, though. And Zelma the woman understood that, too.

What had happened to Elsa, even as hardened a warrior as she was, had to have been traumatizing. Not just because of whatever battle must have ensued, which would have been both violent and gruesome, because there was no way fewer than a baker's dozen of super-powered zombies could have taken Elsa Bloodstone down.

But losing a fight was the least of Elsa's hurts. Even technically dying might not compare to the manner of that death – namely, being overwhelmed, having her bodily autonomy taken from her, and being forever changed into something she didn't want to be, all to assuage someone else's appetites.

No woman would want to relive such a memory. A woman like Elsa Bloodstone would as soon have that memory and whatever brain part held it excised without the benefit of anesthesia than admit it even existed. And now Zelma was asking her to dredge it all up again for them to dissect, like some slimy defense lawyer at an assault trial. She couldn't even imagine how painful that would be.

But what choice did she have? Zelma was convinced they needed that information for their plan to have any hope of success, and Elsa was the only one who could give it to them.

Then Zelma remembered the Thinker's Folly spell she'd suggested to Doc. He'd nixed it, because while it removed his access to his memories, the memories themselves remained, meaning they could be located and appropriated by others. But Elsa wouldn't have to worry about other people picking through her brain looking for information on zombies after the spell was cast. It might work for her.

Or Zelma could even use a simple forgetfulness spell. She was pretty sure she'd seen a Palm of Forgetfulness in the Sanctum Machina. There were a lot of ways this could potentially work, if Elsa was willing

"Could Elsa and I have a moment, please?" Zelma asked, looking over at Nico and Deadpool.

Deadpool shrugged. He'd put his katanas away again, Zelma noted.

"You can have all the moments. You're the time wizard."

Not yet, she wasn't, but Zelma didn't bother to correct him. Explaining the magical nuances to him would probably take more time than making the moniker a reality would.

"Nico?"

The other witch looked from her to Elsa and back again with worried eyes, as if she were afraid one of them might kill the other, but wasn't sure who to be more concerned about. Finally though, she also assented.

Zelma whispered a command to Cloak, who rose from her shoulders and floated over to where Nico and Deadpool stood. The cloak folded itself over in a low bow, then pointed one of its high collars over toward another alcove. When they didn't immediately move, it zipped behind them and snapped its embroidered hem in a shooing motion, like a kindergarten teacher herding students in from recess.

When they were out of earshot, Zelma grabbed another chair from beside the table and pulled it over to Elsa. Then she sat down in front of the monster hunter.

"Listen, Elsa, I can't pretend to know what you went through. It must have been awful, and I get that you don't want to rehash the experience, no matter how helpful it might be to our mission. I struggle with whether it's right to even ask you." She knew Doc wouldn't have thought twice about it, but Zelma wasn't Doc. She didn't want to *be* him. Not really. She just wanted to do what he could do, hopefully without making choices that gave her a Cellar Dweller of her own.

"But what if I could get the information we need from you *without* you having to remember anything?" she asked. "Without you having to relive those memories *ever* again?"

Elsa cocked her head to the side, an eyebrow raising as she did.

"And just how are you planning on doing that, Miss Time Wizard?" Elsa asked. Then she paused and corrected herself. "Beg pardon. Miss *Apprentice* Time Wizard."

Zelma bristled at both the name and the disparaging tone, but she realized that other than getting rid of some zombies, she'd given Elsa no real reason to trust her abilities thus far. There was no guarantee she'd be able to pull off a time loop spell, even with help from Nico's staff.

But she *could* do this spell. She could take this pain from Elsa, and maybe learn something that would benefit their plan in the process. It could be a win-win.

If Elsa trusted her.

"A spell to make you forget what happened, or at least the parts of it you don't want to remember. You tell us – or maybe just me, if you prefer – I cast the spell, and then you never have to think about it again."

Elsa was staring at her, hard blue eyes probing, as if she were trying to see into the librarian's soul. Or maybe to see if she even had one. Finally, the monster hunter sighed and closed her eyes for a long moment. When she opened them again, her gaze was clear and bright and hostile.

"Zelma, darling, what on Earth makes you think I *want* to forget what's happened to me?"

Zelma blinked at the other woman, not quite grasping her meaning. She opened and closed her mouth several times, trying to formulate a reply to the completely unexpected question. She hadn't even considered the possibility that Elsa might not jump at the chance to have those painful memories wiped away.

"Why *wouldn't* you?" she finally asked, unable to keep the utter confusion from her voice.

Elsa sighed again, the anger fading from her expression, replaced with weary resignation.

"It's adorable that you have to ask, really," she replied with a disbelieving shake of her head. "And, surprisingly, I don't want to be the one to burst your innocent bubble. Suffice to say that the memory of what was done to me is what keeps me going. It fuels my rage and my thirst for vengeance. It's the only thing giving me purpose in this poorly scripted freak show now masquerading as my life."

That didn't sound very healthy, but Zelma wasn't about

to try psychoanalyzing the monster hunter. Partly because playing therapist wasn't in her apprentice toolkit, but mostly because she liked her tongue in her mouth, where she could use it, and not hanging out of a hole in her neck, wagging uselessly in the wind.

She did note that Elsa hadn't listed keeping the same thing from happening to anyone else as one of the reasons she kept calm and carried on, which many survivors of similar losses might do. But if trying to save humans from being eaten was what got Elsa out of bed in the morning – assuming zombies even slept – then Zelma, being a human who didn't particularly want to get eaten herself, wasn't about to complain.

"OK," she said when she was finally able to gather her scattered thoughts, "so if remembering what happened isn't a problem for you, then why are you so unwilling to share that information with the rest of us? Especially since there's every likelihood that it will give us a leg up on the very animals that did this to you?"

"Careful," Elsa warned, her eyes narrowing, her voice gone soft and dangerous. "I'm one of those animals now."

Zelma gulped loudly in the tense silence that followed.

Then Elsa threw her head back and guffawed, the harsh sound made more dissonant by the air blowing through the hole in her cheek.

"Relax, you muppet," Elsa said at last, wiping at eyes that held no tears, of mirth or otherwise. "I'm not going to eat you. Not enough meat on your bones to keep me sane for more than a few hours, anyway. Speaking of which… Wilson!" she yelled over her shoulder, in the general direction Cloak had led the others. "Get your butt back over here. It's teatime."

As Nico and Deadpool made their way back over to where she and Elsa sat, the red cloak trailing after, Zelma tried one more time.

"You never answered my question."

Elsa rolled her eyes.

"Has anyone ever told you that you are bloody exhausting? And I can't even *get* knackered anymore.

"Though you're possibly not quite as bright a button as I'd first thought," she added, "so I'll try to speak slowly. Just because I don't want to forget what happened doesn't mean I want to trot it out for story time. Does *that* answer your question?"

Zelma just nodded, trying to keep her expression impassive. Inside, though, she was crestfallen, and her stomach churned with anxiety. She hadn't realized how much she'd been counting on what Elsa might share with them to give her a clue as to how to proceed with their time loop plan.

She was back exactly where she had started – out of her depth. Except now the life preserver she'd been counting on had failed to materialize, and she was about to drown.

CHAPTER TWENTY-ONE

While Zelma's cloak guided Elsa and Deadpool to a more private place to conduct their sordid business, Nico spun Elsa's chair around and sat down opposite Zelma.

"OK, spill," she said. The cloak had only taken her and Deadpool a few stacks away, and while that might normally have been enough to keep them from hearing the two women's conversation, a whispered "Tin can on a string" had made their every word clear to the Runaway.

Zelma shrugged, obviously at a loss. "She doesn't want to talk about it."

"So what?" Nico scoffed. "I've had to do a lot of stuff I haven't wanted to do since this started. She doesn't get a pass just because she's zombified."

"It's a little more complicated than that," Zelma protested, but Nico waved her argument away before she could make it.

"Save it for someone who has an ounce of sympathy," Nico replied, unmoved. "We're heroes. Captain Marvel once said: 'Being a hero is always about sacrifice. It always has been, and it always will be'. And she was right." Nico hadn't been quite as inclined to agree with Carol at the time, but she had seen the other woman's words proven true over and over again since.

"Don't tell me," Zelma replied with another helpless shrug. "Tell her."

"As a matter of fact, I think I will."

Nico rose as Elsa and Deadpool made their way back to the book-laden table and the chairs where she and Zelma sat. Elsa's full lips didn't look any redder, but her overall demeanor seemed calmer than it had been. Which was probably a good thing, considering Nico was about to call her out.

"Zelma tells me you don't want to talk about what happened to you," she challenged the zombie woman, getting straight to the point. "Even though you know it could help us."

Elsa's eyes narrowed as they flicked toward Zelma and then back to Nico. Her lips were now a thin, angry line.

"Zelma tells you right."

"Zelma also told me something else once. She told me to get over myself. And you know what? She was right then, too. Because none of this is about me, or about you. It's about being heroes. And heroes don't get to put their own personal comforts ahead of saving the world. There's another name for the people who do that."

"Oh, oh, I know!" Deadpool exclaimed, raising his hand excitedly. "Is it 'villains'? It's 'villains', right?"

"Yes," Nico replied flatly, not taking her eyes off Elsa, whose murderous glare could have scoured the lead shielding off a nuclear reactor. "That's exactly right. Gold star."

Deadpool gasped in feigned delight. "A gold star? For me?" he said, clasping his hands together in front of his face and probably batting his eyelashes beneath his mask.

Before Nico could actually throttle him, Zelma said, "Cloak!" and the cloak obediently swept up behind the mercenary and wrapped him up in a red cocoon faster than Deadpool could react. Muffled noises of outrage sounded from inside the fabric prison before the merc overbalanced and fell to the floor, rolling around like an over-bundled child in a wintery Christmas movie.

"Poor Nico," Elsa said, her voice dripping pity. "Always needing the world to be black or white. So confused by its many shades of gray."

"It *is* black or white, Elsa," Nico insisted. "Heroes do the right thing for the good of humanity. Period."

"Even if it's not the right thing for their own good?" Elsa shot back.

Nico couldn't keep thoughts of Karolina's kiss or Alice's death from running through her head, of all the losses she'd endured in service of "the right thing". A spiky lump of remorse formed in her throat, and it took her more than one dry gulp to get it down.

"Even if," she agreed, her voice almost a whisper.

"That's bollocks," Elsa said flatly. "It's too much to ask of anyone."

"Yes," Nico agreed again. "It is. You and I both know that doesn't change anything."

But, oh, how she wished it did. She could have laughed. For someone who'd led a team called the Runaways, it turned out she sucked at running away from things. Especially responsibility.

Elsa was silent for a long time, her eyes locked with Nico's. Nico was almost tempted to cast a spell to read the other woman's mind, but that was a Captain Marvel move, not a Nico Minoru one. She had to retain some goth girl anarchist cred *some*where.

"You know," Elsa finally said, seeming to deflate a little, a sight that wrenched at Nico's heart, though she quickly tamped the sorrow down. The last thing she had ever wanted to see was this strong, bold woman made to feel smaller, or less than. The last thing she ever wanted to be was the person making her feel that way. "I used to think I liked you."

"And now?" Nico asked, inwardly cringing, afraid of what the answer might be.

Elsa didn't answer. Instead, she looked over at Zelma.

"Well, crack on, then. Let's get this load of cobblers over with, shall we?"

"Well, gather round, luvs, I'm only going to tell this story once, and I won't be taking questions, so you'd best listen up."

Elsa had turned her chair around and was sitting facing the others. She sat pressed as far back on the seat as she could get, her arms crossed over her chest, one leg crossed over the other, foot bouncing. If it were possible for Elsa Bloodstone to look vulnerable, Zelma imagined this was as close as the other woman would ever get to it.

Zelma sat across from Elsa on her own chair, while Nico sat cross-legged on the floor to the librarian's left, her staff laid across her lap. Deadpool leaned against the table behind them, sulking. Zelma had released him from the Cloak of Levitation's loving embrace on the condition that he behave himself, though she wasn't convinced he was capable of that. The tableau resembled a macabre children's story hour, but no library program would get away with exposing youngsters to the tale Elsa was about to recount.

"I'd just got back from London. I'd popped over to check on the place there – Cullen and I had a bit of a tiff a few years back that brought the house down, and I'm still having it… *refurbished*, shall we say? Bloody contractors move at a glacial pace."

She looked over at Nico, ostensibly addressing the Runaway.

"Did you know there was a time when I completely forgot the house in England even existed? Imagine! Thought the one in Boston was the only Bloodstone Manor there'd ever been, which is bloody daft, when you think about it. Ulysses was *ancient*. It's unlikely he'd have built the first Bloodstone Manor in this squalling brat of a country, is it?" She shrugged nonchalantly, but her shoulders were too tight for pretended flippancy, and her words were sharp and pointed. "But that's the sort of thing that happens when folks go naffing about with other people's memories. Never know what's real and what's implanted, if you can recall anything at all. Nasty business, that." She didn't look at Zelma as she said it, but the apprentice had no misconceptions as to who her words were directed at.

"Anyhoo, for a country with such arse-backwards gun laws, your airlines tend to get their knickers in a real twist when you try to smuggle guns on and off their planes. So I didn't have any on me for the trip back, just a few assorted throwing knives in my checked luggage, a machete, the usual. It's a hop, skip, and a jump from Logan International to the Boston manor; didn't figure I'd actually *need* any firepower. My mistake.

"Hadn't even made it out of the city when traffic just stopped moving. Not that unusual, I suppose – it was afternoon rush hour. And while Boston cabbies might not be quite as hard to rattle as their New York City counterparts, it still takes a bit to get one to run off screaming with the meter still going. Even more than my stunning looks after having flown eight hours nonstop in coach class.

"But a horde of super-powered zombies barreling their way down the Salem Turnpike, ripping the tops off cars like they were sardine tins and gobbling up whatever they found inside could do that to the most stalwart normie, I imagine. Especially when more than one of those supers were big and green and smashy.

"Didn't faze *me* much, of course. But then, not a lot does. Still, I didn't have my guns, and those're the real deal, the custom goodies that can take down biters and shifters and flyers and extradimensional whosits and whatnows. So, the better part of valor being staying alive to accomplish it, I booked it after the cabbie."

"Valiant in the attempt," Deadpool muttered under his breath, but Cloak rustled warningly at the same time and Zelma didn't think anyone else heard.

Meanwhile, Elsa's mouth twisted the tiniest bit; Zelma doubted having fled was an admission the monster hunter was proud of making, especially given the "staying alive" caveat no longer applied. But her chipper bearing didn't waver. She was playing the stiff-upper-lipped stereotype to the fullest, perhaps because every time she relaxed her jaws too much, the hole in her cheek cracked open just a little wider.

"Even in stilettos, I left the cabbie and a few dozen poor blighters in my dust in no time. Not my finest hour, but needs must.

"I didn't make a clean escape, by any means. That lot might've been ruled by hunger, but someone was sane enough to send flyers up as spotters, and it wasn't long before one homed in on me.

"Unfortunately for him, he decided not to share and tried to take me on by himself. Big mistake; I might have looked like easy prey from the air, but I still had my blades. My first knife took him in the throat at fifty yards.

"He kept coming, though, banking a bit as he did, like he thought he was doing evasive aerial maneuvers, silly sod. So my next one hit him at the joint where his left wing exited his back, slicing through bone and severing nerves. He lost control and spun out, slamming into the pavement not ten yards from me."

She looked at Zelma with a wicked smile.

"Good thing Daddy taught me how to dismember things when I was just a tot."

Then she winked and continued her story, and Zelma had no idea if the monster hunter had been teasing her or not.

"Well, people in my business don't last very long if we leave living enemies behind, so I pulled out my machete and moved in to deliver the coup de grace and retrieve my other knives.

"Blighter had been faking a bit, though. When I got up close, he grabbed at my arm, all claw-like, like he thought he was Wolvie or something. He missed, of course, but he *was* able to snag my coat, and then the stupid bugger tried to fly off with me! With one wing out of commission and a knife still sticking out of his throat! Points for stick-to-it-iveness, I guess.

"Now, I know what you're thinking," Elsa said, her eyes bright. She was leaning forward now and talking faster as she worked her way up to some dramatic scene. "I could've just shrugged my way out of the coat and finished it then and there. But, where's the fun in that, I ask you? Also, it's my favorite coat, and there being a bloody good chance my usual tailor was going to be closing up shop – along with the rest of the world – I opted to do the sensible thing and place its safety above my own.

"So I put my machete in my teeth and reached up to grab his arm. Then I climbed my way up him like he was a bit of thick, twitchy rope. He tried punching me with his other arm – the one on the side with the wing that still worked – and he landed a few good ones. But I heal pretty quickly, thanks to the bloodstone, so it was like getting bit by a mosquito. Momentarily annoying, but ultimately inconsequential.

"By that time, I'd reached his shoulder, so I used it as a fulcrum, swinging my legs out and up and trapping his head between my thighs." She looked over at Deadpool, who had opened his mouth to say something. "Not a word."

"I was just going to correct you about the mosquito thing," he muttered. "West Nile Virus is no joke."

Elsa snorted. Zelma was getting better at interpreting the Brit's various odd turns of phrase through contextual clues, but she didn't need any to know that was Elsa-ese for "Whatever."

"It *was* a bit of an indelicate position, I'll admit, but I released his shoulder and heaved with my legs and we both went tumbling back to the pavement, stilettos over ponytails.

"I plucked my machete from my teeth and twisted as we fell, unlocking my legs right before we hit the ground. He landed on the bottom, cushioning my landing, and it took him half a second longer to catch his breath than it did for me to catch mine.

"And that was all I needed.

"I'd ended up basically straddling him, so wasn't in a position where I could swing the machete and do much damage. Instead, I changed my grip on the handle and grabbed the top of the serrated edge of the blade, then placed it across his neck and started to push.

"He'd already smashed his noggin when we landed, and there was some blood pooling around his head, but I didn't know what it took to actually kill – or re-kill – these things yet, so I went with the tried and true. Decapitation.

"After I'd finished playing human guillotine, I got up, cleaned my blades, and started running again, this time keeping my eyes on the skies as well as on the streets around me. Wasn't long before I found myself on the edges of Holy Cross Cemetery. Generally the *last* place you want to be during a zombie apocalypse, but I could see that no graves had been disturbed, so whatever was happening to the suits wasn't likely a supernatural thing. Which actually made the graveyard a pretty safe place to get my bearings, seeing's how the pickings were pretty slim there if you were looking for an ambulatory dinner. Unfortunately, I wasn't the only one with that idea. Just the only one who could keep from attracting unwanted diners."

"Pish," Deadpool said loudly from behind Zelma, his quietude quotient apparently having been exhausted. Zelma raised her hand to have Cloak muzzle him again, but Elsa waved her off.

"No, he's right to challenge me on that one, I suppose. See, he was there, too. Found each other by an aboveground crypt; some tot named Preston, wasn't it?" she asked him, but didn't wait for his answer. "He'd picked the lock on the crypt, but not bothered to relock it behind himself – lot of that going around these days – and I was just trotting on past when the screaming in the chapel started."

Here she heaved an aggrieved sigh.

"Well, Wilson here comes barreling out of the crypt, almost knocking me on my bum, and just keeps going, without so much as a by-your-leave. Seems he'd seen an old woman heading into the building while he'd been fiddling with the lock. Didn't care so much about her, but she had a service dog – *that's* who he was worried about."

"Well, *some*one had to look out for the dog," Deadpool interjected. "The old lady couldn't do it – she was blind!"

Elsa inclined her head, acknowledging the point.

"I recognized him, of course, and seriously considered not following him, but I couldn't take the chance he'd been zombified and was going to snack on some unsuspecting altar servers.

"Well, *he* wasn't a zombie, but there was one there. Balding chap in an outlandish purple and black outfit – no offense, Nico; the combo looks good on you. He was going at the old lady's arm like it was wings night at the local pub. And if I hadn't been there, he would've made Wade his next victim, because that idiot was too busy trying to calm the damned mutt down to watch his own six."

"Hey, be nice!" Deadpool protested. "Bruno was scared!"

Zelma looked over at Nico in confusion, mouthing "Bruno?" at her. Nico shrugged, equally mystified, and mouthed "The dog?" back. Meanwhile, Elsa continued her story like Deadpool had never spoken.

"Luckily, I *was* there, and I grabbed one of the toerag's own silver daggers and stabbed him through the heart with it.

"Unluckily, turns out that spot's not any more vulnerable for these rotters than their throats, and he went for my eyes with his crabbed little hands. Missed, of course, but in dodging him, I danced myself right into the loving embrace of that blue-haired bat, who was now a zombie herself. She spun me around, yelled at me for 'desecrating her husband's memory' and 'ruining the service' – like *I* was the one who'd come in looking for an easy meal, instead of the one who'd rushed in to save her arse. Then she slapped me across the face. Wench.

"Anyhoo–"

"Probably the Rosary," Nico interjected. "It's pretty common to have a formal recitation at the funeral home the day before the actual funeral Mass."

Zelma hadn't had any idea that Nico was at all religious, and judging from the dumfounded looks she was getting from Elsa and Deadpool, neither had they.

"What?" Nico asked defensively, taking in their expressions. "I was raised Catholic. I was even an altar girl, believe it or not. I remember some things."

Zelma wondered if that upbringing was part of what informed Nico's overblown and rigid sense of duty. While the other witch presented a tough, self-protective façade to the world, she seemed incapable of turning her back on people or situations where she was needed, even if it meant risking her own skin.

Zelma also wondered if the silver dagger-wielding zombie Elsa had encountered was the religious fanatic known as the Silver Dagger. He'd carried many of those same weapons throughout his career as a witch hunter, the most powerful of which had wound up safely locked away in Doc's Sanctum Machina. Not safely enough, as it turned out, since Zelma had found it and added it to the collection of artifacts she'd been hauling around in her backpack, just in case it might prove useful. But she figured now wasn't the time to bring it up.

"*Any*hoo," Elsa repeated, "she grazed my cheek with a carefully manicured fingernail, and next thing I know, I'm out of my mind, tearing her half-eaten arm off and beating her to a pulp with it before whirling around to take care of the zombie with the daggers, who'd decided it'd be safer to go for Wade."

"As if," Deadpool said dismissively. "I could have taken care of that guy while taming a lion with both hands tied behind my back. This was just a freaked-out German Shepherd."

"Well, we'll never know," Elsa replied, "since I grabbed him before he could get to you and ripped his balding head clean off. I must admit, I kind of enjoyed that part.

"So I'm just finishing off little old lady leftovers when the priest finally comes rushing out, waving a big old crucifix around like he thinks I'm a bloody vampire, and I ram it down his throat and make a quick meal of him, too.

"By that time, Wade's got the dog mostly settled, and I've got most of my wits back, and my self-control. It's a bit of a standoff then. I'm realizing I've just killed a non-combatant in a fit of uncontrollable hunger that could come again at any time. That I've just become an unwilling puppet to some unknown and frankly gross infection and the next person I got the hankering to snack on might be someone I actually gave a fig about. And him over there realizing the same. Or maybe wondering what to name his new dog. Never can tell with that one.

"And then the dog up and bites Wade and runs out of the chapel with its tail between its legs. And Wade just kind of shrugs, looks at me, and says, 'Where to next?' like it's a given we're partners now... and then it was. And here we are."

She shrugged then, too, and tilted her chin up proudly. Defiantly, even. Making sure they all got a good look at the wound in her cheek that hadn't healed, even though by all rights, given the bloodgem's powers, it should have. The innocuous wound – delivered by an old woman and not a dozen or more super zombies, as Zelma had assumed – that had taken down one of the world's foremost monster hunters with barely a struggle. Making sure they all understood what they were really up against, if they hadn't before. She met and held each of their gazes in turn, Zelma's last. The librarian couldn't read the myriad emotions in Elsa's eyes, but she knew none of them were benign.

She couldn't blame the other woman. As Elsa had rightly predicted, nothing she had revealed told Zelma anything she didn't already know or couldn't have surmised about zombies. Except maybe that they didn't eat dogs, and even that assumption required more data points.

She and Nico had just made Elsa relive a moment that obviously filled the other woman with self-loathing, and for what?

Nothing. It didn't matter that Elsa hadn't done anything to warrant treating herself with such harshness. That she had, in fact, been trying to do the opposite, to do her job – saving people from monsters. That she'd wound up becoming one herself in the process shouldn't be a source of shame to the monster hunter.

But it clearly was, and now that shame had been put on display for everyone else to see. Because Zelma had been so sure she was right and Elsa was wrong, and her confidence had persuaded Nico to follow her lead.

Zelma had held the stake while Nico hammered it home, straight into Elsa's heart.

If there was anyone who should be feeling ashamed of themselves right now, it was the librarian, not the monster hunter. Zelma blinked back hot tears of remorse. This was not who she wanted to be. Leadership without empathy – more, without compassion – was just a more polite way of saying tyranny.

She needed to apologize. But Elsa wasn't going to give her that chance.

"Any questions?" the monster hunter asked, her challenging tone daring any of them to speak.

None of them did. Maybe, because like Zelma, the words were stuck behind a knot of regret in their throats.

"Good. Now that we've got that completely useless drama out of the way, can we kindly get back to the business of taking out the rest of these arseholes and/or seeing you all get yourselves killed trying? Not sure I really care which it is at this point, just so long as we bloody well get *on* with it."

CHAPTER TWENTY-TWO

So they got on with it.

Nico and Zelma spent the next several days poring over spellbooks, but unlike when Zelma had been doing it alone, they weren't looking for a cure. They were looking at time spells. And reality-altering spells. And realm shifting. Anything they could use to move the zombies from the here and now to the elsewhere and elsewhen.

Going into the past wasn't all that hard. Nico had done it before, and even brought someone back with her.

Going into the past and coming back to a timeline that either wasn't altered, or that was only altered in the ways you wanted it to be, was infinitely more difficult.

Even before they'd hit the books, Zelma had asked her about using the Staff of One to create the time loop. But Nico had balked at the suggestion. The staff was powerful, but the spells Nico cast using it – with or without spilling her own blood – were limited by the item's seeming inability to grasp the more subtle aspects of the English language. Once, when she'd faced a different kind of zombie, she had tried to reverse the zombification using the phrase "zombie not". But the staff had interpreted her words as "zombie *knot*", and instead of eliminating the zombie problem, Nico's spell had compounded it, bringing all the zombies together to form one huge knot of mindless meanderers. And of course there was that whole issue of not being able to use the same spell twice. If she did, the second spell would have wildly unpredictable results, like releasing a flock of pelicans when she wanted someone to freeze. Rephrasing was iffy at best. The staff didn't seem to think spells cast in different languages counted, though, so she could do a spell twice if she knew the words for it in, say, Japanese or Spanish. But Nico wasn't fluent in those languages, so it wasn't a loophole she could exploit very often.

She hadn't gone into detail with Zelma, but had made it clear that the staff's power was too inconsistent to trust with a spell that would require such exacting detail and precision. The librarian had frowned, but had taken the Runaway at her word. And now they were knee deep in more magical tomes than Nico had ever seen in her life, and she was pretty sure she was getting a migraine.

One thing the staff could safely do, though, was save them from the horror of stale pantry leavings and microwaveable Tex-Mex.

"Pizza party!"

Instantly, boxes of piping hot delivery pizza appeared in the few clear spots on the table they were using, along with several two-liter bottles of warm soda and bowls of various kinds of chips.

"Now that's my kind of magic!" Deadpool crowed, grabbing the nearest pizza box and a soda bottle and disappearing into the stacks. He never ate with them, because he had to lift up his mask to do so, and he didn't want them to see his face. Nico had originally thought that a little too precious – what was the point in trying to maintain a secret identity anymore? – but Elsa had assured her it wasn't vanity that fueled the mercenary's actions, but self-consciousness. Apparently his facial disfigurements rivaled those of Freddy Krueger. Remembering, Nico set aside an extra pizza for the merc now to help assuage the pang of guilt she felt for having immediately assumed the worst of him. A weak pang, because he was Deadpool and the worst was what he did best. But a pang, nonetheless.

"No pizza by the spellbooks!" Zelma exclaimed, shooing Nico and the slice she was busy shoving in her mouth away from the tome-laden table. "Doc will kill me if he comes back only to discover I've dripped pizza sauce on the *Book of Cagliostro*!"

"'Oo 'ave duh 'ook of 'ageeoh–?" Nico asked around her mouthful, choking a bit on the name. She was surprised Zelma hadn't mentioned it before. The *Book of Cagliostro* was an account of the mystic Cagliostro's life, and was said to include passages from the *Darkhold*, as well as notes from his encounters with a sorcerer from the future. It had been thought lost for decades, but of course Doctor Strange had been the last person known to have held it. It made sense that it would be in his library.

Zelma's look became guarded, and maybe a little… guilty?

"No," she replied quickly, jabbing her glasses up higher on her nose with an annoyed gesture. "Maybe. I don't know. It was just an example."

"Zee," Nico said, having finally finished her bite of pizza.

She wished the staff had bothered to manifest napkins. "Come on. Didn't Doctor Strange use the book to time travel? I'm sure it would be very informative, if nothing else. If it's here, we should use it."

"*If* it were here – and I'm not saying it is – it's far too dangerous–" Zelma began.

Nico gave a disgusted snort.

"*Book of Cagliostro!*"

She squeezed tiny drops of blood from the numerous paper cuts she'd gotten while flipping through more books than any one person should be allowed to own. Cagliostro's missing volume was a potent relic; the Staff of One might need a little extra juice to summon it.

Nico half-expected a tome to come winging through the air toward them from some dark and dusty corner of the library; that was how most of Zelma's books had been arriving. Instead, a tower of texts on the table next to Zelma toppled onto one of the unopened pizza boxes as the book at its base rose to hover in the air before them.

The *Book of Cagliostro.*

Il Libro Di Cagliostro had been scrawled across the book's violet leather cover in a crabbed hand above a golden demon's head with what were either tentacles or electrical arcs stretching out from it in every direction. The foil was so worn, it was hard to tell exactly which they might be, or if the faint yellow lines were meant to represent something else entirely. The book's corners and spine had been bound in a grayish metal. Tarnish suggested it might once have been silver, though that seemed an odd choice for a book intended to last through the ages, as the argent metal, while an effective protection against supernatural forces, was not so formidable when it came to time.

Elsa had been quiet throughout this exchange, not being a magic-wielder herself and unable to enjoy the pizza the two other women had been hungrily downing. But now she and Nico exchanged glances and then looked at Zelma accusingly.

"You've had it all along?" Nico demanded, though it wasn't really a question, since the answer was already apparent to everyone. "When were you planning on telling us?"

"I'm guessing never," Elsa replied for the librarian, whose face had turned red and flustered.

"Hold on!" Zelma protested, her momentary chagrin turning quickly to defensiveness. Her words were directed mostly at Nico, probably because she didn't think Elsa had a dog in this particular fight. "This is a priceless artifact of untold power. I don't know how to use it. And you've already admitted that you can't even always control your Donut Staff, so there's no way I'm letting *you* anywhere near it, either." She paused and waved toward the library's high windows. "Just imagine how much worse we could make things if we messed up one of Cagliostro's spells!"

"So you're afraid to use it," Elsa said flatly.

Zelma spluttered.

"Of course I'm afraid to use it!" she fairly shouted, anger giving her voice a volume and edge Nico had not heard before. "Any rational person would be!"

"And yet…" Elsa said slowly, unperturbed by the apprentice's outburst. Perhaps even amused by it. "You had it out in the open here with all these other books anyway, instead of locked away someplace dark and secret where no nasty blighters trying to save the world would ever stumble across it. Why, I wonder?"

Zelma's eyes widened, then narrowed behind her glasses so quickly that if Nico had blinked, she would have missed it. She almost did anyway, and she was staring right at the other witch, waiting for an explanation.

Which did not seem to be immediately forthcoming. Zelma was clearly wrestling with something, emotions chasing each other across her face too quickly to be named. At last, though, the bespectacled librarian sighed and her shoulders sagged beneath her bulky sweater.

"The nuclear option," she said, shrugging a little.

"Pardon?" Elsa asked, a red brow quirking upward.

Zelma gestured, and the pizza box in front of her moved aside, replaced by the *Book of Cagliostro*.

"The nuclear option. The last resort. The thing you do when everything else has failed, you've run out the clock, and there is no other alternative. When the war is lost, but you're taking your enemy down with you. Mutually assured destruction."

"And you were saving it for, what? A rainy day?" Nico asked.

Zelma rounded on her, angry again.

"The whole point of a nuclear option is that it's the *last* choice you make, not the first one!"

She wasn't wrong. But it didn't matter. They'd been looking for a spell for days now, and they could spend as many more days, or weeks, or who knew how much longer continuing to look, without finding one that fit their needs, or that could be reverse engineered to do so. Zelma knew they had to risk it. She must, or, like Elsa said, the librarian wouldn't have pulled this book out of cold storage in the first place.

"Zee," Nico said gently, "if we don't do something soon – as in now – there won't *be* anything left to save. No Earth. No Doctor Strange. *Not* using the nuclear option is what's going to ensure our destruction. *Using* it might be the only thing that saves us."

Zelma chewed on the inside of her cheek, making Elsa wince reflexively, though Nico wasn't sure either woman was fully aware of their actions. Finally, the librarian-slash-apprentice-slash-would be-world-savior nodded.

"You're right, though I wish to the Vishanti you weren't."

Zelma took a deep breath, then reached out a trembling hand toward the purple cover.

Deadpool chose that moment to wander in, jaws still working on a bite of pizza beneath his mask.

"WhadImiss?"

CHAPTER TWENTY-THREE

Zelma let someone else worry about filling him in. She had the Book to contend with. It wasn't something Doc had ever warned her against using, per se. But that was only because it was something he'd likely never imagined she'd get her grubby mitts on in the first place. He'd certainly be slapping those mitts away if he were in any position to do so.

But before her fingertips could do more than brush over the aged leather, Nico yelled, "Stop!"

Confused, Zelma looked over at the other witch, who was standing now, leveling her staff at the book in front of Zelma.

"Detect traps!"

Nothing happened, and Zelma laughed. Nico's gesture, while appreciated, was completely unnecessary.

"The book isn't warded," she explained to Nico, who was glaring at the gold foil demon's head suspiciously. "Cagliostro was an egomaniac – he wanted people to read his work, to hail his genius. He didn't much care what they used that genius for."

"Sounds like a lovely gent," Elsa remarked sarcastically.

"Sounds like a typical magician," Deadpool replied matter-of-factly, his mouth no longer full.

Zelma couldn't disagree with him. It took a certain amount of hubris to think you could grasp the mystic arts, let alone master them. She didn't think she would ever have found herself playing magician's apprentice if the world of magic hadn't been forced on her; she'd always been more bashful than boastful. And even now that she was learning to understand and wield magic, she didn't think it was about the power itself, or the adulation that came with it. It was about the knowledge. She cared about taming ideas, not conquering the world or reshaping it in her own image or any of the other sorts of nefarious things powerful magic-users seemed to inevitably find themselves doing.

She wasn't looking to become Cagliostro the Second, and she was very much afraid of that happening if she dared open his book and start toying with his spells.

But what choice did she have, now? If she didn't do it, Nico would, and while Zelma respected the other witch's abilities, she had no illusions that Nico's ability was equal to the task of controlling the things that this tome could unleash.

She had no illusions that hers was, either.

But she at least had the advantage of Doc's tutelage. She doubted it would be enough to save them from the repercussions of allowing Cagliostro's magic back into the world, but right now it seemed like the lesser of two evils. And while she wasn't at all convinced you could, or even should, measure good and evil in such simplistic terms, she also didn't have the luxury of pedantry.

Or the luxury of time, despite her protestations to the

others about wanting to keep looking for some other option. *Any* other option.

She'd peeked in on Zombie Doc using the Orb of Agamotto one night while Nico was asleep and Elsa and Deadpool were off seeing to the former's preternatural needs. What she'd seen in the glowing sphere had been the catalyst for her summoning the *Book of Cagliostro* in the first place, even though she'd hoped against hope that they wouldn't have to use it.

Doc was still chained in the basement, but his body had been slumped against the stone wall, his shoulders long since dislocated, the flesh at his wrists shredding against the manacles. She wasn't sure if he'd still be bound to the basement like the Cellar Dweller was if he managed to rot his way out of the magical shackles, but even if so, Zelma didn't like the idea of him wandering free down there. She could sense more than see the Thing in the Basement lurking outside the cell, waiting for just that eventuality. And what would happen then?

Would Doc's karmic bill come due? Would the creature formed from his unacknowledged and unfelt pain and suffering destroy him, finally getting its revenge for the torture that was its mere existence?

Or possibly worse, could the black mass somehow merge with Doc, giving him the use of its intelligence to compensate for the missing parts of his brain? Thereby releasing Evil Formerly Cellar-Dwelling Zombie Doctor Strange on the world? And the universe? All of them?

Zelma couldn't let that happen. It was the very thing Doc had given up his mind to prevent.

Pressing her lips together in a determined line, she took hold of the cover of the *Book of Cagliostro* and flipped it open.

She could instantly feel the rush of magic coming off the words inked on the yellowed pages. The journal had been written in a language she wasn't familiar with, but as she stared at it, the symbols resolved themselves into letters she knew, though all the words had been written backwards.

"What's the point of *that*?" Nico asked, peering over Zelma's shoulder. "If he didn't bother to ward the book, then why scramble the letters? Just for kicks?"

"Did she miss the part about 'typical magician'?" Deadpool asked from somewhere behind the two witches.

"Apparently so," Elsa replied dryly.

Even though she could read the reversed letters, and understand the words, it took Zelma a moment to truly grok what they were saying as she leafed through the thick pages. Because what Cagliostro had written didn't make sense. It flew in the face of everything that Doctor Strange had ever taught her about the mechanics of temporal manipulation. Which, admittedly, was precious little. But it was also counter to everything she'd ever read on the subject.

According to Count Alessandro di Cagliostro, it was possible to travel back into the past without endangering one's present existence. To essentially be a butterfly flapping your wings in the Stone Age and not have to deal with a hurricane in the twenty-first century. To throw a pebble into the pool of time and not create ripples.

"Well, that's great!" Nico exclaimed, still reading over Zelma's shoulder, much to her irritation. Having someone standing so close behind her, even an ally, was worse than waiting for one of the library ghosts to jump out from behind a bookcase – anticipating a threat, but not knowing when or if it was coming. It made all the hairs on the back of the librarian's neck stand at rigid attention. "That means—"

"It doesn't mean anything," Zelma interrupted, frustrated. How had the Runaway survived for this long if she believed everything a sorcerer wrote? "Because it's all, to coin an Elsa-ism, pure poppycock. This guy read the *Darkhold*. He was probably about as right in the head as Fake Spidey over there."

"Rude!"

"Listen," Zelma said earnestly, turning in her seat so she was facing the others and Nico was no longer breathing down her neck. Nico's brown eyes shone with excitement despite Zelma's cautions, Elsa looked bored, and Deadpool was sticking his lower lip out under his mask. "Even if it were possible to go back into the past without affecting your own present – and I don't believe for one moment that it is, because there is *always* a catch – that wouldn't necessarily be true for the rest of the world, something Cagliostro cared nothing about. This isn't some late-night infomercial wonder-working product. It's not going to give you perfect hair or slice through a can or get wine stains out of your carpet."

"Some of us already have perfect hair," Elsa huffed, tossing said hair. Zelma didn't respond to that. She still hadn't found an opportunity to apologize to the monster hunter, and the longer it took her to do so, the harder it was going to be. In the meantime, she didn't want to antagonize the other woman any more than necessary.

"If it does anything remotely resembling what it claims to," Zelma continued, "there's a popsicle's chance in Hell that it does it *well*."

"Oh, yeah," Deadpool said, nodding sagely. "It's like that

skin cream I ordered off the TV one time that was supposed to reduce scar tissue. Turns out it did do that – by burning my skin off completely. And they didn't give refunds. Talk about your bull–"

"Yes, that's exactly what I mean," Zelma hastily interrupted. "Like I said. There is always a catch."

No one spoke for several moments, perhaps still recovering from the shock of Zelma and Deadpool agreeing on something, or from Deadpool's overshare. But Zelma had no real hope that such a minor miracle would end the discussion. Elsa did not disappoint.

"So we use ole Caggie's book and it mucks up the present," the monster hunter said with another toss of her red ponytail. "So what? Isn't that risk sort of baked into the nuclear option? It's not like radiation is generally good for one's health. Still betting on it being better than the alternative."

"Elsa," Deadpool whispered loudly, "I don't think she meant literal nukes…"

"Oh, do stuff it, Wade," Elsa replied, rolling her eyes so hard that Zelma was legitimately concerned that they might pop out and go tumbling across the library floor. She was a zombie, after all.

But the damage was done. Nico was taking Elsa's ball and running with it.

"Right?" she said, her short black hair bouncing with her growing enthusiasm. "It's not like we'd be the ones going back in time, remember? The whole idea was to send *them* back. So who cares if *their* present gets screwed up? Isn't that kind of the point?"

But apparently Nico didn't read as thoroughly as Zelma

did, because she'd skimmed over one of the key constraints of Cagliostro's time-tripping.

"That's just it," Zelma said. "Yes, in theory, we can use the book to open the timestream, even create a loop to lure the zombies into. But there are still some problems with that. The biggest being that if we do, there's only one way to close the stream once it's been opened."

She had their full attention now, which was good, because the next words were so daunting she could barely choke them out. As it was, they were little more than a whisper.

"The timestream must be closed from the inside. Which means somebody has to go in *with* the zombies. And stay there."

CHAPTER TWENTY-FOUR

"Not it!"

Zelma and Nico both looked at Elsa in surprise. In response, the monster hunter shrugged, removing a slender finger from the tip of her nose.

"Just beating gitface over there to it."

"Did she just insult me?" Deadpool asked. "I think she just insulted me. Oh, and also?" he added, touching his own nose. "Not it!"

"Of course not," Zelma said sharply. "Nobody's it. We haven't even decided we're doing this." Then she paused, taking in the expressions on what she could see of the others' faces. None of them seemed to have nearly the same number of misgivings as she did. "... or have we?"

"Closing it behind them won't be enough?" Nico asked, ignoring the librarian's question in favor of her own. It was still an answer, though. One Zelma didn't much care for.

She slouched in her seat, scratching at her temples, where unwashed hair and beanie met in a damp line. She was on edge and nervous, much the same way she had felt when she'd cheated on her driver's test and was scared to death that the DMV employees were going to find out. Not that she was being dishonest with anyone here; she'd been transparent about both her concerns and her own limitations. But she still had that horrible sense of doing something she shouldn't be doing, knowing all the while that discovery and dire consequences weren't far off.

"I don't know," she complained, aware that she sounded like a testy teenager, but not sure what to do about it. She *felt* like a grumpy teen, one whose life was continually being upended by people who just didn't get it. And in this case, what they didn't "get" was that Zelma had no real idea what she was doing, but they still expected her to have all the answers, and that terrified her. "There have to be spellcasters who survived among the infected besides just Wanda. Maybe their hunger would keep them too distracted to magic a way out of the timestream, assuming we figured out a way to get them to enter it in the first place. Maybe not. Elsa?"

"Eh? Sorry, I didn't quite catch that; I was too distracted by hunger."

"Seriously?" Nico asked, a reproachful look on her face. Deadpool giggled behind his hand.

"Almost always, darling," Elsa replied, smiling, before turning her attention back to Zelma. "At this point, unless they have an arrangement like mine and Wade's, if you dangle a bloody flesh carrot in front of them, they won't be sane enough to notice there's a stick in the offing. Of course, the carrot's going to have to be alive to really catch their interest, which may be a bit of a problem."

The gears in Zelma's brain were starting to turn now, mostly of their own accord. She was a pragmatist and problem-solver by nature, even when she'd much rather just be an observer. Or, better yet, not see any of it because she had her head buried in a book.

But her days of hiding in the library had ended when Doc got infected. Now it was step up or get stepped on, and she didn't particularly relish the idea of being squished and scraped off someone's shoe like so much goo.

"I think I have a solution for that, but first things first. Assuming we can use Cagliostro's book to open a zombie-carrot time loop, where do we do it? And how do we get the zombies there to notice the carrot in the first place? From what the orb has shown us so far, there are several little splinter groups, off doing their own thing. We need them all together if this is going to work."

"When was the last time you actually looked in on the rotters?" Elsa asked curiously.

"Ooh, is that what we're calling them now?" Deadpool interjected. "I kind of like it."

Zelma did, too, but she wasn't going to encourage him.

"It's been... a few days," she admitted.

Elsa nodded, unsurprised.

"I think you'll find when you do that those 'splinter groups', as you call them, have either been absorbed or no longer exist. With their food supply dwindling by the day, they *will* have turned on each other by now – they won't have been able to help it. The hunger will have seen to that.

"By now, they'll be running in a pack, like a bunch of starving alpha wolves–"

"Actually, recent science suggests that's not really a thing–"

Deadpool began, holding a professorial finger up in the air and donning a lecturing tone. Elsa silenced him with a single, murderous glare. Then she turned her attention back to Zelma.

"Like a bunch of *starving alpha wolves*," she repeated, emphasizing each word slowly, no doubt for the harrumphing Deadpool's benefit. "Only the strongest ones will be left – hero *and* villain, by the way; 'good guy' and 'bad guy' become meaningless in the face of 'hungry guy'. And they'll have banded together, because they can't kill each other, but they also don't trust each other enough to allow any lone wolves to roam free."

"You seem to know a lot about how they think," Nico commented, brow furrowing in suspicion. Zelma had to blink several times to keep from rolling her eyes. What did the other witch think, that Elsa was some sort of zombie spy, planted with them to learn the secrets of the Sanctum Sanctorum so the zombies could come and plunder it, and them?

Which was almost plausible, if you tilted your tinfoil hat just right.

No, Nico was just being paranoid. Of course, being paranoid didn't mean no one was after you, and it had likely saved the Runaway's life on a number of occasions. But this wasn't going to be one of them.

"Well, they don't call me 'monster hunter extraordinaire' for nothing, darling," Elsa replied airily. "But in this case, I don't need to know how they think. I know how they *feel*. And I know where I would be without Wade. *What* I would be."

Nico didn't seem to have any reply for that.

But Wade did. Of course.

"Aww, she likes me. She really likes me!"

"OK, it sounds like it should be easy enough to get their attention, then," Zelma said, ignoring him. Resigned to this course now, her brain began to run with the idea despite her mountain of misgivings. "So where do we set the trap?"

"Why not where the meteorite or whatever struck?" Nico asked. "End it where it all began?"

"That seems apropos," Elsa agreed, nodding. Then her blue gaze sharpened. "So now why don't you tell us what exactly you're planning on using to bait that trap, hmmm? Or, more accurately, whom?"

Zelma took a deep breath and gathered herself, hardening her resolve. They weren't going to like this part of her plan, but that didn't matter. They didn't have to like it. They just had to follow it.

"Well, that should be obvious. M–"

"Me," Deadpool said from behind her before she could finish.

Zelma turned to the mercenary.

"You?" she asked in astonishment. "What happened to 'Not it'?"

"No offense to Elsa," Deadpool replied, then quickly amended, "well, OK, maybe a little – but you can't rely on appetite alone to keep predators like this interested in the hunt. You can't just make their mouths water. You also have to make their blood boil. You have to be such a pain in their collective rear ends that they don't want to just eat you, they want to tear you limb from limb, chew you up, spit you out, then pick what's left of you up out of the dirt and do it all over again, only harder this time. Meaner.

"None of you ladies have what it takes to annoy someone

to death and beyond. But me?" The mask over Deadpool's mouth morphed into a feral smile, and for the first time, Zelma remembered she should be afraid of him. "I can do it all day."

CHAPTER TWENTY-FIVE

"Much as I hate to admit it, the gobby lout is right," Elsa said after the moment of stunned silence had passed. "Though that does mean I'm going to lose my food source, and therefore what little sanity I have left after palling around with you lot."

"We still have the coolers," Zelma offered. "Those tamales barely lasted forty-eight hours."

Nico looked at her, a little aghast. Was the librarian suggesting they *harvest* bits of Deadpool for Elsa to snack on? But Zelma wasn't joking; her expression was completely serious, even earnest.

Elsa snorted.

"Short-term solution for a long-term problem," she said. "Because that's how it works, right? They go into the timestream – smashing! Brilliant! Still leaves the Earth's population virtually wiped out and civilization in shambles. It'll take decades to rebuild, maybe centuries. If they even can. And, not to be a prig, but I've got my own problems, haven't I? I'll still be stuck like this, only without any palatable means of keeping my wits about me. Might as well jump in the loop myself at that point."

"Not necessarily," Zelma argued. "If I'm reading this right, once we send the zombies into the timestream, it should be like they never existed here. Or anywhere. Or anytime. And if they never existed, none of this–" Zelma threw her hands out, as if to encompass the library, New York City, and the entire world, "–could ever have happened. The timeline should reset. Which means you should become unzombified."

Nico thought she detected the slightest emphasis on the word "should".

"What about me?"

Zelma turned to Deadpool, her beanie inching toward her glasses as her forehead furrowed in confusion.

"What do you mean, 'What about you?' You were never zombified."

"Well, duh," Deadpool replied, his eyes turning heavenward with an aggrieved "you see what I have to put up with?" look. "I *meant* that once everything's back to just regular awful and not zombie-apocalypse awful, you'll get me out, right?

"Don't get me wrong – taunting Avengers into a frenzy is pretty much my dream job. I've got some humdingers I've been saving up for *years*. Wanna hear?" No one did. Deadpool sniffed. "Fine. Anyway, as much fun as it's going to be, I get bored easy. I'm not going to want to do it, like, *forever*."

"Once you step into the stream, it will be like time stops passing for you at all," Nico pointed out. "You won't know if you've been there for ten minutes or ten millennia."

"Oh, I'll know," he insisted.

"We'll get you back out as soon as we can," Zelma hastened to assure him, shooting a wide-eyed, tight-lipped "stop talking" look at Nico.

"OK," he replied, nodding and seemingly satisfied. "Then cut off some Deadpool flank steak to put on ice and let's get this one-merc show on the road."

Things moved quickly after that. Elsa set to work carving some of the choicer bits of Deadpool's rear and a few other places that weren't likely to hamper him much before they healed, chewing on one of the smaller bits as she did.

"Too bad your head can regenerate the rest of your body, but your body parts can't regenerate more of themselves. This whole process would be much simpler," she groused.

Deadpool shrugged, causing one of the cuts she was making on the underside of his triceps to slice off more than she'd intended, but the mercenary didn't flinch.

"What can I say? I aspire to annoy."

While he aspired and Elsa butchered, Nico and Zelma put the rest of the plan together. Using the Orb of Agamotto, they located the remaining Zombie Avengers. As Elsa had predicted, wherever the heroes might originally have been infected, they were all together now, congregated in and outside of Metropolitan General Hospital in Midtown Manhattan. The witches were surprised at the sheer number of supers milling about, but they quickly realized it was because they weren't just dealing with heroes, but villains as well, and those whose affiliations with the concepts of right and wrong were much murkier.

Still, there seemed to be a hierarchy. The A-listers – the figures who consistently made the news, had fan clubs and toy lines – were inside the hospital, taking up the bottom few floors, which included the ER, the cafeteria, the lab, and the morgue. Everyone else seemed to have been relegated to the higher levels of the hospital, which had long since been emptied of edibles, or to the streets outside. There were a lot of petty skirmishes, shoving, punching, and the like, but they seldom devolved into much more than a limb or two ripped off. They were keeping the peace, such as it was.

For now.

But despite Elsa's reassurances, Nico didn't see how the situation was tenable. There were too many of them – hundreds, still. Too many vying for whatever small amount of food they might still be able to scrounge.

Too many still ambulatory with either the power to leave Earth for other hunting grounds or the brains to figure out how.

Some of them were in the hospital lab, which looked less like a place to analyze blood draws now and more like a storage area for equipment from the Baxter Building or the Avengers Mansion, with the Stark logo prominent on most of it. So either Stark himself or Reed Richards was still around, or maybe Sue Storm, who was no slouch in the smarts department herself. And Elsa had said she'd seen at least one of the Hulks, so potentially Banner, as well.

As the orb switched their view from the lab to the morgue, Nico realized how that was possible.

They had humans on ice there, and were using the corpses much the same was Elsa was using Deadpool.

The two witches looked at each other in shock.

"I guess some of the magic-using zombies woke up and got killed, like Elsa said, but it looks like the rest just start harvesting humans to keep themselves somewhat sane," Zelma observed, her face pinched with worry and disgust.

"Do you think they're trying to find a cure?" Nico wondered aloud, though she didn't think that was the case. Any sort of treatment for zombification would have to first be tested on the zombified, but those weren't zombies lying on the slabs and gurneys.

"I think the more humans they eat, the more humanity they lose," Zelma answered, shaking her head. "I mean, they're supposed to be heroes, but they're eating the people they're meant to be protecting. That must have a cost."

"But also a benefit," Nico pointed out. "It helps them stay sane, even if they only use that sanity to figure out how to get more food."

Zelma nodded grimly. "And sane zombies will be too smart to follow Deadpool into the time loop, no matter how tasty he looks or smells."

"Guess we'll just have to make sure there aren't any sane ones, then," Nico replied, and before Zelma could say anything else, the Runaway summoned her staff from its place near the pile of empty pizza boxes. As it flew into her ready grip, she closed her hand around it and said, "Quick thaw!"

The two watched as the power surged suddenly in the morgue, which must have been running on emergency generators. The lights flickered in the silver and white room, momentarily turning the Orb of Agamotto into something akin to a disco ball. Then everything went dark.

Not for long.

There was a blinding flash and a crackle of electricity Nico swore she could feel through the orb, and then the morgue was lit up again, and Ororo Munroe floated there, a good foot off the floor, arcs of lightning bursting from her fingertips to power the freezers. And everything else in the room, and probably the rest of the hospital, too.

Worse, the goddess known as Storm seemed to be looking right at Nico. The Runaway gulped loudly, her mouth suddenly dry.

"She can't see us," Zelma hastened to assure her fellow witch, "but I don't think that worked the way you meant for it to. Unless you *wanted* us to have peeved off zombie deities to deal with on top of just regular sane ones?"

Nico shot the librarian a glare, but her heart wasn't in it.

The other supers who'd been zombified had been mutants and magic-users and assorted other things. Powerful, to be sure, but not supreme being-level powerful. If even the gods could be affected by this plague, they were in deeper excrement than any of them had previously guessed.

But she couldn't worry about that now. She had to deal with *this* god, and quickly, or their time loop plan was finished before they'd even spoken a word from Cagliostro's book.

Luckily, Nico had paid attention in Physics class, and she remembered a thing or two about electricity. Specifically, feedback loops.

In a positive feedback loop, part or all of the input fed into a system got put back into that system, thereby amplifying it. Which was all fine and dandy as long as there was some kind of control in place to keep the loop from growing too big, too fast. If there were no such checks and balances in place, the loop could quickly become unstable, potentially feeding exponentially amplified input into a system until it became overwhelmed and shut down completely, if it wasn't destroyed altogether.

Storm was quite clearly pulling energy from the Earth's electromagnetic field to power the hospital's electrical systems, jagged lines of coruscating white and blue reaching up from the ground, entering through the hero's feet and exiting through her fingers. Normally, the weather-manipulator would work only within existing natural patterns – she would not drain one area of moisture to end another area's drought. But she seemed not to be observing that rule today, perhaps because the hunger she was trying to keep at bay was enough to cloud even a goddess-level intelligence. She was taking energy from the Earth, but not giving it back, instead cycling it through the hospital's wiring and circuitry over and over, to keep the lights on and the food cold.

Nico saw one chance to take out the powerful zombie who would otherwise make short work of her, Zelma, Elsa, and Deadpool combined. She took it.

"Too much positive feedback!"

The result was instantaneous. A woman-sized supernova exploded in the morgue, and the orb filled with a white-hot light so intense it caused both Nico and Zelma to shrink away, covering their eyes in pain. Half a second later, the accompanying shockwave hit the Bleecker Street brownstone, causing even its warded windows to rattle in their panes. Even at this distance, the boom was deafening.

Elsa and Deadpool came running in. Strips of the latter's costume where the monster hunter had sliced her way through to get to the choicest cuts trailed behind him like pennants in the hands of crazed fans.

"Oi, what've you two gone and done now?" Elsa demanded, her voice angry enough Nico could still make it out over the ringing in her ears.

In front of them, the smoke-filled orb began to clear, various supers streaming out of the ruins of Metropolitan General.

"Getting their attention?" Zelma offered weakly.

Elsa assessed the situation in one swift glance.

"Righto," she said. "Time to get to that crash site, then. Everyone ready?"

Zelma nodded, the *Book of Cagliostro* tucked under one arm, her backpack snug under Doctor Strange's cloak. Nico tightened her grip on the Staff of One. Deadpool just shrugged.

Elsa looked at Nico and nodded. The Runaway lifted her staff once more.

"Crater!"

Instantly, they were in Midtown Manhattan, near enough to Metro-General that they could see the black smoke billowing up from Storm's funeral pyre.

Zelma opened the book and began reading from one of the pages, though Nico was surprised to realize she couldn't hear what the other witch was saying. By the looks of it, neither could the others.

But something could, because a white nimbus of light coalesced around the book, then gathered itself into a beam that shot out into the air in front of Zelma. A swirling vortex appeared, spinning in the air like a sideways Catherine Wheel firework. It spat colorless sparks at them, but otherwise did nothing.

Zelma looked over at Nico and Elsa and nodded. The apprentice had worried that simply reading the spell would not be enough, and that her power alone would be unable to open the portal completely, so she'd arranged for backup.

Elsa raised her bloodhand, and a stream of carnelian energy sprang from it, heading for the vortex. At the same time, Nico uttered the spell phrase she'd chosen, from a half-remembered Bible verse.

"A cord of three strands is not quickly broken!"

A pulsing purplish-silver strand of energy leapt from the top of the Staff of One, weaving itself around and into the other two rays of magic. The triple strand struck the vortex dead center and the mystical gyre began to spin faster, its sparks now reflecting the hues of their combined powers. Then, without warning, it stopped and irised open to reveal a star-streaked blackness beyond.

Zelma let out a long, shaky breath, then turned to Deadpool and handed him a page she had painstakingly copied from Cagliostro's journal. Nico thought she caught a whispered word as the paper changed hands; the apprentice was casting a charm spell on the mercenary, one designed to make him look like a walking filet mignon. Even Nico's stomach grumbled a bit in response.

"Once you're inside and we give you the signal, say this word. The paper will disappear, and the loop will close. Then you run like hell. And whatever you do – *don't exit the timestream*. Got it?" The librarian's tone was fierce, her expression stern.

Deadpool took the paper without looking at it and saluted smartly.

"Yes, ma'am! Thank you, ma'am!"

Then Zelma's voice softened.

"Thank you, Wade. We'll get you out just as soon as we can."

Whatever smart aleck comment Deadpool might have given in reply was superseded by Elsa's urgent warning.

"They're coming!"

And they were. Nico looked over to see dozens of zombies

in remnants of skin and colorful suits rushing down the street and through the sky toward them. As arranged previously, the three women gathered around Nico, who tapped the butt of her staff against her boot.

"Ruby slippers!"

The women were through Nico's portal and back in the Sanctum library in front of the Orb of Agamotto in moments, watching as Deadpool ripped parts of his bloody suit off and waved them like a matador's cape at the onslaught, yelling taunts all the while.

"Ding! Ding! Ding! Dinner time! Come and get me!

"You call that fast? My dead grandma has bowel movements faster than you! They smell better, too!"

And then, at the last possible moment, he darted into the opening behind him and disappeared into the blackness like a starship jumping into hyperspace.

The zombies followed him in, every last one. There were a few stragglers, but Zelma blasted them into the vortex with a long-distance Winds of Watoomb spell – Deadpool's signal – and then the portal irised closed as if it had never existed. Which Nico supposed it technically never had.

She was just turning to congratulate her teammates when she saw a shadow pass across the library window. Frowning, she motioned to the others to look into the orb.

"Umm… Zee?" she said slowly, trying to swallow down thickening dread. "I know I'm not from around here, but… there aren't supposed to be *dragons*, are there?"

CHAPTER TWENTY-SIX

Being Doctor Strange's apprentice and having just survived a zombie apocalypse starring super-powered heroes and villains, one would think nothing could surprise Zelma anymore.

One would be mistaken.

Zelma couldn't immediately comprehend what she was seeing and hearing.

Crowds milled about downtown Manhattan, clutching briefcases and purses as they rushed off to yet another meeting that could have been an email. Bicycles and scooters wove miraculously through a near-solid wall of honking cabs. People living their lives as they always had. Humans, not zombies. None of them looking up or so much as missing a step when a flight of dragons passed overhead, or when the sirens piercing the air like birdsong were drowned out by reptilian roars.

Then the orb drew back to give them an aerial view of the city, following the dragons as they flew over a high, thick wall that encircled the entirety of the Big Apple. Inside that wall, it appeared to be business as usual, if you ignored the dragons. But *outside* the wall...

Hordes of demons fought against an immense zombie army, the dragons acting as the hellspawns' air wing, strafing their undead opponents with fire and acid and other things Zelma couldn't name.

"What in the hells...?" Elsa asked, her voice full of odd wonderment.

"Literally," Zelma muttered, but in the next instant, grave-cold horror and incandescent anger washed over her as she finally understood.

Cagliostro's spell was supposed to allow travel to the past without changes made there affecting the future, but it either hadn't worked right or...

That idiot.

But before she could share her suspicions with the others, Elsa reached over and tugged at her sweater sleeve.

"Not that," the monster hunter said impatiently. "*This.*"

She pointed to her cheek. To the smooth, milky skin of her unblemished cheek.

Elsa stuck a finger in her mouth and rooted around inside with it for a moment before pulling it out and wiping the saliva off on her coat.

"It's gone. Nothing rotting on the outside or the inside." She grinned suddenly, a rare, true smile that lit up her face with a beauty Zelma hadn't realized the hard-bitten woman possessed. "I'm me again!"

Nico surprised them both by throwing her arms around the monster hunter and giving her a tight, fierce hug. Elsa surprised them all by not only not stiffening or pulling away, but returning the embrace. She was taller than Nico, even without heels, so she just rested her uninfected cheek on top of the Runaway's head, closing her eyes and letting out a long-repressed sigh.

Zelma shifted her weight from foot to foot, studying the fine weave of the carpet, but finally cleared her throat uncomfortably. She didn't want to interrupt this snatched moment of peace, but she had to. The others had to know.

When she looked up, Nico and Elsa were standing a few inches apart from each other, carefully not touching.

"Listen, I'm super glad you're Regular Elsa and not Zombified Elsa anymore, but… we have a problem," Zelma said.

"You mean the dragons, demons, and rotters warring at the city gates?" Elsa asked. "That's my kind of problem."

"Not that," Zelma said impatiently, then immediately corrected herself. "Well, yes, that. But not for the reasons you think."

"You mean they're *not* there because the universe has finally decided to smile on me and give me the gift that keeps on giving – more monster arse to kick than I can possibly count?" Elsa asked, feigning disappointment. "Drat."

Nico looked like she was trying to bite back a smirk at that, but her question was at least serious.

"What reason, then? What are you talking about, Zee? The spell worked, didn't it?"

"Well, yes… and… no." Zelma sagged into a nearby chair, only now noticing there were no empty pizza boxes scattered about the floor. She didn't know why she'd expected there to be, considering.

"There were only two ways that spell was ever going to work," she said, looking anxiously back and forth from one slightly annoyed face to the other. She had tried to tell them. She should have gone herself. This was all her fault. "Either Cagliostro was right, and nothing would change except the zombies being gone – the post-apocalyptic scenario Elsa outlined. Or he was demented, and the present *would* change – in this case, reverting back to what it would have been if there had never been any zombies in the first place."

She gestured at the hellscape still pictured in the orb.

"But this? This shouldn't have happened. It's not a result of the spell. At least, not directly."

Nico's face paled, so that her skin was almost the same shade as Elsa's.

"You don't mean…?"

Zelma nodded, glad someone else had finally figured it out. "I do."

"Mean what?" Elsa snapped impatiently, her red brows beetling into an irate frown. "Stop speaking magician and speak proper English!"

Zelma looked at Nico. The corner of the Runaway's mouth twitched, but she said nothing. It was up to Zelma to deliver the devastating news. She took a deep breath to steady herself and prepare for Elsa's reaction, which she feared was going to be both explosive and accusing.

Elsa had some history with Deadpool that preceded her zombification; Zelma had heard them talking about having shawarma together. And the mercenary *had* let the woman slice pieces off his rear to keep her sanity intact, though it was entirely possible that was less due to friendship than to some weird thrill he got out of the exchange. But the monster hunter had kept him around, even with his incessant banter and gung-ho screwups, so Zelma was inclined to think there was some level of camaraderie involved, at least on Elsa's end.

Which meant the Brit might not be too happy about Zelma's pronouncement, because if Deadpool *had* exited the timestream at some point, for whatever reason, he was probably long dead. Regenerative factors didn't confer immortality, after all, even if there was some overlap in their benefits.

"Deadpool. He left the timestream."

To her surprise, Elsa just snorted.

"Well, of course he did, luv. Astonished you expected anything else of the spanner, honestly, though I'll admit I'd hoped you had some secret plan up your overlarge sweater sleeve to take that inevitability into account. My bad."

"Wait," Nico said, holding her staff in the crook of her elbow as she formed a T with her hands. "Time out. You *knew* he'd leave the stream? And you didn't say anything?" She looked like a kid who'd just found out her parents had been lying to her about Santa Claus for all these years. Zelma knew what that felt like.

Elsa shrugged, unconcerned.

"I knew Wade was going to be Wade. If you didn't, that's very much a 'you' problem, not a 'me' one."

Nico's face flushed an unpleasant shade of red and Zelma figured she'd better intervene before things went south of the Antarctic.

"Actually, it's an 'us' problem," she said, taking a step forward, as if to separate them, but Nico was already moving away from the monster hunter, hurt and anger warring for supremacy on her face. Zelma had a hunch which one would win, so she took another step forward. "Because we have to fix it."

"Pish," Elsa replied. "How do you propose we do that?

Unless I'm very much mistaken, it's not as if we can step into the timestream and have a kindly conductor waiting there to tell us which stop – or stops – Deadpool got off on."

Before Zelma could come up with an appropriately scathing reply, she felt a tug at her neck. She was about to scold Cloak, but then realized the movement was coming from beneath her shirt, not on top of it.

From the key to the Cellar Dweller's manacles.

Zelma's heart leapt into her throat with a sudden bright hope that she was terrified to let herself feel. Some things about this timeline were appallingly different – where had the wall around the city come from? Who was leading the armies fighting outside of it? And why?

But, if she squinted, some things didn't seem to have really changed at all.

It might not be the present Zelma knew, but this was still the Sanctum Sanctorum. And the key around her neck wouldn't be vibrating if there wasn't still something – or some*one* – chained up in the basement.

Could it possibly be…?

"Nico! We have to get to the basement! Now!"

To her credit, the other witch didn't question her. She just tapped the butt of her staff against the library carpet, saying, "Bleecker Street basement!"

But when they stepped through Nico's portal and appeared in the cellar, Zelma found herself wishing that they'd taken a moment to look in the orb first.

Because it wasn't Doctor Strange chained in the cell.

It was Deadpool, who waved excitedly upon seeing them. And, bound beside him in much larger, non-shimmering but still obviously magical manacles of its own was… a *mammoth*?

Easily ten feet tall, covered in shaggy, brown-black hair with a bushy black tuft on its head as big as a fully grown yucca plant, and tusks that curved out from its body like twin ivory scimitars, it filled the back half of the small cell, rubbing up against three of the prison's four stone walls, and bumping up against its ceiling.

But not even that double whammy could prepare Zelma for the shock of who their captor was. Not least because the librarian had written the brunette woman off as dead, or at the very least, long gone and not coming back any time soon.

Garbed in an emerald-green gown with a plunging neckline, she lounged in an upholstered chair beside a table full of unusually creative torture implements, legs crossed, her toe tapping an impatient rhythm against the cell floor. Almost as if she had been waiting for the trio to arrive.

Given her mastery of the timestream, she very well may have been.

For before them sat none other than Morgan Le Fay. Half-sister to the legendary King Arthur, aunt to both light and dark in the forms of Gawain and Mordred, apprentice to the wizard Merlin.

And hanging about her neck on a gold chain, nestled in her ample cleavage, rested the Eye of Agamotto.

"Ah, *there* you are. I wasn't sure if you'd be joining us or not. Time travel can be very tricky," the Sorceress Supreme drawled, smiling wickedly, "especially when you have no idea what you're doing."

CHAPTER TWENTY-SEVEN

"What are you doing here? Where's Doc?" Zelma demanded, unable to take her eyes off the Eye of Agamotto. Of all the necks in the world it could decide to grace, Le Fay's should not have been one of them. How could the Eye possibly have chosen *her*?

Whatever Deadpool had done when he'd exited the timestream, he'd *really* screwed things up.

"Doctor Strange? Oh, you poor thing," Le Fay said, her full lips drawn down into a fake pout, her tone laced with mock sympathy. "Doctor Stephen Strange, the acclaimed neurosurgeon, never became the Sorcerer Supreme here. He didn't survive the car crash that cost him the use of his hands in your timeline and led to him training under the Ancient One. He never learned so much as a single glamour and was too arrogant to have believed in the existence of magic anyway. Your counterpart here, Ms Stanton, is just a mousy librarian who also knows nothing of magic. She worships me, along with everyone else within the city gates. Because she knows what will happen if she doesn't."

"And what's that, exactly?" Nico asked, her own lips compressed into a thin line, her knuckles white around her staff. "She gets to keep her dignity?"

Le Fay shrugged.

"As much as is possible when you're being thrown into the slavering jaws of a dragon, I suppose," she replied, her tone bored. "Or enslaved by a pain demon. Or, if she's lucky, ripped apart and eaten by the horde of zombies on the other side of my wall."

Zelma didn't know if the Runaway had ever encountered Le Fay before, or if her hackles were up on general principle, but whatever the reason, Zelma was glad of it. Because they were going to have to find a way to get Deadpool out of here – along with what was apparently his new pet, given the way it was trying to nuzzle him – then reopen the portal to the timestream and fix whatever the mercenary had done to make this present so drastically different from what it was supposed to be. And they needed to do it quickly, without alerting the Sorceress Supreme to their intentions. That would be a lot easier to do if Nico's snark could capture and keep the woman's attention.

Elsa seemed to have the same idea, but she wasn't relying on her own considerable skill at snarkiness to keep Le Fay busy. She just started shooting.

Which didn't work, of course. The bullets, magicked though Zelma knew they were, stopped well short of the sorceress, slamming into an invisible shield and falling to the stone floor in a clinking metallic rain.

As Le Fay stood, her face morphing from false pity into a more natural state of irritation, Nico whispered something unintelligible to her staff, and the amulet around the sorceress's throat began to twist and tighten, as if the artifact itself were trying to choke the woman to death. Le Fay sent a bolt of green energy at the Runaway in response, causing Nico to drop the strangulation spell in favor of a defensive one, and the bolt ricocheted away, narrowly missing Elsa as it slammed into one of the cell walls. Stone exploded outward at the impact, showering the women with jagged shrapnel and leaving a smoking crater in its wake.

"Oi, now!" Elsa exclaimed as she dodged the emerald beam and then launched into a high somersault, up and over the spray of rocks. "Watch where you're aiming that thing!"

Whatever shielding Le Fay had in place was apparently only primed to defend against magical attacks, for the monster hunter landed well within the sorceress's personal space, feet barely touching down before she pirouetted into a roundhouse kick, the heel of one stylish boot scoring a line across Le Fay's cheek.

The Sorceress Supreme shrieked in fury and sent a barrage of green bolts at Elsa, who parried them all with orange blasts from her bloodstone. Meanwhile Nico, perhaps in telepathic communication with the monster hunter, took a page from Elsa's playbook, and instead of using the Staff of One to focus spells, rushed in and swung it at Le Fay like a two-handed sword.

Zelma took advantage of the fireworks and fisticuffs to rush over to where Deadpool and friend were shackled. She quickly pulled the glimmering key to Deadpool's manacles out from beneath her shirt and started unlocking them, one by one, the task made harder by the adrenaline pumping through her system and the need to keep glancing over her shoulder to both make sure that Le Fay hadn't noticed her and that none of the deflected attacks from either side were headed her way.

"Aren't you a little short for a stormtrooper?" Deadpool asked, stretching laconically as she unlocked the last of the manacles.

"What?" Zelma asked, startled. Then she squinched her nose at him, perturbed at his continual non sequiturs. "No. You know what? Never mind; I don't care. You're in *serious* trouble, mister. You messed up big time – probably plural. And probably starting with this moldy oldie here," she added as she used a quick "Open Sesame" spell on the mammoth's fetters. "You're going to help us fix every single thing you screwed up or I am going to make it so you never eat another chimichanga or watch another episode of *Golden Girls* again. *Ever*. Capiche?"

"What are you going to do, *Mom*, ground me?" he retorted, then reached over to pat the mammoth on its trunk and began cooing at it. "Who's a good boy, huh? Who's the best boy? Not Deadpool, that's for sure!"

Zelma had had enough. She was not someone who lost her temper often; she almost always felt guilty afterward, like *she* was the one who'd done something wrong, so it was generally better to just swallow her indignation and deal with the acid reflux afterward than to call someone out on their behavior, no matter how obnoxious it was.

But not this time. Because not only had Deadpool not listened to her, he had also created this hellscape they currently found themselves in, a world where Morgan-freaking-Le Fay had usurped the position of Earth's protector and Doc, who was its rightful Sorcerer Supreme, was long dead. And that was just too much.

Cloak's corners whipped up at her thought, grabbing the mouthy merc and slamming him back up against the stone wall, holding him there with his arms and legs pinned and useless, though Zelma made sure to stay clear of his head.

"Now you listen to me, Mr Wade Wilson Deadpool Pain-in-My-Tuchus. I am done playing games with you. I know you think I'm just some silly, meek librarian, but there is a reason Doctor Strange took me on as his apprentice, and it's not because of my great fashion sense or because I can quote the entire works of Shakespeare from memory. I know spells that can turn you inside-out and outside-in ad infinitum for the rest of eternity. Spells that can make you forget everyone and everything you've ever loved – or worse, make you actively seek out and destroy those very things, if they even still exist. I can shunt you off into some empty pocket dimension where there will be nothing to drown out all those voices in your head. You know, the ones you talk so much to keep from having to hear? You think you're unstable now? That the world might be better off without you? That *you* might be better off without you? A few years in a place like that, and you will be begging me to find a way to kill you, a way that you can't regenerate your way back from.

"And I... *won't... do... it.*" She bit off each word with hard, icy precision. "Because Doc is dead now, and it's your fault, and if you can't help me fix it, then you are going to pay, and keep on paying, for as long as the rest of the world has to suffer without him."

For as long as I have to suffer without him, she thought, but did not say.

"And then? I'll let Clea have you."

Zelma wasn't really sure about the legitimacy of that last threat, since this timeline's Clea would never have known Doc, but that didn't matter. If she had to, she'd find *all* the Cleas in all the timelines. Whatever it took.

She was breathing hard and shaking by the time she was finished, with unspent anger and grief and other emotions she couldn't name. She stepped away from the mercenary then, letting Cloak release him. She didn't think Deadpool would attack her, but she readied a seraphic shield just in case.

Still, she wasn't fast enough.

Deadpool leapt at her, his weight bearing her down to the straw-strewn floor, the stink of mildew and fear-sweat filling her nostrils. Above their heads, another green bolt took out a chunk of the wall where they had been standing, the mammoth's bulk protecting them from the resulting hail of stones.

Zelma looked up into Deadpool's masked face, realizing belatedly that she couldn't even really tell what color his eyes were. Wondering if that was going to be the last thing she ever thought before he killed her.

Then he was climbing off her and helping her to her feet.

"Geez, Zelma. Anyone ever tell you you're wound pretty tight?" he asked. "You should really think about a spa day."

Zelma might truly have transported him to the threatened pocket dimension then if Le Fay hadn't come flying across the cell, propelled by a combined blast from Elsa's bloodhand and Nico's staff. The sorceress fetched up hard against the opposite wall, momentarily stunned.

"We should probably get while the getting's good," Nico said as she and Elsa hurried over to where Zelma and Deadpool stood. The librarian nodded and quickly pulled Cagliostro's book out of her pack. The three women had the timestream portal open again within moments.

"Ladies first," Deadpool said, gesturing toward the vortex with a low bow. While he was bent over, Elsa kicked him hard in the glutes, sending him tumbling into the portal. Then she had to leap in after him as the mammoth trumpeted and almost trampled her to get to Deadpool. Nico followed.

Zelma was about to step in after when she reconsidered. She turned to Le Fay, who was still on the floor, dazed.

"Vapors of Valtorr, swirl 'round thy brow
As the Mists of Morpheus envelop thee now!"

As soon as Zelma uttered the spell, a gray haze settled over the Sorceress Supreme. Scant seconds later, she was slumped in the decaying straw, gently snoring. Zelma quickly ordered the Cloak of Levitation to bear the woman's sleeping form over to the glimmering manacles that had held Deadpool not long before. Cloak held her in place while Zelma locked the shackles around the sorceress's wrists and ankles.

"I don't know if they will hold her long – they can't be the same manacles Doc made for his bar tab, since he never learned magic here and never had a price to pay," she said to Cloak. "But they must be similar, or else my key wouldn't have reacted to them, or worked to unlock them. This should at least give us a bit of a head start."

She only hoped it would be enough.

Satisfied that she'd done all she could for the moment, Zelma turned back to the swirling vortex as Cloak resettled itself on her shoulders, then took a deep breath, and stepped through.

CHAPTER TWENTY-EIGHT

The other side of Zelma's portal looked like the intro to that old sci-fi series, *The Twilight Zone*, except everything here was in blazing technicolor, not black and white. Nico felt like she'd been thrown onto some hellish combination of the world's worst amusement park rides, like a Tilt-a-Whirl, Zipper, and Space Mountain all in one, that should come with a strongly worded "strobing lights may affect photosensitive time travelers" warning.

Perhaps even more disconcerting was the fact that there was no sound. She couldn't even hear her own breathing, or heartbeat. Maybe, because they were in a liminal space outside of time, she *wasn't* breathing or pumping blood from her heart to her lungs and brain. But that didn't exactly jibe with her intense need to vomit.

Deadpool was hovering in space several feet in front of her, pretending to backstroke through Escherian triangles as they tumbled slowly past, making a game of it. The mammoth that had been chained with him in the basement cell floated nearby, its legs working frantically to get it exactly nowhere. The poor animal's eyes were rolling back in its head and Nico expected it to start foaming at the mouth any second now. She was surprised it wasn't trumpeting its fear to the entire timestream. Or maybe it was, and she just couldn't hear it.

Elsa was a few feet closer, her hair and the hem of her coat seeming to drift about her as if she were underwater. Unperturbed and ever practical, the monster hunter was checking what ammunition she had left for the guns she was still carrying.

Nico turned slowly, her limbs oddly heavy, like she was pushing her way through jello. Zelma was just stepping through the whirling portal that still showed a small circle of the Bleecker Street basement behind her, and in it, Morgan Le Fay, now bound in the chains that had held Deadpool, and in another timeline, Doctor Strange.

Nico was impressed. But, then, she'd heard some of what Zelma had been saying to Deadpool there at the end. She'd known there was mettle in Strange's apprentice – how could there not be? She'd seen the librarian display it more than once since saving Nico's bacon in LA that very first day.

But Nico had not expected the other type of metal in the witch, the kind forged in fires of both pain and purpose, that stiffened spines and resolve. She would make a formidable Sorceress Supreme should that mantle ever pass to her, though Nico knew that wasn't a title Zelma wanted. No rational person would. Which was why, at least in their original timeline, it was a position chosen by the Eye of Agamotto – and presumably Agamotto himself – and not one that could be applied for on a magical job board. How Le Fay had wound up bearing that title in the alternate timeline they'd just exited was, like the strange affair of *The Phantom of the Opera*, a mystery that would undoubtedly never be fully explained.

Zelma's mouth moved, presumably speaking the words that would close the vortex behind her, though Nico heard nothing. As the portal irised out of existence, Zelma replaced the *Book of Cagliostro* in her backpack, her movements starting out in slow motion, then gradually speeding up to a normal pace.

Nico hadn't heard what spell the other witch cast, but suddenly sound returned, almost painfully loud, the blood rushing in her ears like a roaring river, her breath like a gale-force wind. She winced and instinctively slapped her hands over her ears, as though that would somehow help. The Staff of One was balanced dangerously in the crook of her elbow, and she wondered what would happen if it should slip away into this bizarre space. Would it simply float there beside her, like the mammoth, or would it fall endlessly through this psychedelic void, with her unable to recall it? But then the noises faded, returning to their regular background state, and Nico was able to drop her hands and reclaim the staff before any imagined harms could befall it.

"I can trace Deadpool's path with the Amulet of Agamotto," Zelma said, her voice echoing out into space like ripples in a pond. "I can see where he exited the timestream. More than once. We have to go to each of those times and fix whatever he broke."

"So it's not about getting rid of zombies anymore?" Nico asked and Zelma shook her head.

"No. We have to restore our original timeline; we can't let it end up with Le Fay in charge and Doc dead."

"Why not?" Elsa asked, drifting into view. "At least there's still a decent-sized human population in her version."

"A population enslaved to a maniacal despot!" Zelma snapped back at her, glaring. "We can do better than that."

"Can we, though?" the monster hunter pressed, an ironic devil's advocate, considering it was her job to kill devils and their demonic ilk.

"We have to try."

"But where does that get us?" Nico asked, understanding Zelma's desire to right wrongs, but also seeing Elsa's point. Their goal had been accomplished, one way or another, and humanity's future had been ensured. Even if that future did suck pointy rocks.

But, then, that had never been Zelma's only goal. She also wanted to save her mentor, maybe even more than she wanted to save the world. A mentor who didn't even exist anymore in Le Fay's time.

"I know you want to rescue Doc from his zombified fate," Nico continued, "and I totally get that. I do. I'd love to save my Runaways from getting chomped on, and worse. But resetting things to the zombie apocalypse status quo isn't going to do that. Doc will still be braindead, my team will still be gluttonous ghouls with the murder munchies, and we'll still have to deal with a world overrun by starving supers with no moral compass left. At least in Le Fay's timeline, we only have the one amoral super villain to contend with. And she won't be trying to eat us."

"Don't forget the ones outside the gate," Deadpool interjected unhelpfully. The mammoth trumpeted its agreement alongside him.

"Clearly all C-listers, if Le Fay feels confident enough to leave demons and dragons to deal with them," Elsa pointed out, and Nico flashed her a grateful look.

It wasn't that Nico was opposed to going back and fixing the timeline, necessarily. And she didn't want to keep second guessing Zelma, because she knew how much that stunk. But like Elsa, she wasn't convinced that the timeline they'd just left was any worse than the one they'd started out in. And she needed a better reason to go traipsing about in this seizure-inducing nightmare than Zelma's desire not to disappoint her teacher.

Surprisingly, it was Deadpool who gave it to her.

"I hate to burst your Le Fay fangirl bubble – well, not really, because, eww – but she followed me into the timestream," he said as he petted the spot between the mammoth's eyes, calming it. "She somehow knew we opened the portal, tracked me through the timestream as I was leading the zombies nowhere fast – various entertaining pitstops notwithstanding – and decided that was... what did she say again? 'A waste of their potential'. Said she had a better use for them."

"Let me guess." Zelma's tone was smug. "As extras to help flesh out her little medieval fantasy? Staging a war between all of humanity's worst enemies while she gets to position herself as their savior? In exchange for their fealty, of course."

Deadpool shrugged.

"I dunno," he replied. "Depends on what 'fealty' means." Then he frowned. "And why are we not on fast-forward? Before, it was like me and the *zomboes* were competing for an Olympic speed record! I was winning, of course."

"When we opened the portal for you," Zelma said, "we

needed the zombies gone fast, so we basically shoved you all straight into the timestream, where you got caught by the current. When we opened it this time around, we had a bit more leeway, so I directed us into a... timepool... where things naturally move at a slower pace.

"Anyway, once you tell us where you loused up history, we can go into the timestream proper knowing what to expect. And knowing is, as they say, half the battle."

Deadpool harrumphed.

"I'd prefer to think of the changes I made as 'improvements', thank you very much."

"Yes, Morgan Le Fay as Sorceress Supreme is *quite* the upgrade," Zelma replied sarcastically.

"At least humanity survived under her watch," Elsa replied matter-of-factly "Not so sure it would have done in our timeline, way things were going."

Zelma bristled.

"Only until she gets bored of it all and heads back to a timeline she prefers, leaving humanity to fend for themselves against the zombies *and* the demons and dragons," she argued, and likely would have continued, but Nico decided now would be a good time to intervene. If they started quibbling about which timeline was better, they'd just wind up talking in circles, getting nowhere and wasting valuable time. Le Fay might have been in shackles when Nico last saw her, but she knew the sorceress wouldn't stay imprisoned in them for long.

"We had safely stashed the zombies where they couldn't do any harm to anyone," she said, perhaps a bit too loudly, "except maybe the random, unwary time traveler. If Le Fay purposefully pulled them out in order to further her own designs, it seems reasonable to assume that the survival of humankind en masse isn't high on her ultimate agenda.

"Even so, we don't have enough information to determine whether humanity is or will be better off in her timeline or in ours. There's no way of knowing what would have happened – or might still happen – under our watch until we get back to our own corrected timeline. Which I'd guess doesn't actually exist anymore, thanks to Deadpool's 'improvements.'" She looked over to Zelma for confirmation, since she herself had not taken Time Traveling 101 from Doctor Strange, who had apparently cribbed much of his own curriculum from Cagliostro. The librarian's tight smile didn't inspire much confidence.

But it wasn't like they had a lot of options. Zelma was right, even if Nico didn't fully buy into the other witch's reasons. They couldn't leave things as they were, given what they now knew about how the zombies had wound up in this timeline. Nico almost wished Deadpool hadn't said anything about Le Fay's motives, but that wasn't just water under the bridge, it was a bridge washed out by a tsunami – and probably only the first of many.

"So comparing the two scenarios is sort of like asking if Schrödinger's cat is better off inside or outside of the box," she continued. "There's no way to tell without opening it. So–"

"Well, actually," Deadpool interrupted her, once again sticking a pedagogical finger in the air, "I think that depends on the frame of reference of the observer, doesn't it? What if the *cat* is the observer…?" He trailed off, looking from one woman's face to the next. "What? What did I say now?"

"Are you…" Nico began, then hesitated momentarily because she couldn't believe the words that were about to come out of her own mouth. "Are you actually mansplaining *quantum physics* to me?"

Deadpool's look turned sly.

"*Maaay*-be. That depends on how much you know about quantum physics," he replied archly. Then the pommel of a knife struck him squarely between the eyes before bouncing off his forehead to go tumbling into the void.

"Oww!" he exclaimed, rubbing at the injured spot. "That hurt!"

"What do you know? That was actually worth losing one of my favorite blades for," Elsa said with evident satisfaction. "Now, do shut up, Wade. You're all mouth and no trousers." She didn't pause when Deadpool glanced down at his groin area to check the veracity of her statement. "You don't know onions about quantum physics, and history's gone all pear-shaped because of your shenanigans, so maybe quit while you're ahead for once, hmm?"

Despite the Britishisms and confusing produce references, Nico got the gist of Elsa's meaning, and taking the monster hunter's diatribe as tacit agreement, she continued on as though Deadpool hadn't spoken.

"We have to go with what we *do* know – which is that we at least are trying to save what's left of the world, not enslave it. Maybe we could eventually do that in Le Fay's time, but there, in addition to zombies, we'd also have to worry about both her egomaniacal narcissism and her army of demons and dragons. The odds would be even more stacked against us than they were before we tried the time loop spell in the first place.

"So, on reflection, I think Zee is right. I think we need to go back and try to figure something else out, because the plan to trap the zombies in the timestream obviously had some flaws we didn't foresee, hindsight being 20/20 and all that. And the only way to get back to that precise moment in time is to fix all the moments that were changed along the way leading up to it."

Elsa shrugged.

"Monsters now, monsters then, it's no skin off my nose either way, as you Yanks like to say. Skin off my *cheek* is a different matter altogether." She sighed. "I did rather like being back to my old self, but needs must, I suppose."

"I'm glad we're all agreed, quantum physics debates aside," Zelma said, turning to Deadpool. "So, where to first? Or, *when* to?"

"Manhattan," Deadpool replied, pouting. "Right after the infectoid hit."

Elsa frowned.

"But you were in Boston after the impact. With me."

"Yeah, after I got sent there by a spell Zelma's boss meant for my buddy, Spidey."

"Your buddy?" Nico repeated, surprised. Aside from red suits and slinging wisecracks, she wasn't sure what Spider-Man and the mercenary could possibly have in common, though they were often mistaken for one another.

"Why was Doc casting spells at him?" Zelma asked, her face going pale.

Deadpool gave a half-shrug.

"Probably because Spidey's the one who bit him."

CHAPTER TWENTY-NINE

Zelma felt herself go cold and then numb at the revelation. She didn't know what she was supposed to do with Deadpool's information. She hadn't really thought about the fact that Doc being infected when she encountered him in the library logically meant that someone must've infected him before that, let alone who that someone might have been.

Or, more precisely, she'd swatted those thoughts away like garbage-swarming flies whenever they'd arisen in her mind, unbidden and unwanted. The identity of Doc's assailant was ultimately irrelevant. The fact of his infection was all that mattered.

Still, somehow knowing it was Spider-Man who had brought Zelma's world crashing down around her feet – one of the heroes most known for actually *being* good and not just doing it – was especially bitter. Like it was some cosmic entity's attempt at a very bad joke.

Zelma didn't appreciate the irony.

Nor was she at all pleased to learn that correcting this

"improvement" of Deadpool's was going to require her to not only watch her mentor get infected, but sit by and do nothing to prevent it from happening.

It wasn't just galling; it was unconscionable.

Nevertheless, it was what had to be done. Everything had to be reset, no matter how awful. It was the only way to keep things from becoming *more* awful. And it's what Doc would do, in her position.

Of course, he'd willingly chosen his position. She, arguably, hadn't.

And he'd had his own personal monster in the cellar where he could deposit the pain of such decisions, deferring having to actually feel said pain to the mythical Land of Later. Zelma didn't have that option. She wasn't sure she'd take it if she did.

She also wasn't sure yet what form her own personal magical bar tab might take. Doc had said the bill could range from bruises to depression to worse, so she might not even notice the cost at first, though she supposed that would change the more magic she wound up using.

What she *was* sure of was that the time loop spell – which was ultimately her responsibility – had not only failed, but backfired spectacularly, aided in no small part by Deadpool's inability or simple unwillingness to follow directions. So now they had to find a way to get back to the drawing board, and try something else. Even if that "something else" meant not only that Zelma would lose her mentor all over again, but also that Elsa would have to go back to being a zombie reliant on Deadpool's questionable good graces for her sanity.

Deadpool didn't exactly come out of it a winner, either; he was going back to being walking – or maybe chained up – deli meat. Though Zelma was beginning to think ever letting him out of his cage had been a huge mistake.

And he was going to lose his new pet, which she didn't think the mercenary was going to be too happy about; judging by the way he snuggled close to it whenever he got the chance, the two had already formed a tight bond. But they'd deal with that problem when they got there. For now, they were headed back to the Manhattan from their original timeline, the one sans dragons and a tyrannical Sorceress Supreme. One that would also be, for a brief, blessed moment, free of zombies.

"I guess that's the plan, then. First, Manhattan, to make sure Spidey gets bit. When to after that?" she asked Deadpool, who pretended to look around as if there were some other Destroyer of Timelines she might be talking to. She scowled at him impatiently. "Yes, you. Stop clowning around."

"Remember that old rhyme from elementary school?" he asked. "'Columbus sailed the ocean blue in fourteen hundred ninety-two'? Well, when I wound up there, I *might've* accidentally on purpose made sure he never got across the ocean to 'discover'–" here Deadpool used air quotes around the word, which dripped with sarcasm "–the so-called New World – which, bee tee dubs, wasn't new to the people who had been living there for forever – by making sure the *Santa Maria* and the rest of his fleet sank in the middle of the Atlantic."

"Do we *have* to fix that one?" Nico asked, looking over at Zelma.

Zelma could appreciate the sentiment, but the Runaway knew as well as she did that everything had to be reset, even the wrong turns humanity had made throughout history. Trying to revise events after the fact was part of what had gotten them into this mess.

"You know we do," she replied regretfully.

It did beg more than a few questions, though.

"Exactly how did you accomplish that?" she asked him, trying not to sound too impressed. It wouldn't do to encourage him, even if she was curious how he'd managed to pull off such a neat trick with a horde of super-powered zombies in tow.

"Well, I don't know if you know this, but the Hulk once traveled through time himself and landed on the *Santa Maria*, where he battled Fin Fang Foom – and people say Deadpool is a stupid name! Anyway, I guess he left a rip or something in the timestream, because I was just kind of sucked out of it onto the deck of the ship, and the zombies after me, including Zombie Hulk.

"While Green and Rotting made quick work of Green and Grumpy, the rest of the zombies made sea rations of Columbus and his crew. Triple F managed to escape, and when he did, the timestream suck thing happened again and away we went. But not before all the ships were on their way to Davy Jones's Locker, boo hoo." He pretended to wipe a tear from the corner of his masked eye.

Zelma realized that was probably why he'd been drawn to Doc's confrontation with Spider-Man, as well. Strange had opened a hole in the space-time continuum when he cast the spell that had sent Deadpool to Boston, and that breach had still been there when the timestream carrying the mercenary and his pursuers had looped past.

Which explained another thing she'd been having difficulty understanding – how Deadpool had been able to exit the timestream in the first place, let alone re-enter it again on his own. But preexisting perforations in the fabric of space-time could both suck things out of the timestream and spit them back into it again, so it made sense that the places where he'd made his "improvements" had been where other people had already altered the natural currents of time and space.

"Anywhere else?" she asked, looking meaningfully at the mammoth. Deadpool's new bestie had to have come from a time much earlier than the fifteenth century.

"No. That's it," Deadpool said, his accompanying grin too big and ready to be real.

"Is that a fact?" Zelma replied, one eyebrow lifting skeptically. She'd seen kids who'd lost their library books with that same look on their faces while trying to convince her that it was her system that had somehow misplaced the missing volumes, not them.

It had never once worked.

"And so your wooly friend currently mammoth-paddling in our timepool back there came from…?"

"Oh, you mean Max?" the mercenary replied, trying to look innocent and failing catastrophically.

"You named him?" Zelma asked, not at all sure why she was surprised.

"No," Deadpool replied defensively. "He named himself. 'Max' is just the closest – and politest – I could get to the noise he made when I asked him. Anyway, I couldn't just keep calling him 'Hey, you,' now could I? That's just rude."

"Do tell," Zelma drawled sarcastically. "And so you just… mammoth-napped him from his home? To do what? Take him on a joyride? Keep him as a pet? I'm struggling to understand your thinking here."

"That's pointless," Elsa interjected, smirking, obviously

enjoying herself. At least someone was. "Probably just trying to make himself feel better after his last animal friend bit him and ran off. Or maybe that was his girlfriend? Hard to keep them straight."

"*Also* rude," Deadpool replied, side-eying the monster hunter. "And a little mean-spirited, frankly." He sniffed disdainfully, then looked back at Zelma. "I dunno. Seemed like a good idea at the time?"

"And that's the last thing you 'improved'?" Zelma asked, ignoring their bickering. Honestly, the two reminded her of nothing so much as siblings born too far apart to be friends and too close together not to feel bad about it. Shaking her head, she began ticking items off on her fingers. "Keeping Spidey from getting zombified, stopping Columbus from colonizing the Americas, and acquiring a new mammoth friend? That's it? That's absolutely everything?"

"Isn't that enough?" Deadpool countered, and Zelma had to admit that it was. More than.

"OK, then," she said, looking at her companions. "Are we ready?"

At their chorus of assent, Zelma continued.

"Next stop, Midtown Manhattan, pre-apocalypse. Vishanti help us."

CHAPTER THIRTY

They stepped out of the timestream into the sky above Manhattan, Nico's Staff of One keeping them airborne while Zelma used the Crytorryk Spell of Invisibility to cloak them from view. As they did so, something flashed through the purpling sky, and moments later, they heard a loud boom. Black smoke began to rise into the air not far from where they hovered.

They didn't have much time.

"Where were you when you stopped Spider-Man from getting bitten?" Zelma asked Deadpool, who was pouting because she wouldn't let him ride his stolen wooly mammoth into battle. Zelma would have preferred not to have brought the thing at all, but of course they'd had no choice. They had to take it back to its correct time; they couldn't just leave it languishing in the timestream.

Deadpool pointed toward the pillar of smoke.

"There. The first time, I couldn't see who was biting him until it was too late, but this time I knew who I was looking for, so I stopped her before she got to him."

"Her?" Zelma repeated.

"The Wasp. She was one of the first Avengers on the scene and got chomped early on. I don't know how many others she turned before she got to Spidey, but if she used the same trick on them as she did on him, it could have been a *lot*."

"What trick is that?" Zelma asked, her curiosity piqued. But even as she asked the question, she realized what the answer must be. The Wasp could shrink herself down to the size of her namesake, if not smaller. She would have been able to infect multiple supers before any of them even knew she was there. Though Zelma wasn't as sure about why the size-shifting hero would choose to do that instead of just eating her peers, unless maybe she could paralyze them? Then she could come back and snack on them at her leisure. If she was still wasp-sized when she ate them, just one corpse could last her indefinitely, even if some of the others were discovered and poached by her fellow zombies.

"She snuck up on him when she was all itty bitty," Deadpool confirmed. "I figure she probably would've just stung him or whatever, but his Spidey senses kicked in and he realized she was there. He tried to squash her in midair, but she turned big again at the last minute and attacked him before he could swing out of the way." He paused. "Poor guy, huh? First he gets turned into a web-slinging freak by a spider, then he gets turned into a zombie by a wasp. Guy just has no luck when it comes to bugs.

"But she got hers. Spidey snagged her with a web before she could buzz away again and took a few bites out of *her*. But he forgot all about her and just let his webbing fall to the street with her still inside of it when Doctor Strange flew by. All that red, I guess."

"So you stopped her," Zelma repeated impatiently, not interested in the play-by-play of how her mentor had been zombified. It was bad enough she had to be back here, in the time and place where it had happened, and that she had to let it happen again. She really didn't need a detailed description of the deed itself. "Where, and when?"

Deadpool peered around for a second, getting his bearings, then pointed at the roof of a nearby skyscraper.

"There," he said. "And... right about now."

He'd barely finished uttering the last word when another portal from the timestream opened, ejecting a second Deadpool.

"Ah, there I am," Deadpool One said with some satisfaction. "Right on time."

"*Two* of them?" Elsa said in disbelief.

Zelma closed her eyes, wincing at the sudden throbbing pain in her temples. Of *course* there would be two of them. How in the name of the Vishanti had she not realized that they would be here at the same time as Deadpool's original "repair work"? How could she not have taken that into account in her planning?

Time travel paradoxes were maddening and gave her migraines. Paradoxes that involved multiple Deadpools might be enough to make her head explode.

"I got this," Deadpool One replied, launching himself at... himself.

"Propel," Nico said, using her staff to give him a boost as he left the confines of her flight spell. Zelma assumed that since Nico was just swapping one spell for another, and only for Deadpool, the Runaway wouldn't have to worry about the exchange weakening the effects of the spell that was keeping the others airborne. At least, she hoped not.

But as Deadpool got further away from them, the effects of Zelma's invisibility spell *did* fade, so that by the time he reached his earlier counterpart, he was fully visible. When he hit Deadpool Two, they went tumbling in a tangle of red and black limbs, both bouncing back up to their feet with ease. Zelma had no idea which was which.

"Who the hell are you?" one of them demanded; Zelma assumed the speaker was Deadpool Two.

"I'm Deadpool," Deadpool One replied, sounding affronted.

"No, *I'm* Deadpool," the other one argued.

Another tussle ensued, the twin mercenaries attacking each other so quickly that Zelma once again lost track of the "real" Deadpool.

Then they separated, each pointed at the other, yelling simultaneously, "You're a fake!"

"Wonderful," she muttered. "Now what?"

"Maybe Max can tell them apart?" Elsa wondered, but Zelma shook her head.

"I'll use the Amulet of Agamotto. Once we're sure the Wasp has infected Spider-Man. Then we'll have to get both Deadpools back into the timestream. Before the zombies who are chasing the… second one? First? I don't even know how to refer to him. Anyway, before the time loop zombies come pouring through the open portal after that one."

"What, you don't think doubling the number of infected suits we have to deal with will double our fun? Pish," Elsa said dismissively.

Zelma didn't bother replying to the monster hunter because

she was too busy watching for Spider-Man and Doc while the other two women kept their eyes on the dancing Deadpools and the portal through which the second one had sprung, ready to act should the mercenaries' stalemate be broken or something else begin to emerge from the timestream. It only took a moment for the librarian to spot the red-cloaked Sorcerer Supreme. He was flying toward the impact site, passing a street or two over from the rooftop where the two Deadpools now fought. Zelma saw him stop and hover for a moment, then spin and start back the way he'd come, much more quickly than before. Only to be intercepted by Spidey.

This was it. It was happening. And there was nothing she could do to stop it.

Except that wasn't true, was it? She *could* stop it; she could cast some spell to keep Spider-Man away from Doc and ensure that Doc got back to the Sanctum Sanctorum safely. That he didn't get zombified and that her friends Rintrah and Wong didn't become his first full meal.

But what would that do to the timeline? Could it possibly be worse than a world in which Morgan Le Fay was the Sorceress Supreme and she kept zombified supers around for entertainment purposes? Well, and to punish disloyal subjects, but that amounted to pretty much the same thing as far as the narcissistic half-Faerie sorceress was concerned.

But Zelma knew better. Things could *always* be worse, and even asking that question was just daring the universe to prove it to you.

Still, standing by and doing nothing while she watched Spider-Man closing in on her teacher, knowing what was going to happen to him, was an agony like nothing she had ever felt before. Her heart was a spiked ball of acid, her pulse pounding in her chest and temples like a caged animal, out of its mind with desperation and intent on freeing itself. Part of her was screaming inside, drowning out her thundering heartbeat, telling her to save him, no matter the cost, that she owed Doctor Strange at least that much. While a quieter, more rational and sorrowful part that she could somehow still hear amidst all the emotional cacophony reminded her that he wouldn't want her to.

All *she* wanted was for them both to just *shut the hell up*.

Zelma wasn't some selfish child with an irresolute moral compass. On the contrary, she'd always had a strong sense of right and wrong, even if she hadn't always been inclined to follow it. But she'd grown up a lot under Doc's tutelage, and she'd learned from watching the Sorcerer Supreme that sometimes doing the right thing meant doing the last thing in the world you wanted to do. And that being a good person – not a super hero like Doc, just a decent human being – meant doing it anyway. No matter how much it hurt.

She'd watched him make those choices. The right ones *and* the wrong ones. And she couldn't willingly make the wrong choice now any more than she could pretend she was unable to distinguish between the two.

So she just hovered there, watching, hands balled into white fists at her sides as she began to shake, face twisting into a mask of grief and guilt, tears carving hot tracks down her cheeks. She choked back anguished sobs and the spells she would not, could not, speak.

She watched, unmoving, as the whirling golden oval opened behind the Sorcerer Supreme, a Conjurer's Cone meant to send Spider-Man someplace where he wouldn't be a danger to himself or others. Where that had been in Boston, Zelma wasn't sure. Perhaps Doc had meant to send him to Elsa, figuring she would know how best to deal with the infected web-slinger. That would have been some universe-level irony.

Zelma knew Doc's casting of that spell meant that events were progressing as they had before, that the Wasp had managed to infect Spider-Man, who was in turn about to infect Doc. Her job here was done.

And still she watched, as Spider-Man dodged out of the path of Doc's spell and trapped the sorcerer in his sticky webbing. As the not-so-friendly neighborhood hero latched on to his still-floating prey and pulled Doc's dark head aside to expose his neck. As he bent to feed.

A rough hand on her shoulder spun her around abruptly so that she couldn't see that final, awful moment. Zelma found herself staring into Nico's concerned face, though the lines of worry creasing the other witch's features were blurred somewhat by Zelma's tear-spattered lenses.

"It's done," Nico said gently. "We need to collect our Deadpool and go."

Zelma nodded numbly, her eyes on Nico but her mind still on the scene playing out to its heartrending conclusion behind her.

Oh, Doc. I'm so sorry.

"How can I just stand here and let it happen all over again?" she asked in a broken whisper. "He's my teacher. My *friend*."

Nico's hand was still on her shoulder and now the other witch gave it a gentle squeeze.

"I know, Zee. But we have to set things right. You know that," she replied, her lips twisting a bit as if she were trying to hold back her own tears. Then her grip tightened. "And you know he'd tell you the exact same thing if he were here."

Zelma laughed shortly, a harsh, barking noise. She yanked away from Nico's touch, suddenly angry. But the flash of bitter fire dissipated as quickly as it had come, and she was left feeling defeated and deflated.

Had she failed Doc by not saving him here in the past? She felt like she had, but how could she ever know for sure?

That one was easy. She couldn't. All she could do now was keep moving forward. Stick to the plan, reset the timeline, and carry on trying to find another way to fix things.

No, not trying. *Finding.* She might have failed Doc here, but she was determined not to do it again. Ever.

"No," she said, sniffing and wiping her face with her sweater sleeve. "He'd tell me to stop blubbering and get a hold of myself, because there's still work to be done. And he'd be right, because he almost always is. Was. Whatever." Then she reached up to touch her amulet and a blue ray of light shot out from it to surround one of the Deadpools. "Cloak, fetch!"

The Cloak of Levitation detached itself from Zelma's shoulders and swooped toward the rooftop. As Nico's spell took on the added burden of the now-flightless apprentice, the other witch would have to let go of the spell she'd kept active on Deadpool to return him to the portal, but with Cloak coming to his rescue, he shouldn't need the extra boost from Nico's magic to get him back to where the women awaited him.

But before Cloak could get there, the unlimned Deadpool took advantage of the other's millisecond of surprise at finding himself surrounded by a blue nimbus, and bull-rushed his glowing analogue.

Right off the edge of the roof.

As Deadpool One plummeted, Deadpool Two spent a brief moment assuring himself that the other mercenary wasn't going to catch onto some random piece of equipment and swing back up to re-engage him. Seemingly satisfied, he then turned and went looking for his objective, the now-infected Spider-Man.

But Deadpool Two had not noticed the cloak rushing through the air toward his counterpart. It caught and lifted the falling mercenary, but to Zelma's surprise and annoyance, instead of bringing its burden back to her, it deposited him soundlessly behind his twin.

The other Deadpool turned, but a fraction of a second too late. Deadpool One slammed his head into his counterpart's so hard that Zelma could hear the crack of bone against bone from where she and the others floated. Then he grabbed Deadpool Two's head and brought it down onto his own knee, again and again, until blood sprayed both mercenaries and cloak in equal measure. Only when the other Deadpool was too woozy to stand up on his own did Deadpool One release his grip. He used one hand to divest his counterpart of one of the katanas Morgan Le Fay no doubt had taken when she imprisoned him while the other snaked around to grip his opponent's throat, squeezing. Only when his reclaimed sword was firmly strapped into place did he allow Cloak to bring him and Deadpool Two back to Zelma.

The librarian was fuming at Cloak's apparent disobedience, but she said nothing as it released the two Deadpools to the care of Nico's spell and settled back sheepishly around Zelma's shoulders. They'd be having a chat about this later.

"What do you want to do with this loser?" Deadpool One asked her, shaking the barely conscious Deadpool Two by the throat.

"Throw him back in the timestream before the zombies start coming through," she said. "He has to – *you* have to, whatever – go back in to reset the timeline."

"What'll happen to the me that's here?" their Deadpool asked curiously.

"Nothing," Zelma replied. Then she paused, realizing she didn't really know. "Well, probably nothing."

Deadpool thought for a second, then he shrugged.

"I like those odds," he said, grabbing his counterpart by the scruff of the neck and Elsa's makeshift bum flap to toss him back into the portal he'd come out of. As he did, four zombified Avengers came stumbling out of the opening.

"Finally!" Elsa muttered, exploding the lead zombie's brain with a beam from her bloodgem before Zelma could even register its identity, smiling with obvious relish as she did so. "Bloody snoozefest so far, if you ask me."

The unidentified zombie's decapitated body flew back into that of the zombie behind it – Zelma saw a lot of blue on that one's suit, so it might've been Cap – and knocked him back through the swirling portal. Even as the blue-suited zombie flew backward, he grabbed the corpse of his headless companion and gruesomely started to feed on it.

Then Deadpool One chucked his twin in after them, catching the third zombie dead center before it had a chance to get its bearings, sending it and Deadpool Two both back into the timestream, which instantly closed after them.

Before any of the others could react, Max reached out with

his trunk and grabbed the fourth zombie Avenger – a woman in a white suit, Zelma couldn't tell who – and impaled her on one of his tusks before tearing her head from her torso, leaving part of her spine and brain stem protruding from her neck. Then the creature shook his own shaggy head violently, sending the separated zombie parts plummeting to the street below.

"See? Didn't I tell you he was a good boy?" Deadpool crooned, reaching out to scratch the massive animal behind one of his ears. "Daddy's gonna give you a mammoth treat when we get home. Oh, yes, he is!"

"Which is our cue to leave, I think," Zelma added, leading them back toward their own timestream portal, which was still spinning and sparking where they had left it, though the apprentice had cast a "Nothing To See Here" spell on it, so only the members of their group would even know it was there.

"What about her?" Nico asked, pointing her staff in the direction where the pieces of the white-suited zombie woman had fallen. "Won't her presence here change the timeline?"

Zelma didn't have a good answer for that, but Elsa did.

"Only if she landed on somebody," the monster hunter said. "Wade's bloody pet knew right where to sever the spine to deactivate whatever part of the brain keeps these rotters alive. She won't be infecting anyone else. Not that version of her, at any rate."

"And that's going to have to be good enough," Zelma added, indicating a spot behind Nico, "because we have officially outstayed our welcome."

Nico turned to see what the librarian was pointing at. A Quinjet was headed their way.

"They may not be able to see us or the portal, but they know something's up," Zelma said. "Time to go."

Then she stepped into the light and the others followed her back into the dizzying, kaleidoscopic rush of time.

CHAPTER THIRTY-ONE

As a librarian in the mundane world, Zelma had become a depository for trivia and niche knowledge, depending on the ever-changing needs of her library patrons. Since those patrons were often students who had limited internet or computer access at home, her mini-areas of expertise now ranged from Shakespeare to the laws of thermodynamics to fifteenth century seacraft.

So she knew what she was seeing when she and the others stepped out of the timestream at the spot the Amulet of Agamotto showed her and hovered over the Atlantic Ocean, much as they had over Manhattan, what seemed like both milliseconds and millennia ago.

A Spanish cargo ship drifted on the water below them, flanked on either side by two sleek caravels. The caravels were the two ships popularly known as the *Niña* and the *Pinta*, while the larger ship was *la Santa Gallega*, or the *Santa Maria*. Christopher Columbus's flagship.

All three ships had a three-masted design, with the sails on the first two masts being square for open-ocean speed and the third sail being triangular for coastal maneuverability. Right now, all the sails sagged, and the ships sat becalmed on a windless sea. Aboard the two smaller vessels, fewer than twenty-five men milled about on deck, in what seemed to Zelma to be an aimless manner, but probably wasn't. Roughly the same number of men were currently visible on the deck of the *Santa Maria*, though Zelma knew it could carry three times that amount. She assumed the rest were belowdecks.

As she and her companions watched, an oversized green form and a small, hovering mechanized device of some sort appeared on the aft deck of the *Santa Maria*, eliciting a chorus of exclamations from the crew, who all drew back in fear. They shrank back even further, many drawing weapons and crossing themselves, when a suit of armor suddenly manifested on the Hulk, complete with a crested helmet. Deadpool had not shared this little detail when he'd been relating the tale of his trip through time. Or, rather, been having it pried out of him.

"What the...?" Zelma began, but then she just stopped and shook her head. None of them knew why the Hulk had time-traveled here originally beyond fighting Fin Fang Foom, but she doubted the crew of the *Santa Maria* was his intended target, and, again, he'd originally traveled here *before* Deadpool had shown up with the zombies, so they weren't the opponents he was expecting, either. This did not bode well.

"Looks like it's showtime," Deadpool said, readying his single katana.

"Why didn't you take both of them?" Elsa asked suddenly, pulling out her own weapons.

Deadpool looked at her like she'd farted loudly at a fancy dinner. Well, no. He'd probably applaud if she did that. But *other* people would have given her the same look of faint contempt he was shooting her now.

"Because I might need the other one to fight off all those zombies chasing me. Duh."

"But that's not you…" the monster hunter began, trailing off as she realized there was no good way to complete that sentence. The other Deadpool *was* him, of course, just an earlier version. That the two had been able to coexist in the same time and place was enough to make even an apprentice magician's mind spin. Zelma could only imagine the mental gymnastics the paradox would spark in a layperson's head. Though Elsa was hardly unschooled in magical dealings and was nothing if not pragmatic; it was just as likely that the monster hunter would shrug it off as something not worth worrying about until the second katana was slicing toward her own head.

Right on cue, a second portal opened and Deadpool Two tumbled through it, falling to the crowded deck of the *Niña* below. Deadpool One took a running leap out of the air and dove after his counterpart.

Meanwhile, the lead zombies who'd been after Deadpool Two were much quicker to follow him out of the portal this time. A zombified Hulk bounded out of the spinning mouth, slamming into the ocean below and creating waves that almost swamped the *Niña*. His green head broke the surface quickly, though, and he struck out toward the *Santa Maria*, presumably because it was the biggest ship and therefore promised the largest buffet.

But the Hulk had caught sight of his zombie counterpart now, as evidenced by a mast-rattling roar that set the mammoth to trumpeting in response. Then Zombie Hulk reached the

Santa Maria's heavy anchor chain and used it to vault out of the water and onto the ship's deck to face his uninfected self.

"We can't let that happen," Zelma said in alarm. "They'll sink the ship for sure!"

"On it!" Elsa replied, taking her own running jump out of the sphere of Nico's flight spell, which the Runaway had repeated in a different language to get it to work again here in the more distant past. Like Deadpool, Elsa hurtled down toward the deck of the *Niña*, but she used a few swift, well-timed blasts from an enormous pistol to alter her course, steering herself closer to the bigger ship as she fell, the recoil from each successive shot bringing her nearer to her goal until she landed on its deck with a crash. A quick backward somersault, and she was up on her feet, gun and bloodgem blazing. The crew cowered away from her like they had from the battling Hulks, and Zelma didn't blame them. Elsa looked every bit as dangerous.

In the meantime, another zombie had made it through the portal, the one in the blue suit that Zelma recognized from their brief skirmish in the skies above Manhattan. At first she thought it was Captain America, but quickly realized that the suit's red and white accents weren't in the right places. The zombie was also wearing half of a silver metal mask over the upper portion of his face, leaving the lower portion and his blood-stained mouth free for biting.

She had no idea who he was, only that he was no magic-user, because she had at least a passing recognition of all the magic practitioners on Earth – Doc had insisted on it.

Which meant there was a good chance he didn't have any magical protections, either.

Zelma quickly raised both hands and performed the wave

release motion while she uttered the words of a binding spell. Performed correctly, the spell would call forth translucent red bonds of pure mystical energy that could not be shattered except by supernatural or superhuman means. As with most spells Doctor Strange had taught her, it did not need to rhyme to work, and a rough and fast incantation was often better than a more mellifluous one when it came to combat. However, many gods favored the latter and she had a few seconds, so she chose the more artful route.

"*May the infected foe now be held back*
By the Crimson Bands of Cyttorak!"

Instantly, scarlet lines of power streamed from her fingers to wrap themselves around the blue-suited zombie, enlarging as they went until they were the width of a beauty queen's sash, ten times as thick, and infinitely stronger. They detached from Zelma's hands and wound themselves around the struggling zombie until he was effectively encased from head to toe. He could do little more than wriggle.

That was one down. But while she'd been busy with him, three more had come through, and she was sure there were more on their heels.

"Nico!" she called. "A little help, please?"

Unlike the other witch with her persnickety staff, Zelma had no restrictions on casting the same spell multiple times, and she did just that, encasing two more zombies in ribbons of crimson magic while Nico said something and the liquified brains of the third came oozing out of its various cranial orifices.

Then Zelma had the brilliant idea to cocoon the portal itself in Cyttorak's bands. It wouldn't last long, she knew – the spell wasn't made to bar doors, only to imprison whatever came through them. But casting it should give the team some extra time, and glancing down at the ships where the twin Deadpools and Hulks still fought and Elsa's weapons were having little effect, Zelma knew they needed every last second they could get.

"OK, now let's go save our Deadpool and the Hulk, nab the other Deadpool, and get out of here!"

But as she was about to order Cloak to carry her down to the ships, she saw Nico hesitate.

"What is it? What's wrong?"

Nico pointed the donut end of her staff at the floating mammoth.

"If I want to cast anything more powerful than 'Brain be goo', I'm going to have to let the spell keeping him afloat expire."

"So do it."

Nico frowned at her.

"But he'll fall into the ocean! What if he drowns?"

"Mammoths can swim," Zelma replied. At least, she thought they could. "And anyway, with all of us working together to get rid of Zombie Hulk, even if it does start to flounder, we'll be back in time to give it CPR." How one did cardio-pulmonary resuscitation on a hirsute five-ton elephant was something they'd have to figure out if and when that time came.

The other witch still looked unsure, but she nodded.

"OK, but you're the one who has to break it to Deadpool if we wind up killing his pet."

"Happily," Zelma retorted. "Now can we please *go*? Those bands won't last long."

As if some sea god had heard Zelma's plea, the wind picked

up suddenly, pulling Cloak out behind her like a pennant and turning Nico's hair into a black froth. The smell of ocean brine it carried was strong, but the sudden malapropos vision of Coney Island it conjured was even stronger.

Nico's lips compressed into a thin, displeased line, and she released her spell, letting the mammoth plummet. Screams came from the various ships as the huge creature appeared in midair, having passed beyond the radius of Zelma's invisibility spell, but the poor animal's trumpeted terror easily drowned out that of the sailors. Even the two Hulks stopped fighting each other for a moment, which gave the witches an opening.

Zelma took it, beginning an incantation as she flew toward the *Santa Maria*. She knew neither Hulk could see her thanks to the invisibility spell and hoped to use that surprise to her advantage. She curled the fingers of her right hand into the Karana Mudra and flicked her wrist at the zombified Hulk.

"Bolts of Bedevilment
My foe now torment
Whilst Mists of Morpheus
His ire circumvent!"

Zelma knew that Hulk's change from mild-mannered Doctor Banner was most often triggered by anger, and she assumed the same to be true of Zombie Hulk, so her hope was that the bedeviling bolts would distract him long enough for a calming sleep spell to take effect, quelling that rage and reversing his transformation. Then, once he was in human form, it would be easy enough for Elsa, the uninfected Hulk himself, or even the ship's crew to finish him off.

It might have worked, too, if Fin Fang Foom had not chosen that precise moment to appear.

Rising up out of the water like a sea serpent of old, the alien monster resembled nothing so much as a green bipedal Chinese dragon.

And he was *huge*.

"Nico, can you take care of him? Nico?"

A laugh sounded from behind Zelma. She turned in annoyance to scold the other witch and remind her that none of this was a joke, or even remotely funny, but Nico wasn't there.

Morgan Le Fay was.

CHAPTER THIRTY-TWO

Nico wasn't as sure as Zelma was that mammoths could swim, so her first order of business was to make sure Max landed away from the ships and then did indeed surface after he splashed down in the Atlantic like a chunk of space debris. When his head bobbed up and he spouted water out of his trunk in confused rage, legs busy mammoth-paddling, Nico decided he was safe enough for now and turned to rejoin Zelma.

But several things had happened in that short span of time, and it took Nico a moment to process them all.

The first thing was the weird, anthropomorphized jade-colored sea dragon that was now harrying the *Santa Maria*, and which the armored Hulk had left off fighting Zombie Hulk to attack. That had left Elsa alone to defend the crew from the zombified Avenger, who knew an easy meal when he saw it.

The second thing was the scarlet bonds around the zombie portal starting to give way, a circumstance no doubt helped along by the third thing: the appearance of Morgan Le Fay.

The green-garbed Sorceress Supreme sat astride a non-anthropomorphized dragon the size of a large horse, its scales shining like brass in the sunlight, its wings like sheets of gold foil. Black smoke rose from its nostrils in inky tendrils as it eyed Nico hungrily.

"Going somewhere, witch?" Le Fay asked, which Nico took as her cue to do just that, narrowly avoiding a stream of fire the dragon aimed at her.

She used the Staff of One's inherent teleportation ability to relocate herself to the other side of the sea serpent, which was currently grappling with the armored Hulk and turning the ocean into an oversized wave pool.

She was out of sight of both her enemies and her allies for a few precious moments. She had to make the most of them.

As ever, the urge to run was strong, to save herself and let some deity or other sort out the rest. That was, after all, her MO – she was a Runaway. Not just a member of the team, but their leader, the best of them when it came to getting while the getting was good.

But she had lost that team. She had a new one now, in the form of Zelma and Elsa and even the infuriating Deadpool. Nico wasn't about to lose them, too.

Still, she couldn't save them alone. As powerful as the Staff of One made her, she wasn't going to be able to defeat Morgan Le Fay, Zombie Hulk, the sea serpent that she guessed might actually be the alien Fin Fang Foom Deadpool had mentioned, and the zombies who were starting to break through Zelma's portal barrier. Not on her own.

Nico didn't know exactly where they were over the Atlantic, but she knew Atlanteans had held sway in these waters for thousands of years. Surely there were some around who could help?

"Rise to the occasion!" she said, tapping the butt of her staff against her boot, a motion she knew was unnecessary but that somehow made her spells feel like they worked faster, or better.

But maybe not this time.

She had intended to summon any Atlanteans in the area to come to her and her teammates' aid. Belatedly, she remembered that prior to Namor's birth, most Atlantean-human interactions had been hostile. And Namor wouldn't be born for another five hundred years or so.

Well, crap.

Maybe they'd just ignore the call. That seemed preferable to them answering only to attack Columbus's crew, and probably her teammates and her, as well.

Definitely her. If Namor was any indicator, Atlanteans did not like to be ordered around.

Maybe this hadn't been such a good idea, after all.

But before Nico could think of a way to undo the spell, Fin Fang Foom, armored Hulk, and the robot-thingy that had been following him around like a hover-puppy all vanished. Nico could see all the ships now, and everything that was happening on them. Elsa was a whirlwind of fists, feet, and gunfire aboard the *Santa Maria* as she fought to keep Zombie Hulk away from the crew. The Deadpools had taken a timeout on fighting each other and were standing back-to-back on the deck of the *Niña*, fighting the zombies intermittently tumbling out of the portal that Zelma's fluctuating spell could no longer hold completely closed. Many of the crew of that ship were diving overboard and making for the *Pinta*, which thus far remained unmolested and whose captain was wisely using the rising wind to get out of Dodge. And Zelma was now facing off against Morgan Le Fay and her dragon, dodging blasts of fire and emerald bolts as she tried vainly to shield herself with seraphic energy.

And behind them all, Nico saw something more.

The sea had begun to churn and bubble, as if it were a watched pot that had gotten fed up and decided to boil anyway. And then a dozen tentacles or more burst forth from the tempestuous sea, as thick as redwood trunks and as slick and gray as new headstones.

Krakens.

She had released the krakens.

Good job, Nico.

Now what?

She wasn't sure if her spell just hadn't worked right – she might have used that same phrase before; it was hard to keep them all straight. Or maybe it had worked as intended, and the Atlanteans' response had been to send guard dogs in their stead. Whether to help or hinder didn't really matter at this point, since the creatures were about to swamp Columbus's fleet, making this entire trip back in time a moot point.

Nico had to rejoin the fight. But rushing in willy-nilly wasn't going to help anyone. She needed a plan. All three of her companions could use her help, but they were all also holding their own for the moment. Barely.

Not so Columbus's hapless crew.

The ships were merchant vessels that had been outfitted for a long ocean voyage, not for engaging with pirates on the high seas, let alone sea serpents and other things from the "Here Be Monsters" portion of the map. The men had swords, and a few had what looked like muskets or some other type of early rifle, but even modern-day firearms might have trouble handling a pair of krakens at once.

But maybe not modern-day magic.

Nico tried to remember back to her high school English classes and the mythology they studied there. She'd met actual gods since then, and knew a lot of the stories popularized by Edith Hamilton and other scholars were nothing more than that – stories. Even so, some of them had grains of truth beneath the pearlescence of fiction, and while she was pretty sure krakens were from Norse mythology, she seemed to recall a story wherein a Greek hero had defeated one, or at least something that had looked an awful lot like these bad boys did.

As she struggled to remember, Le Fay's dragon mount winged past in pursuit of a fleeing Zelma.

Perseus! That was it! It was all coming back to her now, though Nico realized what she was remembering was a blend of both movies and myths. In her memory, Perseus had been flying on Pegasus, sitting much as Le Fay was doing now on her golden drake's back. The hero had Medusa's decapitated head in a sack, and when the kraken had tried to attack his one true love, Andromeda, Perseus had withdrawn the head just enough to uncover its eyes, which it in turn had used to turn the sea creature to stone.

Well, if it worked in the movies…

"I'll take bad movie plots for a thousand!" she said, pointing her staff at the krakens.

While she'd been dithering, some of the zombies had decided the krakens looked like easier pickings than the armed crewmen and had flown or swum over to the creatures and begun to attack them. Including Zombie Hulk, whose biggest challenge had disappeared when Armored Hulk, his hovering robot, and Fin Fang Foom had vanished, presumably back to their correct timeline, whenever that was. So when Nico's spell started to take effect, they were caught in it as well.

The transformation began at the tips of one of the monster's tentacles, turning them from the glossy gray of a deep-sea denizen to the flatter hue of worn statuary. One caped zombie had been ensnared by a tentacle right before Nico's casting, and she watched with interest as it first stiffened, then broke in two as the kraken tried fruitlessly to shake off the spell's petrifying effects.

A few other zombies were caught in similar situations, one turned to stone as it gorged itself on the once-soft tissue of the kraken's eye, another petrified as it was being dropped into that same creature's mouth. Zombie Hulk was in the middle of excavating his way through the sea creature's side, stuffing huge handfuls of what looked like whale blubber in his mouth as he went. The petrification process apparently shocked his system enough to trigger the transformation back to Zombie Bruce Banner, who quickly became the Statue Formerly Known As Zombie Bruce Banner. Sadly, most of the zombies who'd opted to try for swim-up or fly-by fast food caught on to what was happening quickly enough to extricate themselves before joining their stoned companions, but any of them the spell took out were an added bonus.

Some were caught up in the huge waves that resulted as the stoned kraken was dragged under the surface by its own weight, but Nico didn't suppose it was possible that they could actually drown.

The crewmen could, though, she realized, as white-capped crests slammed down onto the wooden decks of the nearest ships, washing several unlucky sailors into the sea. Since she couldn't cast another spell until this one was complete without jeopardizing its permanence, Nico used her staff to skim along the water and grab sailors as they surfaced, dumping them onto whichever ship was closest before going back for others.

One sailor had the misfortune of coming up right beside one of the swimming zombie Avengers – the original Hawkeye, Nico thought, though it was hard to tell with half his face rotted away and his hair plastered to what was left of it. She swooped in just as the zombified archer had latched onto one of the sailor's arms and was about to take a bite out of it, kicking out with her heavy hiking boot as she dug her fingers into the collar of the endangered man's shirt and heaved him up and back. She felt a momentary resistance which quickly gave way before she was free, and a glance downward revealed an angry Hawkeye now missing several teeth and part of his jaw as he shouted something unintelligible and lunged futilely after her.

That still left one kraken, but she thought she had an idea of how she might deal with it.

Nico pointed her staff at the enraged sea creature who'd seen its fellow pulled under by a power it didn't comprehend and now wanted to enact its vengeance on the insignificant little krill that were still crawling all over it, and on the ships that had carried them here, into waters where they did not belong.

"You sank my battleship!" Nico shouted.

It was only then that Nico realized that the kraken had

snatched Elsa off the deck of the *Santa Maria* and was even now dangling the trapped woman over the gaping abyss that masqueraded as its mouth.

Bollocks.

Nico was pretty sure that was the word Elsa would use to describe this situation. She didn't know if she had time to redirect the spell, but given that the kraken now had another tentacle wrapped around the mizzenmast of the *Santa Maria*, threatening to pull the ship and its crew under, she doubted she should try. Instead, she used the staff to teleport over to Elsa. The monster hunter was being treated to the full boa constrictor experience by the kraken, with her bloodhand trapped against her side in such a way that she couldn't use it without blasting a hole in her own gut. Which, from the furious look on her face, she might be contemplating doing.

Nico saved her the trouble.

If she tried to cast another big spell right now, she risked syphoning off too much energy from her torpedo spell, but she thought she could manage something small.

"Carpal tunnel!"

Elsa's face registered surprise as the wrist of her bloodhand moved of its own volition, rotating impossibly to face outward so that it was no longer pressed against her, but against the kraken's sea-slimed tentacle.

Elsa didn't need to be told what to do next.

The monster hunter's bloodgem burned through the creature's thick appendage like a hot knife through butter, causing the thing to screech in a way Nico didn't think should be possible for something that lived in the ocean depths. As it did, the tentacle holding Elsa loosened and detached from the rest of the kraken's body, falling into the thing's open beak-like mouth as it did so. Shrill screams of rage turned to gurgles as the kraken momentarily choked on itself.

Nico reached out to catch Elsa by her arm before the other woman could follow the tentacle into the kraken's maw, but was horrified when the monster hunter simply used her as a fulcrum, swinging her body forward and then wrenching her arm away at the last moment.

"Elsa!" she cried, fear skyrocketing her heart from her chest to her throat as she tried vainly to reach out and recapture the other woman's hand. But Elsa just laughed and waved, then spun gracefully in the air and came down, stilettos first, right in the sea beast's closest eye.

And kept going, disappearing completely into the gelatinous orb, as if it had swallowed her in a way its wider throat had been unable to.

"Elsa, *no!*"

Nico tried to go after her, but she was thrown violently backward as her spell finally took effect and the second kraken exploded up and outward with a concussive boom. Nico fetched up against the railing of the *Santa Maria* and was pulled aboard by unseen hands. Then spun about roughly to face a crewman who was yelling at her, speaking in his native tongue so quickly that she couldn't tell if it was Spanish or Italian or something else entirely. At any rate, she couldn't understand a word and she yanked away from him in annoyance. She turned back toward the site of the explosion, just as a rain of bloody pink blobs began to fall in loud plops, covering the ships, their crews, and anything else that moved on them, as well as the ocean surface.

A surface that remained terrifyingly still once the fleshy rain had abated.

She scanned the water for what seemed like hours, waiting for a familiar red head to emerge. Hoping. Even praying, though she hardly remembered how to do that and it just came out in broken whispers.

"Please, please, please, please, please."

Finally, though, she fell to her knees on the slick deck, her head bowed. She was sick to her soul.

Elsa was gone.

And Nico had killed her.

CHAPTER THIRTY-THREE

Zelma was throwing everything she could think of at Le Fay and having all the effect of a swarms of gnats – bothersome, but ultimately insignificant. If not for Cloak, she would already have been toasted like a marshmallow by Le Fay's dragon. As it was, the left sleeve of her favorite sweater was irreparably singed. New fashion rule: Never wear white after Apocalypse Day.

She didn't understand why Le Fay was holding back until she saw one of the Zombie Avengers with the power of flight take a run at the Sorceress Supreme. Zelma thought it was Johnny Storm or maybe Angelica Jones, the hero known as Firestar. All she could really see was a trail of flame as the zombie soared through a blue sky that was rapidly filling with storm clouds. The reason for the weather change became apparent when the sorceress drew electricity from the clouds to unleash a powerful bolt that stunned the zombie, knocking it out of the air. As it tumbled toward the ocean, Le Fay followed up with a Demon Claws of Denak spell. Ugly yellow talons trailing arms that ended in smoke rushed at the zombie's inert form, tearing it to literal shreds before it could hit the water.

On some level, Zelma thought that she should maybe be insulted that the Sorceress Supreme didn't view her as a more serious threat, but if it meant the woman was taking out zombies that Zelma would otherwise have to deal with herself... well, she wasn't going to look a gift nag in the mouth.

Besides, she was more than busy enough trying to juggle both throwing spells at Le Fay and renewing the Crimson Bands of Cyttorak around Deadpool Two's time portal to minimize the number of zombies getting through it. It was only a matter of time before she botched one or the other. Or maybe she'd really outperform expectations and fail at both simultaneously.

But she couldn't spare energy for self-deprecation right now, because Le Fay had the librarian back in her sights, and it looked like she was charging up to cast another electrical spell Zelma's way.

Zelma struck first. While she'd been keeping one eye on Le Fay and one on the portal, she'd been trying to keep the third on her companions, to make sure they were holding their ground and not endangering the timeline any more than could be helped. Not that she was in a position to do anything in either of those situations, considering her own, but she could no more keep from checking on them than she could keep from seeing the magical world once Doc had opened her eyes to it. She might only be a Sorcerer Supreme's apprentice, but she took her responsibility to her team and her timeline as seriously as if it were she wearing the Eye of Agamotto, and not Le Fay.

She had seen Nico turn one of the krakens to stone and had immediately understood the phrase the other witch had used to cast her spell. She and the Runaway were close in age and had many of the same cultural touchstones, including bad movie remakes of fantasy classics.

So, taking a page from Nico's "Perseus v. Kraken" scene, Zelma decided to do what the sea creature in the movie had been too stupid to do – take out the hero's mount.

She didn't like the idea of hurting an animal, but it *was* an evil sorceress's dragon and it *had* ruined her favorite sweater, so she wasn't exactly overwhelmed with sympathy for its plight. Keeping that firmly in mind, she sent two bedeviling bolts at Le Fay, the first designed to make the sorceress dodge, taking her dragon straight into the path of the second.

To Zelma's surprise, the ploy worked, probably because Le Fay was too arrogant to believe an attack could possibly be aimed at anyone *other* than her. Whatever the reason, the sorceress steered her dragon away from one bolt and into the other, where it ripped through the gold foil-like membrane of the dragon's left wing.

The thing screamed, a sound of pure animal agony Zelma would hear in her nightmares for the rest of forever, and then began to lose altitude, flapping furiously with its right wing to try to make up the deficit in its carrying capacity.

Zelma didn't think the creature could do it. Le Fay might well have had a spell up her bell sleeve that could repair the damage the librarian had done, but moments after Zelma's bolt struck home, a large boom sounded behind them, and a concussion wave knocked the Sorceress Supreme from her mount and sent Zelma tumbling.

Cloak righted Zelma almost immediately, and she knew she had mere seconds in which to act. So instead of turning to determine the source of the explosion – one of the Deadpools was the odds-on favorite, with Nico coming in a close second – she formed the Tarjani Mudra with her left hand and moved it in a clockwise motion, summoning a shining golden Conjurer's Cone beneath Le Fay's plummeting form. It was the same spell Doc had used to get rid of Spider-Man, that had snared Deadpool instead.

Normally, the spell would send its subject to another dimension, but she didn't want to start opening up dimensional portals with Zombie Avengers lurking around, even assuming she could find one that was still open for business after Doc's warning had gone out to the other Sorcerer Supremes. She imagined that was the reason Deadpool had wound up in Boston and not Nightmare's Realm when he'd gotten caught in Doc's spell. Because Doctor Strange had sensed even then that interdimensional travel was too dangerous in the face of what was still, at that time, an unknown threat.

So Zelma opened one up into the next best place she could think of in the timeline of 1492 Earth that might hold Morgan Le Fay.

The torture chamber of Tomás de Torquemada, Grand Inquisitor of the Spanish Inquisition.

Most people believed that the use of the iron maiden as a torture device in the Middle Ages was a myth, and that the monstrosity itself did not actually come into existence until the 1800s. However, documents unearthed in a fifth-century fort during the construction of a superstore indicated that Torquemada had almost certainly used that device, along with other horrible creations like the Judas Chair and the ole reliable rack. Doc had confirmed it, though he never told her how he knew, and she'd wondered ever since her first trip to the Bleecker Street basement if the one she'd seen there might once have belonged to the famous Inquisitor.

Zelma wasn't interested in the torture device because of what it could do – enclose someone in an upright coffin while simultaneously impaling them with spikes – but rather in the metal it was made from.

The maiden was constructed of iron. Morgan Le Fay was half-Faerie, and therefore vulnerable to iron. An iron maiden seemed like the ideal holding cell for the sorceress, though sadly Zelma did not believe that the device would succeed in killing her.

Zelma had never tried to direct a Conjurer's Cone to such a specific location before. For that matter, she'd never opened one to anywhere other than the Dark Dimension, and that had been under both Doc and Clea's supervision.

And Morgan Le Fay was a sorceress of far greater knowledge and power than Zelma, as evidenced by the Eye of Agamotto that she now wore about her neck. The only reason Zelma was even attempting this spell was because the sorceress had been stunned by the explosion's concussive blast. Otherwise, she could brush Zelma's magic off like dryer lint, or maybe the slightly more stubborn pet hair. She might be able to do that anyway.

But maybe not if Zelma had some help.

Zelma tore her backpack off and rooted around in it quickly until she found the Scrolls of Watoomb, another little gem she'd borrowed from the Sanctum Machina before she and Nico had first set off on this journey. While Watoomb was a Principality most famous and usually invoked for his control

of the wind, use of his scrolls could also increase the power of
the sorcerer – or sorceress – utilizing them.

"By the power of Weird Watoomb
And the Winds at his command
And by the Seven Rings of Raggadorr
And Cyttorak's Crimson Bands
Into the iron maid's embrace
I do thee now remand!"

A sudden howling wind arose and quickly coalesced into a
single-serving tornado, which promptly engulfed Le Fay. Then
it plunged into the gateway Zelma had opened, sucking the
Sorceress Supreme inside itself in a leprechaun swirl of green
and gold. After, the opening itself shrank to a tiny pinpoint of
light and then disappeared with an audible pop.

"Ha! No one expects the Spanish Inquisition!"

Zelma did feel a small twinge of guilt for sending a fellow
magic-user into the hands of the Inquisition, no matter how
foul that user or her magic. But Morgan Le Fay could handle a
legion of Torquemadas, so the twinge was gone again almost
as soon as Zelma felt it.

The usurping Sorceress Supreme's dragon, meanwhile,
had splashed down in the ocean not far from the *Pinta*, and
disappeared under the water. Zelma watched for a moment,
but it did not resurface. Apparently fire dragons, unlike
mammoths, didn't know how to swim.

Then she turned her attention back to the zombie's
timestream portal, strengthening her Cyttorak spell just as a
half-eaten hand was reaching through the thinning. The bands
glowed with renewed energy, slicing the exposed fingers clean
off. The hewn digits burned to cinders before landing on

the surface of the ocean as flakes of ash which were quickly absorbed into the vastness of the sea.

Only then did Zelma turn to seek out the source of the fortuitous eruption.

Bits of pink goop were still splattering onto the decks of Columbus's fleet and the surrounding ocean, but there was no sign of the second kraken. Zelma quickly spotted Max calmly treading water off the port bow of the *Niña* while the two Deadpools stood back-to-back on that ship's deck inside a hip-high wall of bodies. Zelma still couldn't tell them apart, especially since they were both wearing maniacal grins apparent even through their masks.

Nico, meanwhile, was kneeling on the momentarily zombie-free deck of the *Santa Maria* while one of the crewmen yelled at her, using his hands and gesturing expressively. From his tricorn-y hat, Zelma guessed that it must be Christopher Columbus himself. No regular sailor would wear anything so foppish.

Then she frowned.

There was no sign of Elsa.

Wait. Was *that* why Nico was on her knees, head bowed and, Zelma now saw, shoulders heaving? Had the explosion been Elsa's doing?

Had it been the monster hunter's swan song?

Zelma landed on the deck near Nico, startling Columbus, who reflexively made the sign of the cross before beginning a fresh tirade, this one aimed at her.

"*¡Silencio!*" she snapped at him in Spanish, adding what she thought was the same thing in Italian, for good measure. "*Silenzio!*" Then she put her finger across her lips in the universal symbol for quiet and glared at him, just in case she'd somehow fouled up the word beyond his recognition in both languages.

She turned her attention to Nico, placing a hand on the other witch's shoulder.

"Nico?" she ventured, her voice soft and sympathetic. Zelma had a pretty good idea how the Runaway had come to feel about Elsa, but mourning would have to wait. They still had to reset the timeline, and maybe they'd have to do it again to account for losing Elsa here, instead of back in the twenty-first century, when she was supposed to have technically died and become a zombie.

Gods, but Zelma hated time-travel paradoxes.

She hated seeing people she cared about hurt even more. But it seemed like all she was being called upon to do lately was to either see them hurting or hurt them herself, all in the name of doing "the right thing". Which sometimes didn't feel right at all.

"Nico?" she asked again, louder. Still no answer.

Zelma glanced up at Deadpool Two's portal. As she feared, the Cyttorak spell she'd cast was once again beginning to weaken, and so was she. She'd cast so many spells in this battle that she was surprised she was still standing. She knew she'd probably pay for it later, but right now, all she could do was keep pushing.

But maybe she could get some help.

If Nico was too shell-shocked to be of any assistance, perhaps her staff would work in her stead. Zelma wasn't sure if the Staff of One could be controlled by anyone outside of the Minoru bloodline. All she really knew about it was that Nico wielded it, as her mother had before her. But it was worth a shot.

She bent down and picked up the length of metal. It felt cold and inert in her hands. Dead.

That didn't bode well, but all she could do was try.

She turned toward the *Niña* and pointed the staff at the other ship.

"Deadpools!"

Nothing happened.

"Please?"

Still nothing.

Then she remembered the exchange between Nico and Deadpool in the Sanctum Sanctorum library, how he'd held a blade to the Runaway's throat and she'd just leaned into it, cool as a cucumber.

The Staff likes blood.

Fair enough. Everything needed fuel. Zelma would give it some. She was bleeding from a dozen or more places where Cloak hadn't dodged quite fast enough and Le Fay's spells had grazed her. She picked a spot that still oozed a bit on her jaw and stuck her finger in it, wincing as she reopened the fresh scab to get enough blood to smear on the staff's shaft.

"Fake Spideys!" she said, keeping in mind that Nico had said she couldn't cast the same spell with the same wording more than once. But nothing happened. Apparently, Zelma's blood wasn't to the staff's liking.

It probably had to be Nico's.

Zelma turned back to her friend, whose sobs seemed to be quieting. The upper back of Nico's dress was torn, with pale skin showing beneath. Skin that had been scraped raw and still had bits of wood embedded in it.

They would have to do something about that before the

wound got infected. But first Zelma needed to do the other thing she seemed to be best at: making things worse. With a whispered apology, she bent down and stuck her hand through the tear in the fabric, running her palm along Nico's scored flesh, pressing down so that the wound would bleed more. The other witch didn't react.

Zelma withdrew her hand, which was now red with Nico's blood, and placed it around the staff. For the first time, she thought she felt some energy within it.

"The two Wade Wilsons!"

This time, the two Deadpools rose from the deck of the *Niña*, lifted as if by an invisible hand. They hovered there for a moment, then were hurled at the *Santa Maria* with enough force that Zelma knew the staff was *not* happy about her commandeering its use, and likely wouldn't allow it to happen again.

The red-suited mercenaries hit the deck in twin somersaults, somehow coming up standing back-to-back again, each with their katana still bared, though for the moment, there was no one to use them on.

"It's time to go," Zelma said tiredly, leaning on the Staff of One, which seemed willing to entertain that affront, at least.

One of the Deadpools looked around quickly and asked, "Where's Elsa?"

"Gone," Zelma replied, abruptly having to blink back tears.

"What do you mean, 'gone'?" the other Deadpool demanded.

Nico finally raised her head.

"She means 'gone'. As in dead. Elsa was inside that kraken when it blew."

For long moments, there was no sound other than the

sloshing of waves against the side of the ship and the voices of the men on the other two vessels.

Then the first Deadpool spoke again.

"No," he said quietly. And then both Deadpools took off at a dead run toward the ship's railing, placing their blades in their teeth as they did so, and executed perfectly synchronized dives overboard and into the frothy pink ocean below.

Nico grabbed Zelma's arm to steady herself as she climbed to her feet and then both women hurried over to the railing, along with most of the crew.

"What are they doing?" Nico asked, her voice still thick with unshed tears. But she had wiped her face now and was no longer actively sobbing, so that was a plus.

"If I had to guess," Zelma replied, "I'd say either playing fools or playing heroes. Depends on what they come back up with. *If* they come back up."

This stop on the time-loop trail had gone so far sideways Zelma didn't even think it was in the same dimension as the original plan anymore. At this point, she was just waiting for two Deadpool corpses to come bobbing to the surface, making a complete snafu of this timeline. She didn't know what she and Nico would do then. Go back to the beginning and start all over again? Give up and go back to Le Fay's timeline? Bounce along the timestream until they found a nice, secluded era with sandy beaches and sunshine where they could live out the rest of their lifetimes knowing they'd failed everyone either of them had ever loved?

Maybe they should just jump in after the Deadpools and end it all now to save themselves some heartache.

"You… You don't suppose she could still be alive, do you?"

Nico asked, her voice smaller and meeker than Zelma had ever heard it.

"Can she breathe underwater?" the librarian asked. She wasn't being snide; she truly didn't know. Anything was possible with Elsa.

"Not to my knowledge."

Zelma didn't want to be cruel, but she also didn't want to lie and give the other witch false hope, so she chose not to respond. Which she supposed was still an answer.

A splash sounded not far off the ship's port side, and two masked red heads popped up out of the water. But no red-haired one.

Nico sagged against Zelma, who caught her and bore her weight as best she could as the Deadpools made their way back to the ship without the prize they'd gone diving for. Several crew members helped them up as they climbed aboard, sodden and silent.

It was that at last, more than anything, that really brought it home for Zelma. If you had two Deadpools on your ship and they were both speechless, then you knew it had to be true.

Elsa Bloodstone, monster hunter extraordinaire, was dead.

CHAPTER THIRTY-FOUR

Nico could barely stand. She clung to Zelma's oversized sweater like it was a cable knit life preserver.

Get it together, Minoru.

This wasn't the first time she'd lost a teammate, or even the first time she'd been responsible, directly or indirectly, for a team member's death.

She had a quick flashback of the nightmare that had been the Murderworld-slash-Arena where she and fifteen other super-powered teens had been kidnapped and forced by the ridiculous villain Arcade to fight each other. She'd almost killed Elsa's brother during that so-called "tournament". The irony of her killing Elsa now, when Nico was under no one's control but her own, was not lost on her.

Of course, she hadn't meant to *kill* Elsa. The monster hunter had just picked the wrong monster to hunt, at the wrong time. But that was exactly zero consolation to Nico. She knew Elsa would've had no problems fighting her way back out of the kraken's brain, or wherever she'd wound up after spearing herself through its eye, if Nico's spell hadn't blown the creature to smithereens with Elsa still inside it.

Wrong monster, wrong time, wrong spell, wrong Nico.

Nico knew she was spiraling into an abyss of guilt and grief, but she didn't quite know how to stop herself. Her mother had threatened her with therapy once – in retrospect, maybe that wouldn't have been such a bad thing. At least then she'd presumably have had some tools to fight back against the black wave of despair that promised to engulf her now.

Though she wasn't sure why she should bother. It seemed like no matter how hard she tried to hold things together, everything always fell apart in the end. Someone always got hurt, whether she meant for them to or not.

She should just let the waves take her, let them wash her out into the wine-dark sea, or whatever Homer had called it.

"Nico," a voice said, but it came as if from a long distance, or perhaps through a fog. Nico could barely hear it over the wail of anguish that sounded much nearer to her, almost in her ear. It took her a moment to realize that she was the one wailing, even though she didn't think there was any noise coming out of her mouth.

"Nico!" the voice repeated, louder and firmer this time, and she felt herself being shaken. Suddenly, she snapped painfully back to full awareness, to the here and awful now.

To her surprise, it was one of the Deadpools who was shaking her. He let go of her and stepped back when he saw recognition flicker across her face.

Once he did, she saw that she held the Staff of One in her hand, though she had no memory of grabbing it. Beyond that, she saw the ocean, now a deep, burgundy color, heaving as if in the throes of a terrible storm, though the sky had long since cleared of clouds. Biting wind turned the strands of her hair into briny whips that stung her face. The deck below her feet rocked to and fro. All around her, sailors scampered and shouted, trying to secure the ship, its cargo, and themselves. Zelma had pulled a small statue of a carved wave out of her backpack and was apparently trying to summon a water elemental with it, to no avail. It took the witch a moment to realize that Zelma was trying to calm the waves, not create them.

But if this wasn't Zelma's work... had *Nico* done this? Just by thinking of it with the staff in her hand?

When she and the other Runaways had traveled back in time to 1907, Nico had met a powerful magic-user called the Witchbreaker who had claimed to be her great-grandmother. The woman had promised to teach her time-displaced descendant how to withstand more pain, so that Nico could in turn use more magic, and do it better.

The Witchbreaker had made good on her promise, and when Nico had returned with the others to her correct time, there had indeed been a marked increase in her ability to wield the Staff of One. She no longer needed to verbalize spells to levitate or teleport herself, and she hadn't truly needed blood to trigger her spells since then, even when she did need to speak them aloud, though the letting of blood still seemed to enhance their power and effects.

In the past, it had been her pain, physical or mental, that had been the catalyst that allowed her to access the staff's power, the latter in the form of unwelcome, often guilt-ridden memories. And she couldn't imagine anything more painful than losing both Karolina and Elsa in a matter of weeks.

Still, that would be the last time she quoted Homer, even in her own head, even if she wasn't heartbroken and grieving, if she would ever not be those things again.

"Red sky at night, sailor's delight!"

Immediately, the waves calmed, and the sanguine hue of the water faded, seeming to bleed away into the horizon, giving the sky a faint tint of sunset, though it was still the middle of the afternoon.

Zelma moved to stand beside her, trying surreptitiously to stretch her sweater back into shape.

"We need to go now," she said quietly.

"I know," Nico replied, though the words felt like a betrayal.

"We'll come back for her," Zelma said. "I promise you. We'll have to, to fix the changes to the timeline losing her will have created. But first we have to get Max back to his proper time, to undo whatever happened to make Morgan Sorceress Supreme."

As though he'd heard his name being mentioned, Max trumpeted loudly from the other side of the ship just as one of the sailors up in the rigging cried out.

Something came catapulting over the railing, taking out part of the wood as it sailed over and crashed to the deck, then rolled to a stop a few feet away from where Nico and the others stood.

It was one of the kraken's severed tentacles. Somehow, impossibly, it was still clutching Elsa's body.

Or, more accurately, her corpse.

"Good *boy*, Max!" one of the Deadpools crowed.

Nico rushed over to the monster hunter, falling to her knees at the other woman's side. The Deadpools beat her there, and were already extricating the monster hunter from the kraken's death grip. When they had freed her and stepped away, Nico rolled Elsa onto her back and put her ear to the other woman's chest.

Nothing.

"Zee, help me!"

The librarian hurried over to her, rummaging in her backpack again. As she knelt on the other side of Elsa's body, she pulled out a scroll, its yellow paper cracked and flaking.

"The Scroll of Melsalam," she said, as if that was supposed to mean something to Nico. "It contains the Terranotti Healing Spell. You know, heals you, removes debuffs, sort of like in a video ga–"

"I don't care!" Nico cried impatiently. "Just use it!"

Zelma did, reading the spell off the rolled paper in a language that sounded almost familiar until Nico tried to listen harder, at which point it became gibberish.

And it might as well have been gibberish, too, for all the good it seemed to do.

"I'm really sorry, Nico," Zelma said, her face puckered and contrite. "If it was going to work, it should have been instantaneous."

Nico didn't need to hear anything else.

"I need you to do the breathing while I do compressions," she said, quickly opening Elsa's mouth and using her finger to sweep for any foreign objects. Then she put her hands together on the monster hunter's chest and began CPR.

The two witches continued that way for several minutes while the Deadpools and Columbus and his crew looked on, but Elsa continued to lie there, not breathing, heart not beating.

Not getting oxygen to her brain. Nico knew that, with time, the bloodstone could heal most wounds Elsa received, and her regenerative abilities were almost on par with Deadpool's. But could either of them come back from brain damage? Deadpool seemed to be an argument against that happening.

"Use your staff," Zelma suggested.

"I can't resurrect her," Nico snapped. She'd tried that before. It didn't end well.

"Not that. To restart her heart. With magic, since we can't do it manually."

Nico blinked. That… might actually work.

She picked the staff back up from the deck where she'd left it while she did compressions, and held its circle against Elsa's chest.

She waved everyone away.

"Stand clear!" she ordered. Then, focusing on the staff, she said, "Magically enhanced defibrillation!"

Elsa's back arched as energy coursed through her body. Nico knew that, while hospital television dramas liked to use defibrillation when a patient flatlined, it couldn't actually restart someone's heart. And when a defibrillator *was* used, it seldom made the patient convulse as was typically scripted.

But Nico wasn't using any old automated external defibrillator. She was using the Staff of One, and that could do things a real AED couldn't.

She hoped.

But when Elsa's body flopped back onto the deck and Nico moved the staff to listen for a heartbeat again, that hope started to crumble.

Still nothing.

"That's not what you need to jumpstart," a Deadpool said suddenly.

"That's *right!*" the other one chimed in, nodding and pounding the first on the back like he'd just said something brilliant. Maybe he had, but Nico needed a little clarification.

"What, then?" she asked impatiently.

"Her bloodgem!" the two mercenaries crowed in tandem, which, if she hadn't been in the midst of trying to catch Elsa before she crossed the river Styx, probably would have freaked Nico right the hell out.

Unsettling as the delivery might be, the idea itself was a good one. Besides, it wasn't as if Nico could cast the defibrillator spell again. She had no idea how to say that word in any other language.

Elsa's bloodgem was a much smaller target than her heart, though, so instead of laying part of the staff's circular end on it, Nico placed the balled portion of the staff that connected the circle and shaft over the dull, lifeless stone on Elsa's hand. She prayed to whoever might listen that this spell would work. It *had* to.

"Wait!" Zelma said suddenly, jarring Nico out of the "get 'er done" zone, much to the Runaway's annoyance.

"What now?" she asked, more harshly than was warranted. But Elsa was slipping further away from her every moment, so she was hardly in the mood to be polite.

Zelma was digging in her pack again. This time, she fished out a crystal skull.

"This is the Crystal of Kadavus. I grabbed it when I was ransacking Doc's Mystic Forge. It's supposed to help focus cosmic energies to jumpstart other arcane items. Usually under the light of a full moon over the course of two nights. Obviously, we don't have that kind of time, but the moon is in its waxing gibbous phase; you can just see it beginning to rise. It's not perfect, but it might still help."

Zelma's healing spell scroll had been a flop, so Nico didn't hold out much hope for this little trinket, either, but she took the proffered artifact, anyway. It couldn't hurt, and just might help.

She placed the grinning crystalline cranium on Elsa's hand next to the ball of her staff.

"Give it some juice!"

Nico could feel the energy coursing from the staff this time, almost as if the bloodgem were draining it. Which she supposed it was, considering. She thought she felt some warmth from Zelma's skull, as well, but that could just be wishful thinking. She wondered how much power it would require to reawaken the bloodgem, if even the crystal and the staff together would be enough, and decided maybe the staff could use some more reinforcement.

While she held the staff and skull against Elsa's hand with her own normal hand, Nico used her witch hand to gouge her metal fingers into an exposed part of her thigh where her tights had been torn. She dug her witch fingers in hard enough to break the skin, drawing blood and tearing into the muscle beneath, and then smeared her entire silvery hand with the dark red fluid. She placed her bloodied witch hand on top of her flesh hand, so they were both pressed against Elsa's, with the staff's ball and the Crystal of Kadavus sandwiched between them.

The flow of power stopped abruptly. Nico detected the faint scent of ozone, almost like an overloaded circuit. Elsa's hand grew hot beneath hers, but before Nico could pull them away, a beam of titian light exploded out from the bloodgem, sending Nico sprawling and tearing a hole through one of the *Santa Maria*'s sails.

Elsa took in a huge, gasping breath and her blue eyes shot open. She sat up suddenly, eyes wild, bloodstone primed for another attack. Then she seemed to realize where she was. Her gaze fell on Nico, lying supine a few feet away where Elsa's blast had thrown her, arms outflung, Staff of One another foot or so beyond, Crystal of Kadavus nowhere to be seen. Elsa's eyes widened with alarm and she hurried over to kneel by Nico's side, giving the witch a quick onceover. Seemingly satisfied that she wasn't in immediate danger of expiring, Elsa held out her hand to help Nico up into a sitting position.

"Thanks for bringing me back," Elsa said softly.

Nico felt her eyes filling with hot, stinging tears as emotions roiled within her, warring for supremacy. Fear, relief, gratitude.

"Elsa, I–" she began, but Elsa put her fingers against Nico's lips, and they were so blessedly warm with life that the witch's tears almost spilled over.

"Shh," Elsa said. "You're a right ledge for bringing me back, but let's not lose the plot just yet, hmm? Still got work to do."

Elsa clambered to her feet and helped the still-wobbly witch to stand, then reached to retrieve her staff. She made a face when she handed it over to Nico.

"Sorry, luv."

The balled portion of the staff separating the part Zelma like to call the donut from the shaft was half gone. Looking at it more closely, Nico saw that the metal had been sheared through cleanly. But the staff had been through worse and still worked; she had no reason to believe it would be any different now.

One of the Deadpools gave a low whistle.

"Geez, Ellie!" he exclaimed. "You blew her ball off!"

The women looked at him agog, and Nico couldn't help herself. She snorted. It was funny.

"Someone had to say it," the punster Deadpool said, giving a little half-shrug to go along with his half-smile. The other Deadpool nodded in agreement.

"Anyhoo," Elsa said loudly, speaking over them while shaking her head and rolling her eyes. Her wits, at least, seemed none the worse for wear, especially considering she'd been clinically dead for more minutes than Nico wanted to think about.

The monster hunter turned to Zelma, surveying the collateral damage of their "repair job" with a critical eye. "Seems like we're about finished here, no?"

Zelma's answer came in the form of a blue nimbus surrounding one of the Deadpools.

"Yup. Let me just separate our Deadpool out and then, after we get any dawdlers back in the timestream where they belong and rescue Max from becoming a hairy raisin, I think we can call it a wrap. The Crystal of Kadavus will just have to be a write-off."

Then the apprentice glanced over at Nico. Behind the thick lenses of Zelma's glasses, Nico could see dark circles underscoring her eyes, and her nose was set in a permanent squinch of stress. She looked haggard. Using so much mystic energy in such a short period of time must be taking an incredible toll on the other witch, who did not have a spell-casting staff to rely on.

"Can you round up any leftover zombies while I reopen their portal?" Zelma asked. Then she paused, head tilted to the side as she considered something. "We should probably get rid of any of their bodies, too. Body parts, whatever. What's the phrase outdoorsy people are always using? Oh, yeah – 'leave no trace'. We should probably do that. To the extent possible, anyway."

That was when Nico noticed that the scarlet ribbons of energy encasing the opening to Deadpool Two's timestream were beginning to shred again. Zelma had been maintaining that spell all this time, along with all the others she'd been casting; it was no wonder she looked so exhausted.

The Runaway nodded in response. Deciding on a workable phrase, she said, "Monkeys back in the barrel!" and she tapped her staff against the wooden deck with a metallic clang.

Instantly, the few remaining zombified supers still harrying the crews of the *Niña* and *Pinta* rose in the air, imprisoned in barrels formed of pure light, along with zombie bodies and body parts from not only those two ships, but the *Santa Maria* and the surrounding ocean, as well. Max, who'd apparently been busy liberating some of those parts from their hapless owners, trumpeted in displeasure.

"Don't worry," Deadpool One called down to the mammoth from the deck of the *Santa Maria*. "We'll get you some more bath toys when we get back home!"

Once Zelma had dismissed the Crimson Bands of Cyttorak, Nico sent the glowing barrels with their "monkeys" zooming back into the timestream, and Zelma finished up by sling-shotting a protesting Deadpool Two in after them. As before, as soon as he was through the portal, it disappeared.

Marvel Zombies

Zelma sighed wearily.

"I don't suppose you've got a 'Forget This Ever Happened' spell you haven't used yet?" she asked Nico, inclining her head toward the crewman with the dorky hat. "Better if they only remember a sea serpent or kraken attacking. I know a couple, but honestly, I need a minute. I'm so tired, I can hardly think straight."

Nico understood that. She'd seldom called on the staff's powers so frequently in such a short period of time, and she was experiencing the effects of that overreach herself. Every muscle in her body ached and she had a headache that, left untreated, might produce a Greek goddess. But even as drained as she felt, she was still in much better shape than Zelma.

"I got you," she said. She had just the thing. She bit her lip hard enough to draw blood and planted a crimson kiss on the Staff of One's metal circle. "Confucius says, 'I see and I forget.'"

"That's not exactly what Confucius said," Elsa pointed out with a raised eyebrow as the crewmen around them began to blink and shake their heads, as if awakening groggy from an afternoon nap or a night of too much carousing.

"They don't know that," Nico replied, shrugging. "And if they do, they won't remember it."

Zelma shot her a weary smile.

"Thanks, Nico."

Then the librarian took a deep breath and stood up straight, a determined expression on her face as she looked at the others.

"Next stop, Bedrock."

CHAPTER THIRTY-FIVE

It wasn't Bedrock, exactly. Zelma wasn't sure what it was, but it certainly wasn't a technicolor Hanna-Barbera cartoon with cavemen who worked in quarries and ran around in foot-operated cars. But it wasn't exactly the Stone Age that National Geographic had primed her to expect, either.

For one thing, it was cold. Like, New York City winter cold, though the ground around them was bare of snow. It was bare of most everything, except boulders and large clumps of hardy evergreens. Zelma wondered where on Earth they were. Had they been in their own time, she would have guessed someplace like Siberia, but if they were at the beginning or ending of an Ice Age, there was no telling where they might be. A chain of mountains in the distance with a pair of erupting volcanoes spewing magma and ash into the cloud- and dust-laden sky did nothing to enlighten her.

According to Deadpool, they were somewhere in the neighborhood of 1,000,000 BC. On the prehistory timeline, that meant that dinosaurs had long since been wiped out, and that *Homo erectus* had not yet stood tall, let alone discovered fire. And though there were mammoths in existence at this time, Zelma was pretty sure wooly ones like Max hadn't become their own divergent species until 800,000 years ago.

In short, Max himself shouldn't have been here, let alone anyone for the mouthy merc to have stolen him from. Though, to be fair, Deadpool hadn't yet admitted to pet theft, only "animal rescue". But since there was no way the creature could have been in this era without someone having brought him here, the likelihood of that someone being Max's owner seemed high.

So whomever Deadpool had taken the mammoth from was either a time traveler themselves, or something other than human. Neither of those options boded particularly well for Zelma and her team.

"OK," she said, addressing Deadpool, who was busy petting Max's trunk and whispering in one of the mammoth's floppy ears. "Where to?"

"I dunno," he replied, shrugging. "Ask Max."

Zelma sighed the sigh of a parent whose vocal preschooler did not want to check out of the library with only their allotted number of read along books.

"OK, fine. Where to, Max?" she asked, ostensibly addressing the hairy elephant this time. Of course, Deadpool's suggested tactic would only work if Max *wanted* to go back to his previous owner, which Zelma had a sneaking suspicion was what all the whispering had been about. She wouldn't put it past the self-anointed animal rescuer to try convincing Max to stay with him. She wasn't sure what passed for a mammoth treat in this era, but whatever it was, they could probably top it in the twenty-first century. They had refined sugar, after all.

Though knowing Deadpool, he'd promised the poor

thing chimichangas. Nowhere near an equal trade in Zelma's estimation. But there was no accounting for taste, mammoth or otherwise.

Max, however, seemed disinclined to weigh in on Zelma's internal treat debate. Or, rather, he did weigh in, by moseying over to a solitary shrub as big as a smart car and pulling off large trunkfuls of spiny leaves, which he promptly stuffed in his mouth and started ruminating on.

"Looks like he doesn't want to go back to his previous owner," Deadpool said, quite satisfied with himself. "Too bad. Guess we go home now."

"A-ha!" Zelma cried, jabbing a finger in his face. "So you admit it!"

"Admit what?" Deadpool asked, jumping back, katana half-drawn before Zelma had even finished her accusation.

"That you stole Max! That you didn't just find him wandering around alone and brought him with you because he gave you sad puppy eyes. You took him from somebody. Somebody who probably wants him back."

"I prefer the term 'liberated'," Deadpool said huffily as he sheathed his blade. "The guy who had him before was *really* hot-headed. Besides, if he didn't want someone to take Max, the guy should have kept a better eye on him."

Zelma blinked.

"I'm sorry. Are you *victim-blaming* Max's owner? The guy *you* petnapped him from? Are those actually the words coming out of your mouth right now?"

Deadpool looked over at Elsa, who stood less than an arm's length away from him and had been watching their exchange with amusement.

"Is she OK?" he asked the monster hunter with seemingly genuine concern. "She *can* hear me, right? You can hear me? Nico hasn't cast another silencing spell on me, has she?" The look he sent the Runaway's direction was dark.

"Knock it off, Wade, you insufferable git," Elsa snapped. "Let's get this over with before we have two of you to deal with again. One of you is punishment enough."

Deadpool sniffed. "Now you're just being mean."

"Not yet," Elsa replied, her tone both daring him to push it and promising a marked increase in meanness should he try.

Deadpool turned back to Zelma, clearly pouting. He shrugged.

"I don't know where to go from here. This is about where I found Max grazing when I got sucked out of the timestream and wound up here. I was just making friends with him when the hot-headed guy came running up, yelling, I dunno what. Probably something macho, because caveman. Not known for their diplomatic skills.

"Anyway, Max got all upset and his coat started to catch fire. That's when I knew the hothead was bad news. If it'd been just me, I'd have stayed and taught him a lesson. Made him pay, especially for all those guilt-trippy 'for just nineteen dollars a month, you too can help save an animal in need' commercials with the sad Sarah McLachlan songs I'm forced to sit through at night when I can't sleep. All because of people like him. Well, future people like him. Those things are a crime against humanity. And irony."

That might have been the longest speech Zelma had ever heard Deadpool give. And the most aggravating thing about it was that she couldn't argue with any of what he'd said. She hated those stupid commercials, too, even though she *did* give nineteen dollars a month, like clockwork.

Except maybe not this month, because she wasn't sure banking was even a thing anymore, let alone automatic withdrawals. Nor was she sure there would be any adorable, pity-inducing shelter animals left to save when they got back to their own, corrected timeline. Or people to do the saving, for that matter.

One catastrophe at a time, though. First they had to actually correct their timeline. And that meant getting Max back to his rightful owner; preferably before Deadpool Two showed up with his inevitable zombie entourage.

"Umm… guys?" Nico said, her voice low but her tone urgent. "Does anybody else see the dude with the flaming skull stalking this way looking like he wants to kick butt and ask questions later?"

The others turned to see who she was talking about and Zelma's eyes widened in horror. It couldn't be…

"That's him!" Deadpool exclaimed. "That's the guy!"

Of course it was. Just when Zelma was beginning to think they might get out of this encounter relatively unscathed. That maybe, just maybe, she was getting the hang of this "leading a mission to save the world" thing. After all, she'd cast like, three dozen spells to fight Morgan Le Fay and her dragon, corral zombies, and save Elsa, and they had mostly worked. And even though she was still bone tired and having waking dreams of her bed, she had done it.

She had actually done it.

And now, just when she was starting to believe that she really might have what it took to save Doc, enter a big gun – no, a *Big Gun* – against whom her magic would be virtually useless.

"*That's* the 'hot-headed' guy?" the librarian asked, barely able to get the words out through the hot, thick dread settling in her throat like phlegm. "You stole Max from a... *Ghost Rider?*"

CHAPTER THIRTY-SIX

"Wait, what? Where's his motorcycle?" Deadpool asked in confusion. Nico didn't blame the mercenary. As far as she was concerned, there was only one Ghost Rider, and his ride had way more metal and way less hair.

Zelma shook her head in disbelief.

"You really are a complete–" the librarian began, but then she stopped herself. "No, you know what? Never mind. Like Elsa said, it's my fault for expecting more." Then she took a deep breath, as if to calm herself, and began again.

"There isn't just one Ghost Rider, in one age. They are human hosts possessed by a Spirit of Vengeance, and they can ride around on whatever era-appropriate creature or contraption suits them. Or none at all, I suppose. This one – probably the first one ever – apparently chose Max."

Max trumpeted loudly, as if in agreement with Zelma's assessment.

"Great," Elsa muttered, digging in her coat for the last of her ammunition. "If he didn't already know we were here with his pet, he does now."

"Oh, he knew," Zelma said. "And I'd put that away, if I were you," she added, nodding toward the gun that had appeared like magic in the monster hunter's hand.

"Why, because he'll think we're the bad guys?" Nico asked sarcastically. "Isn't he *already* going to think that, by virtue of the fact that we're standing here with his petnapper? Guilty by association?"

"No," Zelma replied, reaching up to scratch at her beanie nervously. "The Spirits of Vengeance can read hearts and souls. They can determine innocence and guilt with a look, and render judgment in an instant. That gun isn't going to do any good if this one decides your sins outweigh your virtues."

"Darling, I don't have any virtues," Elsa replied, slamming home the magazine she'd finished reloading while Zelma spoke. "I'll take my chances with silver bullets."

"Wait!" Nico said, keeping a worried eye on the rapidly approaching Spirit, currently hosted in the body of a muscle-bound caveman. "Innocence and guilt according to *whom*?"

Zelma looked at her in surprise, one eyebrow arching behind her glasses.

"Well, God, of course. At least that's what they say. I figured you'd know that, being a former altar girl and all."

"Yeah, no," Nico replied, frowning. "Pretty sure there's no section on 'Vengeance Spirits' in the Catechism. Sorry to disappoint."

"It's not me you should be worried about disappointing," Zelma answered flatly.

Nico supposed the other witch was right.

Deadpool, meanwhile, had edged around so that he was standing behind Max, out of view of the Stone Age Ghost

Rider, though his angle still allowed him to see the flame-skulled proto-Avenger's purposeful advance. One hand was on the hilt of his katana, but he hadn't drawn it yet. He was absently stroking Max's pelt with the other.

The Ghost Rider stopped about ten feet away, regarding them with hollow eye sockets. Nico couldn't tell if the Rider was merely curious, or if their judgment had already begun. Her grip tightened on her staff, her palm sweaty, despite the cold.

"Zelma Stanton," the Rider declared suddenly in a booming, otherworldly voice, "you have the scent of sin about you." Flames danced where his eyes should be as his stare bore into Zelma. Nico heard the librarian gulp loudly as the blood drained from her face and she began to tremble. It seemed like it was all the other witch could do to keep her head up and not break the Rider's gaze. Maybe it was. "Envy. Pride. Others. But the fragrance of virtue overcomes. Kindness. Loyalty. Diligence. Chastity." Nico thought she saw a bit of color return to Zelma's cheeks at that. "This is not yet your time for judgment, or atonement."

Zelma sagged and Nico was sure the other witch was going to collapse out of relief, but she caught herself at the last moment and straightened, as became the apprentice of the Sorcerer Supreme. Or someone who was just too damned stubborn to fall.

The Ghost Rider turned his blazing gaze on Elsa.

"Elsa Bloodstone," the Spirit intoned, and Nico realized that it must be the spirit speaking and not the man, because the caveman would neither know English nor, perhaps, be evolved enough for his mouth to form the right sounds. She also realized that this Ghost Rider was rendering verdicts in a way she did not think the motorcycle-riding, chain-wielding spirit she knew of ever had. But Zelma had said "spirits", plural, so perhaps the one that inhabited the caveman was different than the one whose reputation she was more familiar with.

"You also have the stink of sin about you, and you reek of death." The Rider paused for what seemed to Nico like an eternity, long enough that she saw Elsa's finger start to slide off the trigger guard of the pistol she had never re-holstered inside her voluminous coat. Otherwise, the monster hunter didn't seem much fazed by the spirit's fiery regard, although she did refrain from snarkily mentioning her recent demise as a possible cause of her reek-iness, which was perhaps more telling than any physical reaction would have been.

Still, the silence carried on so long that Nico started wondering if the power of the Staff of One and the bloodgem together might not be enough to take out a biblical judgment-bringer and, if so, if she would have to go to Confession afterward.

Finally, the Spirit of Vengeance spoke again.

"But much of that foul odor is the residue of the sins of your father, Ulysses Bloodstone, and not your own, though you are by no means pure. Still, you have done much to counteract the harms he perpetrated, both against others and against yourself. You will be allowed to do more, and perhaps tip the scales. This is not yet your time for judgment, or atonement."

Nico couldn't be sure, but she thought the sigh she heard from Elsa in response was tinged with just a hint of relief. Probably some disappointment, too, knowing how much Elsa liked a good fight, especially one she'd been told she couldn't win. Her finger did move back to the trigger guard, though.

Then it was Nico's turn.

"Nico Minoru," he boomed, and she flinched, because his voice sounded much louder in her ears now than when he'd spoken to the other two women. She resisted the urge to clap her hands over them with difficulty. "You likewise smell of sin, and death. Others have judged your soul innocent, but that time has long since passed."

Tell me something I don't know.

And then he was looking into her soul and her sarcasm burnt to ash beneath his searing gaze. Along with all her excuses, her justification, her rationalizations. She felt like she was being burned alive from the inside out. She suddenly remembered a homily a priest had given one Sunday at Mass about the "Refiner's fire". Nico hadn't really understood then what he'd been talking about.

She did now.

Every white lie she'd ever told, every pang of jealousy she'd ever felt, every ill she'd ever wished on anyone who'd ever hurt her or someone she loved – they all came bubbling back to her consciousness from whatever dark place she'd shuttled them off to, each one scalding its way to the surface through layers of repression, like magma melting through strata of rock, turning her into a creature not of flesh and bone, but of fire and pain, guilt and remorse. Reducing her to one giant, exposed nerve ending.

Though Nico could hear nothing over the rushing of lamentation in her ears, she thought she might have screamed. She knew she wept, but the heat of the spirit's scrutiny evaporated the tears before they could escape her eyes.

She saw the multitude of her sins play out repeatedly in the darkened movie theater of her mind, the reel getting stuck on every loved one's death she had caused – or at least not stopped – over the years. Her parents. Alex. Gert. Molly.

Karolina.

That last clip would not stop, the sight of the young Majesdanian woman being torn apart repeating again and again, ripping away a little more of her heart every time.

Only to finally be replaced by the sight of Elsa lying unbreathing on the deck of the *Santa Maria*. Not just unbreathing. Dead. Because of Nico.

And the sure knowledge that part of the reason she'd wanted to save the monster hunter so badly had nothing to do with Elsa, and everything to do with drowning out the memory of Karolina's dying cries. As if saving one could expiate the sin of not having saved the other.

And as if that was the realization the Rider had been waiting for her to come to, he finally released her from the intensity of his Penance Stare. Nico fell to her knees, trying with all her might not to sob at her unexpected deliverance.

"Good yet prevails in you, Nico Minoru, though it may not always. This is not yet your time for judgment, though you have already begun your atonement."

And then, as Nico hid a surreptitious sniffle, the Rider turned to Max.

"You."

As he said the word, Max suddenly erupted into flames, and Deadpool, who'd been using the mammoth for cover, jumped back with a barely stifled yelp. The fire did not seem to bother the hairy beast, and he trotted over obediently to stand beside the Ghost Rider, who patted his head with what seemed like genuine affection. Then the spirit focused on Max's petnapper again.

"Wade Wilson. Deadpool. You..." the Rider began, then trailed off again, flame-wreathed head cocking to one side, as if puzzled. To his credit, Deadpool didn't pull his usual "Who, *me*?" schtick, but simply stood silently, hands loose at his sides, waiting. "You have faced judgment before."

"Nah, I don't think so," the mercenary replied. "Pretty sure I'd remember a guy with a flaming skull for a head telling me what a bad boy I've been and spanking me with a chain. Because I probably would have liked it."

Nico caught the chain reference immediately. This Ghost Rider didn't carry a chain. Johnny Blaze had, though. Is that who had judged Deadpool before? And if so, why was the mercenary-slash-assassin-slash-ne'er-do-well even still standing?

"No. You have met a Spirit of Vengeance; I can see the mark on you. You have faced judgment, and yet still you stink."

"Hey! Rude, much? Eff wye eye, it's kind of hard to shower when you're being chased by zombies."

The Rider shook his head.

"I cannot determine your innocence or guilt, for your heart and mind are so splintered that you cannot determine those things for yourself. You have faced judgment, and may yet again, but I will not be the one who renders it."

"Whew! That's a load off," Deadpool replied as he drew his sword, much to Nico's horror. "But it's a good thing your schedule just opened up, because I think you might be a little busy with *them*."

Nico, who'd been only been partially focused on the

interaction between Deadpool and the Rider as she strove to recover from her own encounter with the spirit's judgment, had not been paying any attention to what had been happening in the sky behind them. But now she lifted her gaze to the roiling clouds, to see the second portal finally opening, spitting out Deadpool Two.

And this time, Morgan Le Fay was with him.

CHAPTER THIRTY-SEVEN

Zelma rushed over to Nico, and she and Elsa helped the other witch to her feet as the Rider turned his attention to Le Fay.

She could only imagine what Nico had seen in the blazing fire of the Spirit's eyes. The only other time Zelma had seen the Runaway on her knees was when she had not only thought Elsa was dead, but that it had been her fault. Had she been reliving that memory? Or experiencing something even worse?

The Riders were called Spirits of Vengeance, but they could also be instruments of purification, burning away all that they deemed to be impure. But Zelma didn't think this Rider had done that to any of them. He'd looked inside them, to be sure – or, at least, he'd peered into her soul, and Nico's, too, judging from the Runaway's reaction. She assumed he'd done the same with Elsa, but that was based more on what he'd said than on her response; you couldn't even use the phrase "cool as a cucumber" to describe the monster hunter, because she made cucumbers look like hot-house violets. And Zelma still wasn't sure what had transpired between the Rider and

Deadpool, but she did not envy the spirit's journey into that particular mindscape.

Zelma's own interaction with the Stone Age Ghost Rider hadn't been pleasant. The spirit had dredged up her darkest thoughts – not the surface sins, like cheating on her driver's exam or lying to her mother about being a vegetarian so she wouldn't have to eat her meatloaf.

No, these were the things that lived in the shadows, that she didn't want to admit she felt, even to herself. The jealousy she harbored toward those born to magic or to whom it came naturally. Or those, like Nico, whose innate ability was largely augmented by an external source. The feelings of failure and inadequacy being the apprentice to Earth's Sorcerer Supreme constantly evoked, whether because of Doc's disappointment or her own unreasonable standards. Feelings that had only been magnified during this apocalypse, where so far every plan she'd come up with to save Doc had just turned a disaster into a catastrophe. Not to mention the fact of her unmitigated arrogance in even thinking she could attempt such a thing.

Then there were the reasons *why* she wanted to save Doc so badly, even though he had basically murdered and eaten Wong and Rintrah right in front of her, friends whose loss she hadn't even had a chance to process yet, let alone properly mourn. But she had set her loyalty to them aside to help Doc, and it wasn't just in service to the greater good.

And it wasn't because he was her friend and mentor, either, because they had been her friends, too. It was because without him, her access to magic was more theoretical than practical. Sure, with all the resources at her disposal in the Bleecker Street brownstone, she was confident that she could eventually teach herself to become a magician of no mean power. But how long would that take? More years than a regular human like her could count on living, that was certain. Especially with a zombie apocalypse in the offing.

No, she needed a teacher if she wanted to learn real magic in this lifetime. She needed Doctor Strange.

But warring against those dark shadows inside her, the rank selfishness and wounded pride and covert covetousness, there was still light. She had been willing to give her life to save Doc's even before she became his apprentice, and she would willingly do so again, if that was what it took to save him, and the Earth. She'd die for any one of her companions right now, not least because any of them would be more competent to carry on this mission than she was. Well, maybe not Deadpool. But she imagined she'd take a bullet for him, too, if the need arose.

Though she'd also been reminded under the spirit's unflinching, fiery regard, that even those virtues, taken to extremes, could become toxic. Loyalty became blind, unquestioning obedience. A thirst for knowledge morphed into a hunger for power. Duty became twisted entitlement, and even the shakiest confidence could grow into unflappable arrogance.

The Rider had seen all this and more, and made her see and acknowledge it as well. And then he had released her, without passing the judgment she knew he could have. He could have given her a ticket to Hell, or worse, taken her in himself, but instead he'd let her off with a warning.

Because, in his reading of her – and her companions, no doubt – he had also learned why they were here. Not just to return Max, but to fix a terrible mistake, which had only been made because they were trying to save this world's future. Possibly even his future.

A task which had just become all the harder now that Le Fay had apparently teamed up with Deadpool Two.

But it wasn't just the Sorceress Supreme and the Crimson Comedian they had to worry about this time around. During their earlier timestream pitstops, they'd had a short interlude in between the arrival of Deadpool Two and the bulk of the zombies that pursued him. That brief respite had been what made it possible for them to undo Deadpool One's "improvements" and get the timeline moving back in the right direction.

Not so with Round Three.

This time, the zombies poured through the portal on Deadpool Two's heels. Since the opening had appeared in the air, that meant both the mercenary and his zombie followers tumbled to the barren ground, some landing more gracefully than others. A few could fly, so the portal's position wasn't a problem. And Le Fay had found herself another golden dragon, or else rescued the other one from the Atlantic in 1492. She came in hot, with the dragon breathing flames at Zelma and her team and the sorceress herself flinging fireballs.

"Backdraft!" Nico yelled beside Zelma, and suddenly the flames burning their way through the air toward the team reversed course, being sucked back by an invisible updraft to envelop the Sorceress Supreme. Her screams echoed across the empty landscape, though they were shrieks more of rage than pain.

Zelma knew Nico's spell would only keep Le Fay occupied for a short time, but she would have to worry about the sorceress later, because right now she had a dozen Zombie Avengers and worse headed straight for her. She recognized a few of them, and doubted a seraphic shield would do much good against the likes of an undead Thena, the golden-armored warrior Eternal who was often mistaken for the Greek goddess Athena. But Zelma threw one up anyway as she yanked her backpack off and dug through it furiously, like a hungry dog after a meaty bone, or a librarian after a misfiled book.

Meanwhile, Elsa had begun shooting, and Deadpool was running for his counterpart, sword drawn. Nico had shouted "Clay pigeons!" and, holding the Staff of One like a shotgun, started blasting flying zombies out of the sky.

Zelma was deeply disappointed to see that, while the Stone Age Ghost Rider had jumped onto Max's flaming back, causing the mammoth to shoot a jet of fire from his trunk, he did not join in the combat. Instead he held back, merely observing.

Probably some kind of stupid "Prime Directive" rule he had to follow – can't do anything to upset the timeline or something. Good thing Zelma was about to call in reinforcements of her own. Seeing Thena had given her the idea. Or, rather, seeing her and being reminded of her namesake goddess. Zelma's idea was not to fight divinity with divinity – she was not stupid enough to attempt to summon a deity here, especially because whomever she called upon might just smite *her* instead of the zombies, out of sheer annoyance. But there were other things she could conjure that might prove just as useful against these super-powered "zomboes" as Deadpool had called them. All she had to do was find the damned book that would allow her to do so.

How was it that this backpack always seemed to expand

on the inside whenever she went looking for something? It was like the pack had a mind of its own, and that mind had delusions of pocket-dimension grandeur. Then again, it came from the Sanctum Sanctorum, so maybe it did.

Finally her fingers closed on the rough leather cover of the book she'd been searching for and she pulled it out. This blank-faced black book wasn't the actual *Book of Eibon*, but the 1937 limited edition print version put out by Adkins and Jones. Doc had all extant copies of the book locked away in the Sanctum Machina, both the print version and the earlier hand-scribed ones. It had been one of his most treasured tomes, though Zelma had never been clear on exactly why. But since it had caused him to leave this copy out in a display case that Cloak had been able to break into without great difficulty – the wards on the case having recognized the garment as part and parcel with Doctor Strange himself – Zelma wasn't complaining. Still, those wards were a security issue Doc was going to have to fix, if he ever got fixed himself.

Zelma didn't know much about the book that in earlier incarnations was called *Liber Ivonis* and *Livre d'Ivon*, only that it was meant to summon "strange creatures and stranger gods". She wasn't too interested in stranger gods, but strange creatures might be just the ticket. Plus the adjective seemed like a good omen.

She remembered Nico saying, back in the Bleecker Street library before they first set out to fetch Elsa, that you needed a monster hunter to deal with a monster plague. But maybe sometimes, what you really needed was just bigger monsters.

As per usual with tomes of this sort, there was no convenient table of contents, so she flipped through the pages, using the reproduced illustrations as her guide. Many had copied poorly and were little more than blurred black shapes, but one – a giant, furred toad monster – looked like it might just fit the bill. She glanced quickly at the Latin incantation under the drawing, then up at the approaching zombies. Thena led the vanguard and Zelma could see her team reflected in miniature in the Eternal's gore-streaked armor as the zombies advanced.

It was now or zombification.

"*Tibi Magnum Innominandum,*" she began, hoping her pronunciations weren't too far off, given how rusty her Latin was. "*Signa stellarum nigrarum et bufaniformus Tsathoggua sigillum–*"

A familiar male voice cut her off.

"Child, what have you done?"

Zelma whirled, heart thundering, expecting to somehow see Doctor Strange standing there. But of course it wasn't him. The voice belonged to a tall man with long, dark hair and piercing blue eyes who did indeed bear a striking resemblance to the Master of the Mystic Arts. But this man seemed to have antlers either attached to or growing out of his back; whether carved from wood or taken from another animal that didn't belong in this era, Zelma couldn't tell. He also sported a bare chest and what looked like an ancestor of Cloak's – a flowing, red, sleeveless jacket.

And strapped to his muscled chest was the Eye of Agamotto. The *original* one.

And now she understood why his voice had sounded so familiar – because she heard faint echoes of it every time she invoked the Vishanti. He was part of that holy trinity – or at least would eventually become so.

The man standing in front of Zelma now was Agamotto himself, the very first Sorcerer Supreme.

And he was *furious.*

CHAPTER THIRTY-EIGHT

It only took a few moments of the ground erupting around Zelma for her to understand why.

The *Book of Eibon* could be used to summon "strange creatures and stranger gods". She thought she'd been conjuring a creature from the first part of that phrase to fight the horde of zombies now pouring out of the tear in the sky. Instead, she'd conjured something from the latter half.

The gigantic, furred toad-thing was not just some run-of-the-mill monster any would-be demonologist with an internet connection could call forth. Now that it had sprung from the bowels of the Earth, throwing everyone in the vicinity to the ground, Zelma could see its nature more clearly.

Best intentions aside, it appeared Zelma had indeed accidentally summoned a god.

"Not just any god," Agamotto said from beside her. She hadn't seen the OG Sorcerer Supreme approach as she climbed to her feet from where she'd been thrown, away from her companions and closer to Max and the Rider. "One of the Great Old Ones. You have awakened Tsathoggua the Toad-God."

That didn't sound good.

"Umm… sorry?" Zelma replied. She wasn't sure she really was, though, since the better portion of the zombie mass had broken off to engage with the Elder God, including Thena, who'd apparently decided to pick on someone her own size. So to speak.

"You will be, should one of them succeed in infecting him," Agamotto said, again replying to words she had barely thought, let alone spoken.

Zelma rounded on him, angry herself now. Angry *at* herself. She hadn't thought through the consequences of what might happen if whatever creature she wound up summoning became zombified itself. But she hadn't felt like she'd had any other option. Her friends could fight until their last, dying – or more likely zombified – breaths, but Zelma couldn't be the only one who saw how futile it was at this point. When it was just Morgan Le Fay or a few dozen zombies, they'd had a chance. Maybe hovering slightly above the "snowball in Hell" level, but a chance, regardless. But with the upstart Sorceress Supreme *and* not just the Zombie Avengers, but all the super-powered zombies, period? Zelma's money was on the snowball.

Meanwhile, the only ones who *did* have the power to meet this threat were sitting back on their fiery behinds and dispensing untimely castigation. She glared at both the sorcerer and the Ghost Rider.

"Then *do* something! You have to know we can't hope to stop the Wicked Witch of the West and her zombified monkeys by ourselves!" Even as Zelma said it, the Toad-God flicked out a many-eyed tongue to catch a flying super out of the air like a juicy bug. The super, head still free, opened wide, preparing to chomp down on the Elder God's weird flesh. Nico, seeing the danger, used the Staff of One to free the zombie, which Elsa then dispatched with an incendiary round that temporarily blinded Tsathoggua's tongue-eyes in addition to most of the ones crowning its bulbous head.

"You brought her here," Agamotto pointed out, eyes narrowing as he regarded Zelma. She noticed he'd dropped the "child" sobriquet. That hadn't taken long.

"And I'm sure knowing that you have us to blame for it will bring you great comfort when we're long gone and you're still fighting to keep zombies contained to this reality a million years from now," Zelma snapped back at him, a part of her amazed at her lack of deference. But then, this wasn't the Agamotto of her prayers – not yet – nor was he her Sorcerer Supreme, any more than Le Fay was. And both of them were getting in the way of her saving the only person to hold that title to whom she felt any real allegiance.

She thought she heard the Rider snort, but it was probably just Max clearing fire-snot from his trunk.

"Your zombies pale in the face of such threats as Horde-infected Celestials," Agamotto said dismissively. Whatever else he might have said was drowned out by a huge crack of thunder, followed by a rain of lightning. Zelma ducked instinctively, shielding her eyes as she looked up into the cloud-blanketed sky only to see an older, one-eyed version of Thor speeding toward them accompanied by a woman outlined in the flames of a great phoenix.

"You have a Stone Age Thor?" she asked disbelievingly. Moments later, a huge barbarian with a glowing magenta star pattern inset in his muscular chest bounded into view, the rage-maddened expression he wore eerily familiar. "*And* a Stone Age Hulk? Of course you do. What next? Flint Man? Captain Pangaea?" Even as she spoke the words, she saw two lithe figures darting in amongst the zombies, one with a long braid and glowing fists and the other sporting the black mask and tail of a panther.

For a few hopeful seconds, she thought they had come to help, these new Stone Age Avengers. And they did, at first. Glowy Fists and Stone Age Black Panther engaged the Zombie Avengers, while One-Eyed Thor, Star Hulk, and the Phoenix took turns attacking Tsathoggua.

And then Morgan Le Fay recovered from Nico's backdraft spell, and did a strafing run over the witch, the monster hunter, and the two battling Deadpools, bombarding them with emerald bolts as her dragon winged its way past overhead. And Nico, still using her shooting spell as she aimed at the moving sorceress, who was now right over Tsathoggua, missed, catching Star Hulk square in the back instead. Which Zelma realized belatedly had been Le Fay's intent all along.

Because now Nico and Elsa were in the Stone Age Hulk's sights, and he was coming for them fast. And the others – aside from perhaps Agamotto and the Rider, who had yet to act in any definitive way – now viewed them as enemies along with Le Fay, the zombies, and the Toad-God. The sorceress had succeeded in deftly inserting a wedge between Zelma's team and what might truly be the mightiest assemblage of heroes Earth had ever boasted. They certainly appeared stronger than their modern-day counterparts, and perhaps smarter, because while Star Hulk and Glowy Fists – an Iron Fist, maybe? – came running, the others maintained their focus on the Elder God who, of all the potential foes on this battlefield, posed the gravest threat.

That was made clear when the Phoenix, who'd just finished incinerating a half-dozen super zombies, including Thena, was swatted out of the air herself by one of the Toad-God's hairy limbs. The woman went flying, her bird outline flickering as she hit the hardpacked ground and rolled several times, then came up on her knees, groggy. One-Eyed Thor – whom Zelma now realized was Thor's father, Odin – was at the Phoenix's side in an instant, though she angrily shrugged off his help as she climbed to her feet and took to the air again, blasting cosmic fire at Tsathoggua as she did.

Meanwhile, the rest of the flightless zombies had reached Nico and Elsa and the two Deadpools, who had once again put aside whatever differences identical versions of the same person could have and were fighting back-to-back. Star Hulk was ripping his way through the rear ranks of the zombie horde to get at Nico. Glowy Fists – a woman, Zelma saw – fought alongside him, tossing rotters left and right with some truly impressive martial arts moves. She seemed to be trying to get her companion to calm down, a tactic which Zelma could have told her, even a million years later, would only have the opposite effect. There was no sign of the Stone Age Black Panther.

"You have to help us," Zelma said again, appealing to the Rider and the sorcerer. When neither of them responded immediately, she turned to the mammoth. "Max?" The conflicted animal trumpeted flame and looked away.

"Fine. We'll do it ourselves. We'll try to put things right on our own, even though now we have not just a malevolent sorceress and a zombie horde to contend with, but also a giant furry frog deity and your OP buddies. We'll fail, of course, and humankind will either never evolve past whatever stage they're at now, because the zombies wind up killing or eating us all here, or Le Fay will take her undead pets back home once we're out of the picture, back to a world where humans do still exist, but only as slaves to her – the Sorceress Supreme." She glared at Agamotto, jabbing a finger at the green gem that glowed in the amulet bound to his chest. "How you can stand by and let someone like that carry on your legacy is beyond me."

"As opposed to you?" he countered, gesturing to her neck and the amulet Zelma wore.

"Is that the Stone Age version of whataboutism?" Zelma shot back, hands on her hips. "Because A – it's beneath you, and B – it's a bit like comparing apples so rotten not even worms would live in them to crabapples that are still growing and finding their color. I'm not saying I'll ever make a blue-ribbon pie, but even sour, I'm a better choice than her."

"If my legacy is to be that of an apple farmer."

Zelma couldn't believe what she was hearing. Was the world's first Sorcerer Supreme honestly saying he'd rather have an evil, self-serving woman in possession of his Eye than someone like Doc? Or even like *her*? Zelma had no doubt that both she and Doc had done their share of selfish things, possibly even in the name of Agamotto and the other Vishanti, but neither of them were guilty of enslaving humanity to use as zombie fodder in a poorly scripted historical fantasy. That had to count for something, in the grand, millennial scheme of things.

Didn't it?

"The girl is right," the Rider surprised her by saying. "If your aim is truly to shepherd humanity to goodness, you must aid her now."

"I never said I wanted to shepherd humanity anywhere," Agamotto snapped, looking at his fellow Stone Age Avenger in irritation. Zelma got the feeling she'd just become privy to a larger, longstanding argument that had nothing – and yet everything – to do with saving her and her world. "I'm still not entirely convinced humanity is worth shepherding at all."

"But it produces her," the Ghost Rider countered. Nodding toward Zelma. "And her companions."

"And that cackling green harridan up there who now wears my Eye."

"And her," the Rider agreed. "That one is destined to burn, and when that time comes, she will beg for mercy that will not be granted. But she is not meant to burn here, or now."

Agamotto glared at him for another moment before turning to Zelma.

"I will not help you further alter this or any other timeline."

"We don't *want* to alter any more timelines," Zelma assured him, hardly daring to hope that he might have changed his mind. "We only wanted to alter ours, by getting rid of the zombies before they could wipe out humanity, the only way we knew how. As you can see, that plan went horribly awry, so now we just want to reset things by returning Max and then getting back to our own time and trying to stop the zombie plague some other way."

"Max?" he asked, raising one dark brow quizzically.

"The mammoth. Deadpool said that was his name."

"I see."

That makes one of us, Zelma thought, but didn't say. Not that she apparently needed to speak with these two around. Still, she'd been unable to crack the nut that was Deadpool; if the OG Sorcerer Supreme could, more power to him.

Agamotto looked to the Rider again.

"Bring me the thief. Then burn as many of them as you can. Their destruction now will not alter a timeline in which they were never allowed to enter the timestream in the first place." His gaze returned to Zelma, searching. Appraising. "That *is* your intent, is it not? To return to your own time before the spell that allowed this fiasco to occur was cast and ensure that it never is? That the book from which the spell came is never used?"

"*Yes*," Zelma said emphatically, relieved that someone was finally getting it, while simultaneously annoyed that it had taken so long to arrive at this point. She didn't even bother being surprised that he knew about the *Book of Cagliostro*. He seemed to know pretty much everything. It was no wonder he was destined for godhood. "Like I said, that's all we've been trying to do since we realized our mammoth-napping friend had started making 'improvements' to history."

"Taking the Rider's mount improved history?" the sorcerer asked in apparent surprise.

Zelma shrugged.

"I guess Deadpool thought it improved *his* history, because he got a new pet out of it? Who knows with that guy? He's what you get when you take pieces from ten different jigsaw puzzles and assemble them to create a new one. The pieces might all fit together the right way, but the picture they form doesn't make any sense. Not even to him." It was a weird metaphor, admittedly, but the best Zelma could come up with on short notice.

The real answer was that Deadpool was a riddle without a solution. But Zelma didn't think asking Agamotto "Why is a raven like a writing desk?" would advance the discussion in any useful way, so weird-but-probably-at-least-understandable metaphor it was.

Speaking of the red-suited devil, Max and the Rider were back, one of the Deadpools wrapped up snugly in the mammoth's doused trunk. Zelma assumed the Spirit of Vengeance could tell the difference between the two Deadpools. She couldn't do it without using the Amulet of Agamotto; they all looked alike to her.

"Listen," she said as Max set the mercenary down on the ground with surprising gentleness. Perhaps he had liked being Deadpool's pet, after all. Or maybe the Rider had given him explicit instructions not to damage the man. Regardless, Deadpool was a captive audience for a few short moments, and Zelma was going to make the most of them. "What else happened when you 'borrowed' Max from the Ghost Rider? Did you change anything else? Crush any prehistoric butterflies?" She was pretty sure there had been butterflies a million years ago. "Anything like that?"

Deadpool sniffed.

"Of *course* not," he said in that aggrieved tone he favored when dancing around a particularly incriminating truth. "I saved Max from ole Firehead here – because *I* believe animals should enjoy the same bodily autonomy humans do. Which means he shouldn't have to become a walking bonfire unless he *wants* to." Max had released Deadpool and the mercenary had snuggled the animal affectionately before turning and glaring self-righteously at the Ghost Rider, which would have been funny under almost any other circumstance.

In *this* circumstance, it confirmed what Zelma already knew. Deadpool was deflecting.

"OK, so you took Max," she said, regaining Deadpool's attention, though he pointed two fingers at his eyes and then at the Rider several times in an "I'm watching you" gesture. "Did anything else happen before you got back into the timestream?"

Deadpool looked everywhere but at her.

"Wade…" Zelma began, trying on Elsa's warning tone for size and deciding she rather liked it. Cloak floated off her shoulders, readying to mummify the mercenary again at her command.

"OK, OK! I *might* have tripped on something and knocked it over when me and Max were running back to the portal."

Zelma felt icy tendrils of dread snake through her veins.

"What did you trip on, Wade?" she asked, forcing her voice to remain calm, though her heart was slamming against the cage of her ribs. She didn't know what the mercenary was going to say; she just knew it was going to be bad.

He shrugged, eyes growing huge with feigned innocence.

"I don't know, but I think it could have been… maybe… a cauldron?"

CHAPTER THIRTY-NINE

"An *iron* cauldron?" Zelma asked, knowing what his answer would be even before he nodded his head vigorously.

Le Fay's involvement finally made sense. How she'd learned of their plan. Why said plan, which should have been smooth sailing – Deadpool notwithstanding – had become a boat the sorceress was not only aware of, but had chosen to rock vigorously and ultimately capsize.

Doc liked to keep tabs on the more troublesome members of the magical community – where they were, who they were currently feuding or allied with, the status of their powers. It was part of his job as Sorcerer Supreme to monitor existential threats to Earth, but those initiated from within far more often than they came from without. He sometimes shared details with Zelma and Wong, especially the more outlandish or amusing ones. So she'd heard Le Fay's story.

Morgan Le Fay had a thing for Victor von Doom. They had originally met when Doom and Iron Man had been sent back into the past and Doom crossed her half-brother, Arthur

Pendragon. She aided Doom, allowing him to escape back to the future.

Later, Doctor Doom had begun to travel back in time more frequently and often visited the sorceress in Castle Le Fay, where Merlyn had imprisoned her after her many attempts to overthrow Arthur. There, she taught Doom magic lost to the present, and the two became lovers. However, Doom had an ulterior motive for their dalliance and ultimately betrayed Le Fay after getting what he wanted from her – a shard of the sword Excalibur which only someone with the blood of a Pendragon could enchant. Once the shard had been bound to his armor, Doom left Le Fay behind in her prison. She had vowed vengeance, but after several attempts on Doom's life, he had used a spell to trap her in her own cauldron, which he had then sent back in time…

…to 1,000,000 BC.

Which Deadpool had then upended during his own hapless petnapping caper, thereby unleashing the spiteful sorceress and starting this whole miserable chain of events.

Zelma hadn't given any thought to the story when she had looked for Le Fay herself. She'd long assumed the sorceress was powerful enough to have escaped Doom's imprisonment sooner rather than later, so when the Orb of Agamotto had shown Zelma the sorceress's cauldron, she had mistaken it for an "away" message. And she supposed it had been, just not in the sense she'd believed.

She was a little surprised Le Fay hadn't just gone after Doom the second she was free of the cauldron's binding iron, but then she recalled that the Orb had been unable to locate him. Maybe Le Fay had searched for him as well, with similarly underwhelming results. Unable to cross "Take My Bloodthirsty Revenge" off her immediate To Do list, the sorceress had seemingly opted for "Rule the World", or perhaps "Unworthily Become Sorceress Supreme". Zelma wasn't exactly sure how lording it over a bunch of humans in her New Camelot while zombies and dragons fought outside the city for her amusement checked either of those last two boxes, but Le Fay didn't make much more sense to her than Deadpool did, so she wasn't going to spend a lot of brain power trying to figure it out.

Anyway, none of that mattered now – how Le Fay had gotten out, what she'd done while on the lam, why she might have done it. Right now, the only thing Zelma cared about was getting her back into the cauldron. She could think of no other way to keep from having to replay this scenario – or others like it – over and over again, ad nauseum. Emphasis on the nausea.

She turned back to the fray, trying to pinpoint Le Fay, but the sorceress was hardly the only thing in the air right now. Zombified supers still flew about, raining their own versions of hell down on the team, the Stone Age Avengers, and their fellow zombies. Fire, electricity, cosmic energy – it was all on display, a glorious lightshow that really could have used a musical accompaniment that didn't involve screams. Apparently, one or more of them had hit Star Hulk, because he had abandoned his hunt for Nico and was now hurling boulders at the flying zombies – boulders surrounded in nimbuses that glowed with the same violet-pink color as his star brand and had long, streaming, comet-like tails as they arced through the steely sky. Boulders that, when they hit, exploded on impact, creating a

fireworks display that made the zombies' aerial lightshow look
like the work of rank amateurs.

Zelma wasn't sure what had happened to the woman with
the glowing fists or the man with the panther tail; she assumed
they were still unzombified and chopping and kicking their
way toward Agamotto and the Rider.

Meanwhile, the Phoenix swooped this way and that, blasting
at the Toad-God, which had begun spitting out some sort of
purplish acid onto… well, pretty much everything. Hissing pits
were being burned deep into the ground, and Zelma couldn't
tell where they ended, or if they even did. Zombies were being
splattered, body parts dissolving wherever the amaranthine
liquid landed, arms and legs and even heads littering the dirt
and falling out of the sky like sputtering rain. Nico had some
sort of umbrella spell protecting her, Elsa, and Deadpool Two,
but that meant she was fighting hand-to-witch hand alongside
the monster hunter and the other mercenary, who'd apparently
decided to switch sides and fight against Le Fay shortly after
their arrival. Why he'd done so was anyone's guess, but he
could easily defect again. Zelma was pretty sure the only side
any version of Deadpool was really on was Deadpool's.

But for now, the group were holding their own, though
there were more Zombie Avengers than they could hope to
hold back, especially with Le Fay adding her own spells into
the mix.

That, at least, Zelma thought she could help with.

She knew Agamotto wasn't going to help her any more than
he already had, and that Le Fay was more than her match when
it came to magic. But she'd been able to trap the sorceress in an
iron enclosure once before, albeit not for nearly long enough.

She wouldn't be able to do that again, at least not using the same spells; Le Fay would be ready for the Scrolls of Watoomb and all the shiny toys Zelma had produced from her backpack.

Except for the one she'd been saving for last.

The *Book of Eibon* was dangerous enough that Doc had kept it locked up, even within the Sanctum Machina, an area that was itself triple-warded against intrusion and theft. But those protections had been child's play compared to the ones in place around the Crystal of Conquest. Whereas the book – only a reproduction, but still largely usable – had been locked in a display case, the crystal had been stowed away inside a puzzle box that held five different pocket dimensions. Assuming the puzzle could be solved, one still had to choose the correct dimension from which to retrieve the artifact, or risk losing a hand, a soul, or worse.

The puzzle box was a 3-D combination cube, similar to the colorful, best-selling pop culture craze from the 1980s. Like that cube, the puzzle box consisted of twenty-one pieces; a single core piece with three intersecting axes that allowed the six center squares to rotate, along with twenty smaller pieces containing colored surfaces that had to be correctly moved and matched to complete the puzzle. Also like that world-famous toy, there were approximately forty-three quintillion possible arrangements of each of those pieces. Finding the one proper arrangement to solve the puzzle could take someone unfamiliar with the cube weeks. Time they would not have, because, *un*like that popular toy, with Doc's box, once the first piece was moved, if the correct arrangement was not found, the box opened, and the right pocket dimension selected within five minutes, the unfortunate puzzle-solver would be transported randomly into one of those dimensions, none of which were hospitable to life.

Unbeknownst to Doctor Strange, however, his apprentice had been an amateur speedcuber in her misspent youth. Zelma could solve the 3x3x3 pop culture variant of the puzzle in twenty moves, in well under a minute. And Cloak knew which pocket dimension held the crystal, having been the one that placed it there originally, since Doc could not do so himself.

So Zelma had borrowed the Crystal of Conquest from the Mystic Forge along with all the other items, though she knew quite a bit less about it. But the Sons of Satannish had once used it to teleport Ymir the Ice Giant and Surtur the Fire Giant to separate areas of the Earth, presumably aiming to incite some sort of climatic cataclysm – Zelma was sketchy on the details. All she knew for sure was that, if the crystal could teleport entities as powerful as that around, then Le Fay wouldn't stand a chance against it, and Zelma should be able to use it to return the witch back to the confines of her iron cauldron, and maybe this time move it someplace where nobody could unwittingly knock it over, spilling her out again.

Zelma quickly cast a seraphic shield then rifled through her backpack, keeping an eye on Le Fay as she did. The crystal had a very distinctive shape, like two large eight-sided dice made of diamond that had been fused together at the end of the longer axis. She didn't need to look at the pack's contents; she could identify this item by touch alone.

As she felt around, her fingers brushed the rough surface of the terra cotta figurine holding Doc's brain. She'd actually forgotten it was in there, and belatedly realized what a mistake it had been to bring it along on this ill-fated adventure. That it had not already been broken was a miracle attributable only to the Vishanti, whom Zelma supposed there were technically only two of right now.

With a quick prayer to Oshtur and Hoggoth to continue protecting the figurine and its valuable contents, she moved on to the next item, which she identified as the Crystal of Conquest by the fact that its sharp end poked into the palm of her hand, drawing blood.

She closed her fingers around the cool stone and pulled it from the pack. Then she turned her full attention back to Le Fay.

Which turned out to be a grave error.

She had been so focused on the sorceress and the crystal that she hadn't been paying much attention to what was happening around her. She'd been confident that if any threats approached, Deadpool would handle them. He might lack social graces or a filter of any sort, but the man in the red and black spandex could fight like few others Zelma had seen during her apprenticeship, and that was saying something. But she'd simply assumed he'd defend her, forgetting what happens when you assume things.

She was reminded abruptly when a zombie slammed into her from the side, sending her and the pack flying, and knocking the crystal from her hand and the glasses from her face.

She landed on her hands and knees, skidding to a stop not far from one of Tsathoggua's bottomless acid pits, skinning her palms and ripping her jeans in the process. She immediately began feeling around for her glasses, some part of her brain realizing that she must look every inch the cartoon character

Marvel Zombies

sleuth Nico had compared her to. But, like her orange-clad, visually impaired counterpart, Zelma was practically blind without her glasses.

Unlike her, Zelma had more than two eyes to rely on.

Taking a deep, steadying breath, Zelma quickly centered herself, then opened her third eye, immediately tinting the world around her a deep blue. While the extra eye might not provide 20/20 vision on the material plane, it was enough for Zelma to see that the zombie who'd charged her was coming in for a second crack. And as she clambered to her feet, Zelma saw who it was.

"Topaz?"

The empath had been a staple at Bleecker Street well before Zelma arrived on the scene, and still remained on mostly friendly terms with the Sorcerer Supreme, though on the rare occasions she had come to visit since Zelma had been there, the other witch had asked for Wong, not Doc.

Still, even with old blood crusting her full lips, Zelma would have recognized the woman's dark curls and complexion and her penchant for belly-dancing outfits anywhere. Topaz tended to show as much midriff as Elsa, and Zelma wondered briefly if they had the same tailor. Probably not, though; Zelma doubted the brunette witch's clothes came with gun holsters sewn in.

Which might explain how the empath now found herself on Team Ravenous Reanimated, seeing as she had a nasty-looking bite wound over her left hip bone.

It didn't explain why the zombified witch had specifically sought Zelma out, though – a quick glance showed that none of the others had made it past Deadpool's whirling katana.

The only way Topaz would have been able to do so was if the mercenary hadn't seen her, which meant she must have used magic. Zelma could likely only see the zombie now herself because she was using her third eye.

Maybe Topaz had looked at all the available menu items and decided Zelma was the most vulnerable one and would require the least amount of effort to eat. But the librarian had a feeling there was more to it than that.

"This ... all your fault," the zombie witch snarled at her, making a clumsy run at Zelma that the librarian easily evaded.

"Sorry," Zelma replied, catching the magical glow of the Crystal of Conquest out of the corner of her eye. The backpack was not far from it, many of its contents spilled out on the ground, including the *Book of Cagliostro*. She began edging in that direction. "You're going to have to be a little more specific. Lots of things have been my fault lately."

"Time... spell," Topaz managed as she stumbled to a stop and whirled, various bangles and beads clattering in an incongruously cheerful sound. "*Her.*" The zombie's eyes flicked toward Le Fay, who'd gotten the Phoenix's attention now, thank two-thirds of the Vishanti.

"OK, I'll cop to the time spell," Zelma said, readying a quick bevy of bedeviling bolts. "But that wench is *not* my fault."

"Wouldn't be here... without... spell," Topaz answered haltingly, and Zelma realized she must be struggling against the hunger to get the words out coherently.

And the empath was right.

"Should've thrown... grandfather's book... into stream... when... chance," the zombie added, seeming to struggle with the words as she advanced toward Zelma. Several rocks shook themselves up out of the ground to hang in the air before launching themselves at Zelma. "Now… my turn… fix… your mistake."

Zelma dove for the ground, trying to somersault and winding up doing a weird, sideways barrel roll that brought her close to the edge of the acid pit again. She blamed her lack of coordination on the fact that her field of vision was blued over and that her mind was still stuck two steps back, trying to figure out what Topaz had meant.

Not about throwing the book in the timestream, or finding some other way to get rid of it permanently. She was probably right about that, though that wouldn't have stopped Deadpool from leaving the stream or unintentionally releasing Le Fay. But it might ensure nothing like this ever happened again, which could be why the usually-on-the-side-of-good empath wanted her own turn at the book.

No, it was the "grandfather" thing Zelma couldn't figure out.

Then it finally came to her.

Zelma was pretty sure she remembered hearing that Topaz's adoptive father had been the sorcerer Taboo, who had himself been Cagliostro's son. Which would in fact make Topaz Cagliostro's granddaughter.

"Maybe he should never have written it," Zelma countered, climbing back to her feet again. The Toad-God's purple pit had given her an idea, and she took a small step closer to it. "How'd you get bit, anyway? No, wait, let me guess. You were table-dancing for college boys and fell and landed on a zombie?"

Normally, Zelma would never be so catty, especially to somebody as kind as Topaz. But while the empath was fighting hard to hold off the hunger, she wouldn't be able to do so forever, and Zelma wasn't about to volunteer for snack duty. And if Topaz had her grandfather's book when the hunger took over for good… well, Zelma couldn't let that happen.

Topaz snorted.

"Try… harder. Lived with… Satana."

"Yeah, and it looks like you raided her closet before you got chomped, too," Nico said suddenly from Zelma's left. Zelma glanced over in surprise to see the Runaway holding out the librarian's glasses. Over Nico's shoulder, she could see that Elsa and Deadpool Two had been forced back by the zombie horde and were now fighting alongside Deadpool One. "Gotta say, you don't pull it off quite as well as she does. Not for lack of trying, I'm sure."

Zelma took her glasses gratefully and had just gotten them perched on her nose when Topaz made a sort of grunting screech and ran at them, her manicured nails extended like claws. Whatever intelligence had been in her eyes before was gone, replaced now by pure rage and appetite.

The librarian glanced at Nico again and the other witch nodded, having intuited Zelma's plan.

"I'll go low," Nico said.

Zelma took another step back toward the edge of the hole, where the ground was becoming unstable as the amethyst acid continued to leach into the soil. Topaz was almost on her.

And then Nico was crouching, holding the Staff of One out at ankle level, and Zelma was dodging to the side. Topaz's nails caught on her sweater, pulling on threads that snapped like violin strings as the empath's weight and momentum bore her forward. Unable to stop herself, she stumbled over Nico's staff, and tumbled head over heels into Tsathoggua's corrosive pit, disappearing with a fading scream into the darkness.

A slow clap sounded from behind the two witches. They whirled in unison to see Morgan Le Fay standing there, her dragon grounded with a gaping hole in its gut, half a football field behind her.

The Sorceress Supreme smiled snidely.

"Oh, well *done*, girls. You almost looked like actual heroes there for a moment. But I'll be taking that intriguing little book now, along with your necklace, your pretty crystal over there, and whatever other little annoying baubles you have rolling around in that hideous-looking pack of yours, Apprentice Stanton."

Her smiled widened, sending chills down Zelma's spine.

"And then, in gratitude for the incredible ineptitude that got me this *other* little trinket," she said, gesturing to the Eye of Agamotto, "I'm just going to kill you instead of feeding you to the zombies. And it won't even be all that slow."

CHAPTER FORTY

"You can try," Nico retorted, with quite a bit more bravado than she felt. She knew they'd barely been holding their own up until this point, and the combination of Cavemen Avengers and Le Fay's Zombie Groupies was not something any of them could handle. And she was pretty sure Le Fay knew it, too.

But if she was going out, the Runaway was going to make it as painful for the smug sorceress as possible. And if she couldn't manage painful, she'd settle for massively annoying.

"*Fahrenheit 451!*" she said, and leveled her staff at the *Book of Cagliostro*.

Nico was sure the book had been warded against virtually any magical means of destruction that might be wielded against it. But the Staff of One wasn't just any magic, and the power of censorship was something even Cagliostro couldn't have completely defended against. No magician could – if societal fear and condemnation were so easily circumnavigated, no witches would ever have burned at Salem, or anywhere else.

"No!" Le Fay howled, echoed closely by Zelma, who'd begun running toward the book, which was now wreathed in eldritch flame.

Le Fay beat her to it, levitating the flaming tome to her side, but Zelma kept running; apparently it had been the pack she'd wanted to protect and not the book. Which was a good thing, since Nico couldn't reverse the spell she'd just cast, even if she had wanted to.

The Sorceress Supreme couldn't, either, as evinced by her howls taking on a higher volume and pitch. Zelma, in the meantime, had grabbed the pack, and was hurrying over to pick up a twinned eight-sided crystal off the ground nearby.

But Nico's attention had been focused on her friend instead of her enemy, a mistake she realized half a second too late. Because Le Fay had decided to do something with her anger in the interim – namely, end Nico.

A beam of the green energy the sorceress favored came shooting out toward the Runaway, too quick for Nico to dodge.

But not too quick for Zelma, borne aloft by the Cloak of Levitation.

A flash of red passed between Nico and the green bolt. The witch, who knew she couldn't teleport out of the way in time and had been bracing for the hit, felt nothing but the rush of wind as the cloak whooshed by.

For a split second, Nico didn't comprehend what had happened. One moment she'd been preparing to die, maybe even been welcoming the release, and the next she was just standing there, unharmed and confused.

And then she saw Zelma laying on her back on top of the cloak, her stomach sliced open, her hemorrhaging blood indistinguishable from the scarlet fabric on which she lay.

All Nico could see was red, and it was too much.

She leveled the Staff of One at Le Fay.

"You are going to pay for that," she said in a voice gone as cold as her heart, and she had the distinct pleasure of seeing the sorceress pale as she prepared to channel the worst spell she could think of. Not just death. That was too good for the likes of Le Fay.

Endless torment, endless fear, endless, aching loss. The kind of Hell that demons like Mephisto could never hope to visit on the souls in their possession, because they lacked the imagination.

Nico didn't.

Then an ethereal hand closed around her wrist.

"Don't."

To Nico's utter astonishment, the hand belonged to Zelma.

A quick glance showed that the librarian was still bleeding out on the ground; what Nico was seeing and hearing, even feeling, was Zelma's astral form. At least she hoped it was the other witch's astral form, and not her ghost.

"She's not worth it, Nico," Zelma said, exerting gentle but insistent pressure on the hand that held the staff. Forcing it down, though the apprentice was nowhere near as strong as Nico. "The Rider is right there. If you do this, you forfeit the mercy he's already shown."

Zelma smiled at her, gentle, peaceful.

"She's not worth that," the see-through librarian repeated. "And neither am I."

Nico wanted to protest, to cry out that of all of them, Zelma was the *most* worth such a sacrifice, but the words could not break through the dam of sorrow and sobs suddenly lodged in her throat. And she could see the surety in Zelma's eyes. This was what the other witch wanted. Maybe the last thing she would ever want.

Nico lowered her staff.

And then she saw that the apprentice somehow held the twinned crystal in her other intangible hand, which she now pointed at Le Fay. She muttered whispered words Nico couldn't hear – she could never hear the other witch, it seemed; they must teach whispering master classes along with the Dewey Decimal System in librarian school – and an unseen force erupted from the end of the crystal. It slammed into Le Fay, blowing her backward into the shrub Max had been eating from, which Nico only now saw hid a massive iron cauldron. Le Fay disappeared into the iron vessel without a sound, and as she did so, Zelma's astral form likewise evaporated, and the crystal she had been holding fell to the dirt with a dull thud.

Nico didn't have to look over at Zelma's body to know that the librarian was gone. She felt the other witch's absence like the lack of light in a void or air in a vacuum. Sudden and irrevocable.

She might have fallen to her knees then, but Elsa was there to catch her. And Nico saw that the rest of the zombies had finally closed in. The Cloak of Levitation brought Zelma's body over to lay at Nico's feet, and then she and the monster hunter and the two Deadpools were surrounded. The Stone Age Avengers, even Agamotto, were busy with the furry toad-thing Zelma had accidentally-on-purpose summoned, presumably trying to either destroy or banish it. Didn't much matter, since both options meant Nico and crew were on their own.

This was it, then. This was where it all ended, where they failed. Where they died, and humanity died with them.

She looked at Elsa, who tossed her last empty clip at the head of a nearby zombie, lodging it in the creature's eye.

"It's been fun," the red-haired woman said with a wink and a roguish smile.

On impulse, Nico leaned forward, still supported by one of Elsa's arms, and gave the other woman a quick, awkward hug. It wasn't quite the same as telling her that if she had to die, she was glad it was by Elsa's side, but it would have to do.

As she drew back, releasing Elsa's arm, the monster hunter quirked a questioning brow at her. Nico did her best impression of a Deadpool "sorry, not sorry" shrug.

"Indeed," Elsa said, seemingly amused. Then she nodded, all business again, and they stood back-to-back, the Deadpools doing the same beside them, while the Cloak of Levitation hovered protectively over Zelma's corpse.

As Nico prepared herself to face death – not some reaper-toting skeleton or hot brunette with white tattoos on her face, but the actual, true end of her own existence on this earthly plane – she thought of Takijiro Onishi, the man who had come up with the idea of kamikaze pilots in a last-ditch effort to save Japan in World War II. He had gifted his pilots with a version of the traditional samurai death poem, written for them before they left on their fatal mission. Somehow, it seemed fitting that those words be the last ones in her mind when she fell.

In blossom today, then scattered;
Life is so like a delicate flower.
How can one expect the fragrance to last forever?

CHAPTER FORTY-ONE

Zelma wasn't sure where she was.

Well, that wasn't true. She was floating over a battlefield, watching her friends making what was surely destined to be their last stand against the super-powered zombies whose numbers never seemed to dwindle, no matter how many were cut down, beheaded, incinerated, or exploded. And the only ones who could conceivably help them, the OP Avengers, were busy over in the middle of a trypophobic's nightmare fighting the Elder God Zelma had summoned in a foolish attempt to "help".

But, while the scene below her was on the material plane, she wasn't in her physical body, though she could see it down there with her friends, under Cloak's protective shield. And she wasn't in her astral form, either, though she remembered that she had been for a few moments, when she had kept Nico from killing Le Fay out of a desire for vengeance that would only get the Runaway punished herself in the end.

When she had somehow used the Crystal of Conquest to

send Le Fay back into the iron cauldron the sorceress should never have been released from.

Zelma didn't remember anything between the power of the crystal flowing through her astral body and regaining consciousness – or whatever this was – above the battlefield. But she was pretty sure she knew what that gap in her awareness meant.

Only one explanation made sense. If she wasn't in her physical body or her astral body, but she was somehow still here, then that meant she was dead.

Not just dead, but a ghost. A spirit that couldn't move on because of work left undone. But how was she supposed to do that work, now? In this state?

How was she ever supposed to apologize to Elsa for making the monster hunter relive her worst failure, and all for naught? Or tell Deadpool he'd actually been right about frame of reference mattering in quantum physics? Or thank Nico for standing by her when the other witch could have just kept running? Let alone try to verbalize her regret for having led them all here, or her undying gratitude that they had followed?

Zelma tried casting a bedeviling bolt at the zombie currently harrying Nico, but nothing happened. She tried pulling off a sneaker to toss at his head, to distract him, but the shoe wouldn't budge; apparently what you died in was what you haunted in. She doubted hurling insults about the zombie's mother figure would have much effect, but she tried anyway. Zombie Spidey just kept slinging his webs, heedless, apparently trying to get Nico's staff away from her. Zelma couldn't hear what the other witch said over the general din of battle, but judging from the results, it was probably something like, "Call the exterminator", because Spidey and a few other nearby zombies whose powers appeared to be insect-related started to scream, tearing at their own skin like it was clothing that had caught fire. An impressive spell, considering that all evidence pointed to the zombies not being able to feel pain. But Nico was making them feel *something*.

Zelma, sadly, could not say the same. She couldn't even feel anything herself.

But she'd been able to touch things – move them – in her astral form, which really shouldn't have been possible at her stage of magical mastery, though she had definitely leveled up over the course of this journey. Not that it would do her, or Doc, any good now.

But she might still be able to do some good for her friends, if she could affect things in the physical realm. Poltergeists were a thing, after all, right? Even if they weren't actually spirits, if psychic manifestations of adolescent temper tantrums could do it, so could she.

She saw her backpack a short distance from where the lopsided battle raged, near the acid-birthed pit that had served as Topaz's grave. Zelma floated toward it, annoyed that she couldn't just appear next to it or zoom over to it with supernatural speed. Being a ghost was not all it was cracked up to be.

Still, she was there in seconds, not having to dodge spells, weapons, or body parts that went right through her ethereal form. Not that she didn't flinch the first time a beam from Elsa's bloodstone came her way – the monster hunter presumably fought ghosts, too, so there was no telling what her gem might do to Zelma. But it passed through her left arm without so much as pulling a thread on Zelma's sweater, much to the librarian's relief.

And then she was at the backpack, hovering directly over its spilled contents. Not everything had tumbled out of the pack's open mouth, but there were several crystals on top of a scroll, as well as the air elemental statue that was part of the same set as the sculpture Zelma had tried to use aboard the *Santa Maria* to calm Nico's staff-summoned storm. None of which seemed like they would be useful in her present situation, even if she could manage to grasp one.

Still, she had to try.

One of the crystals was the Gaea Shard, which held a sliver of the Elder Goddess's essence. Doctor Strange had once used it to repel the Undying Ones, demons who had reigned over the Earth for untold millennia before the first caveman held the first club. Zelma supposed they could still be around in this era.

But even if Gaea could take care of Tsathoggua and send him back to wherever Zelma had conjured him from, the moment Zelma summoned her – assuming she could – she would be putting the goddess in peril. If the virus or whatever it was could affect Storm, no deity was likely safe, no matter how ancient. And what could the goddess do against the zombies themselves? Gaea dealt with life, and whatever the zombification process had done to these fallen heroes, they were no longer living, even if they couldn't really be called dead.

No, the shard was useless to her in this situation, but the scroll – or rather, scrolls – might not be.

She had used the Scrolls of Watoomb against Morgan Le

Fay back in 1492, more for the power boost than for the winds it could conjure. But now, coupled with the power of the air elemental statue, the supercharged Winds of Watoomb might be enough to whisk all her zombie problems away.

Assuming she could even touch the scrolls and the statue, of course. But a quick glance showed Elsa fighting for her life with a staff she'd liberated from some unlucky zombie, whirling the weapon in front of her like a wooden force field, and Nico reduced to doing the same with the Staff of One. The two Deadpools were faring a little better, but even their limitless stamina seemed to be flagging. She couldn't even see Cloak or her own body anymore; the growing wall of unmoving zombie bodies and the press of still animate ones blocked them completely from view. She was running out of time fast.

"Okay, Oshtur and Hoggoth and un-antlered god-to-be Agamotto," she murmured, trusting that they could still hear her even if no one else could, "I need your favor now like I have never needed it before. We can work out the terms later. For now, *please*, just let this work."

Then, reflexively trying to hold a breath her lungs no longer needed, she reached one hand out for the scrolls and another out for the graven marble of the air elemental statue.

And felt her hands close around them instead of ineffectually passing through.

Vishanti be praised! she thought, but then wasted no further time on gratitude. Nico was bleeding from a blow to the head – not a bite, thankfully – and Elsa was doubled over from a punch that would have downed most fighters. Every second counted now.

*"By the power of Weird Watoomb
And the Winds at his command
By Air's Tower in the East
Watching over this bleak land
Back into the timestream loop
Yon escapees I remand!"*

The Gaea Shard had been lodged in the curls of the Scrolls of Watoomb and Zelma had picked them both up at the same time. And maybe that goddess, though not invoked, also heard Zelma's entreaties.

Because somehow, miraculously, the spell worked.

A gale-force wind blew across the landscape, catching up all the zombies with an angry roar – the truly dead along with those still walking – and hopefully the right Deadpool, and sucking them up in what would easily have been classified as an F-5 back in their proper time. Then the furious funnel bent at a ninety-degree angle and attached itself to the second of the two open portals, spewing its captives back into the timestream.

It was over in a matter of seconds. Then the portal pinwheeled itself closed and the tornado dissipated as quickly as it had formed, leaving only silence and eons of dust settling in its wake.

Silence, and dust, and an impossible warmth in Zelma's incorporeal hand.

She looked down to see the Gaea Shard glowing with a verdigris light, all blue and green and coppery. As she stared at the crystal in amazement, the glow suddenly erupted outward to envelop her, growing so bright she had to close her eyes against the heat and beauty of it.

After a few dizzying moments, the light faded and Zelma

blinked her eyes open again, only to find herself in a supine position, the world gone red and stuffy. She sneezed suddenly, and the burst of air forced the scarlet shroud off her face, revealing the surprised visages of her friends looking down at her.

She was back in her body.

Her *living* body.

She was *alive*.

Oh, thank... wait. The Vishanti?

Whoever. Whatever. She didn't care; she'd figure it out and offer libations later. Right now, as thrilled and relieved as Zelma felt to find herself breathing the blessedly dust-laden air again, they had to finish fixing things, or her resurrection would be a short-lived one.

"Zee?" Nico asked, her eyes sparkling and her voice trembling with amazement and emotion.

"I... think so?" Zelma replied, letting the other witch help her up. Cloak whirled about her like an excited dog welcoming its human back home before settling onto her shoulders.

"Zombie twister was your doing, I take it?" Elsa asked as Zelma tested her balance before letting go of Nico's arm. The librarian nodded gingerly, still a bit light-headed. Which was probably normal for someone who'd been newly resurrected, though Zelma had never thought to question the monster hunter about her own experience waking back up to the world. Not that there had ever been time for it.

Just like there had never been time to apologize, but Zelma wasn't going to waste this second chance that she'd been given. Who knew when she might die again, with no friendly god-types or magical shards around to save her?

"Elsa, I'm so sorry I pushed you to tell your story before you were ready, made you go through all that again. It was callous and insensitive and I'm a garbage friend." Zelma blinked back sudden tears. "Can you ever forgive me?"

Elsa looked at her like she'd grown an extra head before giving a small, uncomfortable laugh.

"Pish," she said. "You were just doing your job. I'd've done the same in your very unstylish shoes."

Zelma thought she might faint with relief – or maybe that was just a side effect of being alive again – but she wasn't done yet.

"And Nico, I never thanked you for sticking with me and this mission, even though you had no real reason to do so. Your faith in me means more than I can say."

Nico looked as flustered as Elsa, her cheeks turning a bright scarlet that clashed magnificently with her hair and clothing.

"No problem, Zee. You've more than proven my trust wasn't misplaced." She smiled kindly at the librarian. "And neither was Doc's."

Some of the tears started to escape.

"Well, so *far*," Deadpool commented, giving Zelma an "I said what I said" shrug when she turned to look at him.

"And thank you for saving my life back in Le Fay's dungeon. If we ever get cable back, you can watch all the *Golden Girls* you want."

"All *right*!" the merc exclaimed, pumping a fist. "You always were my favorite witch, you know. Just saying."

Zelma chuckled, and shook her head.

"Nicely done, Zelma Stanton."

She whirled to see Agamotto and the Ghost Rider, standing

beside a non-flaming Max. The other Stone Age Avengers stood well back, and the Toad-God was gone, apparently banished back to wherever Elder Gods came from. Agamotto was holding out Zelma's olive-hued pack, which bulged again with all its contents back in their proper places. All except the *Book of Cagliostro*, which Nico had destroyed. Good riddance to bad rubbish.

Zelma reached out to take the pack while Deadpool cleaned and sheathed his blade, then hurried over to Max to nuzzle the mammoth.

"You're the one who brought me back?" the apprentice asked the first Sorcerer Supreme.

"That was the Earth Mother," he replied, shaking his head. "Perhaps she witnessed your selflessness and bravery and saw that your work on her behalf was not yet complete."

The Rider, whose own head was no longer wreathed in flames, chuckled at that.

"Gaea seems convinced that humanity is worth shepherding," he said. "Perhaps you'd care to reevaluate your own thoughts on the matter?"

Agamotto's blue gaze met and held Zelma's for long moments.

"I might, at that," he replied. "But for now, I have some time travelers to return home. And you have some holes to fill."

"Me?" the Rider asked, affronted, his voice taking on the echoing quality of the Spirit of Vengeance's indwelling and with tiny pinpricks of light flaring in his eyes. "Why me–?"

But Zelma didn't get to hear the end of his question, because suddenly she and the others were transported back inside the timestream by Agamotto's magic, and their stop was just ahead. She barely had time to marvel at the OG Sorcerer Supreme's sublime temporal command before they stepped out into the middle of a Manhattan intersection and the sky above them filled with purple, lightning-laced clouds.

Deadpool laughed. Gleefully, Zelma thought.

"It's like déjà vu all over again!"

CHAPTER FORTY-TWO

Nico barely had time to glare at the mouthy merc before something plummeted through the scowling lavender heavens and crashed into the asphalt a street over with an impact that rattled skyscraper windows and jarred Nico to her bones. She heard terrified screams and saw streaks in the air and on the ground as local Avengers assembled in moments to assess and contain any possible threat, with no way of knowing that they were already far too late.

The meteorite had struck, and Nico and the other erstwhile time travelers were nowhere close to ready.

They also weren't supposed to be here yet.

The original plan, if surprise appearances from Morgan Le Fay and the progenitor Avengers had not taken front stage, was to have returned to the same point in time as when they had first opened the time loop and then simply... not done that. Instead, they would teleport back to the safety of the Sanctum Sanctorum and return to the magical drawing board.

But Agamotto or some vagary of the timestream had deposited them closer to zero hour than they had anticipated, and even now infected Avengers were starting to stumble away from the impact site, ripping and rending their way through the fleeing crowds, gorging on human and hero alike, killing those of their fellow supers they did not, or could not, turn.

"We have to get out of here!" Nico said to the others, taking a few limping steps away from the nascent zombie horde. With all the adrenaline that had been pumping through her system, she'd forgotten about the wound in her leg from when she was trying to save Elsa. For that matter, her back, head, and left arm all stung from various injuries, minor and not so.

But it was too late. Even as Nico said the words, she saw her friend, Carol Danvers – Captain Marvel – flying backward through the air and fetching up against an SUV in front of her, crumpling its passenger side and setting off its alarm. Turning, Nico saw another Captain, this one zombified. Steve Rogers flung his shield toward Carol, who blew it out of the air with a photon blast as she climbed back up to her feet and cracked her neck, readying for more.

Carol wasn't alone. James "Rhodey" Rhodes was there in his War Machine armor, as were Jessica Jones, Luke Cage, Patsy Walker the Hellcat, and Jennifer Takeda, known as Hazmat, who Nico had been imprisoned with in Arcade's insane Murderworld. Nico's stomach roiled at the sight of the other young woman's familiar bright yellow suit.

But she didn't have time for a trip down Trauma Lane, because Cap wasn't alone, either. Iron Man was with him, a gash in his armor perhaps caused by Cap's shield revealing a chunk missing from his abdomen. Nico was pretty sure she could see some undigested bits of human flesh and bone inside his stomach. She swallowed down bile.

There was no sign of Zombie Hulk – Nico remembered Elsa saying he'd been up in Boston – but the Zombie Thing was there, ready to clobber what his green counterpart wasn't around to smash, as was Zombie Thor. Interestingly, he did not seem to be in possession of Mjolnir; apparently heroes who became zombies and started eating the people they were supposed to be protecting were no longer deemed worthy. Who would have thought?

Jessica Jones and Luke Cage moved in to tag team the Thing, while Rhodey went after Tony Stark. That left Hazmat and Hellcat to try to deal with Thor, which seemed like a bad idea all around.

But then Deadpool appeared, leaping over the hood of an out-of-control taxi, having decided he no longer cared about their planned teleportation, or maybe just needing to scratch his "action" itch. Either way, it effectively forced the rest of them to the aid of Carol's small team, though Nico feared it was a doomed endeavor. Still, Carol was a friend, and even if she hadn't been, Captain Marvel was one of the most powerful heroes in the universe. If anyone could stop this rapidly spreading plague in its tracks, it would be her.

And if there was anyone they couldn't chance getting infected, it would also be her.

Elsa ran over to Carol's group next, bloodgem blasting out bright beams of carnelian light to deflect Zombie Thor's lightning bolts from the uninfected heroes as she did. Nico looked at Zelma, who was digging frantically in her pack.

"Go!" the librarian said. "They need you, too. But we didn't come out of the timestream in the right place or at the right moment. I have to figure out how to fast forward us to the correct time while also teleporting us back to the Sanctum Sanctorum so we don't run into ourselves *or* get zombified."

Nico nodded and turned back toward the fray, retracing her limping steps to where the mistimed portal had been. It had disappeared when the last of the team had exited it, and Nico was unaccountably relieved to see it gone. They had more than enough to deal with now without adding another Deadpool or a disowned Pendragon into the mix.

Nico wasn't sure if these zombies were stronger because they were "fresher" or more well fed, but Cap was having little trouble holding his own against everything Carol was throwing at him. They also looked better – less decayed – than those the team had faced later, not that Nico really had time to swipe right; Hazmat was down and Hellcat came tumbling past moments later, costume blackened by one of Thor's lightning bolts. When the one-time model, author, and star of her own comic finally rolled to a stop beside an open manhole, she lay there unmoving.

Elsa had taken over for the two fallen yellow-suited heroes, blasting away with her bloodgem, while Deadpool had become a virtual food processor, using his single katana with quick, deadly efficiency against a second wave of infected heroes that had followed the first. Nico watched in momentary awe as Deadpool disarmed another sword-wielding super, knocking a weapon up into the air, then catching it and driving the blade through the base of the skull of a zombie coming up behind him, while simultaneously beheading the unarmed zombo with his katana. He finished up by throwing his borrowed sword through the head of a third zombie and kicking the head of his decapitated foe out of the air as it fell, straight into the face of the zombie behind it and yelling, "Gooo-aaal!"

And then Nico saw Hazmat rising up from where she had lain on the pavement, her protective helmet shattered into a half-mask, covering the crown of her head, her eyes, and the left side of her face, like some sort of Crayola-colored version of the Phantom of the Opera. But the torn suit and open wounds revealed something far worse than the horror classic's tragic hero. Jennifer Takeda had been infected, and she was right behind Elsa and Carol, who were fighting side by side at this point.

And they didn't see her.

Nico had only seconds in which to act.

She didn't hesitate. She'd lost Karolina to these monsters and Elsa, too, though she'd been lucky enough to get the monster hunter back. Still, the guilt had been eating her alive ever since. She was *not* going to let it happen again. She was not losing another person she loved.

"Not this time!"

And Elsa disappeared from Carol's side only to reappear at Nico's. Nico grabbed her hand instinctively.

And then they were both being yanked away by Zelma's combined time shift/teleportation spell. The last thing Nico saw as Midtown Manhattan blurred around them was the horrific vision of Carol, her arms pinned to her sides by Zombie Cap and Thor as Hazmat took a bloody bite from the nape of the former pilot's neck.

EPILOGUE

Zelma breathed half a sigh of relief as she, Nico, Elsa, and a still-swinging Deadpool appeared in the Bleecker Street library. But the key still dangling from its chain around her neck was humming, and she didn't expel the rest of her breath until she'd run over to the Orb of Agamotto to check who exactly was chained in the basement.

"By Agamotto's antlers," she said, sagging against the nearby table in relief. "I didn't think I'd ever be so happy to see Doc drooling like a baby and staring off into la-la land."

"By Agamotto's what now?" Nico asked with a startled laugh.

"It looks like we're back where and when we should be," Zelma said by way of reply, concentrating on the orb so it would scan across the city and its outskirts, where there was no wall, and no dragon or demon armies. "We still have a zombie apocalypse on our hands, but at least we managed to uncrush all the butterflies."

"Not all of them," Elsa replied, gesturing to her cheek. "I'm not a rotter anymore. Least ways, not the kind that eats people."

In all the commotion of their arrival and subsequent battle, Zelma hadn't initially noticed Elsa's continued lack of zombification – said lack, courtesy of Agamotto having returned them too soon to their own era. Still, she wasn't displeased by it. And she wasn't going to try and fix it, either. Doing the same thing over and over and expecting different results was either the definition of insanity or of practice, depending on who you quoted, and Zelma had had more than enough of both for now.

"Yeah, well, we are *not* creating another time loop," she said with a smile, surprised and gladdened to discover she was still capable of mirth even after all the horrors they'd been through. "You'll just have to learn to live with being a normal person like the rest of us. Well, normal-ish."

"Stiff upper lip, now, Elsa," Nico added, joining in. "And all that other repressed British stuff."

"Ha ha," Deadpool said suddenly, interrupting their levity with obvious indignation as he cleaned his blade on the back of a cloth-upholstered chair before sheathing it, ignoring Zelma's wince. "I don't see what's so funny. I didn't even get to say goodbye to Max." He crossed his arms in front of his chest, looking downcast.

Zelma felt unexpected tears prick at her eyes and Nico and Elsa exchanged distressed glances before the monster hunter reached out a mollifying hand toward him.

"Listen, mate, I'm sor–" she began, only to be interrupted.

"And you guys are all forgetting the *other* thing that changed," the mercenary continued, still pouting. "When we started, there was one Deadpool with two blades. Now there's one Deadpool with one blade. I want my other sword back. We need to go back and get it from me. The other me."

All three women responded at once.

"Yeah, that's not happening."

"Absolutely not."

"No way in Hell, Wade."

Then Zelma added, "The world can't handle two Deadpools." Which she didn't necessarily mean as a compliment, but seemed to mollify him, nonetheless.

There was another thing that had changed, though it wasn't as visible as a smooth cheek or a missing sword. When Doc had first charged Zelma with finding a way to save both him and the world, despite her assurances to the contrary, she'd had no real confidence that she could accomplish such a daunting undertaking, especially on her own.

But Zelma had proven to everyone, including herself – maybe especially to herself – that she *could* do this. She *was* up to the task. She'd done everything a resourceful magician on a quest needed to do – she'd cast spells, wielded magical artifacts, come up with plans and contingencies, and even found people to help her along the way.

Not just people. Friends. Friends who she knew would have her back through whatever came next.

Well, except for maybe Deadpool.

And if she hadn't yet accomplished the most important parts of a hero's quest – actually winning the treasure and returning home triumphant… well, she'd managed to save one person from zombification, at least. If she'd done it once, Zelma could do it again – maybe even on purpose next time. It was a start, anyway.

"Hey, Nico," she said, "I don't suppose you could get that staff of yours to round us up some pizza again? I'm famished."

Nico nodded.

"I have just the thing."

The Runaway straightened and held the Staff of One out before her solemnly, as if to begin an invocation demanding utmost reverence, but the twinkle in her eyes suggested otherwise.

"Thirty minutes or less!"

ACKNOWLEDGMENTS

As always, I want to thank the folks at Aconyte Books and Marvel Entertainment for letting me play in their sandbox and bloody it up a little this time. Special thanks go to my editor Gwen, who was a fantastic partner to have along on this bonkers adventure. (Even if she did go to the wrong school – Go Cats!)

I also want to give a shoutout to Chad Anderson and Gavin Woltjer for their invaluable assistance, and especially to Carrie Harris, who not only helped me with research, but is also one of the best cheerleaders ever. Thanks also to Kathy and Angi, for helping me manifest my goals and for keeping me accountable, and to Catherine, who is always there.

Last but never least, there's my husband Jeff and our kids: Arthur, Frances, Max, Holly, and David. Thank you for your steadfast love and support through all the curveballs life threw at us during the writing of this novel. I couldn't ask for a better team, or a better husband. Love you!

ABOUT THE AUTHOR

MARSHELIA ROCKWELL (Chippewa/Métis) is an award-nominated tie-in writer and poet. Her novels include SF/H thriller *7 SYKOS*, as well as The Shard Axe series, set in the world of *Dungeons & Dragons Online*. She is also the author of *Sisters of Sorcery: A Marvel Untold Novel*. She has published two collections, and has written dozens of short stories, poems, and comic book scripts. She lives in the desert with her family, buried under books.

marsheilarockwell.com

EPIC SUPER POWERS
AMAZING AVENTURES